I0762284

A NICK FISCHER NOVEL

RIVER WALK MURDER

G.D. OBERMILLER

Published by Frio Press LLC

2025

Cover design by Christian Storm
Interior layout: Lisa Gilliam, lisagilliam.com

ISBN: 978-1-7376459-9-3 (hardcover)
ISBN: 978-1-7376459-5-5 (paperback)
ISBN: 978-1-7376459-6-2 (ebook)

For my dad and my brother and all those who stood the watch

“I must say as to what I have seen of Texas it is the garden spot of the world. The best land and the best prospects for health I ever saw, and I do believe it is a fortune to any man to come here. There is a world of country here to settle.”

—David Crockett, 1836

PROLOGUE

He wore an oversized buckskin jacket and a coonskin cap that fell loosely over his right eye. In his left hand he carried a replica flintlock pistol with an orange plastic muzzle-cap. In his right hand was a genuine, rubber Jim Bowie knife. At fifteen minutes to eight on the fifth of July, the temperature was already eighty-five degrees and climbing rapidly. By noon it would be ninety with matching humidity. Sweat trickled from under young Davy's cap as he led his mother and father along the San Antonio River Walk path. He had been up since the crack of dawn, keeping watch out the double-pane hotel window, and waiting impatiently for his mother and father to wake up. Now, finally on patrol, he breathed the stagnant air that smelled like stale beer and damp tree bark and imagined Santa Anna's men lurking behind every overflowing garbage bin. He smiled to himself thinking about his classmates back in Stuttgart, Germany. When school started next fall, none of them would be able to match his summer vacation story or top the items he brought to class for *etwas mitbringen*. He was already practicing his presentation in English.

Davy spied a suspicious-looking man with a scruffy salt-and-pepper beard leaning against one of the ancient cypress trees lining the river. He pointed his Bowie knife, cocked his flintlock pistol, and crouched in a battle stance like the figurines in the 1836 battle diorama on display in the Alamo giftshop.

The man exhaled a lungful of cigarette smoke and gave him a toothless smile. "Easy, Davy," the man drawled. "I's friendly. You huntin' Santa Annie?" The man wore an Army cap and camo jacket despite the heat and carried a cardboard sign with a hand-scrawled message that read *Iraq Veteran, please help.*

At just under three feet tall, the miniature "King of the Wild Frontier" came face-to-face with the seated man. His mouth opened slightly as he struggled to understand his accent. The missing teeth gave his speech a slight lisp. On paper, he was fluent in English, but this was his first trip to Texas and the locals were difficult to understand.

"I's pretty sure I seen him under that bridge," the man lisped, and cocked his chin whiskers toward the nearby stone footbridge.

"*Danke*," Davy said, slipping into his native tongue. He gazed at the bridge beyond the patio of a Mexican restaurant. The meaning behind the accent slowly sank in. The man had called him *Davy*. He brushed the tail of his coonskin cap over his shoulder and glanced proudly at his mother.

"I heard him, Davy," she said, and handed the man an American dollar.

He nodded. "God bless you, ma'am."

Davy peered into the inky shadows under the bridge created by towering two-hundred-year-old bald cypress trees and close-set buildings. All he could see were a half dozen mallard ducks. He wanted a closer look, but his mother held firm.

"This place is open." She pointed with her chin toward the restaurant. "We're stopping for breakfast."

"*Nein, Mutter, es ist Santa Anna*," Davy said, pulling her arm.

"Santa Anna is just a story," his mother reassured him. "Tell him, Gunther." She turned to her husband. "Why did you buy him that gun?" It was too early, and the sizzling July heat sapped her energy.

"It's part of history—" Davy's father began to explain.

She cut him off for the hundredth time. "You're glorifying it for him. He thinks the gun's real," she said, searching for a table near one of the large outdoor fans.

Davy reluctantly followed his mother to a metal chair beneath a faded green canvas umbrella. The waitress put down her broom and came with a smile, wearing a red-lace apron over a white Mexican peasant dress.

She placed a basket of tortilla chips on the table and gave them each a tall glass of ice water. His father read the laminated menu while staccato mariachi music blared from the restaurant speakers.

Davy announced that he wanted cornflakes, then turned his attention back to the shadows under the bridge. When he adjusted his chair, he could see between the red, white, and blue banners on the handrailing. Being this close to the Alamo fueled his imagination and raised the tiny hairs on the back of his neck. He gripped his flintlock tightly. If Santa Anna was under the bridge, he would be ready.

A pigeon landed beneath his mother's chair. "*Scheiße!*" she exclaimed, startled.

The bird pinched a discarded tortilla chip before his father shooed it away. Then Davy saw something besides ducks floating in the green murky water. It moved slowly out of the shadows and drifted into a pool of sunlight. The bend in the narrow water channel forced the large object directly toward the toothless veteran on the bank.

"*Schau, Mutter!* Look!" he shouted. "Santa Anna!" He tore through the Fourth of July banner, racing to the water's edge.

"Not now," she sighed, pressing the cool water glass to her hot forehead.

"Bam, bam!" Davy shouted, aiming at the object in the water. The toy pistol made rapid metal clicking sounds. The object bumped against the limestone steps, held fast by the current.

Davy suddenly recognized the object. He trembled and dropped the replica flintlock. It was a young woman. Facedown. Dark shoulder-length hair tangled about her head. Small American flags decorated her blue tank top. A black skirt floated above her waist exposing yellow-lace panties and gangly legs that appeared waxy-green beneath the water.

"*Mutter!*" he cried, and his mother was beside him, wrapping him in her arms, covering his terrified face.

"*Es tut mir Leid, Mutter,*" he cried.

"*Nein*, it's not your fault," his mother said, transfixed by the woman in the water.

"It's only a toy gun," his father said.

A tight knot of tourists pushed toward the body. Above the crowd murmur, the restaurant speakers played "Guantanamera." A skeletal middle-aged woman wearing an orange sports bra and lime-green jogging shorts took charge. "You call 911," she commanded the waitress, then she grabbed the floating woman's foot.

"Gunther, *hilf ihr*," Davy's mother demanded.

Before he could push his way to the water's edge, the toothless veteran pulled the woman's head up by her tangled hair. Her face was frozen into a puffy smile, and the skin around her eyes was a shade darker than the rest, as if someone had punched both eyes before she went into the water. The crowd let out an audible gasp.

"She's dead," the veteran pronounced.

The woman with the orange sports bra began to video the scene with her cell phone.

"We're going," Davy's mother announced. She grabbed her son's toy pistol and tossed it into the garbage bin, shooting an accusatory look at her husband.

"Who was she?" Davy asked, staring over his mother's shoulder at the body in the water.

His mother hugged him tightly and took the stone steps up to the street level. "We don't know, just a woman in the river."

"Why did she die?" he asked.

She studied his concerned face, wondering the same question. She couldn't think of an answer. "How about some ice cream?"

"Oil rich boys... had a nice, sweet smile but when you finished meeting with them your socks were missing, and you hadn't even noticed they'd taken your boots."

—Larry Hagman, Actor and native Texan

CHAPTER ONE

DAY ONE

I pressed the button on the limo's automatic window and let my client's dense cloud of cheap leather-and-spice cologne escape. The Alamo City air, though sticky-humid and tinged with exhaust fumes, cleared my head. It was five minutes to nine on a Friday night in early September. I was getting a fat paycheck for providing security for Javier Sosa, an oilman from Mexico City in town to attend a fundraiser for Marcus Antonio Lopez's gubernatorial campaign, and grateful to be working. I hadn't had a paying assignment since the end of July, putting a serious strain on my pursuit of the American Dream. My credit cards were maxed out, and my mortgage payment was past due. Everything I owned was invested in my new Fischer Private Investigations and Security business. Since the bulk of my payment came after the work was done on security jobs, everything I had was riding on me keeping Sosa safe and sound.

My assignment was to escort Mr. Sosa from the airport to the convention center, and after the reception, back to his hotel. He said his personal security team would be in place by then and would take it from there for the rest of his trip. So far, the only problem had been the traffic jam on Highway 281 caused by two local colleges battling it out in the Alamodome for their football season opener. I wished I could say I had a dozen jobs like this lined up, but my business calendar was empty for the next several weeks. Not only was I running out of money, but my girlfriend was urging me to go back to law school. If business didn't pick up soon, I might have to consider her suggestion or a new line of work.

I did have one other prospect. A woman, who wouldn't give her name, had called my cell phone before seven that morning. She was on her way to work but asked if she could come by my office the next morning to meet me in person. It was about her daughter. She claimed she was murdered in July, and the police had come up with zero suspects. I'd never taken a cold case investigation before, but I'd dealt with SAPD incompetence, if that's what it was. I told her I was available.

"Thank you, Mr. Fischer, for accepting employment with minimum notification," Sosa said, getting my attention with a wave of his hand. He compensated for his thick Spanish accent by overenunciating his words and gesticulating with every sentence. "Forgive me for noticing your, uh… your facial scars."

"No problem," I said. "And call me Nick." When I'd picked him up at the airport, he stared for an extra moment at the star-shaped scars that formed a constellation across my brow, courtesy of an IED that shattered the windshield of my Humvee on my final deployment. They were an advantage in a fight. My opponent knew I wasn't worried about ruining my good looks, but I tried to smile at strangers; otherwise, they would get nervous and start looking for an escape. I liked to think the marks added a dash of mystery and hint of danger which attracted the ladies. Sometimes it worked.

As we inched south on the freeway, I caught Sosa glancing at the 750-foot Tower of the Americas built for the 1968 World's Fair. It dominated the flat but colorful downtown Alamo City skyline and towered directly above our destination. The closer we got, the more nervous and chattier Mr. Sosa became.

"Do you know anything about the oil business?" Sosa asked. He didn't fit the Texas-oilman stereotype. He had narrow shoulders made square by a padded tux coat and wore zip-up, high-heeled, patent-leather boots to compensate for his five-foot-nothing stature. "It's a volatile industry," he said, and waited for me to ask why. I didn't bite. I hated idle chitchat mainly because I wasn't good at it. I figured it added to my Gary Cooper persona.

"My job's to protect you," I told him. "I don't care about your business or your politics."

"I like your philosophy. It fits your reputation." He tapped the butt of a Marlboro cigarette against the armrest, then thoughtfully lit it up with a silver-plated lighter. "What's your opinion of Mr. Lopez?"

I rolled the window down a little more to let the smoke escape. Marcus Lopez's face was plastered on billboards all over town. We'd passed four on the way in from the airport. He was an ambitious local attorney whose campaign slogan was "Taking care of Texans." The polls put him in the lead, but rumor had it he was running out of money and desperately searching for a new source of revenue. I'd met Lopez before because my current girlfriend, Sylvia Flores, was trying to make partner in his law firm. I couldn't imagine him taking care of anything other than his ego. Sylvia thought he was the greatest thing since wireless earbuds, so I kept my opinion to myself.

"He's a lawyer and a politician," I said. "That's two strikes against him."

Sosa chuckled. "We are in agreement, my friend, but both are necessary to do business."

"Fair enough," I said.

He checked the proximity of the Tower again to gauge our time of arrival. I didn't mind the accent or even the zipper boots, but something about Javier Sosa reminded me of the kind of used-car salesman who would sell his grandmother a 1972 Chevy Vega. My research showed his main business was with PEMEX—the state-owned Mexican petroleum company. Since PEMEX had recently started refining oil in Houston, maybe he was here to grease the skids for future development in Texas.

"Do you think he is a man of his word?" Sosa leaned forward, anticipating my answer. The question was more complicated than it should be. I didn't care for politics or lawyers, although I'd spent two years in law school. It was Sylvia that kept me from completely thrashing Marcus's character. Since she chose me and we'd been together three years, I couldn't really question her judgment of character.

"Like I said, he's a lawyer and a politician, but since society needs both, Marcus Lopez is probably as good as any."

"Thank you, Mr. Fischer." Sosa leaned back in his seat and lit another

Marlboro. He blew twin plumes of smoke through his nose, then offered me the red-and-white package.

I waved him off. "No, thanks." I'd never picked up the habit. I smoked a cigar on special occasions, but lately those were few and far between, and Sylvia couldn't stand the smell. I preferred smokeless tobacco when I was younger but gave it up when I got out of the Marine Corps and started college. Even Texas professors frowned on holding a spit cup in class.

Sosa tossed the Marlboro package on the seat. "I'll leave those here. Americans don't respect the Marlboro Man anymore."

I thought about telling him the tobacco company had highjacked the iconic cowboy image and that several of the models for the Marlboro Man had died of lung cancer, but I knew Sosa wouldn't understand the irony or care.

"Not much respect for anything," I said. He nodded like we'd shared an inside joke.

When the driver finally made it to the East Commerce Street exit near the convention center, I made a show of checking my weapon. Sosa watched me work the butter-smooth action on my Para Ordnance P14-45 pistol. It was an awesome weapon with the two qualities necessary to win a gunfight—a large caliber and a high-capacity magazine. He seemed curious but not upset, which was a good sign. If I needed to draw a weapon, I liked to know that my client wasn't going to turn into a three-year-old with a bee sting.

I rated every job on a risk level of one to ten. A risk-level-one job was taking Sylvia on a date and fending off the riffraff making catcalls. A ten was the equivalent of storming a safe house in Fallujah, something I'd done in my previous life and counted myself lucky to have survived. This job rated a five. I took all my normal precautions, plus I carried a .38 Smith & Wesson hammerless revolver on my ankle—my weapon of last resort. I'd checked it when I left the house and didn't take it out in the limo. I wanted Sosa to be impressed, but not overconfident. The .38 was for personal protection.

He watched me slip the Para Ordnance back into my leather shoulder holster. The closer we got to the convention center, the more nervous he got. He'd told me in the Skype interview that he was most concerned about protesters. I tried to ease his fear by telling him the local cops would take care of that, but he'd insisted on hiring me, and I was glad to take his money.

The driver made a U-turn on Alamo Street and pulled into a bumper-to-bumper line of limos waiting to drop off other friends of the candidate. Close to fifty people stood behind a police barricade near the entrance. A dozen carried hand-painted signs and chanted a singsong refrain that drifted through the open window.

"No more fracking… No more fracking!" They didn't seem dangerous and reminded me of my small-town high school pep rallies, only they were older and mostly dressed in black.

I'd done my homework on the vocal environmental group after my interview with Sosa. They called themselves Citizens for a Clean County. None of the local members had police records, but they were funded by a national organization with a reputation for chaining themselves to courthouse doors and blocking refinery entrances and pipeline construction sites.

"Looks like the SAPD has your opposition group safely under control, Mr. Sosa. No need to worry," I assured him. He watched the crowd intently and lit another cigarette. The limo inched to a stop at the front door of the convention center where a small group of reporters gathered on the sidewalk.

"Sit tight," I said. Sosa exhaled a lungful of smoke out the window. If the good citizens group was watching, the smoke would be another black mark against him. I dished out last minute instructions: "I'll assess the danger, then open your door. Stay close and follow me to the entrance." Sosa snubbed out his cigarette on the door handle. "Are you ready?" I asked.

"*Sí, vamonos.*" The sweat trickling down his forehead was caused by more than just the heat. Someone or something out there scared him and put me on alert.

The reporters snapped photos as I opened the door and seemed disappointed I wasn't a local celebrity. I unbuttoned the top button on my tux when I felt the wool material stretch a little too tight around the butt of my .45. It had been nine months since I'd put on the monkey suit that Sylvia had picked out for me, and I could tell I needed to get back in the gym before I broke it out again, or better yet, left it in the closet along with the other upgrades Sylvia had picked out in her never-ending quest to transform my style from country boy to urban sophisticate.

The paparazzi displayed their usual rudeness, jostling each other for the best picture angle, hoping for a real celebrity. I checked their hands. They all held mics or cameras, not the kinds of weapons I was paid to protect Sosa from. I scoured the street and the line of attendees waiting at the security checkpoint. It was a black-tie affair complete with a movie-premiere red carpet. Candidate Lopez hadn't spared any expense. I half expected to see Ryan Seacrest on the sidewalk with a microphone, poised to ask me about the latest TikTok gossip.

I counted six uniformed policemen on duty. They looked bored and ready for happy hour. I recognized one of the cops, and we exchanged nods, paying our respects. I'd worked my way through college in Austin as a reserve deputy with the Travis County sheriff's department and still had a few friends on the job.

When I decided the coast was clear, I opened Sosa's door. He took his time getting out and made a show of smiling for the cameras and masking his nerves.

A young female reporter in a loose silk blouse and wavy TV-hair thrust her microphone forward and shouted: "Do you support candidate Lopez's clean county initiative?" I was committed to Sylvia but couldn't help admiring the reporter's made-for-primetime curves.

Sosa was ready for her. "Yes, that's why I'm here." He waved at the protesters.

"Stay close and follow me," I urged him. If we were going to be ambushed, standing in a circle of reporters lit up by camera lights would be a likely place.

Ms. Silk Blouse shouted another question. "Where do you stand on the proposed fracking ban?" I was already taking a step to cut her off when Sosa stopped me with a squeeze to my elbow. He wasn't too spooked to push a little PR.

"The practice of fracking is a perfectly safe and effective drilling technique that is of great benefit to the State of Texas and my country. But I'm here to support Mr. Lopez's candidacy for governor. He understands the strong cultural connections between Mexico and Texas, and he will work hard to strengthen our business relationship. Texas and Mexico can and should always work together." When he finished his prepared speech, he let go of my elbow. I took that as a sign to move forward and maneuvered Sosa around Silk Blouse and hustled him toward the security gate.

CHAPTER TWO

Red, white, and blue political banners and a movie-screen-sized photo of Marcus Lopez's smiling face greeted us inside the convention center. Marcus had just turned forty-five, but his stylishly disheveled hair was free of gray and his light-brown skin was without a wrinkle—courtesy of frequent Botox and salon treatments. I knew because Sylvia loved to share the office gossip. I was twelve years younger, but if you compared our mug shots, nobody would believe it.

On a platform near the bar, a local band played the distinctive San Antonio groove—an eclectic mixture of old jazz standards influenced my mariachi and ranchera music. The locals called it *West Side* sound. The music mixed with clinking glasses and laughter created an atmosphere more like Christmas than Labor Day weekend. All the movers and shakers seemed to think they had a candidate that would roll up his sleeves and get to work. By that they meant support policies that would help their bottom line and pet projects. Marcus drew fawning accolades from the national media because of his calculated support for all the hot-button liberal issues. They considered him the tip of the spear in the battle to turn Texas blue. He had the support of urban voters, and the major newspapers in Dallas and Houston, and of course the *Austin American-Statesman* endorsed him. Compared to the other party's candidate, Marcus Lopez was a rock star. With the election only two months away, it seemed inevitable that

Governor Lopez would take up residence in Austin as the first Democrat to hold the office since 1995.

The hall held close to a thousand of San Antonio's finest, dressed to the nines. There were state and local politicians rubbing elbows with academics and charity foundation presidents all hoping to divert a few donations to their own causes. I felt a little sick to my stomach knowing how much money was changing hands in this room and how much of it was public funds probably diverted from places where it was really needed.

The man on the top of everyone's donor list was Texas oilman and billionaire Patrick Allison, who I knew by name and reputation. As we made our way through the crowd, his presence was hard to miss. He stood six-foot-three, sported a bushy mustache that drooped over his top lip, and wore a silverbelly Stetson Open Road cowboy hat, the same hat LBJ made famous during his tenure in the White House. There were dozens of other men in cowboy hats in the room, but Allison was the sheriff on this western movie set. He was holding court in a corner away from the band surrounded by a ten- or twelve-member entourage that doted on his every word.

Javier Sosa said he had private business, so I reluctantly gave him a pager and watched him make a beeline for Allison. The pager was a panic button. The way Sosa acted on the drive over, I wanted him to feel secure and know I had his back. With the heavy SAPD presence outside and at the door, I didn't anticipate any problems inside the convention center. I spotted two shorthairs with tight suits and earpieces within ten feet of the big man. Obviously, Patrick's personal security. I was satisfied Sosa was safe for the moment.

While my client hobnobbed with the movers and shakers, I headed to the back of the hall to look for Sylvia. I spied her chatting with a group of socialites. She looked every bit as beautiful as the day I met her at St. Mary's Law School. She held a glass of champagne like she was born with it in her hand. This was her element. She was a daddy's girl who grew up tagging along with her father to all the social events in San Antonio. When she appeared at the door of the lecture hall dressed more for Fifth Avenue than first year Constitutional law, all the male eyes turned and watched as she strode confidently down the steps and took a seat next to me as if she had a reserve ticket to a concert. She returned my stare with a polite smile, ignoring my facial scars, jeans and T-shirt. It was the first day of class, and she introduced herself and held out her hand. Her touch sparked an electric jolt. "Are you ready for this?" she said. Her voice was warm and breathy and pregnant with meaning.

Sylvia knew I would be at the fundraiser, of course, but we'd agreed not to make it a date. I was working, and she was there in her official capacity as assistant campaign manager or advisor or whatever she was that week. When Marcus Lopez decided to run for governor, all the staff who had not yet made partner in his law firm took on unpaid roles in the campaign.

I put my elbow on the bar between two younger guys wearing stylishly tight suits and too much hair product and ordered a tonic with extra lime. Sylvia peeled off from the socialites and walked in my direction. The two young guys followed her movements with slightly open mouths. Her red dress was formfitting and slit up to her mid-thigh, and the black high heels accentuated her calf muscles. She glided more than walked across the floor with a model's grace.

"Hello, gorgeous," I said when she was within earshot. I had to speak over the band. She stopped beside me and touched my arm. She knew that always gave me a jolt when she did it in public.

"Why're you here?"

The two young guys shot me an envious look and left us alone.

"I'm working, remember?"

"I meant at the bar, of course," she said and studied my drink.

"It's tonic. I'm just killing time. You look fabulous."

She took compliments without the slightest hint of self-consciousness. "Where's your client?"

"Sosa's rubbing elbows with the rich and obnoxious. He said he didn't need me until later. Last I saw him he was closing in on Patrick Allison."

"Of course. Marcus's biggest client."

"I thought he supported the other party."

"Oh, *Big Tex* likes parties and being the center of attention. Besides, they've been together forever."

"What do you think of the tux? It still fits." I knew she regarded my wearing the penguin suit as a fashion coup in her battle to transform me from a small-town hick into an urban sophisticate.

"I remember picking it out last year. I had to drag you kicking and screaming to Alamo Heights for a fitting." She enjoyed teasing me.

"Hey, but I was the hit of the party."

"Because you insulted my new boss."

"He made fun of the Marine Corps." I remembered opening my mouth and inserting my patent leather shoe while trying to master the subtle art of idle chitchat. It hadn't gone well.

"He was talking about diversity."

"My point was that the Marines should invest in weapons and training killers, not fighting social issues." I knew firsthand that anything that distracted from the mission could get people killed. I also knew I should have kept my mouth shut, but most of the time I can't help myself.

She flashed a perfectly polished smile. Pushing men's buttons was her specialty. She'd had her thumb on mine since the day we'd met.

"What can I say? Your boyfriend's a redneck."

"You always use that excuse, but you're too smart for that. You don't even have any redneck friends." She was right, the only real snuff-dipping, flag-waving, honkytonk-cruising redneck I called a friend was Rocky Velosic. He'd been the quarterback on my high school football team and now was their head coach, but I only talked to him once a year at the Fredericksburg Oktoberfest.

"You want me to turn in my redneck card?" I asked.

She laughed. "I'm just pointing out the obvious. You're more like one of those characters from your Texas history books."

"I'm trying to keep the pioneer spirit alive," I said.

She let out a deep breath and shook her head. It was a sign that I'd made her point. "Don't you have someone to protect?" she chided.

I took her hand. "Yes, I do."

She held my gaze. For a brief moment we were back in law school, agreeing to disagree on a point of law before diving into the twin bed in her studio apartment. Arguing was like breathing to her, she could do it at the drop of a hat, but she could make love in the same breath.

"You're a card that needs to be dealt with," she whispered, not pulling away. I couldn't get enough. Those moments, and that warm, breathy voice, kept me from dismissing our volatile relationship. I wanted to spend a sweaty hour in the limo exploring her perfect body. We moved closer together, shutting out the clamor around us. I breathed in her musky scent and touched my lips to the nape of her neck.

"There you are." Marcus Lopez cut through the crowd, his sharp voice ending our intimate moment.

She pulled on her business armor. Her hand slipped from mine and touched his shoulder. "Marcus, you've met Nick Fischer," she said, instantly dismissing the moment we'd shared.

"Yes, I remember Nick. The ex-Marine." He offered his hand. Said "ex-Marine" like I'd been released from prison. He gave my hand a hard squeeze trying to overcompensate for his lack of muscle tone. Sylvia said he spent a lot of time on his Cannondale mountain bike because he liked the way he looked in spandex bikewear with a matching helmet.

"There are no ex-Marines," I said, and instantly regretted it when I saw Sylvia flash me a look of disapproval.

"Did Sylvia put you on the guest list?" He knew I wasn't on the list.

"I was in the neighborhood. Thought I'd stop by and make a donation."

"Really? I thought your money would be on the other party," he said through a smile so stiff it looked spray-painted on his face.

"Nick's not into politics." Sylvia pinched my arm hard to reinforce the stern look.

"Perhaps he'll change his mind when he sees how much I can do for the people of Texas."

"The Texans I know would rather fend for themselves." I couldn't help myself. This guy rubbed me the wrong way. Sylvia squeezed my arm harder, her way of saying, *Put a sock in it*. So, I added: "But I wish you all the best," and smiled.

"Nick's actually working tonight for one of your guests. Mr. Sosa."

"Right, you're the security guard." The left side of his mouth curled up when he talked, sort of like a lopsided Grinch without the green skin.

"Private investigator."

Before he could respond, my pager went off. Time to go to work. The little red light meant danger or imminent threat. I flipped the switch from casual to combat mode, instantly focusing on the task at hand. It was a conditioned reflex developed on combat patrol that had saved my life more than once.

Sylvia had witnessed my sudden change in attitude before, but when she saw it transform me from her lover into something more lethal, fear clouded her eyes. I'd tried to explain when we first started dating that my reaction to imminent danger or threats was an occupational hazard. Feelings disrupted reaction time, like gravity pulling on a bullet's trajectory forcing it into the ground and away from its lethal mark.

She took a step back.

"Sorry. Duty calls," I said, and rushed toward my client.

CHAPTER THREE

I jogged into the main hall scanning for threats. A quick movement caught my eye, and I squeezed the grip of the Para Ordnance under my jacket. Where was Sosa? I heard a crash to my left and spun in a crouch. A blue-haired grandmother stared down at her broken champagne glass. False alarm.

Her husband glanced at me, then his wife. His mouth opened. Frozen to the spot.

I stood and smiled. "I'm security," I said.

He closed his mouth and nodded. His wife looked up, confused. I patted her on the back. "I'll call a waiter."

I left the befuddled old couple and found Sosa still standing next to Patrick Allison. The court of admirers had thinned to one: a younger blond man who looked to be in his mid-twenties. He was the same height as Allison, and his facial features were almost identical—like twins, only one was frozen at birth and thawed out fifty years later. The two shorthairs with earpieces had backed off to a respectable thirty feet.

"Trouble?" I asked, inserting myself into the group.

Sosa took in my all-business expression. "Oh, sorry. No trouble. I wanted to introduce you." I tried to conceal my annoyance that he'd used the pager like he was calling for a drink refill.

He turned to the other two men. "Nick Fischer, I'd like you to meet

Patrick and Danny Allison. I told Mr. Allison about your willingness to take on my job at short notice. He wanted to meet you."

"Howdy," I said, resisting the urge to slap Sosa for the false alarm.

"Nice to meet ya, son," Allison said with a raspy, Texas drawl and extended his hand in a move that was friendly and rehearsed at the same time. He had an air of self-confidence that came with money and success. Unlike Marcus Lopez, Allison exuded power and influence rather than craved it. He was used to being in charge and the center of attention. I got the feeling I was supposed to be flattered that I'd been summoned for an introduction.

"Call me Nick." I took his big hand and was surprised at his weak grip and how brittle his bones felt compared to how robust he appeared. He sized me up as if I were a quarter horse running the opening race at Ruidoso Downs.

"This here's my grandson, Danny. He just graduated from Texas Tech." He gestured proudly toward the younger man. Up close, there was no question that the two came from the same gene pool. Danny didn't wear a hat, although a sharp tan line crossed his forehead, probably from playing golf or tennis, and his muscles bulged through his tailored tux jacket, signaling he was a gym rat.

"Hey, Nick. Glad to meet you, buddy." Danny flashed a boyish grin. He hadn't quite mastered his grandfather's command and control, but he was working on it. He had a hint of a Texas accent, holding the vowels a little longer and adding in a few more syllables than some words called for. He squeezed my hand while staring openly at the scars on my forehead.

"You're chiseling out quite a reputation in this town, Nick. I'm glad to finally meet you," Patrick Allison said.

I hadn't expected a compliment and wondered what was really behind the introduction. "Thank you, Mr. Allison. I try not to let my clients down."

"Tell you what. Call me Pat," he said. "I hear you take on the lost causes."

"I always root for the underdog."

Allison smiled and motioned the three of us into a tighter circle like we were members of a secret society. "Nick here saved a man from death row," he said and paused for effect. "That's right. That apartment fire that killed twenty people on the east side. The local police nailed the wrong man. Blamed it on that ex-football player from Texas. The one who was drafted by Washington but never played a down. What was his name?"

"Skeeter Davis. He lost his arm in a car accident before training camp."

"That's right. Ol' Skeeter. I'll tell you what, when ol' Skeeter was on the defensive line, there wasn't a running back in the country could get by him. He was hell on wheels. A one-man destruction machine. That boy could flat out play some football. But hell, you got him off, didn't you? You tracked down the real killer."

"That's about it," I said. That wasn't it. The investigation had nearly killed me, but I didn't wanna brag or get into the details unless the man was actually offering me a job.

"How did you know the police had the wrong man? The DA's a friend of mine. He told me all the evidence pointed to the Davis boy," Allison said.

"The evidence doesn't always point to the truth," I said, trying to sound more practical than philosophical.

Patrick smiled at this. This was more than friendly chitchat. There was something on his mind, and he was pressing me for answers. "You do believe in following the law, now, don't you?" he drawled.

"Unless it convicts an innocent man."

Patrick studied me in silence for a full thirty seconds, then nodded. He seemed satisfied, but for what, I didn't know. "Well, there you go. We are in the company of a bon-i-fide hero." Patrick rolled the word off his tongue and touched the brim of his Stetson.

Being enlisted, I'd never been saluted, and the gesture always gave me an uneasy feeling. I studied his face to see if he was serious or making a joke. There was a twinkle in his rheumy eyes, but his expression was hard to read because his mustache covered his lips.

"Mr. Allison is the one who recommended you," Sosa interjected.

"Thank you," I said. That was new information. Why would the big man follow the fledgling career of a small-time private eye? Maybe protecting Sosa was a test for a job working for him. "I do personal security on the side. My main business is private investigations." I wasn't averse to promoting my business as long as it was the subject of our conversation. I produced a new business card. The logo design was simple—two crossed swords below the Marine Corps motto. He glanced at it briefly.

Danny reached over and snagged my card. "Cool. What's semper fi?" Danny smirked, pronouncing it *semper fee*. He'd definitely had more than his share of the free drinks.

I smiled. If those words didn't mean anything to him, I had nothing to say.

"He was in the Marine Corps, Danny," Pat said, winking at me. "Thank you for your service, Nick."

"Can't say it was a pleasure, but I was happy to serve." I had a complicated relationship with the military. I loved my brothers and the fight but hated the mind-numbing bureaucracy. Patrick Allison knew a lot more about me than I knew about him, and that made me uncomfortable. I also got the feeling his cowboy demeanor was all an act. I'd grown up with authentic western men like my grandfather, and Patrick Allison's cowboy image was like his boots, a little too polished.

"See any action?" Danny said, eager for a war story. The kid was an idiot.

"Action's what you do in the Marine Corps, Danny," I said.

"Is that where you got the..." He pointed to the scars on my forehead. He definitely had no manners. I smiled and nodded. I'd had enough chit-chat, and both Allisons were starting to get on my nerves. If he wanted to hire me, he could give me a call.

I turned to Sosa. "You ready, Mr. Sosa?" I caught him off guard. He was enjoying my confrontation with the Allison clan.

"Oh—uh—no," he stuttered, glancing around the room. "I still need to conclude my business with Marcus—Mr. Lopez. Excuse me." He made a big show of shaking hands and thanking Patrick Allison for whatever deal they'd struck, then he took off through the crowd. I nodded goodbye also.

The old man took my hand and focused his watery green eyes on me. "Are you related to Otto Fischer?" he asked.

"He's my grandfather."

"He's a good man."

"I think so." I didn't mention several unfavorable stories that Grandpa told about the Allison family from the early pioneer days.

"Your father was a good man too. Good sheriff. Did they ever find out who killed him?"

"No, they never did."

He waited for me to say more, hoping for some gossip that he could share with his golfing buddies. My father's murder was the last thing I wanted to discuss with Patrick Allison.

"How would you feel about working for me? On salary, of course. I'm always looking for a good man."

There it was. He was offering me a job. He had orchestrated the whole encounter. I had no reason to turn him down. I could use a steady paycheck. But I didn't like being set up.

"I'm trying to make it as an independent, but thanks for the offer."

"I'll keep you in mind if I ever need your services." With no one around but the three of us, Patrick Allison shrank in size and energy level. He glanced at Danny and began to cough into a white handkerchief pulled from his suit coat pocket. It was a deep, lung-rattling cough that heavy smokers get. Danny held his arm for support.

I wasn't sure whether to walk away or wait. He saw my hesitation and held up his free hand. There was one more thing he wanted to say. I waited, looking around to see if anyone else noticed. No one did or pretended not to. The cough shook the old man to his core.

"My grandson could use someone like you around," he finally said, and wiped crimson spit from his chin and mustache.

I nodded. I didn't know what to say. Did he want me to babysit Danny on weekends? Was that the job he was offering me?

"Come on out to the ranch sometime. Danny can show you around. We have some real trophies if you're lookin' for a nice mount for your office wall."

I'd heard about his ranch. It was one of the biggest in the state and had a reputation for exotic trophy animals and extreme privacy.

"Love to," I said. As long as we were being friendly, I decided to satisfy my own curiosity. "Why are you backing Lopez? Isn't he on the other side of the fence?"

The old man's eyes narrowed. He studied me for several moments. I held his gaze.

"Marcus and I go way back. We don't always agree on politics, but I know which horse to put my money on." I waited for him to explain, but he was finished. He seemed to have searched my soul and found what he was looking for. "There are a lot of ways to back a candidate. Take care now," he said.

I nodded and walked to the front door, thinking the first chance I got, I would ask Grandpa about Patrick Allison. I remembered bits and pieces of our family ties dating to before the Civil War, but I wanted to refresh my memory.

Danny followed me like a lost puppy. He carried a drink with lime slices that was probably pure vodka in one hand and an empty cup for spitting in the other. His bottom lip bulged with an inch of Copenhagen snuff. Away from Patrick, he was indulging his vices.

"Granddad likes you," he said, like he expected me to be flattered. He spit snuff juice into the empty cup, then took a big drink from the vodka. "I work out at Lucky's gym on the west side. Mixed martial arts. Just amateur. I started in college. Keeps me in shape." The band had quit playing and were packing up their instruments. Partygoers trickled toward the exits.

"Good for you. Everyone needs a hobby."

"Ever do any fighting? MMA, I mean? Do they do that in the Corps?" He said "Corps" like it was some kind of frat house that offered intermural sports. Brown snuff juice dribbled down his chin while he talked.

I knew Lucky's boxing gym and worked out there regularly, but I didn't share that with Danny. I had a dog, a chocolate Labrador retriever, and didn't want a new puppy. I needed to locate Sosa and get the hell out of there. I was getting paid to wait, but I'd rather get a root canal than spend time in a too-tight tux chatting with the privileged class.

Before I could locate Sosa, Danny said: "I'd like to get a piece of that," and made a hole in his fist and pumped it up and down over his middle finger.

I saw the leer in his expression and followed his gaze to Sylvia. She was turned sideways to us about thirty feet away. The stylishly cut dress accentuated her curves and made me excited and protective at the same time.

Just as I was about to reprimand the kid's behavior, Marcus Lopez stepped up beside her and put his hand on the small of her back. He whispered something in her ear, which produced a laugh. I couldn't tell whether she touched his arm to push his hand away from her ass or if she was flirting with him. Her expression was blocked. His smile was clear. I didn't like it.

"Too bad," Danny said, sounding truly disappointed. "She's with Marcus."

"She's my girlfriend," I said more to myself than to Danny, still trying to process what I'd just seen. Was there something between them, or was she tolerating a paternal touch from an overbearing boss?

"You don't want to mess with him. He's Granddad's lawyer." His flushed cheeks lost some color, and he spit into his cup. His face registered genuine fear. I'd heard Marcus was cutthroat in the courtroom, but Danny obviously meant something more than judiciary tactics. It was a side of the man I'd not encountered.

"What're you talking about?"

"Just sayin', you want him on your side."

Before I could press him on the issue, Sosa shouted at Marcus, "*Esto no está terminado.*" Whatever business deal Sosa wanted with Marcus hadn't gone well. From thirty feet away I could see my client was hot and bothered.

Sosa made a chopping movement with his right hand and stomped toward the door. His zip-up bootheels clicked on the marble tiles.

"Gotta go, Danny. Nice talkin' with you." I put two long strides between us.

"Lucky's gym, killer. I'm there on Mondays and Wednesdays when you're ready to mix it up," Danny shouted.

I waved without looking back. I had the nagging feeling that I'd run into him again.

CHAPTER FOUR

I emerged from the climate-controlled building and took a bucket of heat and humidity in the face. The strange introduction to Patrick Allison and the unsettling image of Marcus Lopez's hand on Sylvia's ass threatened my concentration. Should I worry about it or was I overreacting to something innocent? I loosened the top button of my tux shirt and went to look for the limo driver.

I found him on the sidewalk chewing the fat with a group of his colleagues and asked him to pull up to the curb. Sosa's hotel wasn't far, and with any luck, I'd be home by midnight and free to focus my attention on Sylvia face-to-face. I wondered whether to ask her about the encounter with Marcus or let it go. I wasn't much good at letting things go, but questioning her behavior was always a risky move. Sometimes when I displayed open jealousy, she found it attractive. Other times, she was annoyed. Even hinting that she had something going on with her boss might set her off and ruin my chances of a pleasant evening.

Another thing that bothered me about the evening was Danny's reaction to Marcus. I thought of Sylvia's boss as a pompous ass but never a dangerous man. Underneath the drunk frat-boy bravado, Danny was spooked when Marcus entered the picture. Obviously, he was well connected to the Allison family, and Marcus had a particular hold over Danny. I cleared my mind. At this point, I needed to focus on drawing a paycheck.

Sosa was ready to go and not in a talkative mood, which suited me just fine. The citizens for the environment were gone, probably left right after the media had their sound bite for the ten o'clock news. The SAPD presence had dwindled down to two uniformed officers. I was almost home free.

Once Sosa was carefully belted into the back seat, I told the driver to take Commerce Street to St. Mary's before making the U-turn to Market Street and driving back to the Westin hotel on the River Walk. Bad guys keyed on patterns and obvious moves. It was my Marine Corps training kicking in, reinforced by years of repetition. Using a random route or changing plans mid-stream often meant the difference between life and death.

I checked the street behind us to make sure we weren't being followed, then had the driver take another loop around the block. His downturned lips told me he didn't like it, but he wasn't in charge of security. Sosa was on his second Marlboro and hadn't said a word since leaving the party. I didn't want to pry into his business, but I was curious about Marcus Lopez.

"Your business deal with Mr. Lopez didn't work out?" I tried to sound offhanded.

"It's complicated. The original deal was to provide pipe and equipment for Allison's leases in Edwards County. Marcus wanted to renegotiate." He forced smoke through his nostrils.

"What would Mr. Lopez have to do with Allison oil?"

"Marcus and Patrick are..." He hesitated, searching for an appropriate English word. "Partners," he finally said. I wondered if that was a direct translation. That was something Big Tex hadn't shared during our meeting. Being business partners would explain why he would attend the fundraiser.

He acted like he wanted to say more, but the limo stopped at his hotel. It was time to part ways. The street entrance to the hotel was quiet except for a minivan with a family of four waiting for the valet attendant. They stood on the sidewalk dressed alike in shorts and Hawaiian shirts, looking dazed from a long airplane ride. The main foot traffic was on the river side of the building this time of night. The River Walk was always jammed with tourists and active-duty military personnel on weekend passes. Out-of-state tourists didn't know any better than to visit South Texas in the summer.

The bellhop approached the door, but I beat him to it. I was still on the clock. I wanted to be sure to escort Mr. Sosa safely to his room and into the hands of his regular security team and the mistress he said would be waiting.

The driver popped the trunk and handed the bellhop a single black leather suitcase and a matching carry-on bag. Mr. Sosa traveled stylish and light. The bellhop took the luggage and hustled toward the hotel entrance.

"*Gracias*, Mr. Fischer. You have fulfilled your obligation," Sosa said when I let him out of the back seat. He offered me a wad of Ben Franklins and shook my hand.

"You paid for the full service. That means door to door."

"Please, I can take it from here. I will wire the balance—"

A blast of compressed air cut him off in midsentence, punctuated by a hollow *thunk*. Blood sprayed my face and flooded Sosa's shirt. He spun to the ground with a loud groan.

I pulled my .45 and covered him with my body. From the amount of blood, I knew the shot came from a heavy-caliber rifle. The minimal sound signaled a serious suppressor that masked the shooter's location and told me he was a professional.

The air blast came again. The second bullet took a bite out of the retaining wall, showering us with small chunks of concrete. From the angle, I guessed the shooter was in the parking garage across the street.

The family in matching shirts froze to the sidewalk, watching the mayhem unfold like a movie on a big screen.

"Run!" I yelled. My voice seemed to release their feet, and they took off for the street corner. I pulled Sosa toward the curb and opened the front door of the limo. The driver had wedged himself under the dashboard, shaking uncontrollably.

"Focus," I told him. His wide eyes tilted up. I kept my voice even and calm. "Sosa's hit. I need you to drive him to the emergency room."

"Shit, no. C-call an ambulance," he stuttered.

"He'll be dead before they get here." Another shot smacked the roof of the limo.

"They's still shootin' at us," he stammered and squeezed further under the dashboard.

"Get up and drive," I ordered. I set my pistol on the sidewalk and lifted Sosa into the front seat. The bullet had hit him in the left shoulder. His shirt and coat were soaked crimson-red, and blood flowed out of him like water from a broken pipe. He still had a pulse, but his short, shallow breathing told me that he wouldn't last long. I'd seen it happen too many times.

"You wanna be here when the shooter crosses the street?" I reached over Sosa and slapped the driver's head. "Get the fuck up."

"He-he comin' here?" He scrambled behind the wheel.

I didn't know what the shooter's next move was, but I needed to get Sosa out of harm's way and to the emergency room before I dealt with it. I didn't want to lose a client. He jammed the vehicle into drive.

"One second," I commanded while I stripped off my tux jacket and wrapped it as tightly as I could around the leak in Sosa's chest. "Put pressure on this," I instructed the driver. He reluctantly put his hand out. I pushed it down hard over the coat. "Pressure," I repeated, "or he won't make it. Do you know where you're going?"

He nodded and accelerated away from the curb before I could slam the door shut.

Another whoosh of air. The sidewalk exploded near my feet. I dove behind the next parked car. Whoever was behind the rifle was taking his time and placing his shots.

A city bus lumbered toward me. I waited until it was almost directly in front of the hotel, then dashed across the street. Another shot hit the street bricks. This time I saw a flash of light.

I squeezed off three quick rounds in the shooter's direction. His ultra-quiet weapon hadn't brought an SAPD response, but the booming explosions from my .45 definitely would. I sprinted to the garage's car exit. Sirens approached from all directions.

Tires squealed, and a vehicle descended from the parking garage's upper level. I paused behind the automated ticket booth. If the shooter came this way, he was a dead man. The engine noise receded. I heard a final squeal, then acceleration. The vehicle was headed to the Commerce Street exit on the opposite side of the building.

I jumped the parking barrier and sprinted across the ground floor, hoping to have a shot or at least catch a glimpse of the shooter's license plate.

Instead, I ran headlong into four howling SAPD squad cars with pulsing emergency lights. A spotlight hit me in the face, and a burly uniform trained his service weapon on my chest.

"Drop the weapon! Down on the ground!" he ordered.

CHAPTER FIVE

"You're telling me Mr. Sosa felt threatened by the Citizens for a Clean County, so he hired you to protect him?" Detective Milo Peterson, aka Tomahawk, thumbed through his notes, making a show of checking my story for the fifth time. He had a wedge-shaped nose and a thin face topped by an unruly patch of bleached-blond hair that was reverting to gray at the roots. The skin around his eyes was pulled tight like he'd had some work done, and his short-sleeve dress shirt exposed Popeye forearms.

"Why didn't he contact SAPD?"

"Check your notes from page one. I said I don't know."

His eyes narrowed and he studied his notes some more.

From my awkward position, handcuffed in the back seat of a royal-blue Crown Vic, his silhouette reminded me of a tomahawk, the kind of authentic replica they sold in the Alamo gift shop. That distinctive look and a nasty reputation had earned him the nickname. We knew each other, but he was playing dumb. He was part of that law enforcement crowd who resented ex-military and private investigators, and he had a particular axe to grind with me because he'd been part of the investigation team that pinned a capital murder charge against Skeeter Davis for setting fire to an apartment building that killed twenty people. The case that Allison brought up and the one that made me the St. Jude of private detectives, according to Skeeter's mother.

"Maybe he didn't trust you to do your job," I said. It didn't make sense to me either, but Peterson seemed more interested in giving me a hard time than doing any detective work. There was something Sosa hadn't told me before I took the job. There was a three-way connection between him, Allison, and Marcus Lopez. To find out what it was, I would have to wait until Sosa woke up in the hospital. If he woke up. The possibility that he wouldn't left me reeling. Sosa took a bullet while under my protection. His blood was on my shirt and on my hands. It was bad for his family, of course, but also a strike against my ego and my reputation.

I'd been sitting for over an hour—the first thirty minutes in the squad car waiting for Peterson and his partner to arrive, then the last thirty minutes while Tomahawk made notes and asked stupid questions. Meanwhile, the shooter was long gone.

Peterson turned to his partner, Detective Diana Ochoa. She was a dark-skinned beauty with raven hair pulled into a tight bun and barely a hint of makeup. I could imagine the looks she got from other officers and the whispered insinuations that her detective status came from something other than merit. From the lines on her face, I guessed she was either in her early thirties, or late twenties and very worried about something. From the way she hung on Peterson's every inane question, I put her fresh out of whatever detective training they provided. This was probably her first week on the job, possibly her first night.

"Detective Ochoa, doesn't your grandmother belong to the Citizens for a Clean County?"

She caught his sarcastic tone and played along. "Yeah, that's right. She does, Detective Peterson." She had a slight Spanish accent.

"How old is she?" he asked.

"She's eighty-six tomorrow," she said, flashing a nervous smile that suddenly lit up the car interior.

"Well, wish Granny a happy birthday. Would you say she's a violent person?" Detective Peterson was proud of his sense of humor.

"Homicidal. She once slapped my *primo* for drinking milk out of the carton."

Peterson spit out a loud fake laugh.

"You two practicing that routine for a TikTok video? Ask Granny if she knows where the CCC gets its funding." The cuffs were getting tight, it was after midnight, and I'd had enough of Peterson's clown act. "If your uniform unit hadn't threatened to kill me, I'd have made the shooter's car and this case would be over by now."

Detective Peterson dropped the smile. "A civilian skipping down the street wearing a bloody shirt and waving a .45 is a threat. My officers are trained to react to shots fired. You're lucky I wasn't there. I'd have put you down."

"All right," I said, trying to sound conciliatory. "I get it, they were just doing their job. You're just doing yours."

"Look, Fischer. I know who you are and your reputation," Peterson said.

"Thanks. Now, I'd like to check on my client." I thought I was finally getting through to him.

"That wasn't a compliment." Obviously, he wanted to get something off his chest.

Both detectives stared at me over the dark-blue vinyl seat. It wasn't the kind of stare that's followed by a French kiss and a warm hug. I braced for a double barrel blast of vitriol, the kind I used to get from my Marine Corps DI for standing for inspection beside an unmade rack.

"You found one killer and put that big, one-armed jig back on the streets." Peterson seemed threatened by the fact that Skeeter was innocent and that he was a very large black man. When he leaned further over the seat, I couldn't help imagining feathers dangling from his ears like the ones that decorated the souvenir tomahawks at the gift shop.

"Skeeter didn't do it," I said.

"Maybe, maybe not. He was there. He wasn't innocent."

"He didn't start the fire. He didn't kill those people. You nailed the wrong guy."

"You know how many cases we have to clear every month?" Ochoa jumped into the fray. Her new partner had obviously briefed her on his side of the story, probably as a cautionary tale to a new recruit. "You solved one little case and you're a hero." She raised her dark left eyebrow as she spoke.

I should have let it go, but I couldn't resist. "You're pissed 'cause I don't work on volume? You solve five murder cases a year, but one goes south, and an innocent man gets the death penalty. But hey, you're still at eighty percent. You get a bonus, a promotion, and an invitation to the policeman's ball."

Her eyebrow sank to normal, but she didn't speak. She wasn't going to see it my way no matter how much I argued, because she had to work with Tomahawk. I pitied her.

He opened his mouth to speak, but I cut him off. "Let's talk about recent history. An hour ago, my client was shot in downtown San Antonio by a sniper using a high-powered rifle that sounded more like an air gun. Doesn't that make you the least bit anxious to find a suspect?"

"We found one," he said, still staring at me.

I met his gaze. "Unless you're gonna charge me with the attempted murder of my own client, turn me loose. Mr. Sosa needs armed protection in the hospital, and the real shooter isn't going to turn himself in. You're gonna have to do some real detective work."

"Your job ended when Sosa took a bullet," Peterson snapped. "I don't care if you're a private dick. This case is ours. Stay the fuck out of it. And stay close to home. The DA may still wanna press charges."

"For what?"

"Incompetence for one." He exposed his small sharp teeth in a predatory smile.

For once, I didn't say anything. They weren't going to listen to me, and I didn't want to listen to them any longer than it took to get the cuffs off and out of the Crown Vic. I twisted in the seat and held my handcuffed wrists up. Detective Ochoa reluctantly unlocked them.

"My weapons?" I said.

Peterson examined the Para Ordnance .45 before he handed it over with the S&W .38. "Didn't Remington buy Para Ordnance?" he said, as if that made the weapon obsolete.

"It gets the job done. You forget something?" Both weapons were unloaded.

"I don't remember them being loaded. You should be more careful. Don't forget what I said. Keep your nose out of this case."

I stepped out of the car and strapped my empty pistols back in place. Tomahawk sneered through his open window. I should have kept my mouth shut, but I couldn't resist.

"Think of it this way, Detective. We're on the same team. I only take the cases y'all can't solve."

Ochoa shouted something, but Peterson had the window up and was driving away.

CHAPTER SIX

My pickup was at the airport where I'd left it when I hooked up with Sosa and his limo driver, so I hiked east on Market Street searching for a cab. The bars were still open and filled with tourists doing shots of tequila with Corona beer chasers. I wished I was holding something with lime and salt or a cold beer to wash away the bad taste in my mouth and mitigate the smell of Sosa's blood on my shirt. Despite Tomahawk's warning, I couldn't stay away from the Sosa case. I'd promised door-to-door service, and I'd failed. It brought back the raw, uneasy feelings of survivor's guilt that had threatened to derail my reintegration into society after my final deployment. Those demons were constantly knocking at the door.

When I didn't see a cab, I hit the Uber app on my cell phone and waited for the driver by the life-sized bronze sculpture of the famous cattleman Charles Goodnight that stood guard alongside Quanah Parker, the last Comanche war chief, in front of the Briscoe Western Art Museum. Both figures were so realistic that they seemed to come alive under the dim streetlights. Goodnight's cowboy hat was pulled low on his stoic face, reminding me of Patrick Allison's determined expression when he had been searching my soul. I wondered why he had focused on me. Men like Patrick Allison always had an agenda. Maybe it was my suspicious nature, but I couldn't shake the feeling that the events in the convention center were connected to Sosa's shooting. Had Detective Peterson been interested in doing his job, he would have asked about Sosa's contacts at the fundraiser and followed up with his security detail.

The Uber driver eyed my bloodstained tux shirt. "Must have been some party," he said, anticipating a story.

"The usual," I said, avoiding a conversation. It was far from usual. Not the kind of night I ever expected to spend in the Alamo City. I'd been shot at during the Skeeter case, but that was different. Skeeter had been in lockup, waiting for me to prove his innocence. The gangster who did the crime, and I'd gone after, had a nasty reputation for violence and mayhem. I'd expected bullets to fly, and I wasn't disappointed. The Sosa detail didn't carry the same expectations. Now, I wondered what I had missed.

The driver dropped me off in front of the airport parking garage. I paid my twelve bucks to get out of the short-term parking and swung by the hospital to check on Javier Sosa.

He was out of surgery and his condition was stable. That was welcome news. Still, no chance to ask him any questions. I talked to the head of hospital security and told her what had happened. She said Detective Peterson had briefed her and left two uniforms on the ICU floor. I hadn't expected that. Tomahawk was doing his job. I also talked to Sosa's head of security, the man who should have been waiting outside the hotel. His English was limited, but he seemed confident that his team could protect his boss in the hospital. He was less clear on why he wasn't outside the hotel.

On the drive home, I tried to sort out what had happened. Some details about the shooting seemed out of place. The location was good. The street was quiet. The parking garage provided cover and easy access with multiple exits. Sosa had a regular security team that was going to take over for the rest of his Texas trip. That meant higher security and less opportunity after he left my service. The timing was perfect. The part that bugged me was that the shooter had stayed in position after his initial shot. He would have seen Sosa was hit and assumed it was a kill. The distance wasn't that great, less than a hundred yards. The buildings were close together. If his target was Sosa, why did he keep shooting at me? The thought caused the hair to stand up on the back of my neck. My first thought was that the weapon had to be a military-grade system, but

I'd served three tours of duty and had never heard anything that silent. The constant ringing in my ears was proof of that. The shooter used a high-powered rifle that was Hollywood quiet—that impossibly quiet whisper that can only be reproduced in the movies.

I tried to come up with a list of people who wanted me pushing up daisies. The few enemies I'd made in my fledgling career weren't the kind to hire a sniper. If the gangster involved in Skeeter's case wanted me dead, his thugs would have already come after me. Their style was to roll up next to you on the street corner and open fire with a Glock 19 pistol—the gangster weapon of choice. The scumbag that burned down the apartment building and framed Skeeter was in prison, and his thug friends were too busy cooking and selling more meth to care about me. I crossed him off the list.

Before that, a number of wives had hired me to catch their husbands with their pants down, something I did to pay the mortgage, but I figured the husbands were too embarrassed or too busy remodeling the kitchen for their wives to come after me. The two women I'd caught in compromising positions on behalf of their husbands were happily suing their former spouses. I couldn't see them spending any money to have me killed. I'd been told I had a knack for rubbing people the wrong way. It worked mostly in my favor in the private detective business. I had to ask the tough questions. But I couldn't think of anybody I'd pissed off enough to kill me for it.

I turned right on St. Mary's Street in front of the neighborhood Mennonite church. I lived south of downtown on the border of one of the older neighborhoods of San Antonio called King William, named after Kaiser Wilhelm I of Prussia. So many Germans moved to that area along the San Antonio River in the late 1800s, it became known as Sauerkraut Bend. They built majestic Victorian and Greek Revival homes and enjoyed fishing in the nearby river. After a period of decline, many of the old homes had been renovated, giving the neighborhood a gentrified feel. When I bought the house, I was hoping to cash in on that feeling by buying a fixer-upper on the edge of the main district. I was also trying to impress Sylvia by being a homeowner. When I got around to the fix and repair part, she might be impressed.

I pulled into my driveway and checked for lights next door. My neighbor's name was Rose Gustafson, a retired university biology professor who was born in the neighborhood in 1939. I tried to always check up on her when I got home late. In return, she liked to remind me what day the city collected trash while pointing to my overflowing can.

Sam, my four-year-old chocolate Lab, studied the holes in my ruined tuxedo and sniffed Sosa's dried blood on my shirt. I'd named him after Sam Houston, a hero of the Texas Revolution. Once he decided the holes in my clothes weren't from another dog, he waited by the back door for me to change into my running shorts. He didn't seem to care that it was pushing two a.m. or that I had been shot at and interrogated. We ran every night when I got home. It wasn't his fault I was late. He also knew our evening route usually included a stop at Sylvia's condo, where he could count on an extra meal. You can't argue with a Labrador retriever.

"All right," I told him. "But just this once." He knew I was joking. He waited while I tossed the ruined tux into the corner of the bedroom and pulled on my gym shorts and running shoes.

We jogged to the San Antonio River trail south of the popular tourist loop. It was well lit and paved for most of the fifteen or so miles extending south to the four lesser-known Spanish missions. A welcome breeze ruffled the mesquite tree leaves and Johnson grass lining the trail. Streetlamps illuminated patches of wild sunflowers that a recent rain had revived. The rare summer shower turned everything green and added to the humidity and the mosquito population.

The late-night run was part of a routine that helped me decompress. Seeing Sosa's blood had unleashed memories of my last deployment that I'd been trying years to repress. The steady rhythm on the silent trail eased the pain and tamped the demons back into their black hole. The familiar landmarks were an added comfort and helped ground me in the present. We passed the old US Arsenal that now housed the headquarters of a local grocery chain, and the backsides of a dozen historic buildings including the landmark VFW housed in a restored riverfront Victorian home. Farther north, the buildings got newer and closer to the channel in an ever-expanding condo jungle, but there were no other people around.

Even the motley collection of River Walk homeless had found darker shadows to hole up for the night.

We stopped at the base of a newer two-story condominium complex. The ground floor units all had private patios surrounded by six-foot wooden fences that faced the river. Sam sniffed out the last gate in a row of twelve, then proudly looked back at me. He'd found what he was looking for.

I looked at my watch. It was two thirty a.m. I probably should have called her earlier, but I had a lot on my mind. Sam pawed at the gate. I tested the handle. "It's locked," I told him. "We should probably let her sleep." He wrinkled his forehead impatiently. "Fine," I said. He was right. We both wanted to see her. I punched in the keycode.

Sam surveyed Sylvia's small patio, then went straight for the full bowl of food. She hadn't forgotten. The sliding glass door was open, and I let myself into the dim living room.

Sylvia met me in the dark and wrapped her warm arms around my sweat-soaked T-shirt. "Are you all right?" she asked, with genuine concern.

"Just a little out of breath from the run."

She pushed me away and put her hands on her hips. Her white robe fell open to her waist, exposing a generous portion of her creamy, light brown skin. "Don't play games," she said. "The police questioned Marcus." She pulled her robe closed and secured it with the belt. "Out with it."

I grabbed a Shiner Bock from the sixpack in her fridge she kept for me and flopped down on the couch. Sylvia threw me a hand towel and turned on the lamp.

"Here, dry yourself off."

I explained the evening's events while she examined me for holes in my skin or my story.

Her dark eyes narrowed. "Someone shoots your client, shoots at you, and you take your dog for a jog? No tears? No shouting? You make a sarcastic joke and move on. That's not healthy."

She was probably right, but my people, the people who raised me and the people I admired, didn't show emotion. Other people broke down in tears when faced with death or hardship. For better or worse, we kept it inside, made jokes, and moved on. Sosa's shooting hit me hard, but I had to work through it in my own way. Sylvia only suspected what I kept below the surface. If we stayed together, I hoped I would eventually be able to confide in her.

"What do you want me to do?"

"I don't know. Yell at the wall? Shed a tear? Something to show you're human."

"Yell at the wall?"

"You know what I mean. I'm glad they stopped you before you could chase down an armed suspect in the dark."

Her robe fell open again and ignited an emotion I would let her see. I reached inside the robe and pulled her closer. "You forget my background, counselor. My specialty is chasing down armed suspects in the dark."

"You were wearing a tuxedo, which is probably ruined, and not a helmet and body armor. Do you have to pretend you're a badass all the time?" She let me explore the smooth skin under her robe.

"Who's pretending?"

"Why can't you ever be serious?"

"I'm compensating for my lack of emotion."

"You always do that. Deflect with a sarcastic joke. It drives me crazy. This is a good example of why you should go back to law school."

"Because I lack emotions?"

"Stop!" she said, exasperated.

"Sosa was a lawyer. Look what it got him." I pulled her robe further open, exposing the perfect breasts that never failed to lift my spirits.

"You know what I mean." She took my hands, halting my exploration. "You should have quit after Skeeter's case. Now this? You can't pretend it's safe being a private investigator."

"Driving a car in the Alamo City isn't safe either, but it's necessary."

"Nick, please. Stop the private eye thing. Let the police solve crimes. No more getting shot at. You don't have anything to prove."

"The police don't always get the job done." I sat back and finished my beer.

"So now you're the Caped Crusader?"

"Every city needs one."

She usually laughed at my jokes. She wasn't smiling. "You have a serious problem. You keep everything bottled up. One day you're gonna explode. This isn't a comic book. Your client's in a real hospital."

"And that's why I can't quit."

"Please? For me? Go back to law school." She leaned forward and let her robe slip from her shoulders. Her half-mast brown eyes and slightly parted lips were my kryptonite. It wasn't the first time she'd given me a not-so-subtle hint that the future of our relationship would be short-lived if I continued as a private investigator.

"It's late. We can argue, then have make-up sex, or have make-up sex and argue tomorrow," I said.

That finally produced a smile. She helped me pull my own shirt off and tapped her hand on my chest.

"Are you ever gonna let me in here?" she whispered.

"You're already in." I lifted her by her narrow waist and carried her down the hall.

CHAPTER SEVEN

Sam and I crossed the river on the Navarro Bridge and jogged south toward Market Street. I was hoping detective Peterson's team would be finished so I could look at the crime scene without bullets flying over my head or him asking stupid questions. Once CSI was finished, there was no law against looking. Sosa had taken a bullet under my protection, but he was alive. I'd done all I could. Still, I was too restless to fall asleep. Sosa, Patrick Allison, and Marcus Lopez were linked through business, but what did it have to do with the sniper in the parking garage?

The run and the rack time with Sylvia put my demons back in their cage for now. Sylvia had simply rolled over and conked out. I loved watching her sleep, with her perfect mouth slightly open as if she couldn't wait to wake up and start talking again. That vocal trait was part of her charm for me. I was raised by taciturn people who carefully limited their words to necessary instructions usually disguised as questions or requests. In my grandpa's case, that could mean a week without speaking. His gestures and facial expression filled in the silent gaps, and I was keenly aware of his expectations. "Would you mind replacing the corral post next time you're out by the barn?" he might say. Or "That front left shoe on ol' Roany seems mighty loose." Neither of these statements sounded like orders, but they were, and I understood that from the earliest age.

Sylvia was the opposite. It was as if her emotions were so strong that any attempt to contain them would rip her apart at the seams. The courtroom gave her an outlet at work, and I was happy to serve as a foil to her passion in the bedroom.

While I slipped into the extra running shorts I kept in her bottom drawer and found my running shoes, Sylvia mumbled something about being careful. For her, being careful meant staying home. For me, it meant finding out what the hell was going on. Being warned off the case didn't stop me from wanting to know who took a shot at me and Javier Sosa. Maybe his enemies were from his home country, but why risk killing him in Texas? The murder rate in Mexico was twenty times higher. No one would bat an eye if he got shot south of the border. The *Cártel del Noreste* hung ten rivals from an overpass in Nuevo Laredo and they swung there for a week sporting hand-drawn signs identifying their killers. No one was ever arrested or charged with their killing. A hundred and fifty miles north in downtown San Antonio should be a different story.

A freight train blew its lonely whistle and clacked along the downtown tracks. This section of river had been inhabited for centuries by native tribes, then the Spanish, and finally European immigrants. I wondered if one group was more civilized than the other or if the advance of civilization was just an illusion. Sure, people used Uber instead of wagons and had air conditioning, but they were still killing each other.

I wondered about my encounter with Detective Peterson. It didn't leave me with much confidence he could solve the case on his own. His partner, Ochoa, seemed a bit more intelligent, and definitely easier to look at, but she was a rookie investigator and would have to follow Peterson's lead. I didn't make a habit of interfering with police investigations, but this was personal. Someone had taken out my client and stuck around to fire a few shots at me. In the interest of self-preservation, I needed to find out who did it.

Sam and I entered the parking garage across the street from Sosa's hotel. The crime investigation team was gone and had left behind a few broken strips of yellow caution tape. We slipped past the ticket booth and walked up to the fourth floor. Sam sniffed hopefully at a crumpled orange-and-white Whataburger bag, but it was empty. I picked it up and tossed it in the trash, doing my civic duty.

I checked the angle and found a perfect view of the hotel entrance across the street. Crouching down, I put myself in the shooter's position. He'd chosen well for the first shot, but he hadn't anticipated the cover created by the limo. As soon as Sosa went down, he would have been out of sight for the follow-up shot that hit the retaining wall over our heads. The street was deserted now and so was the entrance to the hotel. I visualized the height of a parked limo and saw where the second bullet had hit.

I moved farther down, re-creating the sequence of events. Once Sosa left in the limo, I guessed the shooter changed position to gain a better angle on me. I found another place that offered a clear view of the sidewalk on the opposite side of the street.

Sam watched me with interest, then started sniffing the empty parking spots. He wasn't a trained police dog, but he could sniff out a wounded deer or a dead dove in a huisache thicket. If I looked for something, he would look too. If I was angry, he would bark. If I was happy, he would lick my hand. He had that Labrador knack for always wanting to be helpful. The parking garage seemed to be swept clean. Sam wasn't so sure. He kept looking. Either Peterson's team had done a thorough search or, more likely, there'd been nothing to find.

Sam whined and pawed at something stuck between the curb and a concrete tire barrier. I scratched his ears. When he didn't give up, I took a closer look. Stuck in the crack was a spent rifle casing. He was a hunting dog and had caught the whiff of fresh gunpowder. It was directly behind where I guessed the last shot would have come from. At that point in the attack, I was returning fire and running across the street. The shooter wouldn't have had time to look for missing brass. He must have ejected the spent round, which took an unlucky bounce, and jumped into his car while I ran to the entrance. Maybe he hadn't counted on my return fire bringing a quick police response.

I took a picture of the location with my cell phone, then snapped a few extra photos of the garage. Sam posed next to his find. The police had been here, searched the place, and cleared the crime scene. I was doing my civic duty. I found a discarded popsicle stick and used it to lift the casing from its hiding place. It was a Winchester .308. Whoever used this had picked a lethal round. I was sure the shooter used a suppressor. If he hadn't, the explosion from the .308 would have echoed off the walls of the Alamo and caused panic along the River Walk. It didn't explain why it was Hollywood quiet. There were no clues on the brass. I got out a poop baggie I carried to clean up after Sam—a yellow plastic sack with the image of a dog doing his business. I couldn't wait to see the look on Detective Peterson's face when I showed it to him.

"Good work, Sam. You might make a police dog yet."

He tilted his head, disappointed that I didn't offer him more of a reward. I slipped the bag in my pocket and looked at my watch. It was four fifteen. We walked to the ground floor and took a shortcut home that crossed the Alamo Plaza.

The lights shining on the adobe bricks of the old mission were a constant reminder that sometimes you had to fight even though the odds were not in your favor. We paused briefly at The Alamo Cenotaph to pay our respects. The massive marble monument depicted the names and larger than life figures of the men who gave their lives in the Battle of the Alamo. It was aptly named *The Spirit of Sacrifice* and was dedicated in 1936 on the one hundredth anniversary of the fight that took place across the street. The names of David Crockett, William B. Travis, Jim Bowie, and James Bonham were forever etched in stone and Texas history.

I read the inscription: *In memory of the heroes who sacrificed their lives at the Alamo, March 6, 1836, in the defense of Texas. They chose never to surrender nor retreat. These brave hearts, with flag still proudly waving, perished in the flames of immortality that their high sacrifice might lead to the founding of this Texas.* I remembered my Marine Corps brothers-in-arms who hadn't made it back from Afghanistan. There was no monument honoring their sacrifice, but their names were etched in my memory and their faces haunted my dreams.

"Morgenstund hat Gold im Mund."
The morning hour has gold in its mouth.

—Grandpa Fischer

CHAPTER EIGHT

DAY TWO

I woke to the sound of rapid-fire knocking, as if Woody Woodpecker were using a hammer instead of his beak on my front door. My head ached, and a familiar nightmare stuck to my skin like sweat from the South Texas heat. It was a replay of my final deployment when our Humvee hit an IED, and I was pinned down while my team fought off the follow-up attack. Yesterday's downtown sniper had triggered the memory. My client was clinging to life in the ICU, and the shooter was still out there. The dream always left me feeling guilty for surviving and helpless for not being able to do anything about it. Despite my conscious effort to lock the demons away, the dream reminded me that they still controlled my subconscious. Not a good way to start the day.

Sam sensed my distress and licked my face. He was like Grandpa, neither ever let me stay in bed and feel sorry for myself. Both would tell me to wake up and get to work.

The knocking continued.

"Easy, buddy. I'm okay. I'm awake." I tried to pacify Sam's concern, then moved to an upright position and rubbed the sleep from my eyes.

At least it wasn't SAPD. I didn't hear the familiar "Police, open up." That was a good sign.

The digital clock read six thirty a.m. Maybe, I thought, I could wait the visitor out. In a few minutes he or she might leave, and I could go back to sleep. Sam wasn't having any of it. Sometimes I wished I were a cat lover like my next-door neighbor. Cats didn't care about your insecurities and weren't concerned about visitors. A Lab needed to be a part of everything. He barked and faced in the direction of the front door. "All right. You win. I'm getting dressed." I knew he was thinking that the visitor was probably bearing food because it was time for his breakfast. His thought process was easy to follow.

I found my shorts and a T-shirt and caught a glimpse of myself in the wall mirror I'd installed for Sylvia's benefit. I looked rode hard and put up wet, but I did have muscle tone. I flashed a smile. A shower and a shave could land me on a magazine cover.

"That's the ticket, you handsome devil." The full-watt grin had won over many potential enemies and never failed to charm the ladies. I turned toward the stairwell. "Roll the cameras, Sam. Let's go meet the early bird."

Sam barked a few times and went to the window to alert the visitor that I was awake and on my final approach. I peered through the peephole to determine the threat level of the caller. I kept a Mossberg 12-gauge pump-action shotgun leaning against the doorframe for anyone not spreading good cheer.

The visitor was a determined-looking woman in her late forties or early fifties judging by the hint of gray and the crow's feet partially covered with makeup. Her attire was modest—a white blouse tucked into a denim skirt that extended to just above her knees. She wore sturdy tennis shoes that had covered their share of dirty pavement, and around her neck was a large silver cross.

Sam barked again. He was focused on the yard, where a younger version of the woman bounced a tennis ball on the sidewalk. The girl looked to be about eleven or twelve—in the preteen stage where she dabbled with makeup and hair products but wasn't afraid to play with a ball or a dog. Sam spotted this trait instantly.

Then it hit me. This was the caller who requested a meeting to discuss her murdered daughter. I left the shotgun where it was and opened the door. Sam ripped through my legs and planted himself in front of the girl and her tennis ball, fixing her with the Labrador gaze.

"Is he friendly?" the woman asked, taking a protective step toward the young girl.

"He's never met a stranger."

The girl knew what he wanted and flicked the ball into the pecan leaves mixed with overgrown grass. Sam had the ball in his mouth before it took a second bounce. No matter how this encounter went, he'd found a friend. Chasing a ball was the next best thing to eating.

Relieved, she extended her hand. "Mr. Fischer?" Her palm was calloused, and her grip was strong. She was no stranger to hard work.

"That's me. Were you the one who called?"

"Yes. My name is Araceli Luna. Lola Davis suggested I contact you. As I said, it's about my daughter, Mr. Fischer. She was murdered. I want you to find out who did it."

Out of habit, I quickly scanned up and down the street for anything unusual—occupied vehicles or people loitering at the bus stop on the corner. I didn't see anything out of place, only the usual rising steam from the dew on the grass and the steady hum of cicadas. Rose Gustafson waved from her front flowerbed. She wore white rubber shrimp boots and a pair of leather gloves. Her gray hair was neatly braided and coiled on top of her head. The pile of brush by her gate was a sign she'd been working since dawn, taking advantage of the relative cool.

"Would you like to come inside?" I offered.

She glanced at the young girl still playing ball with Sam and said something in rapid-fire Spanish. The girl presented herself to me and extended her hand.

"This is my youngest daughter," she said.

"My name is Leticia Luna, Mr. Fischer," the girl said in a clear, crisp voice. She suddenly noticed my forehead scars and sucked in an involuntary breath.

"Leticia!" her mother scolded. "Please excuse her."

"It's okay." I knelt in front of the little girl and smiled. "I was hurt overseas. In the military."

"Are you okay?" she asked.

"It's all healed," I said. That seemed to satisfy her curiosity. It was healed, on the outside. The rest I was still working on. Sam barked, irritated that I'd interrupted his playtime.

"May I play with your dog?" she asked.

"He wouldn't have it any other way. His name's Sam."

I left Sam and Leticia in the yard, led Araceli Luna into the living room, and excused myself while I started the coffee maker and wiped dust from two mismatched mugs. I wanted to be fully awake when Mrs. Luna gave me the details. It wasn't every day someone dropped by before seven to offer me a murder case.

While the coffee maker did its thing, I took the opportunity to study Mrs. Luna. She paced my living room nervously while examining my collection of family photos. She seemed anxious to tell her story. It was a good sign that she was on the level. I got at least two calls a week from someone who wanted me to harass a business associate for screwing them over or a disgruntled worker wanting to stick it to their ex-boss.

She stopped in front of the pictures of my father. There was one of him in his highway patrol uniform and one of him with his cowboy hat and Gillespie County sheriff's badge. I also kept an older picture of him in a Marine uniform, and the triangular mahogany display case with his burial flag.

"Was this your father?" she called to me.

"Yeah," I said, filling the two mugs coffee.

I motioned Mrs. Luna into one of two matching overstuffed leather chairs and placed the mugs on a small carved coffee table from Mexico I'd inherited from my grandma. The only other furniture in the room was a floor-to-ceiling bookcase stuffed with my eclectic collection of Texas history, case law, and my complete collection of Tony Hillerman mysteries.

"I'm sorry for your loss," I said.

Her hands trembled. "Thank you, Mr. Fischer. The pain never goes away. Her killer is still out there. They told me to forget, but I see her face every day." She gestured toward the flag on the mantel. "You know what it's like to lose someone close."

"It was years ago, but I do understand," I said. My dad's murder was still an open wound and not something I liked to talk about. "What did Lola Davis tell you about me?"

"That you were the one to call if there was no one else to turn to."

"Why do you feel that way?"

"The police have done nothing. They said it was an accident. She was found in the San Antonio River. On the River Walk. It was the day after the Fourth of July. They said she was drunk. My daughter never drank."

She took a deep breath. When her hands stopped shaking, she sipped some coffee. I let her collect herself in silence. It dawned on me who her daughter was. The story had made the national news because she was found by a little boy wearing a coonskin cap. As usual, there was no follow-up story. The novelty had worn off. The little boy was the hook for the national news, and he had gone back to Germany with his souvenirs and a story to tell. The dead woman was forgotten. No one cared about her except her mother.

"Did Mrs. Davis tell you that I do private investigation for a living?" I hated coming off as an asshole, but I couldn't afford to run a charity. I had a mortgage on my fixer-upper and an employee who hadn't seen a paycheck in months.

"Oh, yes, of course," she insisted.

"I get five thousand up front to cover my expenses. That does not include seventy-five dollars an hour plus mileage. You don't have to worry. I keep meticulous records, and I'll send you an invoice at the end of each week. This kind of investigation could take some time."

She reached in her purse and took out a new bank envelope. "I pay now?" she asked, offering me the envelope.

I checked the contents and found a stack of hundred-dollar bills. Lola must have mentioned an amount. This bundle was probably at least two months' paycheck. I wondered how far in advance she had planned this meeting.

"Thank you, Mrs. Luna," I said, and handed the envelope back to her.

"It's not enough?" She looked surprised and hurt.

Five thousand dollars would come in handy, but I didn't take money unless I knew I could make a difference. The PI business was built on reputation and referrals. I'd decided from the beginning to pick and choose my cases and my clients carefully.

"The money's fine." I waited for her to take another deep breath. "First, I need to know what happened. I won't take your money unless I think I can help you."

"But I have no one else to turn to."

I stood up. "Give me a moment." I walked back to the kitchen for a coffee refill. "Would you like more coffee?" I called to her.

"No, gracias," she said.

I stopped by the front window on my way back into the living room to check on Sam and her daughter. Sam was crouched at her heel. He would keep her occupied for as long as she was willing to throw the ball. I studied the street again. A black Ford Super Duty pickup drove slowly past my yard. The dark tinted windows blocked my view of the driver. It wasn't unusual, but I made a note of the license number. Getting shot at left me paranoid.

The heavy dew was gone, replaced by heat waves off the pavement. White-winged doves joined the cicadas, adding their slightly mournful notes to the clash of neighborhood noise. Rose was still working on her pyracantha. All the appearances of a normal Labor Day weekend.

I broke out a new spiral notebook and a Bic pen and took a seat behind my desk. "Why don't you start at the beginning?"

Araceli Luna recited her story while I took notes of times and places. Marissa was the first in her family to go to college and she had gotten a scholarship to Texas Tech. She was an ambitious young woman with big plans for the future. Mrs. Luna showed me the newspaper clipping from the day after the body was found. On top was a photo of the boy with the coonskin cap, the story hook everyone remembered. On the bottom was a photo of a man with a scruffy salt-and-pepper beard standing by the River Walk. He had a toothless smile and wore an Army cap and camo jacket. The article said he'd helped recover the body from the river.

The police had found no evidence of a struggle or foul play. An autopsy revealed Marissa had alcohol in her system. A friend said she left a dance club alone around midnight and was never seen alive again. I wrote down the friend's name. I also made a note of the night club near the River Walk. Without any evidence to the contrary, the medical examiner ruled it an accidental death by drowning. Case closed. I took a closer look at the autopsy report.

"Is this all the police gave you?" I asked.

Mrs. Luna nodded. The ME usually listed additional findings at the end of the report. What she gave me had nothing.

"My Marissa never drank, Mr. Fischer. That's how I know the police are wrong." She said this last part with particular conviction.

"She was a young woman out partying with her friends. You said she liked to dance. Are you sure she never drank? Not even a little? She was over twenty-one. It wasn't illegal."

"She was very health conscious. She was studying to be a nurse. One more year and she would have graduated from Texas Tech. My daughter always exercised and took care of herself."

"Did she have any enemies? Maybe her friends were jealous?"

"Absolutely not, Mr. Fischer. Everyone loved her."

I tapped on my notebook. "This is a cold case, Mrs. Luna. Chances are I won't be able to find anything."

Disappointment tugged at the corner of her lips. "But Mrs. Davis said you helped her son," she insisted.

"Each case is different. Sometimes, there's nothing anyone can do. It's hard to take, but accidents do happen. There're times when there's no one to blame. It's better to forget the tragedy and remember the joy they brought to your life." It was the cold hard truth that most people couldn't accept. I didn't want to give Mrs. Luna any false hope. Despite what Skeeter's mother told her, my chances of finding her daughter's killer after so much time were very slim at best.

Mrs. Luna folded her hands in her lap. Her look told me she wouldn't budge from the chair with a front-end loader unless I agreed to take her case.

"Have you discussed your case with anyone else besides Mrs. Davis?" I asked.

"No," she said abruptly. "Absolutely not." Her quick response suggested otherwise, but I would deal with that later.

I tapped on my notebook. "I'll tell you what, let me do some checking and make a few phone calls."

"Mrs. Davis said you were skeptical of everything."

"If I do take your case, I will get to the truth. Are you willing to accept that?" I always asked this last question. Some clients only wanted me to prove their version of the truth.

"Please, find out who killed my daughter."

"If I can help, I'll let you know."

She leaped from the chair and grabbed both my arms. "Thank you. Thank you. I knew you would help. Mrs. Davis was right. You are an angel," she gushed.

"I'm far from an angel," I said, extracting myself from her grasp. "Give me twenty-four hours. I'll consult my associate and do a little digging. I haven't said yes yet."

"Of course. I understand." From the smile on her face, all she heard me say was that I would take the case. "I knew today would be a special day."

"Why's that?"

"Today's Marissa's birthday. She would have been twenty-three."

I opened the front door. Sam lay on his back getting his belly rubbed. He didn't bother to look at me. Shameless.

"One more question. Who was the officer in charge of the investigation?"

"Detective Peterson."

CHAPTER NINE

After months of twiddling my thumbs and racking up credit card debt, my business calendar was suddenly booked. I desperately needed something to keep my mind off yesterday's events, and Grandpa insisted that work was the cure for psychological problems. His well-ordered German temperament offered no excuses for self-pity and eschewed the idea of victimhood. I didn't have a fence to fix or cattle to herd, but now I did have a case to solve or at least investigate. I called the hospital to get an update on Sosa. The helpful nurse said it would be at least another twenty-four hours before I could talk to him. I breathed a sigh of relief. He was still in ICU, but he was stable. That gave me time to find out if there was anything I could do for Mrs. Luna. I called Skeeter next, my associate and one and only employee, to give him a heads up that he might be getting a paycheck this month. After my handy work forced the DA to drop the charges against him, Skeeter became curious about my business. It turned out that he was somewhat of a wizard when it came to electronics, a skill he discovered after the abrupt end to his football career.

"A real paycheck?" Skeeter was skeptical and groggy, with a gravelly voice so near the lowest perceptible decibel level that I had to guess at his response.

"What other kind is there?"

"The last job paid in elk meat." It was true, our client had paid with elk steaks fresh from his New Mexico hunt. But I loved elk, and it was hard to come by in South Texas.

"Compare that to the price of beef and we were highly rewarded." I heard him clear his throat and decided he was sufficiently awake to retain information. "This one already made a cash offer." I heard his three-hundred-pound bulk shift on the bed.

"Give me a name," he mumbled. In the background, his bedside laptop pulsed to life. I gave him Marissa Luna's name and the information her mother had shared, then put the phone on speaker. I finished getting dressed while Skeeter gave me a running commentary of his findings.

"She didn't leave much of a paper trail. There's a Facebook tribute and a few pictures on Instagram, along with her police report courtesy of the Texas Public Information Act."

The nitty-gritty details of cyber research were Skeeter's specialty, which saved me the agony of spending long hours staring at a computer screen. While he wasn't working for me, he made money installing security systems for big businesses around San Antonio and Austin and doing sporadic insurance company background checks. I knew he was as eager to get back to investigative work as I was. I'd thrown the dice when I took on his case free of charge hoping my success would spin into positive publicity and more referrals to boost my fledgling business. Maybe it was finally paying off.

"Well, keep digging. I'll check in with you later."

I left Sam in his backyard pool, cooling off from his playdate and sulking because he held me responsible for cutting it short, and drove to the SAPD headquarters on Santa Rosa Avenue hoping to catch Detective Peterson still in the office. Any other detective I would have called in advance to set up an appointment, but I knew Peterson would tell me to piss up a rope before answering any questions about a case he'd covered and closed months ago.

I was going to use the brass Sam found in the parking garage to work a trade for information. The pressure on him to show results in last night's high-profile shooting would be immense. Javier Sosa was a Mexican citizen. Mexico didn't seem to mind if their citizens were assassinated in their own country, but they took exception to attempts on US soil. This story wouldn't go away without a quick conviction.

Knowing Peterson was a prick, I would have to handle the negotiations as delicately as possible. Not one of my stronger points. I'd waited fifteen minutes for a bag of taquitos at the Las Tapatias drive-through hoping to gain an edge by presenting San Antonio's finest a peace offering.

I parked in the public garage and walked across the street to the white limestone building with small prison windows. The public art on display out front consisted of leftover metal beams painted white and standing on end like unstable teepee poles in a gale force wind. Nothing says "public safety" like a precarious stack of thirty-foot-tall metal poles. Lifelike figures of cowboys and Indians were art I could appreciate. Random poles, not so much.

I recognized the sergeant working the front desk. His name was Hugo Vera, a retired old-timer who came back to work part-time because his wife got tired of seeing him around the house all day. He'd also worked for my father when he was sheriff of Gillespie County and owned a house in Fredericksburg. I'd known him since I was a kid.

"How's the PI business?" he asked.

"Maybe I should have opened a barbecue joint. At least I'd know where my next meal was coming from."

"Hang in there. It takes a while to get established." He'd been offering me encouragement since grade school. "What brings you down here, Nick?"

"I need to talk to Detective Peterson."

When he heard the detective's name, his affable, grizzled face turned sour. "I would advise against it. Tomahawk's been here all night talking to the Feds about your late-night shootout."

"Is he ever in a good mood?"

Vera grinned. "He was happier when he was in the SWAT unit."

"Peterson worked SWAT? When was that?" I couldn't picture the guy having any tactical skills.

"Ten years ago. Before your time."

"Why'd he quit?"

"He was asked to leave. Too many bodies were piling up. Nothing official, but he had a nasty reputation for shooting first."

"This can't wait."

He shrugged. "Don't say I didn't warn you, kid." He buzzed me through to the upstairs offices.

Peterson was in his cubicle wearing the same short-sleeve shirt from the night before, minus the tie. A stack of paper cups threatened to stage a rebellion against the file folders on his desk. I perched three large coffees and a white bag of taquitos in the mix. He looked at me like I'd just asked him to extend his auto warranty. I flashed my best high-wattage smile.

"Who let you in here?"

I ignored the question. "There's eggs and chorizo, eggs and barbacoa, or eggs and brisket. Help yourself." I took the lid off one of the coffees and took a sip like we did this every day. There was a desk next to his sporting a picture of Ochoa and a five- or six-year-old boy with an angelic smile and hair that was dark purple. "Where's Ochoa?"

"Busy. What the fuck're you doin' here?"

"Nice to see you again, too, Detective. How's the Sosa investigation going?"

"You're still the number one suspect."

"So, you got nothin'?"

"It's my case. I told you to stay the fuck away from it."

"It's all yours. I'm here about the Luna case. Apparent drowning victim. Marissa Luna. Found in the river by Davy Crockett."

"Come on, Fischer. I was up all night babysitting the forensics team. I spent two hours briefing the FBI and an hour getting chewed out by the captain for not giving them enough information." He peeled away the foil wrapper on a taquito and took a big bite. "Thanks for breakfast," he said around a mouthful of egg and brisket. "Now, get the fuck out."

I took out Sam's poop bag and dangled it in the air.

Peterson spit his mouthful of breakfast on the floor. "This some kinda joke?"

I kept a straight face, but it wasn't easy. Showing him the poop bag was worth seeing his reaction. "Relax, it's evidence from the parking garage. I was in the area walking my dog and couldn't resist taking a look."

"You interfered with a crime scene?"

"I waited till your guys were gone. This is something they missed."

"A stool sample?"

"Maybe I scared the shit out of him." I was on a roll.

"Take a hike, Fischer." He wiped his face and pointed at the cubicle opening.

I didn't move. "Relax, it's not poop. I was fresh out of evidence bags. It's a .308 shell casing."

That caught his attention. His expression abruptly shifted from irritation to concern. "How do I know that came from the scene?"

"I thought you'd say that." I took out my cell phone and showed him the pictures of Sam in the parking garage. "Actually, my dog found it. Don't worry, he didn't touch it. If he did, you can get his paw prints."

"Funny man. Let's have it." He held his hand out over the table for the baggie.

I held it just out of his reach. "How about a trade?"

"You know that's withholding evidence." The skin on his neck turned red.

"Oh, you're gonna get it. After I take it downstairs and ask Sergeant Vera to run it through the system. He'll have it dusted for fingerprints and do the ballistics. He'd love something to do. The front desk gets pretty boring. You could keep the poop bag."

Peterson sat back in his chair. I saw the wheels turning. He took another bite of taquito, then washed it down with coffee. I expected him to come up with another reason not to share any information with me. I took a step toward the door to prove I wasn't bluffing. "If that's the way you want it."

"All right," he blurted out. "What d'ya wanna know?"

I turned back around. "The autopsy for one. Why were the additional findings left out of the report you gave Mrs. Luna?"

He gestured toward the poop bag. He wasn't giving away anything for free. I set it on his desk.

"Because it showed elevated HCG." He scooped up the bag and tossed it in his desk drawer.

"She was pregnant?"

He wiped his mouth with a paper napkin. His facial expression didn't change. I waited for more explanation. None came.

"You didn't want her mother to know, or you didn't think it was important?"

"Look, the girl was careless. You follow me? Her kind usually are. It was a judgment call."

"Her kind?"

"You some kind of bleeding heart?"

"She was a college student in Lubbock," I said.

"Doesn't change where she came from. She was westside trash."

This guy was a piece of work. "You don't think the father is a suspect? Isn't it odd he didn't come forward?"

"A suspect in what? There's no foul play. We can't prove the father knew about the baby."

"You have fetal DNA. You could ask him."

"The girl had two boyfriends since high school that we could find. They were Facebook friends, whatever that means. They both volunteered DNA. Both came up negative. Like I said, she was careless. The bottom line here is the girl went out dancing, got wasted, and fell in the river. Shit happens. You can tell Mrs. Luna the same thing I told her—her daughter's death was an accident. I thought you were a Boy Scout. I didn't figure you were the kind to take a grieving mother's money and yank her chain." He stood up, ending our conversation.

"A Boy Scout?"

"Yeah, you act like you're working on a merit badge—helping out the underprivileged."

"Who said I was working for Mrs. Luna?"

"She calls me once a week. I figured somebody might have slipped her your number."

"I'm just curious by nature."

He laughed. "Forget about this case. Go find some skirt-chaser to photograph. You're good at that."

I smiled. "Thanks. Good advice. I'll call your wife." I slipped out the hall door before he could respond. I'd heard all I needed to hear.

Halfway down the hall, I ran into Detective Ochoa. She had an armload of files and an up-all-night look on her face. Seeing me didn't cheer her up.

"Busy night?" I asked, hoping to win her over to my side.

"You have no idea."

"I left coffee and a taquito on your desk, if your partner didn't take them."

"You talked to him?" She sounded exasperated.

"Tried to get some information on another case."

"Thanks a lot," she said with a big dose of sarcasm. "He's already pissed 'cause he's missing church." She actually seemed nice when her partner wasn't around.

"Church on Saturday?"

"On the seventh day He rested. He's Seventh-day Adventist."

"Doesn't strike me as the religious type."

She shrugged. "Just do us both a favor and stay away from Peterson."

CHAPTER TEN

A haze had settled over the city by the time I left the station that was a mixture of heat rising off the pavement and a cloud of dust the local meteorologist claimed blew in from North Africa. My eyes and nose started dripping before I could climb into my eight-year-old F-150 and crank the air conditioning. For the last ten thousand miles it had only worked at one speed. Luckily, that speed was high. While the air vents dried the moisture on my face and shirt, I searched the glovebox for an antihistamine. Nothing but an empty package. I'd taken the last tablet during a recent wave of cedar pollen.

The picture Peterson painted of Marissa Luna was of a party girl who had one too many and did a swan dive into the river, quite different than what her mother described. His story about withholding the news of Marissa being pregnant because he was being sensitive didn't hold water. He didn't strike me as the altruistic type. On the other hand, he wouldn't have anything to gain by covering up a murder unless he was involved, and that didn't seem likely. He worked homicide and cleared murder cases for a living. He'd made mistakes before, as I proved in Skeeter's case, but that was partly the DA's fault. Peterson didn't seem like the type who'd close a case if he sniffed foul play. According to Sergeant Vera, he was transferred to homicide for being too gung-ho, not lazy. I couldn't really hold that against him. I'd been accused of the same thing. There was nothing in his report that screamed murder. There was no evidence of assault or rape, and there were no witnesses. If Marissa Luna was murdered, the killer had covered his tracks. Picking up the cold trail wasn't going to be easy.

I turned north on Market Street and admired the red sandstone exterior of the courthouse complex. It looked like something you'd see in Arizona, but still much better designed than the SAPD building. My next move was to track down the place where the police report said Marissa Luna had fallen into the river. I didn't expect to find anything at a stale crime scene, but Peterson's revelation about Marissa being pregnant had left me wondering what else he might have overlooked or withheld. It was a place to start.

I found a rare open downtown parking spot, locked my pickup, and took the steps down to the River Walk. A huge bald cypress tree named for Ben Milam, a veteran of the War of 1812 and the Texas Revolution, stood below the Commerce Street footbridge. He'd survived war, encounters with Comanches, and prison in Mexico, only to be shot in the head by a Mexican sniper while he stopped to relieve himself. Or so the story went. The tree was only a little over three hundred yards from where a sniper put a bullet in my client and Marissa Luna had taken her last breath.

As I walked down the shaded concrete pathway, I got the strange feeling that I was being watched. It could have been paranoia, but it was the same feeling I used to get on patrol in Afghanistan. My mind flicked back to the extra shots fired in my direction in front of Sosa's hotel. Maybe the killer was simply covering his escape, but the fact that he was still out there didn't make me feel any safer. A dust-filled wind rustled the cypress limbs and sent me into a sneezing fit. I needed to find the nearest pharmacy.

The place described in the police report was underneath the Travis Street bridge where the river ran through an urban canyon of buildings and parking garages. Sam and I'd passed the spot a dozen times on our run since that night in July when she entered the water. Below a tile mural of the Alamo, I found an Our Lady of Guadalupe candle, along with a bundle of plastic roses and a white cross held upright in a Folgers coffee can filled with rocks. It was a shrine to honor her death. To the Catholic Hispanics it was known as a *descansos*, a common sight along the highways in the Southwest marking an unfortunate fatal accident.

While I paused to study the scene, a young woman wearing black yoga pants knelt in front of the candle. She had pale skin, a stocky build, and wore her blond hair in a tight ponytail. Her eyes closed and her lips moved with a silent prayer. When she finished, she crossed herself and used a paper clip to attach a five-by-seven photo of Marissa to the coffee can. Then she stood and walked to the flagstones lining the man-made river channel. She pulled a bracelet from her wrist, held it to her lips, then tossed it into the river.

"Tragic," I said before she could turn to go.

She glanced over her shoulder, startled. Her eyes were wet with tears.

I flashed my best disarming smile. "Sorry to scare you. Was that a present for Marissa?" I pointed to the place in the river where the bracelet had sunk.

"Did you know her?" she asked, wiping her face with her fingertips. Her skeptical eyes lingered on my forehead scars. My smile didn't seem to soften my appearance.

"Unfortunately, no," I said, "but I know her mother. She told me today was her birthday."

"Yeah, it's her birthday. But the bracelet was hers. She—she asked me to hold it for her." She wrung her hands while her eyes darted across the river to an older couple walking a toy poodle.

"I'm Nick Fischer," I said, smiling a little bigger. "Are you Beth Renfro?"

That caught her off guard. "How do you know my name?"

"Marissa's mother." I offered my hand. She didn't take it. I realized I was still holding the damp paper towel I was using to wipe my runny nose.

"Were you good friends with Marissa?" I asked.

"Yeah. We went to high school together."

"Do you know what happened to her?"

"She drowned in the river," she said without hesitation, like she'd rehearsed the line.

"How do you know?"

"I was with her that night. We were drinking and dancing. It was a party night."

"Her mother said she didn't drink."

Beth looked taken aback, like she wasn't expecting to be questioned. "Are you a cop?"

"Private investigator hired by Mrs. Luna." I stifled another sneeze and showed my creds.

She glanced at the license but didn't come any closer. "There's a lot of things her mother didn't know."

"Like she was pregnant?"

Beth hesitated, weighing her options for a response.

When she didn't say anything, I added: "Did she have a boyfriend?"

"Not that I know of. She didn't say anything to me."

"Did she dance with anybody in particular that night?"

"No." Her answers came quickly.

"Did she leave with anybody?"

"I told the police everything. No one saw her leave."

"What time did you notice she was gone?"

"Around midnight, I guess. We wanted to get out of there before the bars closed. When I looked around for Marissa, she was gone. The detective said they found her shoe here. It had a broken heel. She always liked high heels." She sucked on her bottom lip. That was all she was going to tell me.

"Thanks for your help."

She immediately turned and walked away. I blew my nose and watched her ponytail dance from side to side as she broke into a jog.

I wondered why she'd lied. I also wondered about the bracelet she'd tossed into the river. The water was less than two feet deep, and the channel was only ten yards wide, yet it was still too dirty to see the moss-covered bottom.

While I wiped my nose and thought about my next move, a man with a scruffy salt-and-pepper beard shuffled out of the shadows. He knelt on the flagstone edge on the far side of the river and stared into the opaque water. He looked vaguely familiar, then I remembered the man in the newspaper clipping. He wore the same Army cap and camo jacket. I hadn't noticed him before; he must have been standing behind the bridge support waiting for Beth to leave.

Suddenly, he stepped into the knee-high water and waded unsteadily to the center of the river. I knew what he was looking for. He fished with both hands in the water and came up with the bracelet. He smiled, exposing missing teeth.

"Hey!" I yelled at him. "Leave that alone."

He turned back toward the opposite bank and sloshed toward the flagstones.

I jumped in the tepid water and splashed after him. "That's not yours," I shouted.

"The lady throwed it away," he mumbled when I caught up to him. "It's mine now. Finders keepers, losers weepers."

I dug in my wallet for a twenty-dollar bill and held it out to him. "Here. I'll trade you."

He quickly snatched the money and handed over the bracelet. I climbed out of the river and examined it more closely. It was gold in color and consisted of three bands connected by a lopsided heart shape. On the inside of the heart were the engraved initials M. L.

The man climbed out of the water and hurried off, holding the twenty above his head.

"Hey," I called.

He picked up his pace, afraid I would change my mind and take the money back. I took out another twenty and waved it in his direction.

"Wanna make another twenty?" That got his attention. He executed a precise military about-face and stood at attention until I caught up with him. "Were you on the River Walk the day after the Fourth of July?"

He scratched his salt-and-pepper whiskers with a wet hand. "Maybe. I spend most days down here. Sometimes I hike over to the Mission. They give out free meals."

"There was a dead girl found in the river that day. Were you there?"

His eyes lit up. "Davy Crockett," he said.

"That's right. A kid dressed in a coonskin cap found her."

"No, it was Davy Crockett. I seen him. He shot her dead."

"Shot her? I thought she was already dead."

He held out his hand. I gave him the twenty.

"He shot her with his flintlock," he whispered as if sharing a secret.

"A toy gun?"

He flashed a toothless grin and laughed. “She looked like a raccoon.”

“Why a raccoon?”

“Both eyes was black. She wearin’ a mask.”

“Two black eyes?”

“Yes, sir. Am I dismissed, sir?”

I studied his anxious face. What did it mean and why wasn’t it mentioned in the autopsy? I wondered if he was making that part up or if he was on the level.

“Sir?”

“You’re sure about the black eyes?”

“Yes, sir.”

“Carry on, soldier.”

He came to full attention, executed a brisk salute, then laughed as he hustled off to spend his fortune.

CHAPTER ELEVEN

There was a parking ticket tucked under my wiper blade when I got back to my pickup. Turns out the space was only free until eleven thirty a.m. I checked my watch. Eleven thirty-seven. The meter maid had my number. I tossed it with the others in my glovebox. That five grand from Mrs. Luna would just about cover my parking fines.

I cranked the a/c and waited for my sneezing fit to subside. Then I took Commerce Street west toward Marcus Lopez's law office. My plan was to catch Sylvia on her lunch break and share the news that I was on a case. It was too soon to say it was murder, but I wasn't satisfied with Peterson's conclusion, and Marissa's friend was less than convincing. My gut was telling me forces besides gravity landed Marissa Luna in the San Antonio River.

Why would someone want her dead? Did it have something to do with her being pregnant? Where did the bracelet fit in? Could it have come from the father? But would he give her what looked like an expensive bracelet and then kill her? Maybe it was a peace offering that she couldn't accept? Why didn't her friend share the bracelet with the police? Was she involved? Was Beth's sweet innocent face simply a cover for something more sinister? The more time I spent in this job, the more I found that the bad guys weren't always obvious. In Afghanistan it was fairly simple: you targeted the man in a turban carrying an AK-47 or wearing a suicide vest. On the streets of San Antonio, evil could carry a rosary or wear a badge.

Noon downtown traffic was heavy as usual. I waited through two lights on South San Saba Street watching a group of teenagers on electric scooters zip around pedestrians in Milam Park. When the light finally turned green, a woman in a white Range Rover cut me off making a U-turn. I honked, and she gave me the middle finger. There were worse places to drive, Kabul came to mind, but The Alamo City wasn't far down the list. Maybe the African dust had everyone on edge.

I stopped at a grocery store a few blocks from Sylvia's office to grab a little token of my affection and a package of antihistamine. She always said she didn't want me to spend money on flowers, but she never seemed to mind when I did. I bought the only bouquet of yellow tulips on display. They weren't the freshest I'd ever seen, but yellow tulips were Sylvia's favorite, and they came with a red vase. I found my miracle drug and got in line behind a guy who just remembered something else his wife wanted him to pick up. He asked if I minded waiting while he went to look for it.

"Why should I mind?" I asked him, sneezing into my hand. He forced a nervous laugh and shuffled toward the frozen food aisle. When I first mustered out of the Marine Corps and heavily sedated with Jack Daniels, I'd have run the shameless lady in the Range Rover off the road and brained the hen-pecked husband with a sack of frozen potatoes, but I was turning over a new leaf and had promised Sylvia that I'd work on my people skills.

Marcus Lopez's law office was a four-story neo-Spanish colonial-style building, complete with a faux bell tower and a Spanish-tile courtyard featuring a koi pond. Its west side location was surrounded by vacant lots, abandoned businesses, and a car body shop. Behind the building stretched neglected tract houses with dirt front lawns enclosed in hurricane fencing. It was the kind of neighborhood Marissa grew up in. Marcus had grown up here too and had acquired most of a city block that he was preparing to demolish and turn into apartments. Sylvia said he chose the location to remind him of his roots, but my guess was he did it to show off to his old west side neighbors.

I parked behind the building and waited a few minutes for the wonder drug to take effect. When my sneezing stopped, I wiped my nose and face the best I could and went inside. Every blank space was covered with election posters featuring Marcus Lopez's smug smile. The signs reminded me of the storm cloud building over my love life. If he was elected, Sylvia would probably go to Austin to serve in his new cabinet. I understood. It was a career move. If she went, I would have to move to Austin with her or settle for seeing her only on weekends. Austin was only sixty miles north, but I was trying to build my own business in San Antonio. Her argument was that I could be a private eye anywhere, which wasn't necessarily true. I did have a few friends in Austin from my time as a reserve deputy for Travis County, but I liked San Antonio. Austin was fun if you were into hipster bands and liked watching the University of Texas play football along with a hundred thousand of your closest friends, but it was one of those college towns that went wild in the 1960s and never really grew up. The city slogan was *Keep Austin Weird.*

San Antonio had history. That was the other reason I'd moved here. Besides having enough people to support my budding private investigations business, Texas history began at the Alamo. I understood the sacrifice now that my enlistment was over. When I looked at the Alamo, it reminded me that the heart of the state still beat and that its soul was still authentic. Maybe I was being naïve, and the spirit had left long before my time, but I wasn't ready to give up hope in Texas or my relationship with Sylvia.

I took the stairs to the third floor and caught a glimpse of my profile in the hallway mirror. The man staring back was operating on three hours' sleep. His fresh black T-shirt was damp with sweat, and he needed a shave. The scars on his forehead had turned purple in the heat, and his nose and eyes were red from breathing African dust. How could she resist that and a bouquet of wilted tulips? I flashed a grin. "You still got it, you handsome devil." One could always hope.

Luckily, her overprotective secretary was away from her desk, so I let myself in. Her office had rustic wood paneling accented with brightly colored paintings depicting blue bonnets, buttercups, and a variety of other native Texas wildflowers. The centerpiece was a three-panel photo of her favorite yellow tulips.

"I came to take you to lunch," I said, trying to sound cheerful. I set the flowers on her polished oak desk.

"I bet you picked those yourself," she said, not sounding impressed.

"I guess tulips are out of season."

"And you got all dressed up." She focused on my dirty jeans still damp from wading the river.

"I can explain. I've been up since six thirty, and my allergies are doing battle with the elements."

"The dust, isn't it? You should take an antihistamine," she said, flipping open a file on her desk. "I can't go to lunch. I've got a meeting in ten minutes. You should've called."

"I'm on a case." No time to beat around the bush. I might as well come clean.

"What case?" Disappointment dripped from the question.

"If I'm gonna go back to school, I'll need money. My GI bill dried up."

She thought about that for a moment. For once, I'd come up with an excuse she might actually buy.

"You have a paying customer? Please tell me it's not one of your lost causes." Her faith in me was overwhelming.

"She offered to pay my full retainer up front."

"Offered? You didn't take the money?"

"I told her I would look into it first and see if I could help her."

Sylvia shrugged. "What's the matter with you? You talked to her, didn't you?"

"Yeah." I knew where she was going with this. It was a new tactic she was using to point out that my business acumen wasn't fully developed.

"And you spent all morning investigating her case?"

"How else am I gonna find out if I can help her?"

"Those are billable hours." She never used to talk like that when we were in law school. We had both volunteered for St. Mary's Center for Legal and Social Justice. Before I became disillusioned with the idea of becoming a lawyer, we had talked about joining the center full-time after graduation. Only a year of working for Marcus Lopez, and she was talking about billable hours. She checked her watch, reminding me I was on the clock. I thought maybe if I told her the details of the case, she would understand my interest.

"She was the young woman found by the kid dressed up like Davy Crockett. Happened on the fifth of July."

She tapped a polished fingernail on the desk. "I remember that." She stood up. I saw a flicker of the old Sylvia who enjoyed the challenge of a mystery.

"What can you tell me about this?" I showed her the bracelet.

"It's a bracelet," she deadpanned.

"Brilliant, Doctor Watson."

"It looks exactly like the one you never gave me." She giggled.

"It belonged to the deceased."

"Where did you get it?"

"I fished it out of the river this morning. Actually, a homeless man fished it out. I paid him twenty bucks for it."

"While you were working for free. How do you know it's hers?"

"I ran into a friend who was with her that night. I watched her toss it into the river underneath the bridge where the police said Marissa drowned."

"Why would she do that?"

"Today was Marissa's birthday."

"You took an offering to the dead?"

"I saved it from the homeless guy. He saw her toss it and was gonna make off with it. If it turns out not to be important, I'll throw it back. Marissa can wear it in the afterlife." I held up the bracelet so Sylvia could see the engraving. "It has her initials. M. L. Marissa Luna."

"Could be a coincidence. If I remember right, the police said it was an accident," she said, crossing to the large window that looked west over the vacant lots. She stared toward the distant rolling hills covered with cedar trees and new luxury homes that she couldn't wait to move into. "You read the article. She was drunk and fell in the river."

"She didn't drink."

"What did the friend say?"

"She lied."

"How do you know?"

"I know when someone's lying. Besides, she was a nursing student with big plans for the future."

"Why would her friend lie? You think she's a suspect?" She tapped her teeth with the Cross fountain pen I'd given her for graduation.

"Maybe they were in love with the same man," I said. "Marissa was pregnant."

Sylvia stopped tapping and turned to me. "Where's the boyfriend?" I saw a flicker of excitement.

"Exactly. No one knows anything about him. She didn't tell her mom or, apparently, her best friend."

"What did the police say about the pregnancy?" she asked.

"Peterson was the detective involved. He didn't even tell the mother. Said it didn't change anything. He checked out two old boyfriends, but neither matched the fetal DNA."

She turned from the window, her brown eyes smoking, and pointed the Cross pen at my heart. "You think it was the boyfriend. And you think the bracelet will help you track him down." She paced a few steps back and forth in front of the window like she used to do while we were studying for tests together in law school. "She told the boyfriend about the baby. He buys her a bracelet and tells her to have an abortion. She says no because she's a strict Catholic, or at least her mother is, and he throws her in the river."

"That's what I was thinking," I said.

"If the bracelet's hers, of course." She tapped the pen on her perfect teeth. "Or she couldn't tell her Catholic mother or go through with an abortion. So, she took her own life."

We looked at each other for a moment, not speaking. I didn't know which was more tragic, Marissa being murdered by her boyfriend or her taking her own life because she thought she had no other options. How many other young women had faced the same dilemma?

Sylvia whispered in my ear: "It's interesting. I get why you wanna go for it. But don't take the case. The firm will hire you. We need investigators. The work is safe, and you'd have time to go back to school."

I wrapped my arms around her, enjoying the warmth of her body and the spicy scent of her expensive perfume. She melted against me. Our lips locked. I wanted to shut the door and make love to her for the rest of the afternoon.

"You don't have to worry about money." She ran her fingertips across my forehead and into my damp, short-cropped hair.

I needed her. Wanted her. But I couldn't keep my mouth shut.

"You know I could never work for Marcus Lopez." The spell was broken.

She pushed me away and walked back to her desk. "It wouldn't kill you to accept help from somebody. You act like it's a sin or something. Do you think Marcus got where he is without help? You don't always have to do everything on your own." It was the first time she'd compared me to her boss. It was a small thing and probably didn't mean anything, but I noticed.

I followed her behind her desk, took her hand, hoping to recapture the moment. "I'm sorry. I know I'm hardheaded. I can't help it. I'm trying to turn over a new leaf. You're a good influence."

"You're so full of shit."

"It's true."

"You'll never change, Nick Fischer."

I leaned in for a final kiss but was interrupted by a cold knock on the door.

A moment later, Marcus strolled in. He saw me holding Sylvia, and his signature smile quickly faded. He stood in the open door like he owned the place, which, of course, he did, but when he surveyed the room, he seemed to claim everything: the carpet, the walls, the double-pane windows, and Sylvia.

"Mr. Anker's in the conference room, Sylvia," he announced.

"I'm ready," she said, quickly dropping my hand and picking up the file and a blank legal pad. She seemed too eager. I knew she wanted to impress this guy to make partner but jumping when he gave the command was not the Sylvia I knew.

Marcus's smile returned when Sylvia stepped toward him. It reminded me of the look he gave her at the convention center. "Mr. Fischer. I heard about your trouble last night. Too bad about Javier Sosa. Do the police have any leads?"

"Nothing that I know of. I'm sure they'll know more when they can talk to Sosa."

"You didn't hear?" He suppressed a smile.

"What?"

"Javier died this morning."

I stared at him, not quite understanding. I'd talked to the intensive care nurse only a few hours ago. His condition was stable.

"Unfortunate," Marcus said. "And, I assume, not very good for your new business." Marcus's lighthearted smile morphed into something harder and much more sinister.

I gritted my teeth and felt the blood drain from my face. I wanted to grip the edge of her desk for support, but I wouldn't give Marcus the satisfaction of seeing me vulnerable. I felt like I'd been kicked in the gut. Sosa's death was on me. New leaf or not, I wanted to wipe the grin off his smug face. I needed to hit someone or something. Instead, I stood stone still.

Sylvia saw the change in me and touched my arm. "Nick, it wasn't your fault." She instinctively stepped between us.

My eyes locked on Marcus. He didn't offer an apology. He didn't flinch or blink. I remembered what Danny Allison had said about him being dangerous. That's not why I let it go. I let it go because Sylvia aimed her big brown eyes at me. My kryptonite. She was a good influence. Smashing a lawyer's face in his own office before he's elected governor might have felt good but would not in any way further my career.

I forced a smile. "Another time, Marcus."

CHAPTER TWELVE

I staggered out of Marcus Lopez's law office listening to the demons beckoning me to follow them back into the abyss. Sosa's blood was on my hands. The voices urged me to stop at the VFW bar for a double Jack Daniels on the rocks. I'd fallen for their siren song after I mustered out of the Marine Corps. Grandpa'd staged an intervention with a recipe for rehabilitation that involved equal parts work and the study of history. He said history taught you that you're not the only poor son of a bitch that's ever suffered in the world, and work kept your mind off the problems that you did have. The siren song was loud and clear, but I knew a double shot of bourbon would only lead to a beer chaser and another shot. I'd wake up tomorrow with a pounding hangover, but no peace. I needed to take Grandpa's advice and focus on work. I mustered all my willpower, passed the VFW, and drove south toward Mission San Juan Capistrano. The Sosa affair could wait. SAPD had more manpower and resources to handle the case, and I'd promised to stay away. I'd keep that promise for now and focus on Marissa Luna.

Skeeter'd agreed to meet me at Isabella's Mexican restaurant across the street from the mission. This was a business meeting. We had a case to solve. Or at least, at this point I felt a strong possibility that Marissa Luna had been murdered. Marcus Lopez was right about one thing—Sosa's death would hurt my reputation. San Antonio had a million and a half people, but it was a small town when it came to private investigators and security. This was worse than a bad Yelp review. It was the kind of thing that might have me searching for a more stable job unless I solved another case.

Isabella's cinder block building was painted bright orange and decorated with Christmas lights—the kind of place that reminded me how close San Antonio was to the Mexican border. I found a rusty metal chair on the concrete patio close to a large outdoor fan. The antihistamine had kicked in, and my nose and eyes were dry despite the still-hazy sky. An older woman wearing a Spurs basketball T-shirt and jeans handed me a glass of ice water and a basket of tortilla chips. She was the owner and head chef, Isabella.

"*Buenas tardes*, Mr. Nick," she said and let out an exhausted sigh.

"No help today?" She had twin teenaged daughters who usually worked the tables and an older son who helped in the kitchen.

"The twins went to college," she said, exasperated. "I don't know what I'm gonna do without them." She spoke with a distinct South Texas Spanish lilt.

"You must be very proud."

"*Sí*, but I can't find help. No one wants to work anymore."

I nodded agreement and ordered a Shiner Bock with a plate of beef enchiladas from the lunch-special menu on the chalkboard and a double cheeseburger for Skeeter with iced tea. It was after one, but the place was doing big business on Saturday afternoon. Tejano music filled the parking lot, and a group of workers in blue overalls were getting their weekend started with an ice bucket full of sweaty Corona longnecks.

I was on my second beer when Skeeter crossed the parking lot. The workers turned to gawk when he stepped on the patio and made his way toward my table. He stood six-foot-seven, weighed in at three hundred pounds, and his left arm from the elbow down was made of titanium and capped with a double hook that could grip a hammer or pinch the edge of a paper napkin. He cut an imposing figure that sometimes worked to his advantage and sometimes, like when he was on trial for murder, worked against him. People had no trouble believing Skeeter could kill another man. He hadn't always been an introverted computer wizard. Before the auto accident that took his arm, he had completed a stellar career on the gridiron for the University of Texas and had just been drafted by the Washington Redskins. One night of wild partying put him on a different career track.

He pulled up a chair and placed his small black backpack on the table. It held his assortment of electronic gizmos that accompanied him everywhere. Sweat dripped from his forehead and soaked his T-shirt. The workers turned to each other, eyes wide, holding their hands out to indicate Skeeter's size and the prosthetic double metal hook that replaced his hand.

"You always make a grand entrance," I said.

"They're not watchin' me. They're wondering why I'm stupid enough to sit next to a dude who looks like a psycho-killer."

"Psycho-killer?"

"I swear, sometimes you look like you're ready to slice someone's ear off."

"Fair enough. Lot on my mind. Busy twenty-four hours."

"You should have come to the house."

"You know what happens when I come over. I like visiting, but we don't have time to spend the next three hours eating and listening to your mom." Ever since I'd tracked down the guy who framed Skeeter for murder, I was the honored guest in the Davis household and a visit to her house always involved a full home cooked meal and an hour or two of reminiscences about my gallant effort to rescue her son. "I love adulation, but we got work to do."

He smiled. "Now you talkin'. Show me the money."

I scanned the parking lot. A black Ford Super Duty pickup had backed into the far corner of the lot near the street. I checked the license plate. It was the same one that rolled down my street that morning. It could have been random, but I doubted it.

Skeeter noticed my reaction. "What's up?"

"That black Super Duty cruised my house this morning."

He glanced over his shoulder. "Coincidence?"

"In a county of two million?"

Skeeter shrugged and studied my face. "You gonna tell me why you're jumpy, or do I have to guess?"

"Javier Sosa died this morning."

"And that pickup is…"

"Probably a coincidence."

Skeeter shook his head. "I thought he was recovering."

"He was. When I talked to the nurse this morning, he was stable."

"That explains your killer attitude. It ain't your fault, man. You did your job. You're lucky you didn't take a bullet."

"I should have. That's what I was paid to do."

"I know you got into some shit overseas that you never talk about. I also know when there's work to do, you're ready to go. I admire that. Seeing you stay focused helps me get through the day." He held up his prosthesis, reminding me that he had a history too. I wasn't the only poor son of a bitch suffering in the world.

"Yeah, well, Grandpa said work was the answer to everything. Give yourself a goal and go after it. Keeps your mind off your problems."

Skeeter smiled. "Good advice. We goin' after Sosa's shooter?"

"Detective Peterson told me to stay away from it."

"Since when did that ever stop you?"

"For now, I wanna focus on the Luna case. We have a paying customer."

"Sweet." He held out his open hook. "When do I see some of it?"

"Soon. My next stop is to pick up our retainer."

Isabella brought our food. While we ate, I brought Skeeter up to date on what I'd gotten from Detective Peterson about Marissa Luna. It didn't take much to convince him that Peterson had bungled the investigation. He had an even lower opinion of Tomahawk than I did, having been on the receiving end of his crime-fighting work. I also told him about finding the bracelet and the peculiar answers Marissa's friend gave me. When we finished eating, I showed it to him.

"Put that massive brain of yours to work. How can we use this to get to the boyfriend?"

He held it up with his prosthetic double hook. "It's a Robert Byrd. The bands are gold. Very nice." He pulled an Apple iPad Pro from his backpack and touched the screen. Moments later he brought up the jeweler's catalog. "It's called a Mother's Love bangle." He whistled through his teeth. "You say her friend threw this in the river?"

"That's right. She kissed it and tossed it."

"The gold version retails for four grand. For twenty bucks, you got a great deal."

"Can you trace who sold it?"

He scanned the website. "No, but the Byrd factory store in Kerrville might have a record of the engraving. It's open today till six."

I checked my watch. It was close to two. Kerrville was in the general direction of Grandpa's ranch, and I was due for our weekly visit. I needed a dose of Grandpa's wisdom.

"Sylvia okay with this job? She must have been pretty upset. You gettin' shot at and all."

"Your job's electronics, big guy," I snapped.

He raised his plate-sized hand in surrender. "Enough said."

Isabella handed me the check. I gave her a twenty-dollar bill, which covered two lunch specials and a five-dollar tip. That and the homemade tortillas were why I kept coming back.

I scanned the parking lot when we stepped off the patio. The black pickup rolled to the street and turned north. If I saw it again, it wouldn't be a coincidence.

Skeeter followed me to my pickup. "You sure your head's straight?"

"What do you mean?"

"You lost a client and got shot at with a high-powered rifle. That's enough to rattle most people."

We stood for a moment gazing at the brownish sky punctuated with puffy cumulus clouds. "You worried about your paycheck?"

He gave me a disgusted look. "Smart-ass. You know it's more than that."

"Yeah, everything's under control. Let's go to work."

I opened my pickup door. "By the way, how does your mother know Mrs. Luna?"

He cocked his massive head. "She don't. Mrs. Luna just showed up at the house and started asking questions. You know how my mom is."

CHAPTER THIRTEEN

Araceli Luna lived in a working-class neighborhood on the west side not far from Marcus Lopez's law office. The house stood behind a dirt yard surrounded by a chain-link fence on a street lined with cars and identical houses. An angry Chihuahua guarded the porch. Before I could knock, Mrs. Luna opened the door and scooped up the feisty animal.

"Mr. Fischer, come in." She scolded the pooch and set him down inside. He spun around four times on the threadbare rug and jumped into a chair which I guessed was designated for him.

In the cramped front room, pictures of Marissa covered the walls. Baby pictures started at the door and went counterclockwise around the room depicting every stage of growth through college in a patchwork collage. Sadly, the growth stopped at college. Those final smiling pictures showed a Marissa full of life and expectations.

Mrs. Luna offered me lemonade, which I gratefully accepted. Then she left me in the shrine room while she disappeared down a hallway. I knew what it was like to lose someone close and not know how they died. My father was killed when I was sixteen years old. He died serving the community, doing his duty. He had volunteered to put himself in danger and accepted the consequences. As the elected sheriff of Gillespie County, he was paid to confront the criminals who killed him.

For Mrs. Luna it was different. Her daughter wasn't a volunteer, nor was she paid to protect and serve. She was a sweet innocent flower cut down before her life could bloom. The idea made my blood boil. Mrs. Luna had lost a daughter and a grandchild, and no one could tell her why. The police said it was a tragic accident brought on by too much alcohol. I wanted to find the truth.

The ancient window-unit air conditioner provided a constant mechanical hum and made the floorboards vibrate. I heard ice cubes dropping into glasses in the kitchen while I examined the photos of Marissa more closely. The last photo was stamped with the date July 4, the day she died. Marissa wasn't wearing a bracelet. That was odd. If someone had given her an expensive bracelet, she would have been wearing it. That meant someone had given it to her after the picture was taken, or the gift had resulted in an argument.

Mrs. Luna came back into the room. "I'm sorry. I had to make fresh lemonade. My daughter and her friends drank the pitcher from this morning." She handed me a sweaty glass.

"When was that picture taken?" I asked, pointing at the Fourth of July picture.

She didn't have to think to answer. "At six o'clock. Her friend Beth came to pick her up. She took the picture." Her lip quivered. "Beth had a print made and gave it to me for her birthday."

"You saw Beth today?"

"This morning."

"Did she say anything about this?" I took out the bracelet and handed it to her.

She ran her calloused fingers over the delicate features. "Is it real gold?"

"I think so. Look at the engraving," I said, pointing to the letters under the heart shape.

"Where did you get it?"

"Her friend Beth had it. I saw her today on the River Walk. She said it was Marissa's."

"I've never seen it before. Marissa would have shown it to me." She handed me the bracelet, and I sat down on an orange couch that must have been in style when she bought the house. Mrs. Luna sat in the matching chair. She folded her hands in her lap and looked at me with anticipation.

I dreaded what I had to tell her, but if I was going to get the truth, I had to ask the hard questions.

"Did you know Marissa was pregnant?" I waited for the full meaning to sink in.

She slowly dissolved into tears. I got up and found a box of tissues. She blew her nose. It took a full five minutes for her shoulders to stop shaking. She would have made a wonderful grandmother.

"I spoke with Detective Peterson. He withheld the information. He said it didn't change the case and he didn't want to... well, to see you like this."

She took a deep breath and blew her nose again. "Thank you for telling me," she said. "Now you see, it is even more important to find who did it."

"You had no idea? She never told you?"

She shook her head. "No, she didn't."

"I believe Marissa's death was no accident. That doesn't necessarily mean that she was murdered. Would she take her own life?"

She took the suggestion like a slap in the face. Her nostrils flared. "Not my Marissa. No." She was emphatic, but I had to be sure.

"Getting pregnant without a husband and having to face you and your... family creates a lot of pressure."

"She always knew I was here for her no matter what happened. We were very close. She was a happy child. The night she... the night she was murdered, she kissed me goodbye and said, 'Don't wait up, Mama.'"

"But why didn't she tell you about the pregnancy?"

She looked at her hands, trying to justify this to herself. "She came home from Lubbock the last week of June. After a summer class. The first session. It was an English class she said she needed to get out of the way before her senior year. She spent the mornings sleeping. Said she needed the rest..." Her voice trailed off. "Now I know why. In the evenings, when it was cooler, she went running. Maybe—maybe she was waiting until after the holiday to tell me."

Marissa didn't kiss her mother goodbye because she wanted to go commit suicide on the San Antonio River Walk. She wasn't making plans to cut short her senior year. I knew from experience that people didn't subject themselves to exercise when they're too depressed to go on living. When I came home from my final deployment—scarred inside and out—the last thing I wanted to do was go for a jog. The only time I left the house was when I ran out of beer or Jack Daniels. I put on thirty pounds, grew a full beard, and was angry at the world. I'd looked into the abyss and wondered if it offered any relief. Moving back in with Grandpa was the only thing that brought me back from the dead.

Maybe Marissa had made a decision about the baby that the father didn't go along with. I doubted it was an answer that her Catholic mother would condone. These were all questions detective Peterson didn't ask and didn't have answers to. Marissa had a secret that she took to her grave. I had to find out what that secret was.

"Mrs. Luna, I'll take the case."

The tension left her neck and shoulders. Relief washed over her. "Then you believe me?" she asked, letting out a sigh. "Mrs. Davis was right. You are a saint."

"I'm no saint. I can't work miracles, but I will do everything in my power to find out what happened to your daughter."

She got up and lit a Saint Jude candle on the mantel. I recognized it from the identical one in Skeeter's mother's house. "Mrs. Davis called you the Saint Jude of detectives. Saint Jude is the patron saint of lost causes. I will keep this candle lit and pray for you every day."

"Thank you, Mrs. Luna."

She handed me the envelope full of cash.

I didn't believe in the power of saints, but I took any help I could get. "One last question," I said. "Who gave you Mrs. Davis's name?"

She pursed her lips, deciding whether to tell me or not.

"If I'm going to find the truth, you can't hold anything back."

She went to the mantel and picked up a worn family Bible. Inside was a newspaper clipping. She handed it to me. I read the familiar headline from the local newspaper: Local Private Eye Presents Evidence to Exonerate Ex-UT Football Player.

"Where did you get this?" I asked.

"Someone left it in my mailbox two weeks ago."

CHAPTER FOURTEEN

All roads west of the Alamo City snaked through the geographical region known as the Texas Hill Country, a jumbled collection of rugged limestone and granite hills that stretched west from the Balcones Fault to the southern tip of the Great Plains. It was where I grew up and where I always felt at home. When the Fischers settled the area in the late 1840s, it was a dangerous frontier between western civilization and native culture dominated by the Kiowa and Comanche Indian tribes. That confrontation left an indelible impression on the settlers who bore the brunt of the fight and their descendants. I was proud my family had lived it and survived, and grateful to have my grandpa as a living link to their experience.

I was headed to the factory headquarters for the Robert Byrd jewelry store located in Kerrville about sixty-five miles out of San Antonio. If I could get the name of the person who had the expensive bracelet engraved, it might lead to the father of Marissa's unborn child. And the father might lead to the killer. I also wanted to pick Grandpa's brain about Patrick Allison. He told stories about the ancient family feud between the Allisons and the Fischers, but Grandpa also kept track of Patrick's recent business because it had an impact on his property. An Allison-controlled company was building a gas pipeline across the family land.

The ranch was only a short detour off the main road to Kerrville, and I was past due for a visit with Grandpa. I'd told Skeeter everything was under control, but it wasn't. Sosa's death threatened to send me over the edge. I needed a reality check. Our weekly visits weren't a formal thing where I checked in with him like an AA counselor. But seeing him reminded me what being human was all about. He set the example and showed me how to pick myself up and keep on living.

I turned off on Grape Creek Road and noticed that a familiar homestead ranch house that once stood on the corner had been torn down to make way for a new construction. Each trip, I counted more new development in the back country. The old homesteads like Grandpa's were getting harder to find unless you knew where to look. The narrow road was paved now, like more and more of the backroads, to accommodate tourists driving sedans while searching for that authentic rural-Texas experience and staying at one of the many new bed-and-breakfasts. Sam hung his head out the window, enjoying one of his favorite pastimes. Number one, of course, was duck hunting. He was bred to be in the water searching for birds. But if he couldn't hunt, he settled for hanging his bulky head out the passenger window.

I slowed down behind a herd of brightly colored bicyclists—a group of twenty or more all in orange-and-black stretch outfits with matching helmets. There was no room to pass, so I followed them at a crawl until I got to Grandpa's road. The nearby town of Fredericksburg had been attracting weekend bicycle enthusiasts since the '70s, and each year there were more clogging the roads. Grandpa's road was one of the few left unpaved, which thankfully reduced bicycle traffic, but his newest neighbor'd threatened to change that. He put up a large plywood sign showing the smiling face of a cartoon llama. The caption read, "Petting zoo open on weekends" and listed a contact phone number for private parties. Grandpa said he petitioned the county commissioners to pave the road.

A neat row of limestone rocks marked the entrance to the ranch. It was a remnant of the original stone fence put up in 1848 by the first Fischer to land in Texas. Every spring since I could walk, I'd helped Grandpa replace the stones that the weather, animals, or gravity had forced to the ground. He always quoted his favorite poet while we worked. "Something there is that doesn't love a wall," he'd recite. I agreed. I was one of them. Repairing a rock fence was Grandpa's way of keeping me busy and out of trouble. It was hard, back-breaking work that for the most part worked just as Grandpa said it would.

Sam leaped over my lap when I opened the door, and sprinted for the cool spring-fed pond at the head of the driveway. I opened the gate and heard the distinct hum of a Cessna engine. The blue-tipped wings cleared the trees and buzzed close enough to the ground for me to see the slightly crooked smile on Grandpa's face. He was too old to be flying this low, but nothing scared him, and no one was going to tell him how or when to fly. Still, it didn't keep me from reminding him that I'd like to keep him around for another twenty years.

I drove with the windows down breathing in the familiar mixture of cedar, fresh-cut hay, and late summer buttercup flowers. I passed the tidy limestone-block house and barn built before the Civil War and crossed the creek before climbing the hill to a level section of land Grandpa used as a runway. I stopped at the small Quonset hut and let the caliche dust settle around me. The field was five hundred yards long and half as wide. Landing and taking off was tricky because of the cedar trees on one end and the abrupt limestone cliff on the other. When the conditions were right, Grandpa only used half of it just to prove he could.

Today, the conditions were right. He swooped over the limestone cliff and touched down like he was practicing carrier landings in the Indian Ocean. He tipped his gray sweat-stained cowboy hat to me when the aircraft coasted to a stop. He didn't wear a rattlesnake-skin hatband or trim his mustache to look like Charles Goodnight. He didn't have an image to maintain.

The only indication of his age was that he took more time than he used to climbing out of the plane, still favoring the knee he had replaced last year. At over eighty he had no intention of slowing down. The khaki work shirt and Wrangler jeans he wore was the same uniform he'd worn ever since I was old enough to remember. The only other shirt he owned was a white Cinch shirt with pearl snaps grandma had given him for Christmas. That one was reserved for church and Oktoberfest.

"*Wie geht's?*" He spoke with a German-Texas accent, because he'd grown up speaking German, the language of our ancestors that was all but extinct in Gillespie County. He and a handful of the old-timers kept the language alive when the spirit moved them to get together and swap stories about the old days.

"Couldn't be better. Nice landing."

"Saves tires," he said, straight-faced. He was modest to a fault, detested a showoff, and would never consider drawing attention to himself.

We shook hands. His grip was still strong, and his large palms were thick from years of outdoor work. I could remember only two occasions that he'd ever greeted me with more than a handshake. One was at my dad's funeral when he put his hand on my shoulder. I was sixteen. The other was four years later at Grandma's funeral. He did the same thing. That touch was the most emotion I'd ever seen him display.

"You keepin' your nose clean?" he asked. His voice was raspy from years of smoking cigars and breathing Hill Country dust.

"I stay busy."

"Work is good," he reminded me. He'd been reminding me of the virtue of work my whole life but hearing him say it made all the difference in the world. We got in my pickup and headed to the house.

"One of these days, I'm gonna peel you off a mountaintop and there won't be enough left to bury. The neighbor will call me after he sees a puff of smoke."

"The neighbor wouldn't bother. That's why I'm up in the air—chasing his damned llamas from my hay. He called the game warden on me last week for shootin' at one of his miniature horses."

"Why'd you do that?"

"To scare it from my field. That honyock comes here from Dallas once a month and calls himself a rancher. His damn petting zoo causes more traffic up and down my road. They come in my gate asking to take pictures of the house. I've got no time for such nonsense. I have livestock to tend to."

We traveled in silence for five minutes. Neither one of us felt the need to fill in the gaps in conversation. My dad had been the same way. We could go for days without speaking. I never knew that was unusual until Sylvia pointed it out on her first visit. She couldn't understand how three people could sit in a room for thirty minutes without speaking. Silence drove her crazy.

"Get any rain?" I asked. To a farmer or rancher, speculation about the weather was an expected staple of conversation.

"Dry as a bone." He pointed to the dead, ankle-high grass lining the road. "I'll need to start feeding hay early this year. The price is gonna go through the roof."

Sam ran up the road to greet us, his coat covered with mud. I opened the door and let him jump into the back seat. He immediately put his paws on Grandpa's shoulder and began licking his face. Labradors had no qualms about showing affection.

"Ah, teach this dog some manners," Grandpa growled, but gave him a playful pat on the head, and Sam happily settled down on the back seat. I noticed Grandpa studying my profile. When I slowed to cross the creek, he asked: "Your fancy girlfriend don't come?"

"Tied up at work," I said. Sylvia was a little too refined for Grandpa's taste, and he never missed a chance to remind me without overdoing it. He was always charming when she came with me, but I don't think he ever referred to her by her name. He waited for me to say more. When I didn't, he didn't press me on our relationship. He changed the subject.

"I read about that business with the sniper."

He was asking if I was okay, physically and mentally. He didn't need to spell it out. In his own way, he was better than a trained counselor. The one I'd been ordered to see before I was discharged wanted me to talk about my feelings, which only increased my guilt and anger. For Grandpa, mentioning the event was enough. The weekend he turned my life around, I drove out to see him after a weeklong bender. He listened to me cry in my beer until I fell asleep on the porch. The next morning my keys were gone, and my pickup was in the barn. We didn't talk about my feelings. He let me mope around and sober up for about a day and a half, then he put me to work rebuilding fences. It's hard to feel guilty about being the only one of your platoon brothers to come home alive when every muscle aches from digging post holes in the hot sun.

I slowed to let a cottontail rabbit cross the road.

"You working another case? Something besides that shooting?" he asked.

I told him about Marissa Luna and what I'd found so far pointed to murder instead of the official ruling of accidental death.

"You think the Luna girl's murder and Sosa's shooting are related?"

"So far, I can't connect the two."

"If they are, it's gonna open a can of worms. You ready for that?"

Was I? Would I be able to do what it takes to find the truth, or would I let my demons get the best of me? I was here to answer that question.

"Stay a few days. Give yourself some time. Fence needs work," he said.

We both knew what he meant. I parked in the shade of an oak tree near the deer-high fence surrounding his vegetable garden. Since before the Civil War, the Fischer family had gathered in this yard, worked out their problems, and found the strength to carry on. I let the minute stretch to five. Enjoying the moment alone with Grandpa and watching the oak leaves flutter in the dry wind. I felt the fire in my belly begin to cool. Just the mention of fence work drove my demons back into their cage. A mockingbird landed on a low-hanging branch and stared at us expectantly through the windshield.

"I'm good," I said. To the casual observer our interaction was a practical, businesslike exchange about building fences and investigative procedure, but to the initiated we'd plowed the depths of emotion as deep as any Shakespeare play. If I didn't come up with any leads on this trip, at least I'd accomplished my first goal.

I looked at the old man and smiled. It was time to move on to the second reason I was here. "I wanted to ask you about the Allison family. My client met with Patrick Allison the night he was shot. He introduced me to him and his grandson. Allison said he knew you. Offered me a job."

His eyes narrowed, and the lines around his mouth deepened into canyons. I waited for Grandpa's response. The mockingbird ran through his repertoire of songs. I waited some more. Sam whined from the back seat, anxious to take another dip in the spring water. I let him out.

Grandpa finally cleared his throat and spit out the window. "You're gonna work for Patrick Allison?" His tone suggested I was considering joining the local Al-Qaeda affiliate.

"I didn't take the job. I wanna find out if Patrick could be mixed up with the Sosa shooting. You know that family. What do you think?"

"What do I think? Hell, dirty tricks and murder have been part of that family's business model since before the Civil War."

CHAPTER FIFTEEN

Grandpa pulled a Churchill from his breast pocket and clipped the end. He struck a kitchen match against his Wranglers and produced a cloud of smoke that obscured his face until I unrolled the passenger window behind him. We'd driven southwest from Gillespie County toward Mexico through the southern edge of the Hill Country. The air was dryer and the vegetation dwindled to prickly pear cactus, sparce mesquite, and huisache brush. Grandpa pointed out a tiny dot on the horizon that he said was an oil derrick. There was nothing wrong with his eyes.

"Take the next gravel road," he said, then tapped his cigar ash into my unused ashtray.

It'd been thirty minutes of silence since I'd brought up the name Allison. I had to be patient. Anticipating the story from Grandpa was part of the ritual I grew up with. So was lighting his cigar. I'd heard different versions of the story over the years, both from Grandpa and my father. Each time, the emphasis was a little different depending on the timing. When I was younger, Grandpa highlighted the nostalgic parts of the story of how our family picked up the pieces after the Civil War and maintained the family homestead. Because of the Allison company's pipeline threat, and my admission about Patrick's job offer, I expected I would get the bloody version of the story.

Grandpa cleared his throat and spat out the window. It was story time.

"In 1848, the Fischers were newcomers from Prussia, and men like Allison didn't trust us. We spoke German, wore funny clothes, and brought our own tools and customs. Some of the newcomers were also Catholic, another mark against them. They'd just lost a fight to reform the autocratic government of the German Confederation and faced the wrath of the aristocracy. Naturally, they wanted their own land and freedom. America offered freedom, and Texas promised land. Two things they couldn't get in the old country. The trouble was a whole passel of people wantin' the same thing had gotten here first. Folks from Tennessee and the southern states saw big promise in Texas, especially after the 1836 Independence. As is usually the case, the folks that got here first figured they had a better claim to the land. The Allisons were part of that earlier crowd. His family threw in with Houston and routed Santa Anna at San Jacinto. They didn't like liberal German politics or the Catholic religion. Allison belonged to a group called The American Party—second and third generation settlers. All were immigrants, but they got here first, so they figured they had a larger say in how the country was run. Same old story. Been that way since the beginning of time. Third generation don't trust the second. The second don't trust the first, and they all hate the newcomers. The American Party held secret meetings and dreamed up ways to control elections in their favor all over the state."

He paused to relight his cigar. Another part of the ritual. I'd given up asking him not to smoke in the pickup. He took it as more of a suggestion, and his generation didn't follow suggestions from anyone under fifty. I watched his stoic, unchanging face out of the corner of my eye while following the white ribbon of dusty caliche road. Something about listening to Grandpa tell a story put society in perspective. He could filter through the gibberish of the world so that it all made sense. I wondered if I would ever get to pass on that legacy to my grandchildren.

"The Civil War added fuel to the fire. The Fischer family and the majority of Gillespie County did not vote to secede from the Union. There were other loyal counties from Central Texas and a few along the Red River. They supported Lincoln and the Union, that's why they'd immigrated. Allison, and the majority of Texas, saw it differently. They were loyal to the state." He paused to blow a cloud of cigar smoke at a fly that had found its way into the cab.

"What happened to Allison during the war?"

"Allison joined the Confederate Army. He was with that group who chased down the German Unionists trying to make it to Mexico."

"Allison was part of the Battle of the Nueces?" This was a part of the bloodier version of the story that was left out when I was younger.

"The Nueces Massacre," he corrected. "Allison assumed command after that bloodthirsty Lt. McRae was killed outside of Brackettville and ordered the murder of nine wounded captives. He lined them up and shot 'em in cold blood. The poor families of the German Unionists weren't allowed to collect their dead till after the war."

I knew he could go on about the details, but we were running out of time, and I wanted him to skip ahead. "Was our family part of the Unionists?"

"No. The Fischers decided to stay home and defend their land. The Kiowas and the Comanches stepped up their raiding during the war. All the men of fighting age were conscripted, leaving easy pickings for the bloodthirsty savages. And to top that off, instead of protecting the families, the hometown militia harassed all the Germans suspected of Union sympathies. They caught hell from both sides of the frontier."

"What happened to Allison?"

"The old man took advantage of the turmoil. By the end of the war, his family had more land and cattle than any bill of sale could account for." He blew another cloud of smoke at the fly, then cleared his throat and spit out the window. The oil derrick loomed large on the horizon. I guessed we had another ten minutes to go on the dust-choked road.

"Right after the war, your great-great-great-granddad, Johann Fischer, caught Allison's son-in-law, Roland McCarthy, with a string of Fischer horses. They were tied to the hitching post in front of Doebbler's Inn near Grape Creek all wearing the Fischer brand. Johann waited until Roland came out on the steps and confronted him in front of six witnesses. Roland said he found the horses along the creek. Johann called him a liar and pointed to the brands. Roland's hand went for his pistol. Johann gave him both barrels of his shotgun. Johann gathered his horses and rode home."

Grandpa turned in his seat and stabbed his cigar at me. "That was the last time a Fischer talked to a member of the Allison family."

I suppressed a smile, knowing that was the punchline, and family tradition called for at least a minute of respectful silence in case the storyteller wanted to add his own spin in an epilogue. A mile of dusty road later, I said: "I didn't know I was supposed to be holding a grudge."

"Patrick was made in the mold of his ancestor, just as you are. Just as we all are."

I liked to think people made a choice to act good or evil, but Grandpa believed who you were and how you acted had much more to do with where you came from and how you were raised. I looked at my watch. Only two hours before the jewelry store closed. I would save that argument for another day.

A cattleguard and locked pole gate blocked the entrance to the oil lease. I pulled to the side of the road and let the dust settle. "This might be a bust," I said, thinking we'd driven out to the middle of nowhere for nothing.

"*Wie hast du es eilig? Abwarten und Tee trinken.*"

I laughed. I knew he was telling me to be patient because he'd been repeating the same German aphorism to me all my life.

As if on cue, an oil field water truck stopped at the cattleguard. The driver got out and opened the gate. I waved, pretending I'd been waiting for him. "I'll get the gate," I yelled. He drove on without looking back, and I followed him.

CHAPTER SIXTEEN

Stacks of drill pipe, machinery, and a dozen metal storage containers were scattered over a muddy ten acres surrounding the oil rig. The buzz from huge power generators and bone-jarring clanging continued twenty-four hours a day until the drill bit hit its mark, the company ran out of money, or the bottom dropped out of the market. It wasn't a business for the weak or faint of heart. When we got within fifty yards, a guard wearing an orange hard hat and black uniform emerged from a portable building. He slipped on his sunglasses and ear protection, then waved the water truck through. He held his hand up for us to stop. He was a big man in his early thirties with five days' growth of beard and a Santa Claus belly.

"What is it you're looking for out here?" Grandpa asked me.

"I don't know exactly. I'll know it when I see it."

"Usually, it's Texas equipment that ends up in Mexico. That's why that fellow is wearing a sidearm," Grandpa commented. I'd noticed the Glock 9mm on the guard's utility belt.

"I'm just curious about the business connection between Lopez, Allison, and my dead client." Sam stuck his head out the window and sniffed at the guard.

"Halt!" the man shouted above the head-pounding roar. He stood five feet from the door with his hands resting on his wide hips. "What's your business vit Allison Oil?" His accent was distinctly German.

Grandpa heard his voice and leaned toward my open window. "*Wo kommen Sie her?*"

"*Ein Mitdeutscher?*" The guard's eyes lit up like he'd just found a long-lost relative. He stepped forward and let Sam lick his hand. Seeing a Labrador and an old man speaking his native tongue seemed to put him at ease.

Grandpa winked at me and got out of the pickup. The guard immediately joined him near the bumper. They shouted at each other in German. My knowledge of the language was limited to hello and goodbye, and a few German table prayers Grandma'd taught me. After the initial greeting I was lost. Grandpa said something about water, and the guard gestured toward his trailer.

"I'll wait here," I shouted. Both waved. Grandpa was happy as a clam getting to speak German. His small group of Texas-German speakers was down to just a handful, and they only got together once a month.

When they disappeared into the trailer, I let Sam out and we headed for the nearest container. A half dozen other workers in hard hats were busy on the rig itself, but no one was within a hundred feet of my pickup. I ducked out of sight behind the row of containers. Sam made a beeline for the nearest mudhole, wasting no time cooling himself down in the muddy overflow from the tanker truck. I tried the handle on the first container and found it open. It was the kind loaded onto semitrailers and stuffed with equipment I'd never seen in action. Working in the oil field was one of the few jobs I hadn't done. I recognized the PEMEX red-and-green logo with the Mexican eagle head. Sosa and Patrick Allison were definitely in business together. This was Mexican equipment on an American rig.

"*Halt dich munter*," Grandpa shouted.

That was my signal. I pretended to zip up my fly as I stepped around the front of the container and saw the guard and Grandpa standing by my pickup. The German guard shot me a suspicious look, but Sam immediately rushed to him and rubbed his muddy coat on his legs. It was just the distraction I needed to get safely back into my pickup.

"*Halt dich munter*," the guard repeated and let out a belly-shaking laugh. It was a German-Texan salutation I'd heard Grandpa use all my life. According to him, it meant *keep your chin up*. The native German had probably never heard it before but seemed to understand.

"What'd the square-head have to say?" I asked when we were safely back out the gate.

"He's fresh off the boat. Looking for a Texan wife. I told him to try San Antonio."

"Good advice."

"What did you find?"

"I found PEMEX equipment. The containers are full of it."

"Hell, the Mexican oil company has gas stations in Texas now," Grandpa said. They own a refinery in Houston."

"Sosa told me his deal with Allison fell through because of Marcus Lopez."

"That's funny."

"What?"

"The guard said he worked for Marcus Lopez."

CHAPTER SEVENTEEN

The Robert Byrd factory store was a collection of single-story limestone-block buildings located near the interstate in Kerrville, a medium-sized Hill Country town which supported a university and an annual folk music festival that drew musicians from around the country. The artesian jewelry maker had over a hundred stores in three other southern states, but it had all started in the Texas Hill Country. I parked under a shade tree near the showroom. The heat from five to six in the afternoon could be lethal in the first week of September, and Sam would have to wait in the pickup. The parking lot was empty as I'd hoped. I was going to have to get creative to find out any info about the bracelet, and I didn't want interference from other customers.

When I'd dropped Grandpa back at the ranch, he warned me again about getting involved with the Allison family. I didn't tell him that things may have already gone too far. After a hundred and fifty year hiatus, our families were once again on a collision course. I hoped it didn't come down to a shootout in front of the general store. It was curious that security at Allison's drilling site would be handled by Marcus Lopez. Clearly their relationship went beyond attorney-client. Did one or both have a motive to kill Javier Sosa? To get any further, I'd have to find out what Skeeter was able to dig up. Right now, I needed to focus my attention on the paying gig and finding out what happened to Marissa Luna on the Fourth of July.

I caught a glimpse of myself in the side mirror. My burnt-orange

Longhorn cap covered the scars on my forehead and my polarized shades masked eyes made bloodshot by African dust and lack of sleep. I wouldn't be stepping out on the model runway anytime soon. I rehearsed my winning smile. With the help of the hat and the glasses, I didn't look too bad. "That will have to do, partner," I said.

Sam licked my cheek. I had his support no matter how I looked. He whined, tired of riding, and immediately jumped out when I opened the door. He made a beeline for a manmade pond behind the showroom that, I discovered too late, was covered with multi-colored, semi-domestic ducks. By the time I got him back in the pickup, it was fifteen minutes till closing time, we were both covered with mud, and the ducks were in the next county.

I walked into the store tracking pond scum and dripping sweat. This wasn't exactly what I'd planned, but I decided to wing it. The half dozen glass display cases featured handcrafted silver earrings, necklaces, and bracelets. Sylvia raved about the designs, but on closer inspection they all looked the same to me. A young female clerk was busy polishing the countertops near the register. When she didn't look up, I cleared my throat and plunged into my cover story.

"Not too busy today," I said, trying to establish a rapport.

The nametag on her shirt read Tiff. She glanced at the clock on the wall, trying to decide if I was worth a sales pitch and the commission that came with it or if she should continue her cleaning duties and let me fend for myself. She no doubt had a boyfriend to meet or homework to do.

"I know what you're thinking, Tiff," I said, laying on the charm. "You're thinking I'm on the hunt for a last-minute gift for my wife or girlfriend. Am I right?"

I took off my hat and glasses and set them on the glass countertop. That got her attention. She stopped cleaning and came over. She was in her early twenties, probably a student working her way through the local university. She had rodeo-queen good looks and was dressed in casual western, with a thick blond braid reaching the top of her sequined jeans pockets.

"Excuse me," she said. "We close in fifteen..." She paused midsentence. Her eyes lingered on my forehead with a mixture of fear and expectation.

"Don't worry, I'm friendly." I flashed my disarming smile. "I'm sorry about the mud," I said, pointing at the splashes on my jeans. "My Labrador found your duck pond."

Her expression suddenly softened. "Mine does that all the time. Where is he?"

I pointed out the door. Sam was in the driver's seat scanning the sky for returning ducks and sulking because I'd locked him in the cab.

"He's adorable." Sam had won her heart and eased her fears.

"I'm in a real jam," I said, and showed her the bracelet. "Do you recognize this?"

"It's ours. A Mother's Love bangle." She walked to a display case and showed me two identical bracelets made of silver. "Yours is gold. Most of the ones we sell are silver. It's our specialty."

"Could you tell me where it was sold?" I handed it to her so she could take a closer look.

She examined the engraving. "No, but I can tell you this was a special order."

"This is gonna sound crazy. And I'm totally embarrassed. My wife had a baby shower in July. July fifth. Now, the baby's here and everything's fine. But here's the thing… my wife is trying to send thank-you cards to everyone and I… Well, I tossed all the cards."

Tiff looked at me like I'd just bit the head off a live rattlesnake. She was adding the mud and the dirty pickup with the Labrador to my description of dumping the cards and coming up with every dumb cowboy she ever dated. I'd gotten the story from Rocky, my redneck high school buddy. Throwing gift cards away was his explanation for why his second wife left him, but I suspected it was only one of many problems she had with his behavior.

Tiff took an involuntary glance at Sam through the glass door. I knew she was almost convinced I was telling the truth.

"If you can't do it, you can't do it. I told my wife it's just a bracelet. She can send out a generic thank-you note and call it good." I turned toward the exit and grabbed the bracelet from the countertop like it was made of plastic.

"That bracelet cost four thousand dollars," she blurted out, sounding slightly hostile. She was a sister-in-arms with my imaginary wife. "Not including the engraving."

"Wow, I never would have guessed."

She raised her left eyebrow like I was a country bumpkin who had a lot to learn. "What were you thinking, throwing out the cards?" She suddenly sounded twenty years older. Her voice shifted from rodeo queen to scolding ranch momma.

"I thought I was being helpful. It was a big party. Everything was a mess." I tossed a hundred-dollar bill on the counter. "I'd like to buy her another bracelet too. Something to smooth things over."

She raised her eyebrow again. I'd seen that look before too—the look that said, *you cheap bastard*. I pulled two more hundreds out of my pocket, part of Sosa's final tip. Ranch Momma was making me feel guilty for a social faux pas I'd invented.

"I think that's a good idea," she said, after she saw all three bills were the same denomination. "I can imagine your wife's worried sick about this. I know just what she'd want." She walked toward the front door. "Let me check the sales records from the first week of July," she said. "I gotta lock the front door first. The guard will check it at six and I get in trouble if it's open." She flipped the deadbolt on the front door, and I followed her into the back office. While she booted up the computer records, I glanced at the photos on the wall. One by the back window caught my eye, a picture of a younger Patrick Allison standing by a man near the same age at some sort of ground-breaking ceremony. The inscription below read, "Boys and Girls Camp Number One."

"Who's that next to Patrick Allison?" I asked, pointing to the picture.

She didn't have to look up from the computer records to answer. "That's the owner, Robert Byrd. Mr. Allison and the Byrd family have been partners in a charitable foundation for years. Do you know the Allisons?"

"Our families have known each other for a long time. Used to be neighbors way back in the day."

"Really?" she said, not believing a word.

I studied the picture. Could Patrick Allison be carrying on the family's murderous, cutthroat legacy? He didn't act particularly bloodthirsty at the fundraiser. But I wasn't naïve enough to believe in appearances. A smile and a charity donation didn't preclude a person from being a cold-blooded killer. Despite the heat, a cold chill ran up my spine.

"Here," she said. "On July second we did an engraving on a gold Mother's Love bangle."

"So, you sold it here?"

"No, it was a special order for the La Cantera Parkway store in the mall off I-10 in San Antonio."

"Who bought it?"

"You'd have to check with the store."

"Can you call them?"

"I really shouldn't be doing this, you know?" She checked her wristwatch. It was ten after six.

"Ya gotta help me out. I've been sleeping in the baby's room for three weeks. On top of the nine months before that. I'm goin' crazy, if ya know what I mean." I ducked my chin and lifted my eyebrows.

Tiff's cheeks turned red, and she stifled a smile. "Okay," she said and picked up the phone. She called whoever answered by her first name and explained some of my phony story. Something the clerk said made Tiff laugh. I'm sure it was at my expense. I knew I was letting Rocky and the brotherhood of good ol' boys down, but what the hell. I was on the job.

While Tiff talked, I picked out a bracelet in the three-hundred-dollar range by the register. As long as it fit my cover story, I might as well buy something for Sylvia and see if it would have a better effect than the over-the-hill yellow tulips. I glanced at the engagement rings in the next case. Six months ago, I'd been ready to take the plunge. Sylvia'd taken me to meet her parents, and I'd taken her to meet Grandpa. Neither family was impressed with our choice of mate, albeit for opposite reasons, but we both managed to ignore their admonitions. Then she started working for Marcus Lopez and he threw his hat in the ring for governor. Now, I wasn't so sure. Instead of taking the next step, we seemed to be taking two steps back. She had a high-paying job and was on the cusp of a political move to Austin. According to her, I was stuck in a dangerous profession that offered no hope for the kind of money she craved.

"You weren't kidding about knowing the Allisons," Tiff said, returning with a big smile.

I didn't say anything. I hadn't told her a lie, but it was a complicated relationship, so I wasn't sure exactly what she was referring to.

"That bracelet was sold to Danny Allison."

I thought maybe I'd heard her wrong. After spending an hour listening to Grandpa relate the sordid history of the Allisons and the Fischers, maybe my mind was playing tricks on me.

"Allison?" I asked.

"Yep, Danny Allison. He bought it and had it engraved."

The cold chill came back. Was it a coincidence, or were Marissa and Sosa linked somehow through the Allison family?

CHAPTER EIGHTEEN

A bass-boosted techno sound reverberated from the dance club and rattled the no parking sign near the front door. Some might call it music, but to me it was annoying noise. I was waiting in line behind a trendy group of partygoers dressed like extras in a *Mad Max* movie to get a first-hand look at the place Marissa visited on her last night on earth. Finding Danny Allison's name was my first solid lead, and I wanted to move on it quickly by retracing her steps from the murder scene and establishing a link with Danny.

The building was an unlikely venue for a trendy night club. The owners had taken a turn-of-the-century building, with elaborate white-stone arches, and added stainless steel and graffiti highlights to give it a modern twist. The security guard wore black leather armbands with metal studs and a matching dog collar. When he checked my ID, I asked him if he was a friend of Mel Gibson. He gave me a blank stare. I'd changed into dry Wranglers, clean boots, and a black, long-sleeve Cinch shirt. It was my go-to casual wear and usually wasn't out of place anywhere in Texas.

The walls inside were painted black and overlaid with green-and-purple glow-in-the-dark graffiti. There were pieces of chain-link fence lining the dance floor and blocks of concrete used for tables giving the place a post-apocalyptic feel. The decorator must have been the same person in charge of the artwork displayed in front of the public safety building.

When my eyes adjusted to the laser light show, no one was doing anything that remotely resembled dancing. Growing up, Grandma had insisted I learn the two-step and the polka, which required partners to hold each other and attempt to step in time to the music. The only touching on this dance floor came from forced contact because of the limited space. Conversation was out of the question. After five minutes, the throbbing noise and lights were already giving me a headache.

I searched the ceiling for surveillance cameras, found two on the bar and four on the dance floor. If they were operating the night Marissa was here, I might be in luck. A bouncer stood guard near the office. He looked in his late twenties with a serious steroid addiction. All his exposed skin was covered with tats. I had one tattoo I'd gotten on my eighteenth birthday, a small Chinese character representing family. It was an act of rebellion because Grandpa insisted that I not get a tattoo, so naturally, I had to get one. Grandpa smiled slightly and shook his head when I showed it to him. I didn't understand the irony until after I mustered out of the Marine Corps.

I approached Muscle Man and held up my private eye credentials. He didn't smile or talk. Probably a side effect of the 'roids. I pointed to the office door behind him. He shook his head. At least he could communicate. I leaned in close to his ear.

"I need to see the manager!" I screamed.

He shrugged. This guy was in bad shape. He wasn't wearing ear plugs, so I guessed that his hearing was shot to hell. I'd promised Sylvia that I would avoid violence at all costs, but I had a lead and was anxious to get results. I sent my right elbow to his neck. He was a couple inches taller than me. So, the move was a natural uppercut. That got his attention. He dropped to the floor, clutching his throat. No one seemed to notice. I stepped over him and through the office door.

The back room was partially soundproof. Only the muffled, throbbing bass could still be felt when I shut the door. A man in his forties looked up from behind a metal desk. His thin hair was streaked with pink dye, and he wore a black T-shirt with a white skull and the name of some music group he thought was important. His earlobes were stretched over black disks the size of silver dollars. Classy.

"You're in the wrong room, asshole," he said. His voice was thin and cracked like he'd spent years talking over that noise outside. His demeanor matched his outfit.

"You the manager?" I asked, moving to the side of the desk.

He shifted in his chair to keep me in front of him. I caught sight of a pistol grip in the open desk drawer. His hand went for it.

"You don't need that," I said, taking a quick step forward and slamming the drawer closed.

"What the fuck?"

I let go of the drawer, and he cradled his smashed fingers in his lap.

"I'm a private investigator." I held up my credentials.

"So what? You fucked up my fingers, man. Piss off." He stood and looked at the door, expecting help.

"Your bouncer's recovering. He didn't want me to come in either."

"Are you on something, man?"

"No, but I wouldn't mind a couple of Tylenol. The noise is killing me."

"Where's Gino?"

"If that's your bouncer, he'll be okay in fifteen minutes or so. I'm on a case. A murder. The victim was a young female. This was the last place she was seen alive. Having been here for five minutes, I'm not ruling out suicide induced by noise and laser lights."

He picked up his cell phone. "I'm calling the cops." He didn't think I was funny.

"Call 'em. When they get here, I'll show them the weapon in your desk and the bag of coke." I'd spotted the bag of white powder on the table behind the desk when I first walked in. I grabbed it and held it up to the light. "Nice stash. Probably helps get you through the night in a place like this."

"Easy with that, asswipe."

"I wanna see the tapes, amigo. Surveillance from July fourth. The night Marissa Luna was murdered."

"I don't know nothin'," he sneered.

I grabbed the black disk in his right ear and pulled it toward his desk. So much for people skills. I needed information. "You sure about that?"

"Look, a detective came in and took everything from July second through the fifth. I didn't ask for them back, 'cause I don't care. Why should I? Talk to the cops."

"Why didn't you just start with that?"

"Fuck you. Let go of my ear, man. Jesus."

I let him go. His hand went to his ear. He was going to need a bigger disk.

"Thanks for your time." I walked out and closed the door.

Gino was standing up and leaning against the bar. The goth barmaid handed him a shot of something. No permanent damage. I headed for the exit before he could notice me. The fact that Earlobes didn't ask for the tapes back didn't mean he didn't care. It meant he had backups. I needed Skeeter's expertise.

From the club to the River Walk was only a short distance. I took my time and checked my watch to gauge how long it would have taken Marissa. The crowd was heavy on a Saturday night, but nowhere near what it would have been on the Fourth of July. A dozen drunken airmen from the local base shuffled by me in single file. Their haircuts were so new I could see the razor marks above their ears. A group of middle-aged men dressed alike in jean shorts and new I Heart Texas T-shirts asked me to take their picture. They said they were in town for the facial hair competition. Anything to attract tourists. Each sported an elaborate mustache and beard combination that would put General Custer to shame. Everybody was having a good time.

It took me fourteen minutes of leisurely walking to get to the Travis Street bridge. The Our Lady of Guadalupe candle still burned for Marissa beside the bundle of plastic roses. The white cross was still standing upright in the Folgers coffee can. Her picture clipped to the side seemed to be urging me to find her killer.

I studied the parking garage and the buildings that formed a canyon over the River Walk, then checked for surveillance cameras under the bridge but didn't see any. Why had Marissa come to this place? There were a few restaurants to the north, but they would have been closed. There was easy access to the street, so whoever killed her could escape without notice. Maybe she had taken a walk with Danny. This part of the River Walk was well lit but decidedly less crowded than the loop to the south. It seemed a good place for a private conversation or to execute a murder and make it look like an accident.

CHAPTER NINETEEN

Thirty minutes later, I was sipping a cold Shiner Bock and waiting for Skeeter at the Esquire Tavern. It was near the dance club but far enough away that I didn't have to feel the music. The crowd was a little older and the setting more laid-back, less concerned about the apocalypse.

Skeeter didn't share my love of the Alamo and didn't care for the River Walk. He called me a tourist for spending time in a place most of the city's inhabitants avoided because of the traffic and lack of parking.

The tavern patrons seemed to fit his description of tourists. A heavyset man wearing a Hawaiian shirt and cargo shorts sipped an oversized frozen margarita at the end of the bar. His female companion wore a matching shirt and a new pink straw cowboy hat. Both had white skin burnt to a cherry red from overexposure to the South Texas sun and looked like retirees visiting from Minnesota. Three women in the next booth wore white socks under their Birkenstocks, and tie-dyed shirts. They could have been from Austin, but I guessed farther abroad. A younger, hipster couple in matching skinny jeans were taking selfies in front of a signed team picture of the Spurs basketball team, the new heroes of the Alamo City. I had to admit, the tourists had taken over downtown.

When Skeeter walked in, I signaled him to the booth in the back. As usual, everyone in the bar turned to look when he entered, which reminded me of what he said about my own appearance. I still thought a huge man with a metal hook drew more attention.

"How'd you know I wouldn't be out partying?" His normal voice rumbled like dynamite exploding inside a mine shaft.

"Because you're always working."

He squeezed into the booth, and his belly expanded over the edge of the table.

"You wanna sit at the bar?"

Skeeter noticed my focus. "I'm all right," he said and chuckled. "You all calm, cool, and relaxed. Good visit with Grandpa?"

"Couldn't survive without him."

"You should make those visits twice a week and maybe you wouldn't come off as such a hard-ass."

"Thank you, Oprah. Maybe I like being a hard-ass. It's good for business."

"Right. That's why we been so busy these last few months."

"Point taken."

"And why can't I be Dr. Phil?" He pinched a napkin with his prosthesis, dabbed his sweaty forehead, and pretended to be offended.

"Because you're black."

"Man, you racist." He loved to pull the fake race card just to watch me react.

"That's why I got you off death row. I wanted one more giant black man on the street when I organize the next Klan rally."

The mine shaft exploded, shaking the table.

"Anything new from your research?" I asked.

"Nothing about Marissa Luna, but Sosa, Allison, and Marcus Lopez are tight. Land, oil, mineral rights. Lopez handles every aspect. Most of his law firm is occupied with the Allison family. Allison oil and the family cattle operation does business with Sosa in Mexico."

"Grandpa took me to one of Allison's drilling rigs. I found Mexican equipment, and the security guard said he worked for Marcus Lopez."

"If that's Heights Security, they're part of his law firm."

"He has private security?"

"He's high profile. Especially now, running for governor."

"Nothing about Marissa Luna?"

"Everything her mom told you checks out. She was a good student, focused on graduating, and didn't drink. Definitely not a suicide."

"I agree."

"How'd it go at the Byrd Factory?"

"Danny Allison bought the bracelet and had it engraved."

"Allison? The Allison?" Skeeter sat up straight and glanced around the tavern. "You think Sosa and Marissa's murders are connected?"

I shook my head. "Too early to tell. I wanna find out if Danny boy was at the dance club with Marissa. I need help with the security cameras."

He dropped the napkin and smiled. The mention of an electronic puzzle focused his attention. I explained the situation with the surveillance cameras at the club. Skeeter had an immediate answer. He almost seemed disappointed it wasn't more of a challenge.

We drove to the dance club and waited across the street until closing time. The manager exited through a side door and walked to the parking garage. I took out my lock-picking tools and selected what I thought I would need to access the building.

Skeeter put his hand on my arm, nodding toward the tools. "Why'd you even call me?"

"You said you needed access to the system."

He flashed a smile that a ten-year-old might give Grandma when she needed help with the remote control. "I got this," he said. He opened his laptop with his metal hook and tapped a few keys. "I installed the system. I knew guys like you'd be tryin' to break in with tools like that." He pressed one last key. "Let's go."

Something he'd done unlocked the door and disabled the security alarm and we were inside the building in minutes. Without the throbbing sound, the laser lights, and the horde of post-apocalyptic dancers, the empty room turned into an abandoned warehouse.

Skeeter led me to a different office where the server and backup tapes were kept. He plugged in his laptop, then plopped down in a too-small chair.

While we waited for the tapes to download, I told him what happened in Kerrville.

"She just told you the information, even though that's illegal?"

"You underestimate how charming I can be for a country boy."

"You took Sam, didn't you?"

"He had nothing to do with it," I protested.

"Right." Skeeter pulled his laptop in front of him and tapped a few keys. "What do you know about Danny Allison?"

"He's rich, spoiled, and just graduated from Texas Tech."

"Why'd he buy Marissa an expensive bracelet, then kill her?"

"Because he's got money to burn," I said.

"Sometimes these rich kids don't get their money until they come of age." He brought up a university database that he shouldn't have had access to and started reading Danny Allison's backstory.

"He's a weekend warrior. Amateur MMA fighter. He joined the Tech boxing club his freshman year. Must be pretty good. He won a few tournaments. He played rugby, so he's not a complete loner. His grades were average or a little below, counting his freshman year. Someone must have given him a pep talk. They went up just enough to graduate on the five-year plan. This is interesting…"

"What?" I was twiddling my thumbs while I watched the gentle giant work.

"His daddy went to Tech and so did his grandpa."

"How'd you find all that?"

He smiled. "All here in the university records. Both are prominent alumni and big donors. The son would have had to attend the family college. Probably part of his trust agreement."

"How's that?"

"His family's filthy rich, but he goes to school in Lubbock. Not exactly the Ivy League. He plays rugby and likes to fight MMA. How many rich kids you know do that?"

I saw his point. "He's not flashing money around like you might expect with the Allison family fortune behind him. He should be doing the Formula One circuit and flying off to ski the Alps in a private jet. Danny boy spends his weekends getting his ass kicked."

"Actually, he's pretty good, judging by his record," Skeeter said.

"He's twenty-three. Let's say he doesn't get paid until he's twenty-five, and Grandpa placed certain conditions on the first payment," I said.

"Like graduate from the family alma mater," Skeeter said, nodding.

"And not getting arrested." I was thinking of Danny standing next to his grandpa in the convention center trying to look sober and respectable.

"I'll bet he has to join the family business." Skeeter turned the laptop so I could see a picture of Danny, Patrick, and Marcus Lopez standing in front of an oil derrick somewhere in West Texas wearing hard hats and matching Oxford shirts.

"What happened to his dad?"

"Died in a plane crash. Private plane. He was the pilot. Danny was with him. Happened between here and Lubbock during his first year in college."

"Could explain the bad grades. That must have hit him hard."

"He did get himself under control. I wonder if there were any more conditions on his trust fund," Skeeter said.

We looked at each other across the table. Both thinking the same thing. "Don't get some girl pregnant," I said.

"Bingo," Skeeter said and unplugged his laptop. "I got what we need. We gotta go."

"What's the hurry? I thought you installed the system."

"I did. I installed a failsafe in case someone like me did what I'm doin'."

"That doesn't sound good." I followed him through the office door.

Skeeter looked at his watch. "We have thirty seconds. The alarm goes off here and at the police station. The building locks down."

"You're joking, right?" I yelled as we ran for the side door. I could see myself trying to explain this to Detective Peterson and watching him laugh while he shoved us both into the back of his Crown Vic. A half step from the door, an ear-piercing screech shattered the silence. The annoyance level rivaled the pulsing techno sound without the bass. I grabbed the door handle.

Locked.

"Told you," he said.

"You couldn't get us out before the alarm went off?"

"The download took longer than I thought," he yelled over the noise.

Sirens outside wailed above the alarm. I didn't want to end up face down on the parking lot twice in one weekend.

"I can't face jail again, man," he shouted. "Get us out of here."

We ran for the emergency fire exit.

The front door burst open.

"Police!"

We ducked behind the bar and scrambled toward the exit. I reached up and pushed the red handle. A light above the door began to flash. Outside, we slammed the door, and Skeeter leaned all his three hundred pounds against it. We waited ten seconds, then fifteen. Skeeter felt the door move against him.

"Here they come," he whispered.

I added my weight to the door.

We felt two sharp bumps, then a voice yelled: "This door's blocked. Check the perimeter!"

CHAPTER TWENTY

The pounding on the door stopped, and the policemen inside retreated.

"Let's move," I whispered.

We sprinted down the alley and back to my pickup. Technically, we were breaking the law. Nothing we found in the tapes would be admissible in court, but the details of this case were starting to point to a cover-up, and I didn't really care about building a case. I wasn't a cop. I humbly considered myself a competent investigator, otherwise I wouldn't have quit law school to open a business. I enjoyed the pursuit and I had to admit that the occasional adrenaline rush beat the hell out of shuffling paperwork or even arguing a point of law. The endgame for me was finding the truth.

On the short drive back to my King William neighborhood, I thought about what I had so far. I'd uncovered the name of the likely father to Marissa's child and a possible motive for killing her within a few days. Why hadn't Detective Peterson made the same discoveries? Incompetence or cover-up? I was leaning toward the latter. The other reason I'd gotten into this business was to fight for justice when incompetence or corruption occurred. Marissa deserved justice, and right now I was the only one on her side. Peterson had been too quick to label Marissa as west side trash. The only thing that fit his narrative was her place of birth, and the ease with which he dismissed her life made my blood boil.

When we got back to my place, Sam stood by the back door ready for his run. "Not tonight, partner," I said. I gave him a piece of leftover beef brisket. He took it but didn't forgive me. "I'll make it up to you. I promise." He turned his back to me and lay down.

Skeeter observed the exchange and shook his head. "You and that dog."

"You're just jealous."

We watched the dance club surveillance video on the TV in my front room. Skeeter rolled the tape in fast motion beginning at six o'clock on the evening of July fourth. The stringy-haired manager went through the cash registers, and the muscle-bound bouncer took up his position at the end of the bar. The waitress wiped down the shot glasses and loaded ice in the cooler. We watched the comical, frenetic movements of the young people on the dance floor for half an hour with no sign of Marissa or Danny Allison. It was like watching a *National Geographic* documentary on some lost Amazon Rainforest tribe. The ritual dance consisted of an up-down movement combined with arms flailing about. The dress code was a mixture of preppy, urban hip, and jeans and boots, the Texas standby. Most of the participants were college age and younger—the only people with enough stamina to withstand the grinding assault to the senses. It went on for hours, fueled by alcohol and open drug use. I started to wonder if Detective Peterson had reviewed any of the tapes.

It was three a.m. We'd stopped by the twenty-four-hour pizzeria to stock up on snacks. In my experience, food and lots of coffee were essential for the tedious chore of reviewing surveillance tapes.

The good part about it was that there was no sound, and Skeeter manipulated the images so that we could watch eight camera views at once. Two on the bar, four on the dance floor, and one each on the front door and the back entrance.

At nine thirty Marissa and Beth entered from the street side. They walked to the bar and ordered drinks. Marissa wasn't wearing the bracelet, or any visible jewelry. She wore the blue patriotic tank top and the black skirt I recognized from the crime scene photos. I watched closely to see if Marissa's mother had overstated her sobriety. The barmaid squirted water in a glass with ice and added lemon. Marissa took a thirsty drink. She poured Beth something with carbonation in a copper mug topped with lime.

"That's a Moscow mule," Skeeter said, sounding full of himself.

"How would you know? You don't drink."

"I had one last week for a special occasion. Vodka, ginger beer, and a twist of lime. Very refreshing."

"You had a date?"

"Why are you surprised?"

"'Cause you haven't had a date since last October."

"How do you know?"

"I set it up."

"She still calls me."

"That's because you installed her security system. Who was your date with?"

"I took my mom to Applebee's for her birthday," he said. He was a good son.

We watched Marissa and Beth sip their drinks and search the crowd. A guy in a skin-tight silver T-shirt waved his rainbow-colored Mohawk in their direction. The girls looked at each other and giggled as Mohawk pranced in front of them. He hopped from one foot to the other and gestured toward the crowded dance floor. The girls shook their heads. Mohawk persisted. He inserted himself between them and ordered a drink. When he turned, he brushed his hand across Marissa's breast. She grabbed the thumb on his right hand and twisted it up behind his back. Mohawk looked shocked and in pain. He backed away and left the girls alone. I ruled him out as a suspect. Marissa would have kicked his ass.

I was beginning to like Marissa. I wondered where she had learned that move. At the same time, of course, I realized she was dead. Whatever training she had wasn't enough to keep her alive. That told me the killer was persistent and brutal, and made me even more determined to catch him.

The girls continued to watch the crowd and giggle. They looked young and innocent and full of life. I wanted to shout, "Go home!" at the screen. But, of course, Skeeter and I could only watch the inevitable. It was like seeing a video of a train wreck before the fatal accident. The passengers were all happy and clueless that death was rushing to meet them.

They left their drinks on the bar and went to the dance floor. Not a good thing to do in a place like this. We watched the drinks for any sign of tampering until the barmaid swept them into the sink.

By eleven thirty on the video time stamp, the Fourth of July crowd was double what I'd experienced. Just watching it made my ears ring. There was still no sign of Danny Allison. I was beginning to think risking jail time to get the tapes was a big waste of time. Maybe Marissa's friend was telling the truth about their night. And maybe Peterson had done his job.

I put on another pot of coffee. Skeeter and I were taking turns concentrating on the crowd. When there was enough caffeinated liquid accumulated in the pot, I siphoned it off into my mug and took a drink. It contained the double shot of wake-up that I needed.

At eleven forty-seven on the time stamp, Danny Allison walked through the door. He wore designer jeans and square-toed cowboy boots.

"Speak of the devil. There he is."

"And he's lookin' for someone," Skeeter said.

Danny's white Oxford shirt was pressed and tucked into a western belt. He searched the room, then waded into the crowd. He didn't wait for people to move. If they didn't step aside, he gave them a persuasive shove. More than a few didn't seem to like being pushed. One young woman gave him the finger. Danny didn't notice. He never even looked back.

I searched the other cameras but couldn't find Marissa. "Where is she?"

"In the restroom."

"You didn't put a camera in the ladies' room?"

He didn't dignify that with an answer. Even the idea irritated him. He once used his hacking skills to take down a porn site that used public restroom footage.

Danny ordered a drink and put his back to the bar, doing his best Gene Autry imitation, fresh off the trail and looking for whiskey and some action. We spotted Marissa exiting the restroom alone.

"Where's the friend?" I asked.

Skeeter shrugged. Marissa went straight to the bar. She obviously recognized Danny and approached him directly. When he saw her, he pushed away from the bar and reached to hug her. She held up her hands to stop him. Without the sound, it was impossible to judge their conversation, but she wasn't happy, and it looked like Danny was making up an excuse for being late. I recognized the body language because I'd done it a few times. It was some version of: *Sorry, honey, there was a lot of traffic.*

Danny reached into his perfectly ironed shirt pocket and brought out his ace in the hole. The bracelet. Four grand worth of *I'm sorry I'm late.*

"That's it," I said. "That's the bracelet."

The angle didn't give a great view of her expression, but even from above it looked like her face registered shock. In the next breath she hit him. Hard. She used a flat right hand and caught him on the lower cheek. In the color video, his skin turned crimson. He grabbed her by the wrist. She hit him with the other hand. Good for her. Too bad she hadn't carried a pistol.

Danny grabbed both her wrists and pushed them down to her sides. The bouncer at the end of the bar did nothing. What a waste of skin. Her friend was nowhere in sight. The whole encounter lasted less than a minute. Marissa stopped struggling, and Danny let her go. She took a step back, said one last thing. Danny held up the bracelet in a gesture of surrender. Marissa took it and walked out.

Danny stayed at the bar and watched her go. She walked out of one camera and into another. Halfway between the bar and the back entrance, she ran into Beth. The two hugged briefly. Marissa wiped her cheeks with her fingertips, clearly crying. Beth held her hand and seemed to ask pointed questions. Marissa held the bracelet out to Beth. She shook her head, refusing to take it. Marissa insisted. Beth finally gave in and put the bracelet in her purse. Then Marissa took a step toward the back door. Beth started to follow, but Marissa waved her off.

"Why did she lie to me? Beth obviously saw that Marissa was upset."

"Maybe she was too drunk to remember."

"Maybe someone else got to her."

"You think Danny threatened her?"

I didn't answer. He let the tape roll forward. We watched Danny finish his beer. He didn't seem too upset. At least, he didn't smash his head against the bar or stomp his boots. Ten minutes later he looked at his wristwatch and walked out the street-side entrance.

"Didn't he come in on the other side?" Skeeter asked.

I nodded and sipped my coffee.

"He would have known the place had security cameras," Skeeter continued.

I finished my coffee, letting Skeeter blast the air with questions we couldn't answer.

"You gonna solve this case or play dumb?"

I held up my hand. "I'm thinking."

"In that case, I'll just shut the hell up." Skeeter stalked off toward the kitchen.

I picked up my spiral notebook and wrote down the timeline from the video. Danny left at twelve twenty-eight. The time of Marissa's death was listed between one and three a.m. He had plenty of time to walk to the Travis Street bridge, but had they set up a meeting? Did he know which way she would walk? He could have followed her progress from bridge to bridge, waiting for a moment when she was alone.

If Detective Peterson had seen this, it wasn't in his report. There was no mention of Danny Allison as a witness or as a suspect. The report didn't mention a fight, the bracelet, or the friend taking it. The question was, why?

Skeeter came back into the room. "What now, Sherlock? Do we grab Danny Allison and haul him down to the police station?"

"Fightin' with your date doesn't automatically lead to murder, even in Texas."

"But you have the bracelet."

"It's not enough. We need to mark him as the boyfriend before that night." I took my empty coffee mug back to the kitchen. "Check on Sam tomorrow, in case I don't make it back."

"Where you goin'?"

"Lubbock. It's where Danny and Marissa must have hooked up."

"Be careful."

"Something going on in Lubbock I don't know about?"

"Nothing's ever going on in Lubbock. Be careful because Danny's last name is Allison. That family has more money and connections than AT&T."

I doubted the Allisons were that rich, but I got his point.

Skeeter took an Uber home, and I trudged upstairs. Sam followed. It was four forty-five. He jumped on the bed and curled up on a pillow. I flopped down beside him. Two nights in a row burning the midnight oil. I felt like I was studying for finals, or worse, going out on patrol.

I thought about calling Sylvia, but it was late, and the antihistamine had made me drowsy. That was my excuse anyway. We needed to have a long talk about our future. She asked me if I was ever going to let her in. I'd told her she was already there. The truth was, I didn't know if I could ever let her in.

"Wer rastet, der rostet"
He who rests, rusts."

—Grandpa Fischer

CHAPTER TWENTY-ONE

DAY THREE

By six the next morning, I was fighting coast-to-coast truckers mixed with local traffic on Interstate 10. Even the Labor Day holiday didn't diminish the perennial bottleneck created by the Texas Department of Transportation who, in their infinite wisdom, had cut the eight-lane freeway to one lane west of San Antonio, then moved all the road crews to the south side. No one seemed to know when or if the twenty-mile stretch of road would ever be fully reopened. The limited sleep was catching up to me, and that first ten miles felt like taking a lap around the Talladega racetrack. But I had a lead, and Grandpa always told me when there was work to be done, sleep could wait.

Ninety miles and a large coffee later, I took the exit for State Highway 83 at Junction and turned north. The road narrowed, the traffic thinned, and my pulse returned to normal. Lubbock was a six-hour drive—five and a half if you pushed it—through arid, rolling hills that was once the sole domain of Comanche Indians following free-range buffalo. With the complete demise of the herds and the tribes, dry hills were all that was left. The advance of western civilization wasn't only thwarted by hostile tribes. Cemented caliche over limestone bedrock combined with limited water made farming impossible and ranchers required over a hundred acres per cow to survive. There was life here to the trained eye. Kit fox, prairie dogs, white-tailed deer, antelope, black bear, and mountain lions thrived along with the world's largest population of Mexican free-tailed bats, but until the discovery of oil in the Permian Basin in the 1920s most people avoided the region.

I stopped in Ballenger for more coffee and topped off my gas tank. I was making the drive to find out if Danny and Marissa left any trace of their relationship in their college town. No one seemed to know they were together in San Antonio. If they did, they didn't admit it. The mother was out of the loop, and Marissa's best friend from high school wasn't talking. I had contacted Kelly Hoffman, a former Marine officer I knew. She worked for the university police force now and had agreed to help me out even though it was Sunday on a holiday weekend. In fact, she seemed a little too eager to see me, and I wondered what that was all about. The last thing I needed was another woman to complicate the tenuous relationship I already had. I sensed a hint of flirtatiousness in her voice, but maybe it was just my overdeveloped ego playing tricks on me.

At the end of the vast expanse of rolling limestone hills the landscape leveled off into the Llano Estacado, a pan-flat red-dirt farmland that stretch west to the Rocky Mountains and linked with the Great Plains stretching north to Canada. Before the farmers took over, the area was an endless sea of grass first described by Francisco Coronado in 1541 as "so vast, that I did not find their limit anywhere...with no more landmarks than if we had been swallowed up by the sea. There was not a stone, nor bit of rising ground, nor a tree, nor a shrub, nor anything to go by." Now, there were manmade landmarks and a few trees planted by the farmers, but the pan-flat landscape still made it one of the loneliest places on earth. Lubbock seemed to rise out of the dark-green, irrigated cotton plants that stretched in neat rows as far as the eye could see. I followed the signs to the university and found an empty parking spot next to the new crime lab building. The one thing Lubbock had was plenty of free parking.

I'd texted my arrival to Kelly, and she was waiting for me on the front steps. She had the wholesome good looks of a farmer's daughter, which she was. She was born and raised five miles south of Lubbock and had joined the Corps as an MP after getting a degree in forensic science. She still wore her blond hair cut short following the female military standard and looked like she could ace the Marine physical fitness test.

"Fischer, you scallywag. I wasn't expecting you till after lunch." She took off her lab coat and extended her hand.

I glanced at her new sergeant stripes and name badge. She had traded one uniform for another. She looked good in both. I shook her hand. Her palms were calloused from lifting weights and helping her dad on the farm. Her nails were painted blue but filed down so they didn't interfere with the instruments she worked with in the lab or the bales of hay she bucked on the weekends.

"You look like you just got off the obstacle course," I said.

"Who says I didn't?" She laughed and gave me a playful tap on the shoulder. She definitely had muscle tone.

"Thanks for giving me a little time."

"Of course. Us jarheads have to stick together. Let me give you the short tour."

She showed me the unit's new Rapid DNA instruments. They could process DNA samples in two to three hours while a perp was sitting in a jail cell. A process that normally took months now could put a suspect in jail before he was back out on the streets or clear him before he was locked away.

When she was done, I followed her to her office. She had a collection of Marine Corps paraphernalia including a picture of us together on the base in Afghanistan. That was a surprise. I didn't think we'd been that close. I hadn't kept a picture of her. She sat behind a metal desk and watched me study pictures of other bases I knew.

"Make you wish you'd stayed in?" she asked. I detected a hint of longing in her voice.

"Not me. But I was enlisted. It was a whole different Corps than you experienced."

"Don't give me that BS, Fischer. I did everything y'all did, and extra because I was female." She laughed and seemed to be waiting for me to argue her point.

I got the feeling she wanted to swap war stories. She didn't seem to be in any hurry, and I wondered if her excuse about working on Sunday was really true. The building was otherwise empty. I didn't want to hurry her and seem ungrateful, but as much as I was enjoying her company, I was hoping to get some information and hit the road. When the silence stretched for another minute, she sensed my impatience.

"What was the name of your suspect again?" she asked, booting up her desktop computer.

"Danny Allison." I spelled the last name. "He's more of a person of interest. I'm trying to establish a link between him and the murder victim."

"Let me run his name in the law enforcement database and see what pops up," she said, and typed a few keys to access the files.

While we waited, I asked if she liked being back in Lubbock or if she preferred South Texas. She kept her eyes on the screen and didn't answer. The last time I saw her was when she was stationed in San Antonio. She had called out of the blue, and we met for a beer. I'd just started dating Sylvia at the time.

"My family's here," she finally said. "This job is what I've always wanted. We have one of the most sophisticated labs in the country. Last year we got approval for the upgrade by the FBI. We stay busy." She scrolled through a list of names, then stopped. "I got a hit on your boy."

I got up to look, but she swiveled the screen to block my view.

"I know you told me about this on the phone, but you *are* on this case, right? The mother hired you to find the killer?" She was a good MP and had transitioned into a by-the-book civilian policewoman. I gave her the details again, starting with the bracelet and what Skeeter and I found on the surveillance tapes. She listened and nodded.

"She was pregnant," I said, finishing my explanation. "Everything points to Danny Allison as the father. He didn't come forward or lift a finger after the body was discovered."

Kelly's features hardened. The story definitely left Danny smelling like week-old roadkill. She studied my expression, then nodded, convinced. She turned back to the monitor and read Danny's record.

"There was a sexual harassment report filed his sophomore year. The woman was a foreign exchange student from China. She dropped the charge and moved back home."

"That won't help."

"Here's another one the following year. Same charge."

"Another foreigner?"

"Nope, this one was a local."

"Spread the love."

"She dropped the case too."

"Is that unusual?"

"Not really. Even with the MeToo movement, if the guy's got money, he can hire the best lawyers and private investigators to dig the dirt. Pretty soon the case starts to fall apart, and the victim gets cold feet or settles out of court."

"He does have money and a high-powered lawyer. But not the best private eye."

"What makes you say that?"

"I'm the best, and I don't work for him."

She smiled. I always liked that smile. Bright, clean, crisp. The kind of smile that turned heads even if it was hiding under a helmet. I turned back to the screen. If I stared any longer, she might think I was flirting. Maybe I was and wasn't willing to admit it. The idea made me feel guilty. I didn't wanna complicate my relationship with Sylvia any more than it already was.

I made notes on the details of the last complaint against Danny, then offered to buy her lunch. Instead, she took me to the university cafeteria and paid with her punch card. The food reminded me of military meals, which were hard to describe but stuck to your ribs. I was starving after the drive, so I took a plate of meatloaf with mac and cheese on the side, because there was a long line waiting for chicken fried steak. Coastal universities had a more vegan-friendly menu, but Lubbock was in the heartland and had too many farmer's kids to be too politically correct. Kelly met me at the iced tea dispenser, where she watched me fill a glass with unsweetened tea.

"What are you, a yankee?" She laughed. "No one drinks unsweetened tea in the South."

"I'm watching my weight."

"Don't say that out loud," she whispered.

We took our trays to a corner table. The sound of clacking silverware and ice being dispensed provided a constant undercurrent to our conversation.

"How's your girlfriend, the Victoria Secret model?" she asked.

"She modeled furniture for her dad's store, not underwear." I laughed. I knew Sylvia and Kelly would never get along if they ever met.

"Whatever, I'm surprised she lets you do this kind of work."

"If I did what other people wanted, I would have stayed in the Corps."

"You'd be a gunny by now."

"Or busted back to private."

"I always wondered how a guy like you that has a problem with authority ended up in the Marine Corps."

"My dad was a Marine. I had something to prove."

Kelly sensed that she'd strayed into territory that I wasn't ready to talk about with her. She didn't press it. We finished lunch listening to the clanking of silverware against plastic trays and the murmur of college gossip. I searched the faces of the students. *This is where Marissa should have been*, I thought, starting her senior year, laughing and eating meatloaf without a care in the world. Instead she'd ended up in the San Antonio River. The thought made my blood boil.

CHAPTER TWENTY-TWO

The incessant North Texas wind greeted me outside the cafeteria, filled my eyes and nose with red grit, and laughed at my weak-kneed response. I laughed back and popped an antihistamine, wondering if the original inhabitants, Comanches, suffered from allergies. I got in my old F150 and drove west on Broadway. In the ten minutes it took to reach the city limits, I'd passed a dozen Baptist churches. Lubbock County had a high concentration of the faithful, which was why for most of its history the county had been dry. For decades, thirsty residence had to travel to the county line for a taste of anything stronger than root beer.

I was looking for the Buena Vista Mobile Home Village—the trailer park listed as the last known address for Valerie Martin. She was the coed who filed a sexual harassment claim against Danny Allison last year, then dropped the charges. I wanted to know why she'd changed her mind and if the young woman knew Marissa Luna.

A neglected plywood sign marked the entrance to the Buena Vista. The advertised *good view* was a red haze of wind-blown cotton fields to the south and unobstructed pan-flat cow pasture to the north. So flat, ranchers used to say, that if you stood on an apple crate you could see the Canadian border. I was sitting in my four-wheel-drive pickup and could only see as far as the dairy farm across the barbed-wire fence. I was raised on a ranch and didn't need to roll down my windows to know what the giant mounds behind the milking sheds were made of.

The single-wide mobile homes formed a large circle laid out over five acres with a portable office building in the middle. A few had small grass lawns, but most were surrounded with red dirt and gravel. There was only one road in and one road out. No need for the GPS. I passed the office and drove the loop checking the mailboxes for Valerie's address. Two of the occupants were resting in the shade of their retractable porch awnings, rocking away the hot afternoon. I wondered if they were immune to the dairy stench and constant blowing dust.

The trailer park seemed an odd place to find an acquaintance of the very affluent Allison family. Was there a pattern to Danny's pick of female companions? This trailer park wasn't so different from Marissa Luna's neighborhood. I wondered what he was looking for.

I found the number and parked in the gravel driveway. The trailer had a worn wooden porch that was missing a few railing boards, and a loose awning that flapped in the wind. Rust showed through the light blue paint, but it wasn't the oldest in the park. Someone had mowed the small patch of grass out front and the junk in the driveway was kept to a minimum. I'd lived in worse places. Nothing stirred behind the windows, so I knocked on the metal door.

I heard a medium-sized dog barking inside but no human activity. It was Sunday afternoon. Maybe Valerie worked weekends or was honoring the Sabbath in one of Lubbock's many churches. A stout older lady wearing a red apron over a flower-print dress waddled across the street toward me. She looked like she'd just hurried home from church to pull a pot roast out of the oven.

"Can I help you, son?" she asked in a nasal Panhandle twang and placed her hands on her portly hips.

"Do you know Valerie Martin?"

"Yes, I do. She moved on some time ago. Let's see… at the end of last year. November, I think. She's got a condo on the north side, closer to town. I still have the forwarding address. She was getting monthly checks in the mail. Didn't want to miss any. I think it was financial aid."

I told her I was from the university and needed to ask Valerie a few questions. It only took a minute for her to shuffle back to her trailer and find the forwarding address. If every trailer park had a friendly neighbor, the private eye business would be a snap.

The address she gave me was in a much newer residential area fifteen minutes from the dairy farm, but a world apart. This area north of the city was home to a country club, golf course, and a collection of gated communities. Valerie's condo was in one of them. A bored-looking guard sporting a droopy mustache and wearing thick, wire-framed glasses met me at the entrance.

"Howdy, I'm Valerie Martin's brother, Tom. It's her birthday today, and I drove up from Austin to surprise her. She's in 3304."

He stared at me and chuckled. "Her brother?" he asked, like he knew more about Valerie than I did. "I'll have to call." He was thin, and his breath smelled of cigarette smoke and vodka masked with peppermint candy.

"It's a surprise, Doug." I read his name off his nametag. I took out a twenty, folded it in half, and held it between my fingers, palm up. "I'll sneak you some cold beer. What d'ya say?"

I had him with the beer offer. He took the money and buzzed me through the gate. The complex had a cozy, round pool on each end and thirty units, all with a private garage and a covered patio. In the center was a tree-lined park with a paved trail and a half dozen picnic tables. The units were two stories and put together with terra-cotta bricks, dark wood trim, and shake shingles. It was quite a step up from the trailer park across the fence from the dairy farm. If Valerie was getting financial aid, she wasn't using it to pay for school. That or she had won the lottery.

I knocked. After a few minutes, bare feet slapped on a tile floor inside. I got out my private investigator credentials and held them up to the peephole. The door opened, and a strikingly pretty young black woman squinted against the bright sunlight. I understood why Doug hadn't believed my family story.

"What's this about? Who're you?" She didn't sound happy to see me. Judging by her appearance and her disheveled hair, she was not an early riser. The oversized man's white T-shirt she wore covered her petite frame down to her knees and contrasted sharply with her ebony skin.

"Valerie Martin?"

She studied my forehead scars and hesitated like she regretted opening the door. "Yes."

"My name's Nick Fischer." I smiled and tried to sound apologetic. "I'm a private investigator looking into a sexual harassment case against Danny Allison."

She stood up straight and focused on my ID. I had her full attention. She was nervous and crossed her arms over the thin T-shirt. "I don't have anything to say," she blurted out.

"This is important. There was another incident. A student named Marissa Luna. Do you know her, or have you ever heard the name?"

"Never heard of her."

"Ms. Martin, if you'd let me come in, I'd like to ask a few questions about your case."

"No. There's nothing to it. I dropped the charges. I already explained. That was a year ago. It was a misunderstanding. I can't talk about it."

"Please, just—"

She slammed the door in my face. It wasn't the first time someone had done that, and it wouldn't be the last. I didn't push it. If she wouldn't talk, she wouldn't talk. Walking back to my pickup, I thought about her last line. *I can't talk about it.* Did she mean she didn't want to, or she was prevented from doing so by a legal agreement? I suspected the latter.

I checked the handle on her garage door. It was open. Why lock it when Doug the security guard was on duty? Valerie Martin had a new BMW. White with cream leather seats. I wasn't a car guy but guessed it was worth north of fifty grand. How did Ms. Martin go from a trailer park overlooking a dairy farm to a luxury condo and a Beemer while going to school and working at a bar? And why did she get a big pay out when Marissa got a bracelet and a trip down the river?

I waved to Doug on my way out. I knew he was looking forward to a cold beer on a hot day, but I had things to do. I searched the work history Kelly had found for Valerie and drove to her last known place of employment. It was a bar near the university named the Library. The owner knew how to attract college students. I was expecting a trendy, upscale nightspot where frat boys met sorority girls and jocks wore tight jerseys to show off their muscles. Maybe Danny stayed late one night and offered Valerie a ride home after work. Maybe he'd used the same line on Marissa.

From the outside, the Library didn't look like much. It was in an older part of town across the street from a car dealership. Parts of the street were still paved with red brick left over from the nineteenth century. The sign on the outside said they didn't open until seven on Sunday, but the door was unlocked.

I paused to let my eyes adjust to the dim lighting and to soak up the air conditioning. The North Texas air was less humid than San Antonio, but it was hot enough in September that it didn't matter. A hundred degrees was a hundred degrees no matter where you stood on the planet.

The place had the feel of an old high school library but smelled like hops and orange peels. An ornamental collection of used books was stacked against the back bar. It was the kind of place I wouldn't have minded spending a few hours in, but I had work to do.

The bartender wore a Pink Floyd T-shirt and a manbun. He didn't look up until I tapped the little library bell on the counter. He was young, hip, and annoyed.

"We're closed," he sneered.

"I just wanna ask you a few questions."

"We're a little busy getting ready for opening. Why don't you show yourself out?"

I flashed my private eye credentials. "It's about an employee."

He ignored the license and pulled a tray of shot glasses from the washer. "You a cop?"

I wanted to say I was Rodney Dangerfield, but I knew he wouldn't get the reference. Nobody respected private eyes anymore. "Private investigator," I said. Manbun was getting on my nerves. It had been a long day following a short night, and I still had a six-hour drive back to San Antonio. I wanted to grab his trendy ball of hair and slam his left ear on the counter, but I figured he would shit himself and call the cops, so I flashed my best disarming smile instead. I was working on my people skills.

"I'm not asking much. Answer a few simple questions, and I promise not to slice off your topknot with my Buck knife."

He looked puzzled, trying to figure out if I was kidding or not. I stopped smiling and held his gaze. He seemed to notice my scars for the first time.

"All right, all right. Fuck, dude. Ask your question." He backed off a few steps.

"Does Valerie Martin work here?" I asked as politely as I could.

A female coworker poked her head out of the back room. "Everything kosher out here?"

Manbun looked at me. I smiled again.

"Yeah, no problem," he said.

She ducked back inside. He placed another tray of dirty glasses in the washer. "No, man. She left a year ago. Bitch said she didn't need the job."

"Not a happy ending?"

"She left on Thanksgiving weekend. Busy time. Home game for the Raiders. We had to cover for her."

"Were you friends before that?"

"I wasn't her type."

"What type is that?"

"Rich," he said. He didn't have to spell it out. I knew the type. Every university town had gold diggers. It cast doubt on her accusations, but since she dropped the charges no one would ever know the truth.

"One more question. Do you know Danny Allison or Marissa Luna?"

He shook his head. "Sorry, no."

I laid a twenty on the bar and walked out. I had a pretty good idea where Valerie Martin got her money. I couldn't prove it, of course, but it wouldn't take too much digging. Skeeter could find out. Paying hush money didn't make Danny Allison guilty of murder, but it established a pattern of behavior.

Outside, the wind still laughed, but the drugs had kicked in, and I had too much on my mind to take offense.

CHAPTER TWENTY-THREE

I crossed the river at the Eagleland Drive trailhead behind my house and followed Sam north on the River Walk trail. At that point, the water was contained in concrete banks and lined with trees and overgrown grass instead of bars and restaurants, but the path was paved and well lit. I thought of using an alternate route through the city to avoid the narrow confines of the trail and increased risk of ambush but brushed it off as being too paranoid. Still, the Allison name had popped up in two murder cases. Too much for a coincidence. I ramped up my precaution level to seven, which meant checking my backtrail and packing my .38, even if it rubbed my ankle raw. At under a pound, it packed a punch and could neutralize a threat at short range. A half mile further up the trail the rough grass turned into a manicured park that received more regular maintenance. I began to relax. The air was warm and humid, but it felt good to be moving after the long drive to Lubbock. The late night runs with Sam never failed to reduce my stress level and help me put my world back in perspective.

When Sam and I hit our six-mile-an-hour pace, I tried to sort out what I'd learned so far. Danny Allison fit all the requisite criteria. He had means, opportunity, and motive. He also had a history of harassing women. Unless I was way off base, he'd paid at least one woman to buy her silence. Marissa may have wanted money. Or the baby could have jeopardized Danny's inheritance and family reputation. Killing her was his only way out. Greed was a powerful motivator.

What I needed was proof that he was the father of Marissa's child. That would require a DNA sample from Danny to match the fetal DNA from Marissa's autopsy. Kelly had agreed to run the sample through the rapid DNA test at her lab. The only problem was getting a sample of Danny's DNA. He wasn't gonna give it to me voluntarily. Either I had to convince Peterson he had probable cause to get a court order, or I had to squeeze a sample out of him myself.

Before I could finish the thought, a punch on my arm spun me to the ground, followed by a muffled pop. My brain processed sniper fire. Warm blood soaked into my T-shirt. The whiff from another bullet flew past my head. I recognized the sound. The same compressed-air pop that took out Sosa.

I pulled Sam into the shadow of a palm tree beside the trail, keeping the trunk between us and the shooter. He whined and sniffed my bloody arm. Another round hit the tree, showering us with bark. This time I saw the flicker of light from the muzzle blast. The shooter was in a parking garage across the river, less than a hundred yards away.

Sam crouched next to me, the loose skin around his forehead curled into a question mark. He thought it was a game until I pulled the .38. Any kind of gun meant the hunt was on. He didn't yet realize we were the prey.

The wound began to throb, but I still had control of my fingers and could move my shoulder. The bullet had missed the bone. Careful not to expose my body outside the tree, I ripped a strip from the bottom of my T-shirt and wrapped it around the wound. The loss of blood was making me lightheaded. I needed to fight against shock. If I passed out, the shooter would move in for the kill.

Sam and I waited. His body tensed for my gunshot or a command putting him in action. I kept my .38 ready but knew I was unlikely to hit anything outside of twenty-five yards. Five minutes went by. I checked my watch. Nine thirty. I carefully scanned the area. Climbing the retaining wall behind the tree was out of the question. The move would leave me exposed for at least several seconds. Beyond that was an empty parking lot. Further exposure. I had no doubt the shooter had a night-vision scope and would be able to see even the slightest movement. He had picked a good location for an ambush.

I studied the parking garage. The structure provided ideal cover and an easy getaway. It also would be empty tomorrow for the Labor Day holiday. No one was coming to the rescue. My mind wandered to the countless nights I'd spent huddled with my platoon brothers waiting for a dawn attack. This time, I had no platoon and no way to call in support. I didn't carry a phone on our runs to avoid the distraction. That hadn't worked out too well. Someone had literally reached out and touched me with a sniper round.

Sam's mouth hung open, dripping from the heat. He would last the night, but the lack of water wouldn't be good for him or me. I checked my makeshift bandage. The blood flow had stopped, only to be replaced by painful burning, and my muscles were starting to cramp.

Another bullet splintered the tree trunk and ricocheted into the limestone retaining wall, spraying the grass with white dust. The angle was different this time. The shooter had changed positions. He was on the move, and I wouldn't be able to wait him out until morning. The plan I was forming was risky, but so was the alternative. If I stayed behind the tree, eventually, the shooter would find an angle for a clear shot.

Sam was anxious to move. He looked at me and whined, waiting for me to make a decision. "I'm working on it," I said, to calm his nerves and mine. I shifted to a standing position and examined the space beyond the ten-foot retaining wall. The dirt along the edge was removed in preparation for new landscaping. That was the first bit of luck all night. If I could get over the wall, the depression looked deep enough to provide cover. From there, I could inch my way to the bridge and out of sight. I scratched Sam behind the ears. He understood something was going on that involved him.

"All right, Sam," I whispered. "Time to play Rin Tin Tin." I pointed with a flat hand to the shadow under the bridge. He focused on the signal. He knew from countless hours of training and hunting that a dead bird lay in line with my outstretched finger. He only needed to stay online until he found it. His muscles tensed, anticipating the command. The shooter wouldn't be expecting a sprinting Labrador. The move was risky, and I hated to lie to Sam, but it was the only plan I could come up with. "Forgive me, ol' buddy. I'll make it up to you." I scratched his forehead, then yelled, "Fetch."

Sam took off like a bat out of hell, following my pointed fingers like he was trained to do. Two steps into his run, I heard the first pop. Sam kept moving. A miss. I focused on the edge of the ten-foot retaining wall and my dive over the ledge.

The next shot would be the real test. A good marksman will miss the first running shot but compensate for movement in the next round. With any luck, the shooter wasn't that good.

The second shot came and missed. Sam kept going. It was my turn next. I lunged for the wall, vaulted the ledge, and squeezed my bulk behind the narrow lip of stone, crushing my face against the dirt. If any part of my body was exposed, the next shot would hit me. I braced for impact.

Another whoosh of compressed air. The bullet hit the rock wall twenty yards away. No yelp from Sam. Another miss. Both of us were safe for the moment. The plan had worked. The long hours I'd worked with Sam as a puppy training him to follow my point to a downed bird had paid off. I lay still for five long minutes. Nothing. No shot. My muscles began to cramp. A colony of ants explored the sweaty hair on my forearms and discovered the sticky blood farther up. I tried to blow them away, but my breath seemed to piss them off and made them cling harder to my skin. I waited a moment longer, then slowly began to crawl forward.

The sweat on my legs and arms turned the dirt mixed with mulch into mud that stuck to my skin like paste. If it took more than fifteen minutes to cover the distance to the bridge, Sam would realize there was no dead duck and lead the shooter directly back to me.

I inched forward, using my toes and outstretched fingers. In boot camp, I'd been forced to crawl through mud under barbed wire spaced eighteen inches off the ground wearing a backpack and carrying an M1. Our drill instructor fired live rounds above the wire to simulate combat conditions. The training paid off. I knew how to keep my butt down and keep moving.

Ten yards short of the bridge, the city crew had already planted landscaping, and tiny vines were starting to sprout. Going forward would put me in full view of the shooter. I checked my watch. It had taken fifteen minutes to get to this point. My forearms and calves ached. The bullet wound throbbed. I was dehydrated, and the tiny ants continued to feast on my arm.

The open ten yards to the bridge might as well have been a hundred. It reminded me of the old WWII movie where the prisoners had tried to dig out of a German POW camp only to come up short of the tree line in an exposed no man's land. They'd been caught and returned to the prison. They were lucky.

I didn't fear death. Combat patrol had taught me to stay alert and in the moment. My only thought was to escape and find the son of a bitch pulling the trigger. If the attack was meant to scare me, it didn't work.

A splash brought me back to the present. Sam was in the river searching for that imaginary duck. The distraction I needed. Now was the time to move. I jumped to my feet and sprinted to the bridge. I could feel the target on my back. I heard the whoosh of compressed air and braced for impact.

CHAPTER TWENTY-FOUR

The bullet hit the retaining wall behind me. Another miss. I breathed a sigh of relief, but at the same time felt something wasn't right. I wasn't that lucky. The distance was easily in the kill zone of a trained sniper. He'd picked the perfect time and location, which meant he'd done his research. The same was true with Sosa's ambush. The guy was a professional, but he wasn't sent to kill. The attack must have been designed to scare me or send a warning. Was I getting close to Marissa Luna's killer? I thought about the Super Duty I'd seen at the restaurant and in front of my house. Could I have been followed to Lubbock? It didn't seem likely. I'd daydreamed through most of the trip, but I would have noticed a tail on the isolated road. Maybe Valerie Martin made a phone call and tipped off whoever was buying her off that I was asking questions.

Sam scrambled out of the river and shook his wet coat. I thought of circling back behind the parking garage and trying to get a glimpse of my attacker, but I remembered what happened with Sosa, I was again on foot with a pistol in my hand wearing a bloody shirt. I decided not to press my luck. Instead, we used the cover from the bridge to put some distance between us and the parking garage. Sam and I'd had enough excitement for one night.

The shadow of a U-Haul truck parked across the street from Sylvia's condo gave me cover to study the front entrance and let the adrenaline rush slowly subside. When I was certain I hadn't been followed, and my pulse returned to normal, I knocked. Sylvia opened the door wearing a pair of my boxers and a pink tank top. She gasped at the mixture of mud, sweat, and blood that caked my skin.

"What happened?" She pulled me inside. "Is that blood? Are you hurt?"

"Just a flesh wound."

"Oh my god." She checked the bloody makeshift bandage.

Sam inserted himself between us and rubbed his wet, muddy self against her bare legs.

"Sam, you're filthy," she said, and led him out the back door. I could hear her fill his bowl with fresh water. "Has he eaten?" she called through the door.

"Give him some food. He earned it." I heard her toss a cup of dry dog food into another bowl while I grabbed a beer from her fridge.

She returned and led me to the couch. "Out with it," she demanded.

She put a towel down on the couch, and I sat beside her and took a long drink. "I played lead-ball with a shooter between here and the McCullough bridge. Sam saved me from being KIA." The beer ushered in a bone-numbing tiredness.

"What does that mean? You were attacked? Speak English," she insisted. "I'm not in the Marine Corps."

I realized that I'd slipped back into military jargon out of habit, because the sensation of the attack was so familiar to my deployments. The strange part was that I was sitting in my girlfriend's condo drinking a beer, when I felt like I should have been debriefing my platoon and gearing up for a counterassault. "Someone shot at me from a parking garage while I jogged along the River Walk. I didn't see who it was."

Sylvia grabbed her cell phone. "I'm calling the cops, right now."

I took her hands. "No. Not now."

"When? After you're dead?"

"It was the same weapon that took out Sosa."

"Why would he be trying to kill you?"

"I don't think he is." I pressed the cool beer bottle to my forehead. I was still trying to wrap my head around what had happened.

"Damn it, Nick. What does that mean?"

"It was a warning. If he wanted me dead, he wouldn't have missed. The guy was hired to scare me."

"Listen to yourself. What're you doing? If you can link this to Sosa's shooting, you have to notify the police. It's an active investigation. Peterson warned you specifically to stay away."

"Then what? Ruin my reputation? Marcus was right. Sosa's death was not good for my business. I was responsible for him."

"Nick, Sosa's death was not your fault."

"I know that. But I think his murder and the Luna case are connected." I told her what I'd discovered about the bracelet and about Danny's track record in Lubbock.

"Danny Allison?"

"That's right. And tonight, after I told Mrs. Luna I'd take the case and found a connection with Danny, the same shooter who put a bullet in Sosa came after me."

"How could they be connected?"

"An Allison is involved in both."

"You don't know that for sure. Quit now and let the police handle it."

I clenched my jaw and kept silent. I knew she wouldn't like my answer.

When I didn't speak, she shook her head. "Take a shower," she commanded. "You're filthy. I'll fix you a sandwich. Then you need sleep. You look like hell. We'll talk about this in the morning."

She was right. It had been a long time since the meatloaf at the Tech cafeteria. I felt like I'd been ridden hard and put up wet. She directed me to the shower, ordered me to strip. I stepped under the warm running water while she tossed my filthy shorts and T-shirt in the trash.

When I was done, she wrapped me in a towel. "You're shaking."

She was right. With the adrenaline rush gone and the danger passed, the reality of coming close to death sank in. She led me into the bedroom, stripped off her pink tank top, and pressed herself against me.

"At least consider getting help." She ran her hands through my short hair and kissed me.

"You know I will," I said.

"Liar."

"Don't dig up more snakes than you can kill."

—Grandpa Fischer

CHAPTER TWENTY-FIVE

DAY FOUR

Sam woke me with a yip and scratched his nails on the sliding-glass door. The concrete slab in the unshaded ten-foot-square patio was heating up and did not meet with his approval. I heard Sylvia in the kitchen and smelled coffee. My arm was sore as hell, a throbbing reminder of unfinished business and the new, and very real, threat that had raised its ugly head on the River Walk.

I found the clean pair of shorts and a T-shirt that Sylvia had laid out on the bed and went outside. The calendar indicated it was fall. The Longhorns had played and won their first football game and dove hunting season had started, but the weather still felt like summer. I sprayed Sam down with the garden hose and watched the high cirrus clouds drift over the city. Grandpa called them "mares' tails." They either signaled rain was on the way or clear skies. I couldn't remember which. I popped open the patio umbrella so Sam would have shade until I was ready to go, and went back inside to face the music.

Sylvia was showered and making toast. "How's the arm?"

"Sore, but I'll live."

"Until next time?" It was a loaded question.

"I'm not gonna run and hide."

She studied me while I took a couple of eggs from the fridge and got out a frying pan.

"You think Danny Allison killed Marissa Luna?" She was in lawyer mode. The soft cuddly sex kitten was safely tucked away. She was switching tactics and had me on the stand, ready to grill a hostile witness.

"He was with her the night she was killed," I said, cracking the eggs into the hot pan. "He's an amateur MMA fighter, easily capable of drowning her. And he was the father of her unborn child. Something I'm sure his family wouldn't have approved of. Means, opportunity, and motive." I found the pepper shaker and gave the eggs a generous sprinkle.

Sylvia shook her head like she was scolding an impudent child. "How many males in a Texas bar play amateur sports?"

I knew where she was going with this. "Twenty percent." I dumped my over-easy eggs onto a paper plate and sat down. Sylvia handed me a piece of toast.

"More like eighty percent, which was probably two hundred men with means and opportunity." She had always been better at arguing than I was.

"I'm not a numbers guy. Anyway, he had a fight with her. I've got it on video."

"Why didn't the police see it?" she asked and handed me the butter dish.

"I don't know. Maybe Peterson didn't watch all the tapes."

"What about the motive? How do you know he's the father of Marissa's unborn child?"

"He gave her an expensive Mother's Love bracelet."

"Some men buy jewelry for women as a token of affection." She wasn't going to let me off the hook easily.

"I brought you flowers." I remembered I'd bought her a bracelet at the factory store too but decided not to bring it up. She wouldn't believe me now until she saw it in my hand.

"Dead flowers." She poured us both more coffee and sat down.

"Now you're being picky." She was enjoying shredding my theory. "What about his prior history? Two women accused Danny Allison of sexual harassment. At least one of them benefited financially. You can't defend him for that, counselor. The guy's a dirtbag."

"Will those women testify in court?"

"Well, no. They both dropped the charges."

"Unfortunately, you have nothing that will overrule the police theory. There's still a reasonable doubt. Being a dirtbag isn't a crime or half the men in Texas would be behind bars."

"What about the terms of the trust fund? You work for Marcus. You must have heard something."

She shook her head. "I can't tell you that."

"Come on. We're trying to establish a link here. All I wanna know is if there were conditions for him to inherit the money. I'm not gonna take it to the DA."

She sipped her coffee and looked out the window. Her legal mind was searching for an answer. It was at the heart of our disagreements from the time I decided to drop out of law school. She was thinking of courtroom rules. I was thinking of justice. She was considering what could be proven in court. I was thinking of the truth. Two totally different concepts.

"I just wanna know if a pregnant girl could interfere with his inheritance."

Her lips pinched together. I didn't think she would answer. The silence stretched on for a full minute. An eternity for her.

"Yes," she finally said.

"That's pretty close to a motive. The silver-spoon-sucking frat boy was willing to murder his girlfriend and unborn child so he could maintain his rich and privileged lifestyle. You know in Texas that counts as killing two people. The charge is capital murder, counselor. That means a minimum of life in prison." I caught sight of my reflection in the door of the microwave oven. My face was flushed and my forehead scars glowed red.

"If convicted. You still don't know Danny Allison is the father."

"All I need is a drop of his blood."

"Even people you decide are guilty are allowed a rigorous defense. It's called due process. You can't be judge, jury, and executioner."

"I'm not a vigilante."

"Then let the system work," she insisted. We were both standing in front of the fridge.

"I will. But Marissa Luna is dead, and nobody was held accountable!"

I saw disappointment in her eyes. I heard Sam barking and realized I was shouting.

"Don't look now, but you're showing emotion," she said.

I took her in my arms, but she felt different. Nothing like the night before. I knew this issue between us wouldn't go away. She studied my face, searching for some indication that I would reconsider, that I would walk away and let the police and the DA handle everything. They'd had their chance and done nothing.

"When we were in law school, we both wanted to fight for the little guy—the underdog who couldn't fend for himself," I said.

"I was young and naïve," she said. She meant I still was.

"I gotta go."

"Nick…"

I turned toward the back door.

"We…" She started to say something, then changed her mind. "Be careful. You still don't know who's shooting at you."

CHAPTER TWENTY-SIX

I joined a handful of people waiting at the neighborhood bus stop. Sam shamelessly solicited affection. He assumed everyone wanted to pet a Labrador if given the chance. I studied my yard across the street. Breakfast and the night's sleep had renewed my strength, if not my relationship. That would take more time. "We," she'd started to say. What did that mean? We, what? She'd never been shy about sharing her thoughts, but today she stopped short.

The traffic was light because of the Labor Day holiday, and the high school down the street was closed. Kids were sleeping till noon. A flock of white-winged doves dive-bombed a rooftop and reminded me that I was missing opening weekend for hunting season for the first time since I'd mustered out of the Marine Corps. This case was giving me a bad feeling. Maybe the mares' tails were a bad omen and had nothing to do with the weather. I tried to think of what Grandpa had said about them, but I still couldn't remember.

I checked the porches and the parked cars lining the street. Four houses down, I spotted the black Super Duty Ford pickup with dark tinted windows. This time I could make out the outline of two men in the front seat. I couldn't see their faces, but they seemed familiar. This definitely wasn't a coincidence. Whoever was in that pickup was waiting for me.

The bus arrived and blocked my view. Two of my neighbors got out. They worked the night shift as civilian employees at the local military base. Sam and I said hello. They were unaware of the potential danger. Like the doves on the roof calmly pecking seeds, most people felt safe in their own neighborhood where hunting was supposed to be off-limits. When the bus pulled away, the black Super Duty was gone.

Rose Gustafson was backing her pickup out of her driveway, so I stopped to open her gate. She rolled down her window and looked me over like my grandmother used to when I'd stayed out all night with the boys in high school.

"You look like a man on a mission," she said. "Are you on a case?"

"Just out for a jog." I didn't want to involve her in any details.

"Humbug. I know you better than that. You didn't come home last night. I've seen that look before. You're after somebody. Even Sam looks all wound up."

I glanced at Sam. He cocked his head, wanting me to share the details of his escapades knowing it would earn him the respect of the cat lady and a dog biscuit. Maybe another time. I shrugged. "He's just happy to get out of the house."

"Well, be careful," she said. "Would you mind keeping an eye on my place? I'm going to Seguin to visit my sister."

"Happy to. Drive safely."

"I always do. Don't forget, tomorrow's trash day." She nodded toward my overflowing can, then drove away. I'd missed last week's pickup. I wondered if she braved the freeway or took the back roads. I remembered her complaining about cataracts.

There was a scrap of white paper trapped under my windshield wiper blade. My first thought was another parking ticket, but this was a torn piece of a takeout bag from Whataburger with a note scrawled in pencil.

Stay away from Luna. Next time I won't miss.

I read it again. So, it *was* a warning. I thought of the Super Duty. What other surprises had the writer left? I checked under the hood, looking for signs of tampering, but didn't come up with anything. No obvious prints on the windows. I checked the perimeter of the house. Sam made a show of sniffing the bushes and barked at one of Rose Gustafson's cats, trying to be helpful. To Sam, cats were always guilty of something. I unlocked the front door and searched the house. Everything seemed in order. The surveillance cameras were intact. Nothing was missing, and no one had done my dirty dishes or laundry.

I threw a set of gym clothes in my duffel bag along with a handful of cotton swabs, bandages, and a Ziploc baggie. My wound was sore, but the injury didn't affect my grip or arm strength. Had the bullet hit the bone, the hollow point would have mushroomed and torn out most of my muscle. I would have been in the hospital with a missing arm. The first aid gear was for Danny Allison. The note pissed me off. I had no intention of staying away from Luna, and Danny was my prime suspect. He had already challenged me to a fight. If he left a little blood on the canvas, there was nothing to stop me from having it analyzed.

This case had taken on a new dimension. It wasn't just about justice for Marissa and closure for her mother. It was about self-preservation.

CHAPTER TWENTY-SEVEN

Lucky's gym was on the west side of San Antonio, an older part of town not connected to the upscale north or the newer expansion to the far west. It was a low-rent area that housed Marcus Lopez's office and Marissa Luna's home. Instead of the fashionable Hill Country views filled with cedar trees and limestone rocks, it was covered with a dense sea of green trees that flowed in every direction. I rolled down a street lined with two-story apartment buildings, car repair shops, and Hispanic food markets. The businesses showed their age, but they were open even on Labor Day. The area bustled with a gritty working life. Taco trucks and one-room restaurants offering fresh tamales were abundant. In the last twenty years, the only new addition to the local economy was the dollar stores that sold everything except fresh produce.

The gym was the anchor store for a strip mall that also housed a Mexican restaurant, a tattoo parlor, and a barbershop. It was a big two-story building that had once been a discount furniture store. Caesar Hernandez, or "Lucky," bought the building and the mall with earnings from an impressive welterweight professional career. He was an aggressive, Mexican-style boxer that pummeled an opponent to a round-one TKO in his late forties. Now he trained and managed a stable of young up-and-comers.

High school kids loved the place because he let them work out for free. It was Lucky's way of giving back to the community. He wouldn't let them in unless school was out and they showed him passing grades on their report cards, but it was the Labor Day holiday, so the place was packed. A skinny girl not much more than thirteen was swinging for all she was worth at a punching bag twice her weight. A half dozen other kids were in the corner working the speed bags. Lucky was leaning on the center ring ropes watching two featherweights dance around each other.

"Mix it up," he shouted at them. Both seemed reluctant to throw a punch.

"Hey, champ," I called to him. "Those your new prospects?"

He smiled, exposing two missing teeth. When he went outside the gym, he wore two gold replacements. In the gym, he kept the false teeth in his pocket.

"Why don't you get dressed and teach them a few moves, huh?" Lucky let me spar with the young guys he was training in the heavyweight division. I wasn't a natural boxer but could hold my own in the ring, and he liked that I could take a punch.

"They look like eighth graders," I said.

"They wanna be fighters, they gotta learn. What you workin' today?" he asked, keeping his focus on the young fighters.

"I'm gonna try my luck upstairs. I wanna hang out with the cool kids."

He raised an eyebrow. I never went upstairs, which explained why I'd never met Danny.

"Don't hurt those guys. I need them healthy to pay rent."

I didn't say anything. There were no guarantees I wouldn't break Danny's neck.

Four years ago, Lucky partnered with an ex-Army Ranger who offered mixed martial arts classes on the second floor. The clients were tough guys and wannabes who watched MMA on TV and figured they should get in on the action. Lucky was cashing in on the craze. Danny Allison was a wannabe tough guy who got a taste of MMA in Lubbock, and he and his trend-following crowd had made Lucky's gym the in place to train.

There were free weights in one corner and practice mats in the other. In the center was a sparring ring, where two women were doing their best Ronda Rousey imitation, huffing and panting and shouting each other down. A handful of guys practiced Brazilian jiu-jitsu moves led by Lucky's partner, Jerry Muth. He wore black pajamas and looked like Chuck Norris with a gray ponytail. Everyone called him Sarge.

The wannabe tough guys on this floor all wore specialized, name-brand outfits and shoes that they bought on the MMA websites. Most of them decorated their exposed skin with RockTape, the popular kinesiology tape that was supposed to relieve pain and provide joint support. I was five years older than everyone on the second floor except Sarge and could use joint pain relief, but the red, green, and black strips looked more like a fashion statement than anything useful—like wearing a baseball cap backward on a sunny day. The kids downstairs were in gym shorts and T-shirts issued for free by their school's athletic department. They came from the west side streets, where it took more than money or colored tape to be a tough guy.

I found Danny Allison doing barbell curls and watching himself in the mirror. He wore a string tank top that let him admire his muscles without interference. Strips of black-and-green RockTape covered his knees and both elbows. He was bulky but not cut like a bodybuilder, which meant he probably did some cardio. Skeeter said he'd won a few tournaments, and I wanted to know what I was up against. I never had any doubts about who would win this fight, but I liked to study my opponent ahead of a fight if I got the chance. He had an inch of height on me and about ten pounds that he probably packed on with whey protein. The happy-go-lucky facial expression on his face didn't change whether he was looking at himself in the mirror or the other guys on the floor.

Sylvia didn't say how much he would inherit, but the Allison family was one of the richest in the state. Skeeter compared them to AT&T. Had Danny weighed the money against Marissa and his unborn child? If it was less than a million, would he still have killed her? The more I thought about it, the angrier I got. Spilling Danny's blood would be a pleasure.

He racked his barbells and finally saw me. "Nick. Didn't think you'd show up." He said it like he'd challenged me to dual at high noon.

"You said Monday." I matched his schoolboy grin. I wanted him to stay cocky and at ease until after I laid him out on the canvas. "You up for this?" I pointed with my gym bag to the center ring.

Danny stepped toward me wiping his face on a monogramed towel. "Always."

"I'll get changed." I went to the locker room and stowed my street clothes. By the time I came back out, a small crowd of Danny look-alikes were gathered around the ring. Lucky stood at the ropes. Word had spread fast. I set my bag down just outside the ring, so I had easy access to the swabs and the plastic bag.

"My gym. My rules," Lucky said loud enough for Danny and the dozen or so onlookers to hear. Sarge joined the crowd and nodded at me. We'd traded stories over beers at the VFW a time or two. He was the real deal. Someone I wanted in my corner.

Danny sauntered over. "Sure, anything you say." He exposed his perfect white teeth, trying his best not to look worried. He was standing on the balls of his feet and had his shirt off and his shoulders back and chest puffed out.

I didn't smile, transitioning into fighter mode. I stayed loose and flat-footed. "Fine," I said. "We use the four-ounce gloves." I didn't wanna be here all day. The heavier gloves had too much padding.

Lucky looked at Danny, then back at me. "Okay but use headgear."

"Done," I said, effectively taking Danny out of the negotiations. Making psychological points—playing the adult in the room.

Lucky handed us the padded headgear. I slipped in my own mouthpiece and climbed into the ring, holding the ropes apart for Danny. Another signal that I was in charge. He noticed the skin-tone patch on my upper arm.

"That gonna interfere?" he asked, pointing to the bandage.

"I'll manage," I said and walked to the opposite corner of the ring.

Danny's cheering section barked encouragement. I stood rock-solid while Danny danced for the crowd. He put on a shadow-boxing show, stretched, and showed off a combination roundhouse and front scissor kick. All very impressive. The routine telegraphed everything I needed to know about his fighting style.

"Aren't you gonna warm up?" Danny said, still bouncing on the balls of his feet and wasting energy.

I didn't say a word. His frenetic movements told me he was nervous, ready for the punching to start.

Lucky made his way to center ring. "Looks like somebody's got somethin' to prove here," Lucky said to both of us. He'd been in the fight business too long not to know what was going on. He fixed me with a cocked eyebrow and whispered so Danny couldn't hear: "I don't want nobody hurt. We clear?"

I shrugged. I wasn't going to promise anything.

Danny glanced at his buddies for support. One said: "Take the old man out." Nobody had ever called me "old man" before.

"MMA rules. Stop if I tap you out. Got it?" Lucky barked above the noise.

"Got it," I said, keeping my focus on Danny.

"Yeah, man," Danny said. He held his gloved hands out. I bumped them hard.

The fight was on.

Danny held his arms up and flexed his muscles. He'd never been in a street fight against an equal opponent. He was showing off for the crowd instead of keeping his attention on me.

His first shot was a left-hand jab. I dodged and slapped it away, moving just enough to keep him off balance. My hands were at the ready, but lower than my shoulders. I wanted him to build up his confidence and start into the kick combination that he'd been practicing. That was the knockout move he was dying to unleash on me.

"You don't have much style," he shouted through his mouthguard.

He was already breathing hard. Nervous energy. He threw another left-right combination. I batted both down and hit him with a backhand just to give him a taste. The blow caught him on the chin below the headgear. His neck snapped back. He felt it.

"The Marine Corps doesn't give you points for style," I said.

Danny recovered from the blow. I gave him credit for taking a punch even though I'd only given him a taste. He tested out a roundhouse kick that grazed my wound. Pain shot down my arm. Danny noticed and tried to throw another kick in that direction. He smelled a weakness. His muscles tensed. He was ready to kick my ass.

"How do I measure up to your military standards?" he said. He was fishing for a compliment, still playing cocky.

"You tell me. Do you have what it takes to be a killer? Maybe you already have a taste for blood." I watched him for a reaction.

"I'm just playing around," he claimed, but I saw a slight change in his attitude. He wanted to hit me with everything he had.

"Are you a killer?" I asked. I saw a faint hint of recognition in his eyes like he knew what I was talking about.

He swung a couple more punches, trying to get me to move into the corner so that he would have enough room for his kick-punch combination. I stepped back and let him have all the room he needed.

"You know where this came from?" I asked, holding up my bandaged arm. "Someone took a shot at me."

"Dangerous work," he said.

"It was a warning. You can tell whoever did it, I won't back down."

"You're one crazy dude. How would I know who did it?" He wasn't going to give me a confession. Not then anyway. He wanted to kick my ass.

I saw his kick-punch combo coming before he executed it. His body language telegraphed the attack like the scroll of a Star Wars movie. I crouched low to the mat and waited. There would be enough blood for a dozen DNA tests.

The roundhouse came and went. I moved as little as necessary and felt the breeze on my cheek as his foot cruised through empty air. He did have strength and speed. That kick had probably taken out a dozen opponents in Lubbock. I saw the disappointment on his face when he didn't connect.

The scissor kick came next. He had good form but no imagination. I pressed back against the ropes, and he landed on the balls of his feet. The combo came next. I leaned into the hook and took it on the shoulder. My arm burned. Danny noticed my reaction and smelled blood. I needed to finish him off before he hit the mark again.

He flashed his right jab. The move I'd been waiting for. I stepped inside of it and let go with my own right hand. The punch landed just under his nose—that space not covered by the headgear. I wanted plenty of blood.

When he tried to duck, my left elbow hit north of his mouth. The bone snaped. Blood gushed from his nose and lip like water from a breached dam. Danny collapsed on the canvas. Lucky slipped through the ropes and knelt beside him. He shook his head at me.

"What?" I said innocently. "It was a fair fight. The kid challenged me."

I grabbed my bag through the ropes and pulled out the cotton swab and a baggie. Danny's nose soaked the cotton with blood. Lucky popped an amyl nitrate in his face. Danny came around slowly.

"Take it easy. Don't get up too quickly," I said. I was playing the adult again. His eyes swam in his head. He never knew what hit him.

"Wha—what happened?" Danny stammered.

"You got your ass kicked, kid," Lucky said.

Lucky waved me out of the way. "Go home. He's learned his lesson." Lucky was the only one in the room besides Sarge who knew what I'd just done. In his prime, he could have done the same to me.

I slipped the blood sample into a plastic baggie and put it in my gym bag. I didn't bother to change clothes. The group of Danny's friends gave me a wide berth and nodded their admiration. They'd just seen their champ get beat by the "old man."

Outside on the street, a bronze F-350 pickup with oversized tires and a chrome roll bar took up the first three parking spots. The license plate read *Danny Won.*

Clever. But this time, he didn't.

CHAPTER TWENTY-EIGHT

As much as I hated long drives across featureless landscapes, there was no faster way to get Danny's blood sample to Kelly's lab in Lubbock than to drive it up there myself. My plan was to keep the pressure on and force the shooter to come after me again. He'd started the deadly game. I would finish it.

I didn't really have any doubts that Danny was the father or that he was Marissa's killer. The only remaining question was, how was Marissa's death connected to Sosa? I spent the five-hour drive racking my brain for answers. Sosa couldn't have been directly involved because he had been in Mexico in July. Skeeter had checked on his whereabouts. The timing of Marcus Lopez's takeover of Allison Oil seemed significant. Both Marissa's murder and the business transaction took place in July. He could have found out about the murder and threatened the Allison family. Maybe his business with Patrick at the fundraiser had been to secure blackmail payment. By the time Lubbock emerged out of the late summer cotton fields, I was no closer to a viable link. The one thing I was sure of was that whoever took out Sosa was now shooting at me. The weapon used was identical.

The panhandle was enjoying much cooler weather than South Texas, and Lubbock traffic was heavier than usual. Texas Tech was back in session. Red-and-black signs supporting the football team decorated every streetlamp. Tuesday marked the second week of classes. From my own college experience, I knew week one was devoted to pledge week, which translated into drunken parties and freshman orientation. Week two was when the professors began dishing out assignments and, of course, it was football season.

Kelly had used her connections with the San Antonio medical examiner's office to get a sample of the fetal DNA and was waiting to run the test. She said to meet her at the back door by the air-conditioner unit, so I parked on the street and stepped out with Danny's blood sample.

I caught Kelly looking the other way anticipating my approach from the parking lot. She was unaware of my presence, and I paused in the shadow to observe the woman I barely knew who had agreed to run a DNA sample on an exclusive piece of equipment under FBI supervision. Did she have an ulterior motive for helping me out? I couldn't decide. Thinking about it made me feel guilty for taking advantage of her. I was committed to Sylvia, or at least that's what I kept telling myself. Why was I thinking about this female former Marine?

When she turned her face into the light, I involuntarily took a sharp breath. She wore her normally tightly wrapped hair loosely curled around her oval face, accentuating dark-red lipstick. I'd never seen her dressed as a civilian. Her lab coat was open, exposing tight jeans and a western belt with a turquoise buckle that matched a set of ostrich-skin boots. Her black shirt was a silky material that sparkled in the halogen light and clung to curves that I'd never noticed before.

"Hey there," I said. "You look amazing."

A shy smile spread across her made-up face, and her cheeks turned a shade redder. "You're late," she said and swatted at the moths circling the outdoor lamp.

"My old pickup won't do over seventy. You got a hot date?"

She gave me a hug. "Yeah," she said, like I should have known. "You owe me dinner. The test is gonna take three to four hours. Did you think we were gonna wait in my office?"

Her hair smelled like lavender and fresh-cut roses. I checked my own clothes self-consciously. I had on my usual Wrangler jeans and boots. Not my best boots, but at least they weren't muddy. My button-down shirt was clean, but I'd been in a pickup for six hours.

She laughed and took my arm. "You look fine. If I'd asked you to dress up, you'd have worn the same thing."

I was going to say I had a tux, but I remembered it was torn and bloody. We walked side by side down the hall to the lab. This area of the building was still buzzing with activity even at nine in the evening on a holiday. The express lab was doing a booming business.

"You have one ahead of you," she said. "I've already loaded the fetal DNA."

I waited in her office while she prepped the sample and loaded the machine. It gave me time to take a closer look at her collection of photos and memorabilia. There was a snapshot of her father on his tractor, and one of me in Afghanistan. We were the only men in her collection of photos. My picture was taken before I took a face full of glass. It was hard to remember what I looked like without scars. Kelly had never mentioned it or asked me about the attack, but we'd had only one face-to-face contact since she resigned her commission. I remembered telling her about Sylvia because we'd just started dating. After a few beers, I probably said more than I should have about our chemistry. A couple of days later, Kelly called to tell me she was taking a job in Lubbock, her hometown. That was three years ago. Did Kelly sense a change between me and Sylvia? I thought back to our conversation. I couldn't think of anything specific I'd told her.

Kelly knocked and came inside. "All we can do now is wait," she said with a smile and a raised eyebrow. She slipped off her lab coat, revealing the tight-fitting outfit.

"Never saw you out of uniform." She looked too good, and I was tongue-tied and probably overthinking her intentions.

She spun around on her bootheels. "You like? We never went out on a date before." She took my arm and led me out the door and down the hall. I felt her warmth and smelled a hint of lavender. I wasn't prepared for this.

We used my pickup, and she directed me to her favorite steakhouse on the west side of town away from the throngs of hungry students. It was a cozy place with white tablecloths that strived for upscale, but jeans and boots were always welcome in a Texas steakhouse.

I ordered a beer even though the place was proud of their wine selection.

Kelly selected a Malbec. I occasionally drank wine, but it put me to sleep, and I was staring at a six-hour drive back to San Antonio.

"How's Sylvia?" she said. No beating around the bush.

"Honestly, I'm not sure." For whatever reason, I felt comfortable confiding in her.

"What does that mean?" Our drinks came, and she took a large sip of Malbec.

"I think her new job reminds her of the lifestyle she grew up with." I was trying to break down my own thoughts into pieces I could understand and explain.

"She likes money and everything that goes with it," she said. "Her boss has it. You don't." She had a way of cutting through the BS.

"The thing is, I don't know if she knows it. I don't know if she's aware of what she wants." I was being honest. I really didn't think Sylvia knew what kind of a life she was after.

"I never met her, but she seems very high maintenance. I can't believe you hooked up with her." She took another sip of wine. "How's the campaign going?"

"Marcus is ahead in the polls. Unless there's an October surprise, he's movin' to Austin."

"She's going with him?"

"I don't see any way around it."

Kelly took my hand under the table. Her hazel eyes didn't have the depth that Sylvia's had or the exotic passion. They were open and direct. What you saw was what you got.

"I know what I want," she said.

I took a swig of beer to avoid eye contact and Kelly's full-court press. "So, you're having the T-bone medium rare?" I didn't want her to finish her thought.

She smiled and squeezed my hand. "Medium well. I like mine a little more cooked. I could eat two. I'm starving."

The waiter appeared wearing black pants and a white button-down shirt, a college kid working his way through the semester. Kelly let me have my hand back, and we ordered our meal. I didn't want to shut her out.

She was going out on a limb for me, but on the other hand, I didn't want to lead her on. Kelly sensed my discomfort and shifted the conversation.

"What happens when you get the results of the DNA test?" she asked.

"If it's a match, Danny had a motive. It would cut him out of the family fortune."

"Only if he knew about the baby," she said.

"He bought her a Mother's Love bracelet. He knew. And I think they argued about it the night he killed her."

The college kid brought the steak. I cut into it. The meat was red and juicy and perfect. I nodded to the waiter and took a bite. There weren't many places that served steak this good. I closed my eyes and enjoyed the smoky, rich flavor.

"If it is a match, you're going to go back to San Antonio and shoot him in the head?"

"What do you take me for, a Neanderthal?"

"Yeah. Look at your steak." She pointed to the bloody half-eaten portion on the plate. "Your German palate was formed before they invented fire." She said it with a smile, but she meant it. "Am I gonna have to spend my vacation time getting you out of jail?"

"I'm not gonna shoot him. Not yet. I'll give him a chance to confess first."

"Danny Allison is not the kind of person you confront on your own. I know you don't trust the police and this Detective Peterson to do his job, but you don't have a choice."

I grinned at her, but I was dead serious. "Of course," I said. "I wanna see Danny on trial. I wanna see him sent to prison. I want justice."

She studied my expression. I expected her to argue. Instead, she smiled. "That's what I thought you'd say."

"One thing I wanted to ask you."

"Shoot."

"I talked to a homeless guy who saw Marissa's body when they fished it out of the river. He said she wore a raccoon mask. She had two black eyes. It wasn't mentioned on the ME's report. What would cause that?"

"Well, she could have been punched in the face."

"In both eyes?"

"She chewed her steak and washed it down with Malbec. "She also could have hit her head and fractured the base of her skull."

"Could that have been the cause of death?"

"Definitely. And it would cause the black eyes. That should have been in the report."

We finished our meal without speaking. On the walk back to my pickup, our hands brushed against each other, and our fingers laced together. The move felt natural, like we'd done it before. Her hand was warm. The stars were out, and the wind had taken the night off.

When I stopped to open the passenger-side door, Kelly put her arms around me and nestled her blond head into the curve of my neck. "It's getting late. What if the test's negative?"

"I'll stay. That would mean I have to start all over. Since Marissa was in school here until the first of June, the father was either a student or a local."

"That might take a while," she said. Her lips were close to my chest. I could feel her heartbeat. "You'd need a place to stay."

"You're offering to put me up?"

She answered with a kiss. She tasted like warm honey with a hint of Malbec. She pressed harder. We held the pose for an extra minute. I couldn't help thinking how different Sylvia felt and tasted. She drank pinot gris and her lips were closer to jalapenos than honey. The two couldn't be any more different.

"I know what you're thinking," she said.

"Are you kidding? I'm a Neanderthal, remember? You're pressed against me. There's only one thing on my mind. Keep it up, and I won't be able to control myself."

Kelly smiled. Even in the dark, I could see her blush.

"You're lying. You're thinking of your fancy lady in San Antonio." Her smile faded, and her hazel eyes bored into mine.

"Kelly, I—"

She cut me off with a finger on my lips. "No explanations." She kissed me again.

Her cell phone buzzed. She slowly took it out and saw the caller ID. "It's the lab." She listened, then disconnected. "Call me next time you're in town."

"Alles hat ein Ende."
Everything has an end.

—Grandpa Fischer

CHAPTER TWENTY-NINE

DAY FIVE

What was left of the storm clouds were now turning pink along the eastern skyline signaling the end of a very long drive home from Lubbock. The puddles in my driveway reminded me what Grandpa'd said about mares' tails. The moisture was the remnant of a hurricane that struck the Pacific Coast and traveled far enough inland to answer the prayers of South Texas farmers. It hadn't made a dent in the West Texas drought. The early morning AM radio host who kept me awake on the drive speculated that South Texas had more pull with the Lord or at least were more insistent in their prayers.

Before getting out, I studied my house for signs of movement. All was still and quiet, but something was off. There was mud on the sidewalk. Closer inspection showed the mud formed tracks leading across the lawn and up the front steps. The tracks weren't big enough for Skeeter. He wore a size sixteen when he could find it. Eighteen if he ordered online. These tracks were sized nine or ten, and the toe of the print was deeper than the heel. Whoever made the tracks was in a hurry.

Rose Gustafson's house was dark and silent. I remembered she'd asked me to watch her place while she was gone, which meant feed her herd of cats. She always left enough for them to survive a week in her absence, but I made a note on my phone to check on them later.

I followed the muddy footprints to my front door and found a two-inch gap in the doorjamb. Splinters around both deadbolts showed someone had used something large and heavy to smash through the door. The extra locks I'd added as a precaution had barely slowed him down. I pulled my .45 and pushed the door open, listening for any indication that the intruder was still inside the house. The only noise came from the ever-present cicadas and a vocal mockingbird welcoming me or the new day from his perch on top of my pecan tree. Perhaps, I thought, he was trying to tell me what had happened. Too bad I didn't speak mockingbird.

Sam should have met me at the front door. "Sam." I called but got no answer. I caught a whiff of something pungent, like Sam had pooped in the house. That was unusual. He could come and go as he pleased through the doggy door and had been house trained since he was a pup. I followed the muddy tracks upstairs. A Texas tornado had touched down in my bedroom. Even a loose board I'd neglected to fix had been pried up to expose the empty space beneath.

The mud was dry. Whoever left the tracks had been gone at least two hours. I took a breath and called for Sam again. No answer. A cold chill ran down my spine. His absence left the house feeling abandoned.

The same tornado cut a path through my office downstairs. Business papers and books were scattered everywhere. The locked cabinet meant nothing. The padlock was cut. The contents dumped. Hopefully, the security cameras Skeeter installed had captured a face. The alarm should have triggered a police response. Somehow the intruder had bypassed that and the locks.

The one place he hadn't disturbed was the fireplace. I'd left the burnt log from the second week of January, the one week cold enough to light a fire, to disguise a hidden compartment. I lifted the grate and a layer of bricks. The metal safe underneath was still intact. I set it on the Spanish coffee table and sorted through the contents. Surveillance tapes, the engraved bracelet, and my notes were untouched.

Something else had happened down here besides a ransacking. The poop stench was stronger here, and I realized it was coming from the kitchen. "Sam?" I called again. Still no answer. By now he should have been licking my hand and pointing toward the back door for his daily exercise. He could usually be counted on to at least bark at strangers, unless he decided they were friendly, or they were bearing food.

I followed my nose around the bar and into the kitchen. Sam was on the floor. A half-eaten cheeseburger lay beside his body. The pool of blood on the hardwood floor was still tacky to the touch and had soaked into the green kitchen rug in front of the sink. I sank to my knees beside him.

"Sam?" I whispered. My stomach turned over. He was my constant companion and had even saved my life. What kind of sick bastard would shoot a dog? I choked back the urge to unload last night's steak in the pool of blood.

I put my hands on his still-warm chest, feeling for any signs of life. There was something there. It was faint, but his heart was still beating. I put my cheek against his wet nose. His breathing came in faint shallow puffs. He was still alive. Barely. A wave of relief washed over me.

"Sam, goddamnit! You scared the hell out of me." I kept my hand on his chest to reassure myself he was still alive. "Hang in there, boy. I'll get you to the doc." There was a small entry wound behind his left ear. I grabbed a kitchen towel and wrapped it around his head. Someone had tossed him a hamburger and pressed a small-caliber weapon to his ear while he ate.

I took a ragged breath, still fighting the urge to throw up. The sudden panic that had morphed into relief quickly morphed into anger.

"I will find who did this and make them pay," I promised. I stood and searched for my phone to call the vet, then noticed something else just beyond the pool of blood. The shooter had taken Sam's collar and nametag off and left it on the floor on top of a note scrawled on my own spiral notebook. It was a list of names. *Sam, Sylvia, Grandpa, Clarence.* Sam's name was crossed off the list. On the bottom it read: *I'm going down the list. One a day till you back off.*

CHAPTER THIRTY

I wrapped Sam in a bath towel and carried him to my pickup. His mouth was open, and his tongue lolled out to the side. "Hang in there, buddy," I whispered, awkwardly looping the seatbelt around his limp body. I slammed the F-150 in gear and called the vet. After the third ring I was connected to an emergency call service who arranged to have the doc and his team meet me outside the office. I'd never had to use an emergency vet service, but I was glad it was available.

Sylvia's name was next on the list. The note said one a day. Sam's name was crossed off the list. Was he counting Sam as today or yesterday? What time had he tried to execute my dog? I hit speed dial for Sylvia. She picked up on the fourth ring.

"Nick?" She sounded half asleep.

"Are you all right?"

"I'm fine. What's wrong?" She hated to get up early, and I could hear the irritation in her voice.

"Where are you?"

"Where do you think? It's ten till seven in the morning."

"You're in danger. Whoever shot at me and killed Sosa, shot Sam. He left a note threatening a list of people. You, Skeeter, and Grandpa are on the list. Sam was on top. You're next."

"Someone killed Sam!"

"Someone tried. He lost a lot of blood, and he's unconscious, but he's still alive. I'm on my way to the vet now."

"You called the police, right?"

"I will, after I find Danny Allison."

"Nick—"

"I know what I'm doing. How fast can you get to your office?"

"Thirty minutes, why?"

"Leave now. You can finish your makeup or whatever in the car. When you get there, stay put. Don't leave your office for any reason. Marcus has security for the building. I'm sending Skeeter to watch the parking lot."

"You're scaring me."

"I'm scared too. And pissed off. Whoever did this is getting desperate. That means I'm getting close."

"Nick…"

This time, I didn't cut her off. The silence stretched for thirty seconds. An eternity for her. When she didn't speak, I said: "What is it?"

"When this is over, we need to talk."

"Whatever you want. Just, please do what I asked. You are in danger."

"Okay, Nick." She disconnected. I knew what *we need to talk* meant. It was what she'd started to say the other night. But for now, that talk would have to wait.

I called Grandpa next. Going down the killer's list. As usual, the phone rang and rang. After eight times, I disconnected. It was a landline without an answering machine. He wouldn't be caught dead indoors after seven a.m. I remembered the sign for the neighbor's petting zoo. I wondered if he could get a message to Grandpa. I wasn't sure what I would say to him. *Be careful. Go to town.* Where would he go? The Fredericksburg stockyards were closed on Tuesday. He could go to the Lutheran Church. There was a morning Bible study group that met every morning at eight. He could call on one of his rancher buddies, but I would have to come up with a much stronger reason, or he would simply check the loads on his shotgun at the front door, and maybe carry his ancient Colt 1911 out to feed the livestock, but he wouldn't change his routine. When this was over, I would insist he get a cell phone or at least install an answering machine.

The last name on the list was Clarence, aka "Skeeter." He answered on the first ring, and I briefed him about Sam and the threatening note.

"You didn't get a call about the break-in? There was no police response?" he asked.

"Nothing. The guy must have disabled your system. Check the surveillance footage to see if you caught anything on tape."

"On it. The feed goes to my computer."

"My guess is you won't find anything. If the guy was good enough to bypass the alarm, he's not gonna show his face on camera."

"I'm looking at him now," he said. "Athletic guy, just under six feet, wearing a black windbreaker, surgical gloves, and a ski mask."

"So much for security."

"Your house is over a hundred years old. It wasn't made for that kind of system."

"We'll talk about that later. Leave your house. Take stuff for a couple of days. Don't go home until this mess is over. Your name was on the list."

"My name?"

"Yeah, Clarence. Your real name."

"Sonofabitch!"

The morning traffic buzzed outside my window. Sam's mouth was still open, and the bath towel was now soaked with blood. I put my hand on his chest. He didn't look up. His breathing was shallow, but his heartbeat was steady. I hoped that was a good sign.

"Whoever did this is gonna pay," I said.

"Stay calm. Don't do something you're gonna regret," Skeeter said.

"I am calm, cool, and collected. But I'm not waiting around to take a bullet or watch anyone else get shot. This asshole has stepped way over the line."

"You about to go all Afghanistan. I'm just saying take a step back right now and assess the situation. Somebody shot your dog and threatened your family. You loved that animal, and you want revenge. Make sure your head's clear."

"He left a list, Skeeter. You're on it," I said. A purple Dodge Charger cut me off, and I cursed and slammed on the brakes. Sam nearly tumbled off the seat before the seatbelt caught his fall. I put a hand on his bloody shoulder.

"Listen, you ain't takin' down a gangbanger. This guy's got connections that you or I can't access."

"You wanna quit? I'll wave the two weeks' notice and mail your final paycheck. Consider your debt paid in full." I knew that sounded harsh, but I couldn't help it. I was angry.

Skeeter didn't reply. I heard him breathing. I set the cell phone on the seat and put it on speaker. The wave of emotion was gone, and in its wake was stone-cold focus.

"I'm with you," he finally said. "Do me a favor. Let's meet and make a plan."

"Fair enough. Get me the number for a petting zoo in Gillespie County."

"Not what I expected…"

"I can't reach Grandpa, and the zoo is next door."

"Got it. Where are you right now. I'll come to you."

"Pulling into the vet's office on Quincy near North Main," I said.

"You're two blocks from Lulu's. When you're finished with the vet, go in and order two cinnamon rolls for me and coffee. Give me twenty minutes."

I agreed and disconnected. The vet and two assistants met me in the parking lot with a small stretcher and rushed Sam inside. He wouldn't know the extent of the damage until he took x-rays. The bullet had passed through Sam's skull. That wasn't a good sign. If he lived, there might be permanent damage.

I had to force myself to leave. There was nothing I could do but sit and wait for the vet to do his work and Sam to wake up. What I had to do couldn't wait.

CHAPTER THIRTY-ONE

Lulu's cinnamon rolls were legendary among Alamo City commuters, and I was forced to circle the block and find a place to park on the street. Skeeter was still a few minutes away. I took a deep breath and let my muscles relax. My neck and shoulders were tight, and I realized I'd been doing isometric exercises on the wheel in the heavy traffic. Things were about to get western.

I found a table that two uniform cops were just leaving and shoved their dirty plates aside. They both looked well fed and ready to take on San Antonio riffraff. I wondered how their day stacked up against mine, and if they would face the kind of person who could take an innocent life for no other reason than to send a message or because that life interfered with the family inheritance. That's what I was up against.

Had Danny led such a sheltered life that killing meant nothing more than a business transaction? When I took a life in combat, I took comfort in knowing the evil that life represented. I'd watched the enemy behead women and children and murder my brothers in arms. When I went hunting, the animals I killed were part of the food chain and thinning their numbers helped control population density and preserve habitat. The hunt itself was infused with ritual and the spirit of the pioneers. Killing for sport, pleasure, or monetary gain represented evil.

The young waitress stood beside me for a full minute before I realized she was there and waiting. I looked up when she cleared her throat, and forgot to smile.

She took an involuntary step back. "You okay?" When I didn't answer immediately, she pressed on. "Would you like to order, sir?"

"Two large coffees and two cinnamon rolls," I said. She rushed off to fill the order. Normally, I ordered the migas plate with scrambled eggs, tortillas, and refried beans, but this morning I had no appetite. My brain flashed the picture of Sam's bloody body on a continuous loop. Even the sweet smell of melting butter on cinnamon couldn't mitigate the churning in my stomach.

Skeeter texted me the petting zoo number. I called the number. Nobody home. I left a message explaining who I was and that I needed to contact Otto Fischer, his next-door neighbor. When Skeeter arrived, I was on my second cup of coffee. The young waitress came back and offered to heat the cinnamon rolls she'd left for him.

"Let me see your hands," he said.

"What for?"

"Let me see them."

I held my hands above the table.

He studied them. They were rock steady.

"Somebody's gonna feel pain," he said.

"You think I'm a vigilante?"

He didn't have an immediate answer.

"Well?"

"I'm thinkin'."

"Did I shoot the guy who set you up?"

"Point taken. But this is different."

"I didn't kill him because I wanted him to stand trial and prove the cops and the DA got it wrong. I'm not gonna shoot Danny for the same reason. When I'm finished with him, he might wish he were dead. He's gonna confess to killing Marissa and her unborn child. Capital murder. I'll let the State of Texas execute him."

"What about Sosa?"

"What about him?"

"How's Marissa's murder tied to Sosa?"

"When I find Danny, I'll ask him."

"How you gonna get to him?"

"I'll light a fire under Marcus Lopez. He's the Allison family lawyer and Patrick's business partner. He'll know where Danny is."

The waitress brought back the hot cinnamon rolls with a new pad of melted butter on top. Skeeter cut into one of them with a knife and fork and shoved a large slice of buttery cinnamon dough into his mouth. He couldn't help himself. Pleasure spread across his face like a ripple on a lake.

When the moment passed, he said: "What if he tells Danny to run?"

"Danny won't run. He's too arrogant. He thinks the sun rises and sets in his asshole. Think about it. He paid off a girl in Lubbock, he murdered Marissa because she got pregnant, and he shot Sam to get me off the case. He's not scared of me or the law. He thinks he's untouchable."

"Maybe he is." He took another bite. "You said Patrick is buds with the DA. The family lawyer is gonna be the next governor. Add that to a mountain of financial resources, and you have a young man who may just be above the law."

I held his gaze and felt my skin turn hot and my forehead scars burn. "That's where I come in."

He stopped chewing and studied me. "Man, you a force of nature."

"I'm gonna bring Danny in. In the meantime, stay armed. I want you to watch Sylvia."

"The note said he was coming after me? What did it say?"

I handed him the note. "How'd he get my real name?"

"Maybe he read it in the paper." I was thinking about the article that Mrs. Luna had showed me. The one that someone left in her mailbox.

He read the note and swallowed hard. "I need a shotgun. You know I can't hit the side of a bus with that pistol you gave me." It was true, he wasn't a marksman by any stretch of the imagination.

"Got you covered," I said and finished the last of my coffee. The tables around us were empty. Most of the patrons had gone to work. Rush hour was over for them.

"You want me in her office?"

"No one will touch her there. Too many people, and Marcus has security. Stay in the parking lot. She should be getting to work about now.

Track her car and set up surveillance at her condo." I grabbed the check and Skeeter followed me to the front counter.

"This is Marcus's business card with his personal cell phone number written on the back. I'm gonna pay him a little visit. I wanna know who he calls when I leave his house."

"You think he'll reach out to Danny?"

"I'm countin' on it. Can you trace the number?"

Skeeter took the card and smiled. "Man, do you know who you're talkin' to?"

"Right, I forget you're the tech wiz. I'll give you thirty minutes." I knew he loved a challenge. "Keep your phone charged." For a tech guy, Skeeter had the hardest time keeping his array of gadgets charged. I paid the bill and left the waitress a twenty. She'd earned it.

"Be careful. Marcus Lopez is starting to sound more like a gangster than a politician."

"I think he's both."

CHAPTER THIRTY-TWO

Marcus Lopez lived in a newer gated community in the fashionable far west side of the Alamo City outside Loop 1604. It was one of a dozen gated communities popping up like fungus on a rotten log and pushing the rural road system beyond capacity.

The location reminded me that Marcus Lopez and the Allison family had more resources than I could match. If I was going to beat them, I would need to take actions they wouldn't expect. Both Marcus and Patrick operated in a world where money and influence mattered and would fight with both. I'd never cared or had access to either one. My moves had to come from places they didn't expect. If I caught them off guard, they might make a mistake that I could take advantage of. The DNA match between Danny and Marissa's unborn child was my ace in the hole. They showed their hand by shooting Sam and leaving the threatening note. It was time for me to put my cards on the table.

There was no guard on duty at the metal security gate, only a keypad providing community access. Sylvia brought me to the Christmas party last year and had given me the code. I punched in the numbers. Nothing happened. Naturally, the code was changed. I needed an alternative plan. Marcus's house backed up to the community golf course, and I checked Google maps for an alternative route. Before I could zero in on his house, a landscape service truck stopped and punched in the new code. I followed him in and down a row of identical limestone houses.

A foursome dressed alike in white polo shirts and Panama hats rolled down the center of the street in a four-seater golf cart, lost in conversation. They didn't see my pickup and didn't seem to care if anyone else was on the road. I wondered if I would be as carefree when and if I reached retirement age. I putted behind them until I found Marcus's address.

His house bordered the immaculate fourteenth fairway of the community golf club of which Marcus was an avid member. He kept his golf cart and clubs in a shed the size of a guesthouse near the back gate. He could call the grounds crew and start eighteen holes anytime he wanted. At the Christmas party, he had insisted that Sylvia and I pay close attention to his version of the finer things in life. Sylvia was impressed.

Marcus had a wife and two kids. I counted on them being long gone by eight o'clock on a Tuesday morning. His wife was on the board of directors at one of the local banks, and school was back in session after the Labor Day break.

The structure of Marcus's house broke with the limestone-block McMansions lining the street. His was a three-story glass-and-steel building that reminded me more of a post office, but it was unique. I'll give him that. I wondered how it ever got approved by the HOA committee. A security guard stood by his front door sipping coffee and staring at his phone. He was not quite Skeeter's size but could have been his younger brother. He wore a black uniform and watched my pickup roll slowly past the house. I stopped at the end of the cul-de-sac and waited for him to get bored again and go back to sipping coffee and scrolling through his phone. It didn't take long.

From the end of the cul-de-sac, I walked between the houses, pretending to look for survey stakes, then slipped over the chain-link fence into the fairway. From there I backtracked to Marcus's yard, betting that he wasn't too worried about home invasion. He'd grown up on the west side and probably figured he could take care of himself. The back gate was open.

The pool guy was squatting by the large oval-shaped pool checking the pH level. He didn't seem concerned when he saw me. Neighbors probably came and went by the back gate all the time. I waved a greeting and he nodded. There was no guard on the expansive back deck, so I let myself in through the double glass doors.

The ceiling in the back room was a spacious three stories high, larger than most hotel lobbies. I remembered the sunken fireplace in the center surrounded by two white leather couches from the party. The only thing missing was the twenty-foot-tall Christmas tree. A wide staircase along the wall led to rooms on the second and third floors. I heard the distinct musical flourish from the NPR morning radio program.

"Pool service," I called. I didn't want Marcus to step out with a gun in his hand.

After a few moments, Marcus leaned over the second-floor railing. He blinked, obviously groggy with sleep. He had on gray dress pants and a white T-shirt. Specks of shaving foam dotted his neck. After a beat, his eyes adjusted to the light streaming in through the floor-to-ceiling windows. Recognition kicked in.

"Hi, Marcus," I said. I pointed to his neck. "You missed a spot." If I'd met him at his office, I would have been talking to Marcus Lopez, high-powered lawyer and politician. I wanted Marcus the family man with something to lose. I wanted him to feel vulnerable, like I did kneeling in my kitchen holding my bleeding dog.

"Nick? What the hell are you doing here?" The wheels were turning.

"Thought I'd stop by for a chat before work."

"How did you get in here?" He glanced behind me, expecting to see his guard.

"You mean, through security? Piece of cake. You want real protection, hire me."

"That didn't work out too well for Mr. Sosa," he said.

"Cheap shot. Turns out Sosa wasn't the target. I was." I held up the bandage on my arm. "He tried again, but it was just a warning."

Marcus wore leather, hard-soled slippers that clacked as he descended the staircase. "Sounds like you should be talking to the police. Why tell me?"

"The shooter is your client."

He didn't answer until we were face-to-face. "Who're you talking about?" He probably had a dozen clients who would pull a trigger or hire a hitman if they felt threatened.

"Danny Allison."

If that surprised him, he didn't skip a beat. "You're out of your mind."

"How about some coffee? It's been a long night. Someone shot my dog."

"You need to leave."

I ignored him and followed my nose toward the coffee I'd smelled when I came in. Marcus trailed behind me, his slippers echoing down the wide hallway lined with family photos. The kitchen was an open design with granite counters and recessed ceiling lighting.

An older woman wearing a white apron over a blue uniform stood polishing the silver cutlery by the sink. Marcus dismissed her in Spanish, and she disappeared reluctantly into the back of the house. He fiddled with the settings on his coffee machine.

"It has to do with the death of Marissa Luna, a college student found in the San Antonio River on the fifth of July," I said.

Marcus was turned away from me. I saw the tension in his back. He was listening. The coffee machine came to steaming life. He placed a cup the size of a soup bowl near the spout.

"What's Danny Allison's connection to this?" he asked, handing me the bowl of coffee.

I took a sip and had to admit it was good. Better than what my drip coffee maker could produce. Not as stout as Grandpa's stove-top percolator, but not bad. Marcus made himself a cup, and we sat across from each other on polished, metallic barstools.

"This is really good coffee."

Marcus watched me and waited.

"The dead girl was carrying Danny's child." I watched him closely for a reaction.

Marcus didn't blink. Didn't move. He was waiting for more explanation. That was all I was going to give him. He was too polished as a lawyer to betray his feelings.

"You know this how?"

"Danny's DNA matched the fetal tissue."

Marcus took a sip of coffee. "And how did you obtain a DNA sample from Danny Allison?"

"That's not important."

He took another sip of coffee. "So, Danny knew a girl who drowned in the river. Now you think he's shooting at you and killed your dog?" His lips curled into a patronizing grin.

"Wounded my dog," I corrected him. "If he was dead, I wouldn't be paying you a courtesy call or giving you a heads-up about your client. I don't like being threatened."

"And what will you do with this information?"

"I'm taking what I have to Detective Peterson as a concerned citizen. He handled the original case. With the new information, he'll have to reopen the case."

He sipped more coffee and seemed to be calculating his next move.

"You know Detective Peterson?" I asked.

"I know *of* him. He seems competent." Not a choice of words I would have used.

"Why not have Danny stop by the police station and confess?"

He forced a laugh and set down his coffee cup. "You want me to bring Danny in, so he can confess to a murder that he didn't commit based on evidence that's inadmissible?"

"Sounds reasonable."

"Get the hell out of here," he yelled, his face turning red. I wondered how long it would take for his temper to flare. "If you make one move against Danny Allison, I will have you arrested." His voice climbed to a higher octave. "You can't come into my house and threaten me or my clients. I'm going to be governor of Texas. I'll bury you!" He paused to catch his breath. He didn't just have an anger management problem. He was showing signs of coming unglued. A vein popped out on his forehead, forming a column from his left eyebrow to his receding hairline. "The Allison family is one of the most respected families in Texas. I will not have you impugning their reputation with ridiculous accusations." He was falling back on money and connections for support, just as I calculated he would.

"The word on the street is that you and Patrick had a falling out."

He scoffed. "Nothing could be further from the truth. Patrick Allison and I have been close friends for twenty-five years."

"Close enough for you to cover up a murder?"

The vein on his forehead throbbed. He reached for his cell phone and hit the speed dial. So far so good. I hoped Skeeter was ready to trace the call. I finished my coffee and stood up.

I'd accomplished what I came for. Marcus was rattled and making phone calls. One of them would be to Danny. "Just remember, I have the DNA. Danny can run, but he can't hide."

CHAPTER THIRTY-THREE

I pulled into a convenience store off Loop 1604, topped off my gas tank, and waited to hear from Skeeter. Ten minutes later, he came through. Marcus had made four calls. He was rattled. That was my intent. Skeeter started to explain how he intercepted the calls, but I cut him off. I knew he enjoyed showing off his skills, but I was in a hurry.

"Just give me the details."

"Fine. The details. The first call was to the Heights Security Company."

"That was the guard on his front porch."

"The second was to Danny's cell phone. No answer. The third was to Lucky's gym, and the fourth was to the Dominion. Still no answer."

"Where the hell's Danny?"

"Mexico?"

"Let's hope not. Keep monitoring. Let me know if he connects with Danny."

I called Lucky. Danny hadn't worked out since our MMA fight. He said he'd call me if he came in. That left the Dominion. Skeeter had a connection that worked security who might help me gain access, but it was a long shot. I could wait outside the gate and hope that he came out. That could take days.

The Dominion was an exclusive neighborhood with a high concentration of very pricy real estate that was home to some of the Spurs basketball players, a few Hollywood celebrities, and at least one famous country music singer. Unlike Marcus's neighborhood, the security gate was manned twenty-four seven, like an entry point on the Mexican border with really nice landscaping. The residents were serious about security and willing to pay for it. If Danny was behind the gate, I wasn't going to get him out.

While I was sipping coffee and watching the 1604 traffic slow to a morning crawl, Skeeter called back. Marcus had connected with Danny at the Allison family ranch in rural Edwards County. He wasn't privy to the conversations, but the exchange lasted two minutes. Bingo. My surprise move worked. I'd located Danny. Now, I just needed to get to him before Marcus and the Allison family circled the wagons.

I took I-10 northwest, passed the turn to Grandpa's ranch, and got off at Kerrville. From there I followed the Guadalupe River west through a narrow, winding limestone canyon, which blocked out cell phone reception. Unlike the trip to Grandpa's ranch, which over the years showed increased cell coverage and dozens of newer houses, the more isolated western edge of the Hill Country nearer to the Mexican border resisted the advance of civilization. If anything, with the rise of border crossings and cartel influence, the facade of civilization was slowly eroding away.

The Allison spread was a sprawling forty-thousand-acre ranch that in its own way seemed part of the resistance. From the paved two-lane state highway, I turned south on a caliche road marked only by a row of mailboxes. There were no signs identifying the road. No name and no number. It wasn't from neglect or oversight. The Allisons didn't invite casual visitors.

The white ribbon of caliche wound through rolling limestone hills covered with oak motts and cedar brush. A pair of vultures floated in circles looking for carrion, their wide black wings buoyed by the updraft from the canyon. The road then dipped into the Nueces River bottom where giant pecan trees that gave the river its name, meaning *nuts* in Spanish, mixed with ancient, gnarled oaks covered with ball moss. A tom turkey scurried across the road, stopped to take a closer look at my pickup, then disappeared behind an outcrop of gray, weathered limestone. The area was a favorite outlaw hideout in the nineteenth century, and a who's who list of infamous characters like Butch Cassidy and the Sundance Kid had made the trek up this isolated canyon escaping pursuit. There were modern tourist cabins farther downriver and a guest ranch along Hackberry Creek that fed into the Nueces, but this part of Texas had escaped the growth that threatened to overwhelm Grandpa's ranch near Fredericksburg. This was the Texas outback.

After three more unmarked turns, the road emerged between two eight-foot game fences. The GPS showed I was getting close. Rocky Mountain elk, tiny Asian sika deer, and a dozen giant, bluish Nilgai antelope grazed on the sparse, dry grass behind the fence. All the animals stopped and stared at my pickup, expecting a handout. If my meeting with Danny Allison went south, there would be no cavalry or posse of Texas Rangers coming to my rescue. I'd only had cell phone reception twice since I'd left Kerrville. Near the main gate, I had zero bars.

I did a mental inventory of my weapons. The .45 was in the glovebox, the .38 on my ankle, and I'd packed a Colt AR-15 that held a twenty-round magazine. I glanced at my reflection in the sideview mirror. The man I saw was hard, driven, and extremely pissed off about what happen to his dog and the threat to his family and friends. I needed to use that force and all the self-confidence I could muster because I was straying into territory where I'd never gone before. I was alone, facing unknown odds in what for all intents and purposes was a foreign country. I tried to flash my signature smile, but it came across more like a grimace. "Improvise, adapt, and overcome, you handsome devil." The man in the mirror nodded.

The entrance to the Allison ranch looked more like a control point to a forward operating base in Afghanistan than a friendly cattle and exotic game ranch. A huge stone arch featuring the YA cattle brand in use since before the Civil War was set back fifty yards off the road, and concrete security barriers forced drivers to zigzag on approach. The stone guardhouse featured a Texas flag and a red-and-black Texas Tech banner along with four surveillance cameras that covered the front, the back, and down the fence in both directions.

A security guard in his late twenties with an overdeveloped neck stepped out of the guardhouse. He wore a black Heights Security uniform matching the guard in front of Marcus's house and a mustache that was a dead ringer for the one Burt Reynolds wore in *Smoky and the Bandit.*

His left hand signaled me to stop. His right hand rested on the butt of a Glock 17.

I drove through the zigzag pattern, keeping an eye on his right hand, then stopped and got out holding my hands at shoulder level. I didn't want any misunderstanding. Burt looked jumpy, like he was expecting trouble.

"Howdy," I said and flashed a good ol' boy grin.

"Can I help you, sir?"

"I'm lookin' for Danny Allison." I took another step forward and put my hands down.

Burt watched me, keeping his hand on the weapon. "Do you have an appointment, sir?"

I figured that confirmed Danny was there, otherwise he wouldn't have asked about an appointment. "No. Danny's expecting me."

"You'll have to call in at least twenty-four hours in advance."

I stepped closer. Inside his comfort zone. "I'm here now. Call him. My name's Nick Fischer. Tell him it's about Marissa Luna. He'll see me." I gave him my practiced I'm-gonna-kick-your-ass look and waited for his reaction.

Burt wasn't intimidated, but he decided to make the call. He went back to the guardhouse and used the landline phone mounted on the wall.

A few minutes later, he hustled out and punched in the key code for the gate. "You're clear, Mr. Fischer. Sorry for the delay. Stay on the main road for two-point-six miles. It's paved to the house. Be careful of the animals. They're usually near the road this time of day. Feedin' time." He said "feedin' time" like it was the highlight of his day.

I pulled my .45 pistol from the glovebox and rested it on the console beside me. Getting into the Allisons' isolated property was the easy part.

CHAPTER THIRTY-FOUR

The paved two-lane road through Allison's pasture had fewer potholes than the street in front of my house. The ranch had the look and feel of a state park. But even the family fortune couldn't keep the grass from turning brown in the late summer drought. No amount of financial resources could mitigate the effects of nature.

I kept track of the milage, so I'd know how far I'd have to run in case things went south. My unexpected move had worked on Marcus Lopez. He'd gotten flustered and pointed me in the right direction. But like a trick play on the gridiron, it's never as effective the second time. The defensive coordinator always found a counter move. Once Marcus and Patrick Allison figured out I'd connected with Danny, the shit would hit the fan. The digital clock on the dash read five thirty. It had been a long day, and it wasn't over yet.

The exotic animals rushed my pickup looking for a handout. The tiny spotted antelope came first. So close I could touch them out the window. The Rocky Mountain elk herd was next, led by a trophy six-by-six bull. He stood in the middle of the road, daring me to drive off without leaving his daily hay ration. I couldn't help him, so I honked the horn. The noise startled a kangaroo lounging in the long shadow of a mesquite tree. I wondered if they hunted them or raised them as pets. I also wondered if the animals missed their natural habitat or if they were like humans and just adapted to their surroundings. The tight security and exotic animals added to the strange aura that surrounded the isolated Allison family ranch.

At two-point-two miles I topped a ridge overlooking the sprawling ranch compound. There were towns in West Texas with fewer buildings. Seven of the structures were larger than my house, including a three-story newer home and a stable big enough for fifty horses. On the other end of the compound, corrals stretched over a ten-acre area. Near the road, there was a garage the size and shape of an airplane hangar. An older single-story structure sat behind the newer buildings, put together with smaller limestone blocks that were darker in color and weathered with age. Obviously, the original homestead. Its design resembled Grandpa's house.

A massive oak tree in the yard supported two kids' swings and shaded a white picnic table. Five men worked near the corrals. Two were loading hay onto a one-ton flatbed truck, the crew the bull elk was waiting for. Danny's bronze F-350 with the oversized tires and chrome roll bar sat beside the garage.

There were no signs of an ambush, no rifle barrels in the windows or silhouettes in the shadows, but before I drove into the yard, I pulled my Colt AR-15 from behind the seat, locked in a twenty-round magazine, and jacked a shell in the chamber. I hadn't lived through three deployments by taking unnecessary chances.

I slipped my pickup into second gear and let it idle downhill toward the open garage. Danny strolled out of the original ranch house, carrying an AR-15 and a pistol in a waist holster. He looked anxious but wasn't pointing the rifle at me. As I got closer, I noticed he had a bluish tint under both eyes and his nose was swollen from the pounding I'd given him. His bottom lip was packed with snuff.

I stayed seated and watched Danny approach with the AR-15 slung over his left shoulder. If he made a move to point it in my direction, I was ready. Movement in the open garage caught my eye. An older man in a weather-beaten straw cowboy hat stepped out of the shadows. He had a revolver in a leather holster on his waist and a look of concern on his dark leathery face.

Danny's eyes were glassy like he'd just polished off a six-pack or something stronger. The swelling made it difficult for him to hold the snuff in his bottom lip, and brown tobacco juice dribbled down his peach fuzz chin.

Two more men stood in the shadows behind the cowboy. They wore the same black security uniform as Burt and the guard in front of Marcus's house. Both carried AR-15s and wore tactical belts with pistols and extra ammo.

I examined Danny's rifle. It sported a Marauder D-750 night-vision scope that cost more than my old pickup. The kind the shooter would have used to hit Sosa and fire at me along the river trail. It also had a suppresser: an oversized tube with air vents attached to the end of the barrel to reduce the sound and recoil.

Danny held up both hands in a welcome gesture. "Come for a rematch?" He tried to smile, but his swollen face interfered. More brown juice trickled down his chin and he wiped it away with the back of his hand. He looked like he'd just come from the dentist. I kept the cowboy and the two guards in the corner of my eye while I unrolled the window.

"Tell your boys to stand down," I said.

"It's okay," Danny said to the guards. "Mr. Fischer's here for the evening hunt."

The guards reluctantly retreated inside the garage. The cowboy stayed where he was. Danny peeked into my open window, noticed the butt of my AR-15.

"I wasn't expecting you so early," he said in a loud voice. He held his hand up to the open window. I shook it. He spoke under his breath without moving his swollen lips. "I told them you were here for the evening hunt. Take your rifle and step out of the pickup."

I wasn't sure what he was up to but having my rifle in my hand made me feel safer. I tucked the .45 behind my belt and stepped out.

"Night huntin's the best," he said, switching back to his loud voice. "That's when the hogs come out to feed. They're out of control. Eating all the grazing reserved for the exotics."

We both glanced at the sky. The sun was setting behind the rugged limestone cliff, casting a shadow over the ranch compound and painting a handful of puffy clouds bright orange. It was easy to see that the first Allison had chosen this place for privacy and defense. The cliff made a wide U on the west and north side of the homestead. To the east and south, the terrain sloped downward providing a panoramic view. Comanches, outlaws, or a posse couldn't approach without being seen for at least half a mile.

"Tell me about Marissa," I said.

Danny threw me a nervous glance. "*Quédate aquí, Juan. Iremos solos,*" he said, indicating we would go alone.

Juan shrugged. "*Cómo no,*" he said and walked into the barn.

When Juan was out of sight, he turned back to me. "I'd rather talk away from the house. Do you mind?" It was a request, not a command—a tone he hadn't used before. Maybe the beating had softened him up.

"Makes no difference to me."

The cowboy reappeared driving a four-seater, all-terrain vehicle. He left the motor running, nodded to Danny, and got out.

"Gracias, Juan," Danny said.

Juan walked toward the men loading hay.

Danny hopped into the driver's seat, and I climbed in beside him. He propped his rifle in the gun rack between the seats. I kept mine in my lap. I wasn't sure what was going on, but I wanted to be prepared. He took off on a caliche road that followed a meandering creek bed choked with willow trees.

"Hogs like to come to water just after dark. They're smart. You rarely see them in the daytime." While he drove, he pulled a sixteen-ounce can of Lone Star beer from the ice chest on the back seat. He offered me one. I declined. He cracked his open and hung his head out the doorless side of the ATV, washing the snuff from his mouth before he took a long drink.

Twilight was turning into night. The shadows from the cliff deepened and the thick olive-green brush turned a soft gray. Danny was doing twenty miles an hour on a dirt road without headlights. Brush slapped the sides of the vehicle and the oversized tires slid sideways on each turn. I let him go for fifteen minutes, listening to his nervous, rapid-fire hog hunting spiel, obviously memorized for hunting clients, then I reached over and turned off the engine. The ATV coasted to a stop. I took the key out of the ignition.

"I don't care about huntin' hogs," I said, jamming my left leg against his AR-15. In case Danny went for it. "Put your hands on the wheel."

He shifted uneasily, then followed orders. I unsnapped the holster on his waist and pulled out an Infinity .40 caliber Smith & Wesson pistol. Not a sidearm the average Joe could afford. Every Infinity weapon was made from each customer's specifications. His was a beautiful collector's piece. The stainless-steel barrel was hand engraved with a medieval knight doing battle against a fire-breathing dragon. It wasn't hard to believe that Danny thought of himself as a young knight from a royal family.

"Nice pistol," I said.

"Graduation present from Grandpa." Danny was nervous and talked fast.

I eased my own pistol out of my pants so that I could sit back further in the seat. Then pointed it in Danny's general direction. The AR-15 was too bulky to maneuver in the small cab of the ATV, and I wanted to be ready when I told Danny I knew what he'd done.

"How come security's so tight? What're y'all afraid of?"

"Coyotes, cartel drug runners. All kinds of crazies. Animal rights activists too," he said. "That anti-hunting crowd is persistent. The Allison name is a high-profile target. Sometimes they try to sneak on the ranch. Disrupt our hunts. That kind of thing."

"You know why I'm here?"

"Yeah, Marissa Luna."

"She was murdered. You killed her so she wouldn't keep you from your inheritance."

His eyes bugged out of his head. "No, sir! You got that wrong."

"She was pregnant when she died. You're the father. That's capital murder."

Danny's face flushed, and he shifted in his seat. The crickets chirped a warning that darkness was coming. A frog on the creek bank joined them. There was no wind. The air was dry and started to cool as soon as the sun went behind the cliff. I waited for Danny to speak. A minute stretched into two.

Finally, he said: "That's why you came to the gym... for a blood sample?"

"That's right. I matched it to the fetal DNA from Marissa's autopsy."

Danny repacked his bottom lip with snuff. He seemed to need it to think clearly. "How'd you get the results so fast? Don't that take months?"

"You thought you had more time? Is that why you're still here?"

"I wasn't gonna run. I didn't kill her." He spit out the door. "You saw the police report. It was an accident."

"Bullshit."

"I swear to god." His voice cracked like a teenager's.

"Then why are you trying to kill me? Why did you shoot my dog and threaten my family?" I grabbed his shirt collar and squeezed it tight around his neck.

"I didn't do any of that."

I loosened my grip before he blacked out. "You're on the video surveillance from the dance club. You fought with her. You bought her a four-thousand-dollar bracelet. You told her to have an abortion. She wouldn't do it."

"No. That ain't what happened. I wanted the baby. That's why we fought. *She* wanted an abortion." His eyes watered.

"You're lying."

"She promised to wait for the abortion until we talked about it again."

I shoved him back across the seat. "Where did you go that night after you left the club?"

"Home. The Dominion. I was there by one. You can check with security."

"Why didn't you come forward?"

He stared up at the sky, searching for an answer in the Milky Way. "Detective Peterson came to my house. He asked a few questions. He checked my alibi. That was the end of it," he said. Tomahawk had failed to mention this to me.

"I know about the girls in Lubbock. I tracked down your ex, Valerie Martin. She moved out of her trailer park and bought a BMW. There was another the year before. She moved back to China. How much did you pay *her*?"

Danny spit out the door. "That's one of the problems with being an

Allison. Everybody knows the name and knows you're rich. I tried to date girls that didn't know or didn't care. Valerie found out. She made up that BS about the rape. Hell, she's the one invited me to her place. She set me up. She wanted money. She wanted everything. No one believes the guy. You're guilty if you open your mouth. Marissa was different. She didn't know who I was from Adam. She'd never heard of my family, and she didn't want anything to do with them when she finally found out. She was refreshing. When she got pregnant, I was the one who wanted to make a family with her. She wanted a career. She wasn't ready to be a mother. I would've taken care of her. That's all the other girls wanted—my name and my family's money. Marissa didn't want it. She wanted to make it on her own." There was just enough light to spot tears streaming down Danny's swollen cheeks. If he was acting, he was good.

"Is that a .308?"

"Yeah."

I pulled his AR-15 out of the rack and popped a round into the chamber.

His muscles tensed, ready to jump if I leveled the rifle at him. "I didn't shoot your dog. I didn't threaten you. I swear to god," he said and wiped his cheeks with the back of his hand.

"Why the suppressor?" I knew what it was for, but I wanted to hear Danny justify using one on the ranch.

"The noise doesn't scare the game. You can shoot two or three hogs out of a herd before they run. Helps with the recoil, too. It's easier to keep the scope steady on a second shot."

I stepped out of the vehicle and brought the weapon to my shoulder. The view through the lens was amazing even in the low light. The Marauder scope was better than what I'd used in the Marine Corps. I swept the scope over the side of the cliff. Found a mesquite tree about four inches in diameter clinging to a rock. The range finder in the scope read two hundred and seventy-five yards. A simple shot for a trained sniper.

I handed Danny the rifle. "Hit that mesquite tree at two hundred and seventy-five yards."

He swept the cliffside with a smooth, practiced motion. "I see it," he said and pulled the trigger three times in quick succession. The sound was quiet, but not the soft compressed air sound I'd heard on the street. The empty brass flipped in an arc and landed in the dirt. This wasn't the rifle that had shot at me. If it was, he had done something else to modify the sound. I picked up the brass. Still warm. Danny watched me tuck them into my jeans pocket. He held the rifle pointed in my direction. I knew what he was thinking. One shot would end this conversation. I wondered if he had the guts to kill me at close range. I didn't give him a chance to decide.

"Look at me," I said. When his eyes shifted to my face, I grabbed the rifle out of his hands and leveled the scope on the tree. There were three neat holes in the center of the trunk less than a half inch apart. Danny wasn't a military sniper, but he was a good shot. I pulled the magazine, ejected the live round, and tossed the ammo on the floorboard.

"If you didn't kill her, who did? Who's threatening me?"

Danny shuffled his boots in the dirt.

"Are you protecting someone? Did your grandpa find out about the baby and have Marissa killed?" I was losing patience. If he wasn't the one who killed Sosa and shot at me, he knew who did.

After a full minute, he cleared his throat. Miles away from Patrick and Marcus, I hoped he was finally ready to come clean.

Suddenly, the small clearing lit up like a sports arena. A dozen spotlights converged on the cab of the ATV.

"Drop the rifle!" a voice shouted from behind the wall of lights. I heard metallic clicks and recognized the sounds of weapons being prepared to fire.

"Better do what he says," Danny said.

I put the rifle on the ATV seat and raised my hands. Four bodies appeared in silhouette. The closest one held a Glock pointed at my head. The others held AR-15s aimed at my waist.

"Step forward," the man with the Glock ordered.

I couldn't see their faces because of the glare from the bright lights. The silhouettes of their weapons convinced me they were serious.

"It's okay, Ricky." Danny addressed the man with the Glock. "We were just getting some target practice." Danny's voice was high and thin. He was scared. Whatever was happening, I got the feeling Danny wasn't in charge.

One of the guards grabbed my rifle and .45 from the ATV. Ricky frisked me. He didn't find the .38 in my ankle holster. Not that it mattered. He took my pickup keys and put them in his pocket. I was outnumbered and outgunned. Shooting it out with a five-shot revolver was out of the question.

"Change of plan," Ricky said. "We'll take him from here."

"Why?" Danny asked.

"Orders," Ricky said.

Two of the men grabbed my arms. When they dimmed the spotlights, I noticed that Ricky and his team all wore the same black uniform. Heights Security Company. I did a quick scan of the perimeter. Eight men altogether. They had walked up on us in the dark while I argued with Danny. I'd been so wrapped up in the interrogation, I'd dropped my guard.

They led me fifty yards down the trail to where four ATVs and a pickup were waiting.

"Put him in the backseat," Ricky ordered. He holstered his Glock.

My mind was racing for a plan. Anything. If I disappeared out here, no one would ever find me. The two guards tightened their grip on my arms and shoved me toward a four-door Toyota. It was now or never. If they got me into that pickup, I'd never see the sun come up.

"What the hell are you doin'? Danny, tell these goons you're coming with me."

Ricky pulled his Glock and aimed at my head. There was silence. A coyote yipped, followed by another, and another. They were starting their night hunt.

Finally, Danny said: "Sorry, Nick."

"Sorry, Nick?" He sounded lost and defeated. "What does that mean?" I jerked my arms free of the guards and took a step toward Danny. "Who's in charge? Do you run this place, or do they?"

The guard on my left grabbed my arm again. I slipped his grip and kicked his knee. His partner swung the butt of his rifle at my head. I ducked and shot a flat hand to his throat. He dropped to the ground, gagging. I grabbed his rifle and leveled off on Ricky.

"Back off!" I shouted.

Something hard hit the back of my head. My knees buckled.

My world went black.

CHAPTER THIRTY-FIVE

I came to with a splitting headache and numb fingers from the tight zip ties cutting into my wrists. I was crammed into the back seat of the Toyota pickup flanked by two black-uniformed guards. The dome light showed they were the same two I'd seen in the garage. Both held AR-15s pointed in my direction. Another guard in the front passenger seat had an AR aimed at my chest. Ricky drove. I'd been in worse situations, but it had been a while.

Ricky eyed me in the rearview mirror. "Rise and shine jarhead."

Danny must have filled them in on my military background, which would explain the extra precaution of three armed men and the zip ties.

I checked the time on the pickup's console. 8:30 p.m. I hadn't been out more than ten minutes. "Everybody knows where I am, Ricky," I croaked. "My answering service, my employees, even my girlfriend. If I don't show up by midnight, they'll sound the alarm," I lied. No one was coming to my rescue. I didn't have an answering service, and I hadn't told Sylvia where I was going. Skeeter knew, but he wouldn't sound the alarm for at least forty-eight hours. I'd warned him about getting too anxious if I didn't check in immediately. I didn't want him blowing my cover or compromising my position. Now, I was rethinking that strategy.

Ricky chuckled under his breath. His three companions played dumb. The guard pointing the rifle from the front seat was clearly enjoying himself. He wouldn't hesitate to shoot me.

"Where's big Patrick, Ricky?" I asked. "Is he on the ranch? Let's go talk to him."

"You know Mr. Allison?"

"We're old pals. Our families go way back. Before the Civil War."

Ricky didn't respond. He didn't care about history. Or maybe he wasn't working for Allison at all. Since he wore the same uniform as the guard on duty outside Marcus's house, I wondered who was in charge. I checked out the window. The dome light made it difficult to see where we were until the road descended into the family compound. He stopped beside my pickup.

"We'll escort you back to the main gate," Ricky said.

One of the men opened the back door and pulled me out. Another cut the zip ties and opened my pickup door. I got behind the wheel. The front seat rifleman got into my passenger seat and trained his weapon on my waist. This had to be a setup, but I couldn't figure their angle.

Ricky handed me the keys. "Follow me. Don't try any combat moves. Lonny has an itchy trigger finger."

I started my pickup and backed up slowly. When I pulled in behind Ricky, the two ATVs with the spotlights followed me. I glanced at Lonny and his AR.

"How long have you worked here, Lonny?" I asked casually.

He didn't speak. I gathered the Heights Security Company trained them not to talk or hired them because they couldn't. I liked the fact that they did have some training. I hated to think some gun-happy cowboy traded his spurs for tactical boots and took the night shift. I goosed the engine just a tiny bit to see what he'd do. The pickup jumped forward quickly, closing the distance between the bumper and Ricky's Toyota. Lonny jerked his head forward. I let off the gas and fell back ten yards.

"Sorry. Foot slipped."

Lonny's eyes narrowed and refocused on me. He'd done what most people would do at the sudden change of speed, he looked forward to see what we were going to hit. He forgot his primary duty was to guard the prisoner. He should have kept his eyes on me. Maybe he hadn't gotten that far in his training. It was information I would use to avoid at all costs a one-way trip into the dense brush where neither my body nor my pickup would ever be seen again.

"So, do you work for Allison or Marcus Lopez?" I asked.

Lonny nodded. "Uh-huh." Great conversationalist. I imagined him as Death personified wearing a black hoodie and pointing silently toward my final resting place.

I thought of that first patrol outside the wire in Afghanistan. The sergeant instructed our platoon to write out a will and sign it. Nothing heightens the senses like knowing you face death. Everything I had at the time went to my grandpa. With my dad's death, he was the only Fischer in our immediate family. I'd always counted on someday extending the family tree, but that possibility didn't seem to be in the cards.

I looked at Lonny. He pointed silently straight ahead.

I'd beaten Death before, maybe I could do it again. I braced for a final desperate fight. The brush was cleared on both sides of the road. Ricky's headlights picked up a dirt track that split off to the left. I slowed to increase the distance between our vehicles. A quick turn and acceleration could throw Death against the door and give me a split second to redirect the barrel of his AR. It was my only chance.

"Pick up the pace, sport," Lonny said.

"What's that?" I stalled, waiting for the turn-off, and let my right hand rest on the seat closer to his weapon.

Seconds from the dirt track, the lights from the main gate suddenly came into view at the bottom of the hill. I hesitated. Maybe Death wasn't leading me into the brush. I had to make a choice. Trust Ricky, or grab Lonny's rifle and mount a counterattack. There was no guarantee I'd survive either.

Ricky stayed on the paved road. He didn't seem any more trustworthy than Death, but I followed him anyway. At the last moment, he turned away and I stopped in front of the gate. Burt hustled over to the keypad. Ricky got out and walked to my open window.

"Thank you for visiting the Allison ranch," he said, almost sounding sincere. "I hope you had a good hunt." The engine exhaust created a white fog under the gate lights.

"I'd like to come back. I didn't get the trophy I was after," I said.

"I'm sorry." Any pretense of sincerity evaporated. "You wore out your welcome."

"Where's my pistol and AR?"

"We'll arrange to have you reimbursed."

"Who do you work for? Allison or Marcus Lopez?"

"Have a nice night," Ricky said.

"Fuck you very much." I couldn't hold back.

Ricky smiled and walked back to his pickup. Lonny got out and slammed the door, looking less like Death and more like the redneck he was. In my rearview mirror, I watched the four guards on ATVs form a semicircle around my pickup. Clearly, I wouldn't be welcomed back.

San Antonio was a two-hour drive. I had enough adrenaline pumping through my veins to keep me awake for the rest of the night. The pieces of the puzzle were falling together. The picture of Marissa's murderer looked more like Patrick than Danny. Maybe he didn't want the family name tarnished or the bloodline diluted, so he staged the murder to look like an accident.

As soon as I had cell phone service, I called the animal hospital. It was after hours, and I had to leave a message to call me with an update. I didn't like the idea of Sam waking up in a cage alone. He hated the vet's office as much as I hated hospitals. Something about the antiseptic smell or the fact that I'd known too many friends and relatives who went there to die.

My next call went to Skeeter. I briefed him on my visit to the outback and told him what Danny had said about being home by one and asked him to check with his contact at the Dominion. I knew it was a waste of time to question his family and the staff. They would do and say whatever Patrick wanted them to. It would be much harder to fake the security video.

He filled me in on his surveillance. Sylvia'd gone to the grocery store and to the gym after work. She'd gone home after that. He was watching her condo from the street with intruder cameras on her front and back doors. If anyone tried to get in, an alarm would go off on his laptop. She was safe, for now.

I knew one thing from my meeting with Danny—he knew what happened to Marissa that night. If I hadn't been thrown off the property, he would have finally told the truth.

I parked on the street a few houses down from my fixer-upper and, as exhausted as I was, spent fifteen minutes watching for signs of movement.

I checked the other cars on the block. Nothing seemed out of the ordinary. Rose Gustafson watched television in her front room with her favorite white cat perched on her shoulder. I was glad to see she had made it home safely.

Just as I concluded it was safe, my phone rang. I jumped when it chimed and moved quickly to muffle the sound. It was Skeeter. He'd called his contact at the Dominion. They had Danny on video checking in at 12:57 a.m. on July fifth. That part of Danny's story checked out.

When I went inside, the mess was cleaned up, and Sam's blood was gone. Skeeter had come over and taken care of everything. I was grateful for that. I'd gotten very little sleep in forty-eight hours and wanted a shower and a nap. My head was throbbing. I'd gotten away from Allison's thugs with a knot on my head. Next time would be different.

I stripped out of my musty clothes and spent fifteen minutes in a hot shower. In the military, any shower over five minutes was called a "Hollywood shower." I was pampering myself after a hard day. When I finished, I stumbled into the bedroom and called Sylvia.

"Where have you been?" she asked.

"On a safari," I said as cheerfully as I could.

"Don't you dare make a joke."

"Everything's under control." I tried to sound convincing, but I didn't believe it myself. Events were, in fact, spinning out of control. I wasn't sure who was after me or where the next attack would come from, but it would come soon. I didn't want to give her any more details, and I didn't want her advice.

"I know that voice, Nick. You're holding out. Tell me what's going on," she insisted. "Marcus told me you went to his house. What were you trying to prove?"

I let the uncomfortable silence stretch while I stood and paced my small bedroom. A little bell was going off—a gut feeling that she'd shared our conversation with Marcus. "What did you tell Marcus?"

"Nothing he didn't already know."

"I mean before today. Did you tell him about me going after Danny Allison?"

This time she went silent. I listened to her shallow breathing and watched my reflection in the bedroom window. Had I been the topic of lunchtime conversation or maybe he'd called her into his office and questioned her about my investigation. I hated to think she shared our conversations willingly.

"Did you talk about my investigation?"

"Allison is his client. Of course he'd wanna know."

"Did it ever occur to you that he might be involved?"

"In what? Murder? You're talking nonsense. Marcus would never do anything like that."

"I've gotta go." Her response left a bad taste in my mouth.

"Won't you tell me what you're gonna do?"

"That depends. Are you gonna tell Marcus?"

"That's not fair. No, of course not." She sounded angry. I didn't care. I was angry too.

I tried to think of an answer that wouldn't come back to bite me if she did share it with Marcus Lopez. "I'll take what I have to Detective Peterson and ask him to reopen the investigation."

"What if he says no?"

"I'll drop it. There's nothing more I can do." I didn't have any intention of contacting Tomahawk again or giving up on the case, but I wasn't going to share that with her. Not now.

"I know you better than that. Your gut tells you he's guilty, and you'll keep going till someone gets arrested or killed. This time, it could be you."

"We'll talk later."

"I'm worried about you, Nick. You're in over your head."

I disconnected. What could I say to that? I knew she was right. The reflection in the window suddenly looked like Death pointing silently toward my bed. I took the hint, turned my back, and fell onto the mattress.

"Geld regiert die Welt."
Money rules the world.

—Grandpa Fischer

CHAPTER THIRTY-SIX

DAY SIX

I woke drenched in sweat and needing another Hollywood shower. Fractured pieces of my final deployment mixed with a dream about my dad's murder, Sam's bloody body, Sylvia in bed with Marcus Lopez, and Grandpa sending smoke signals from his hayfield. The demons were active again, and my subconscious was rolling every possible unpleasant thought into a horror movie marathon curated by Death himself. Maybe Sylvia was right, I was in over my head. I found my spare pistol—a Springfield XD .45—loaded it and went downstairs to fix breakfast. It wasn't the Para Ordnance, but it had a thirteen-round magazine and would get the job done. A loaded weapon and a full stomach may not help me tread water, but it would make me feel much better.

I called Skeeter to check on his surveillance. He answered on the second ring. No one had gone in or out of Sylvia's apartment, and he was hungry. I told him to follow Sylvia to her office and wait for me. I'd bring him breakfast. I called Grandpa next and listened to his phone ring, and ring. I tried the petting zoo number and got the answering machine. I left another message.

My next call was to the vet. He said it was still too early to know the extent of the damage from the gunshot wound. The swelling was going down, and Sam's vital signs were stable. There was nothing more I could do for him except pray and wait. I fixed myself some eggs and venison pan sausage while I considered my next move. I knew asking Peterson to reopen the case was a waste of time, but there may be a way to go around him and still get some help.

I'd done the unexpected by confronting Marcus Lopez and showing up unannounced at the Allison ranch. Danny hadn't given me a confession, but he and Marcus were rattled. If I didn't press my advantage, Marcus and Allison would mount a quick counterattack using their money and influence and squash me like a bug on a windshield.

I finished breakfast and called Detective Ochoa. She answered on the first ring. She gave me her cop voice, flat and aggressive. I guessed she was already sitting at her desk in the station.

"What is it, Mr. Fischer?"

"I have new information about the Marissa Luna case." I heard her breathing, but she didn't answer right away. I guessed she was checking the floor to see if anyone was within earshot or walking away from Peterson's desk.

"Give it to me," she finally said. Her voice was a whisper this time.

"I'd rather tell you in person. Is Peterson with you?"

"No, he took the day off. Can you be at the station before eight?"

I checked my watch. Seven fifteen. I would have to hustle. "I'll be there," I said and disconnected.

I got dressed and took the .308 casing from my dirty jeans pocket, put it in a proper evidence bag, and dropped it into an accordion folder. I gathered my notes, the bracelet, and the surveillance tapes, and dumped them in with the casing. Then I made copies of the DNA comparison from Kelly's analysis and added the warning note the shooter had left on the kitchen floor. To make it look official, I wrote Marissa Luna on the side of the folder with a black marker. Nothing got a lawyer or detective's attention like a folder with a label. It gave them something to stamp a number on and file.

I put the folder in the leather briefcase Grandpa'd given me for Christmas while I was still in law school. I rarely used it anymore, but I was making every effort to look professional for Detective Ochoa's sake.

When I'd shaved and combed my short hair, I took one final precaution and added my sheriff department issued Kevlar vest under my button-down shirt. When I quit the department to go to law school, Travis County was in the process of upgrading their equipment using a federal grant. I got to keep the used but still serviceable bulletproof vest as a separation gift. The September day was hot, and adding an extra layer was like wearing a plastic suit at the gym, but I wanted to live through the day.

I stopped at Las Tapatias and bought another bag of taquitos. Cops always liked free stuff. Maybe the breakfast would soften the blow. I was going to tell Ochoa that the case she and her partner closed as an accidental death was really a murder case involving one of the richest families in the state and the leading candidate for governor. Not something a detective wants to hear on an empty stomach.

The public lot across the street from the station was nearly full at 7:45 in the morning. Each car that passed reminded me that the shooter had twice used a parking garage to hurl .308 bullets in my direction. Whatever shit I took for wearing the vest was worth it. At the entrance, I paused to scan the surrounding windows and rooftops. The move triggered memories of the constant threat of urban snipers on deployment. I never thought I'd have to keep my head down in the Alamo City.

I felt a presence beside me and jumped back, drawing my Springfield .45 from my shoulder holster. Instead of a killer, a cross-dressing prostitute in black stilettos and a leather skirt raised her hands and smiled. After a long night, black facial hair was starting to show through her heavy makeup.

"Easy, officer. Are you late for work?" she said, exposing large yellow teeth.

I holstered my pistol and mumbled an apology. She didn't seem spooked or surprised. My nerves were strung a little too tight. If I didn't relax, I was going to hurt somebody.

"Aren't you in enemy territory?" I asked.

"It's time for my nap. Jail's air conditioned." She smelled the taquitos in the greasy paper bag. "Come on, suga. Do mama a favor and feed me a big taco."

I shrugged. I'd worked crowd control in downtown Austin with the sheriff's department and knew what she wanted. "You stopped the wrong guy. I'm not a cop."

Before I could say she looked good in heels, she abruptly stepped into the street. A police cruiser swerved to miss her and slammed on its brakes. She got her wish, an air-conditioned room and a hot meal.

I stood inside the entrance to let my temperature return to normal before announcing myself to Sergeant Vera. He studied the restaurant bag and my Kevlar vest, then he sighed and shook his head.

"Just like your father," he said. "You won't let this go, will you? Stubborn as a barn-sour mule."

I shrugged. "What can I say?" No one had ever compared me to my father or a mule, but I got his point.

He chinned toward my bulky shirt. "You expectin' trouble?"

"I've already been shot at twice. And somebody put a bullet in my dog."

"Damn, is he all right?"

"I don't know yet. He's alive. I took him to the vet. I found him in my kitchen with a hole in his head."

"Jesus." He clicked his tongue. "You need anything, let me know. I owe a lot to your daddy. I'm not as fast on the draw as when I worked for him, but you know I have connections."

"Thanks. That means a lot, but I think I got it handled." I knew Vera would help out of loyalty to my father. I didn't want that kind of help. It was my case. I was getting paid to get justice for Marissa, and I thought I still had a few cards left to play. I didn't want to call in a favor yet. "I'm here to see Detective Ochoa. She's expecting me."

Vera nodded, appraising me. "I figured that. Peterson's off today."

"What's your take on her?"

"She's competent. No nonsense. One of the good ones. She'll be an asset to the department if she can survive working with Tomahawk."

"Good to know."

"But don't bullshit her or you'll have a short meeting."

"Duly noted. How's your wife?"

"Happy as a clam, now that I'm out of the house."

"I can imagine what it would be like putting up with you all day long."

He laughed and told me to wait on the bench while he called upstairs. I watched a dozen plainclothes and uniform officers hustling to work. The usual police station collection of hookers, gangbangers, and drunks were housed in the detention center a couple blocks west. I should have felt safer surrounded by law and order. Instead, I was jumpy, wondering when and where the counterattack from Allison or Lopez would come.

Ochoa was at her desk reading a case file. I opened the bag of breakfast and handed her one of the coffees. She smiled and seemed more relaxed without Peterson around. The attitude was much more attractive. She wore a stylish white blouse with gray slacks, and her dark hair was pulled into a tight ponytail that showed off her high forehead and prominent cheekbones.

"Thought you could use some breakfast," I said.

She tasted the coffee. "Beats the crap we get here." She studied my bulky shirt. "What's with the vest? You pretending to be a real cop today?" She dived into the breakfast bag and took out a chorizo and egg taquito.

"Someone took a shot at me. I think I know who." I opened my briefcase and took out the file. Ochoa suddenly seemed interested. My briefcase and the file with Marissa's name on it had the intended effect. That and the bulletproof vest got her attention.

One by one, I placed the items on her desk. The .308 casings, the bracelet, and the DNA results.

"More shell casings?" She caught a large dribble of orange chorizo grease a second before it landed on her white blouse.

"These are from Danny Allison's rifle. He has a fancy night-vision scope for huntin' hogs. And he uses a suppressor."

"Danny Allison? Patrick Allison's grandson? You think he killed Marissa Luna?" She couldn't hide her amusement.

"Danny killed her because she was pregnant. It would have jeopardized his inheritance. Or Patrick killed her because he didn't want an illegitimate heir. Take your pick. Maybe they were in it together. They also tried to kill me because I know the truth." I pushed the DNA report in front of her.

She wiped her hands on a napkin and read it over. "Who authorized this?"

"Doesn't matter. Danny knew he was the father."

"You talked to him?"

"That's right. I visited his ranch. Nice spread. Heavy guard. And I wanna report my weapons stolen. A Para Ordnance .45 and a Colt AR-15 in case they decide to use them to shoot somebody else."

"He confessed?"

"Our conversation was cut short."

"What does that mean?"

"Ranch security escorted me off the property before he could finish."

"You were trespassing?"

"No, I was invited in. I just wore out my welcome."

"You know what Peterson's gonna say," she said.

"That's why I came to you. There's more than enough for you to reopen the investigation."

She stood and glanced over the empty cubicles. "Between you and me, I didn't like what Peterson did with the Luna case."

"What do you mean?"

"I mean, he shut me out. It was my first case, and he said it was open and shut. I got the feeling he didn't want me involved."

"Did you look at the surveillance tapes from the dance club?"

"We saw them. We did see Danny. Peterson checked his alibi."

"That's not in the report," I said.

"Because he's Patrick Allison's grandson. Peterson didn't want to involve him in a media frenzy."

I picked up the bracelet and showed her the engraving. "Danny bought this and had it engraved with Marissa's initials. It's gold and worth four grand. That and the fight the night she was killed should give you probable cause to get a warrant for his DNA."

"We already cleared the case. My advice is to drop it, or Peterson will come after your license. The DA's a close personal friend of Patrick Allison. There's no way he's gonna reopen the case to press charges against Danny."

"I can't drop the case."

We stared at each other over her desk. I knew her hands were tied with bureaucratic red tape. It was the reason I hadn't followed my dad into law enforcement. He'd complained to grandpa every night at dinner after he was elected sheriff about the list of regulations that interfered with keeping bad guys off the streets even in rural Gillespie County.

She took a sip of coffee. "I've got a half dozen other cases waiting for my attention. A gangbanger shot up a Walmart 'cause he didn't get last week's fifty-percent discount on a flat-screen TV. Three murders last weekend were linked to a cartel turf war."

"Patrick Allison gets a pass because you can't handle the workload?" I understood her dilemma, but Marissa Luna deserved justice too, even if it was a busy crime week.

Her skin flushed and sparks flew from her brown eyes. "*Pinche gringo.* You think I'm giving you the runaround because I'm lazy?" She stood and pressed her fingertips down on the desk. Her knuckles turned white. This was a side of Detective Ochoa I'd never seen. She had backbone, strength, and plenty of fire. Sergeant Vera was right; she'd make a good detective.

I met her gaze. "Somebody took a shot at me and put my Labrador in the hospital. He left a warning note." I pulled out the note and tossed it on the desk in front of her. I'd saved it for last. "Sam's my Labrador. He was shot and left for dead."

She relaxed her arms and let out a long breath. "I'm sorry to hear that. You're sure this is connected to Sosa?" She studied the note through the plastic baggy I'd put it in.

"He used the same weapon."

"If you're yankin' my chain…" She didn't finish the sentence.

"It's unmistakable. There can't be two shooters on the loose in San Antonio using the same ghost-quiet suppressor." The glass doors opened at the far end of the room. Two detectives wearing dark suits entered. They held up playing card coffee cups in greeting.

"Like I said, I can't help you," she said loud enough for the two detectives to hear. Then she pulled a business card from her top drawer and wrote her cell phone number on the back. Both suits looked my way before sitting down at their desks. "This is my personal cell," she said in a low voice. "I'll do some digging."

I took the card and handed her one of mine. "I appreciate this. My opinion of the SAPD just went up a notch."

"We're not all assholes. In the meantime, do me a favor, keep your head down and stay off the grid. I don't wanna add your name to my list of murder victims."

CHAPTER THIRTY-SEVEN

I knew Detective Ochoa couldn't open a full-blown investigation on her own without bureaucratic approval, but I'd won over an ally in the department. Considering the odds stacked against me, I had to take what I could get. Back on the street, I took Commerce west toward Marcus's law office and speed dialed Sylvia. When she didn't pick up, I let it go to her voice mail. "Hey, babe," I said. "Call me when you get this." After last night's phone call, I knew she was still angry. But whatever impasse we'd reached in our relationship didn't matter. The threat was real. Sylvia's name was on the list. Her life was in danger.

I wondered what my dad was thinking before he served the warrant on the drug house in rural Gillespie County. He'd gotten a tip about a little girl being held inside the trailer, but he hadn't gone in right away. He'd waited for the judge to issue a warrant, which took twenty-four hours. He'd followed the rules as he always did. When he got to the trailer house, the little girl was already dead, and the occupants were waiting for him. The Texas Rangers' report said Dad's pistol was empty. He'd used two seven-round M1911 magazines and six blasts from his Mossberg pump shotgun. In the end, it wasn't enough, which was why I always carried an extra, large-capacity magazine and a backup .38 revolver on my ankle. The volatile chemicals the drug gang used to cook meth went up in smoke. Everything, including my dad, burned to a crisp. The official story was that the perps burned with their drugs, but there was a rumor that they staged the fire and had gotten away. Dad had gone in alone with his .45 pistol and a shotgun. Fearless. But he was dead and so was the little girl he tried to save. If I stormed the Allison ranch, I would end up the same way. Danny Allison was the key. If I could get him alone away from his security guards, I felt certain he would give me the truth.

At 9:30 a.m. I rolled into the parking lot of Marcus's law office building. Skeeter drove a pristine four-wheel-drive Dodge Ram pickup, which didn't stand out in Texas. The only two vehicles not pickups or SUVs in the parking lot were Sylvia's Toyota Camry and Marcus's Lexus LS 500.

I backed in beside Skeeter and handed over the bag of food.

"'bout time." He inhaled one of the tacos. "You bring my shotgun?"

For a guy who didn't like guns, I was glad he understood the danger of the situation. "I think you're gonna like it."

I waited for a woman in a red skirt and high heels to walked to her Silverado and drive away, then I handed Skeeter a Remington 870 Express shotgun. It had a short barrel and a pistol grip, the kind of weapon you didn't want pointed at you.

Skeeter smiled. "This is more my style."

He pulled it in through the window and admired its sleek design. The weapon was a toy in his huge hands. He tested the trigger guard to see if it was big enough for his finger. It fit, but there was no room to spare. I handed him a box of double-aught buckshot. He looked at them both, then back at me. Puzzled. He didn't know how to load it.

"Think you can figure out how it works?"

"I'll Google it. Piece of cake," he said.

He handed me a GPS tracking device. "You wanna do the honors?"

"My pleasure."

The tracker was the size of my thumbnail and attached to the car with a magnet. I walked to Sylvia's Toyota, pretended to examine the back tire, and attached the GPS under the rear bumper. I didn't want to answer questions if Marcus's security team was watching the parking lot.

Skeeter smirked when I returned. "You shoulda been an actor."

"I saw that move in a movie once."

"They're having auditions at the Community Play House for *A Christmas Carol*. You'd make a good Scrooge."

I looked at him to see if he was serious. "Thanks," I said. "I've got plans for Christmas."

"I do lights and sound for the productions. Been doin' it since high school."

I'd known Skeeter two years and never knew he was involved with community theater. I guess it never occurred to me to ask him.

"Call me if anything unusual happens," I said.

"Like what?"

"Like somebody takes a shot at you with a .308 rifle."

"How do I know if it's a .308?" He chuckled with his deep rumbling voice.

"Funny man. Just don't forget to duck."

Any thought of storming the Allison ranch with Skeeter went out the window. He wouldn't be any help in a firefight or know how to reload and cover my back in an ambush. Taking him could get him hurt or worse. I was going to have to come up with a plan that didn't involve a direct assault to get Danny away from the Allison ranch.

Skeeter chewed his bottom lip, the action he took when he wanted to clear the air.

"Spit it out," I said.

"You sure she needs protection?"

"What the hell are you talking about? You saw the note."

He shrugged his huge shoulders. "Maybe she knows more than she's lettin' on."

"You think Sylvia's involved?"

"When it comes to women, your thinking always gets fuzzy."

I felt my face flush, but he was right. Sylvia'd already breached my confidence. "She's still on the list. Right now, we need to focus on preservation. Are you in or out?"

He studied my face for a long moment. "I'm in."

"Then let's get to it."

"What's the plan?"

"Danny's the key. I need to get him off the ranch."

"How you gonna do that? You go out there again, you ain't comin' back."

"I'll reason with him," I said and smiled.

Skeeter smiled back. "You do that. That's what you're good at."

CHAPTER THIRTY-EIGHT

I found Lucky working with a lightweight southpaw in the downstairs center ring. Since the local schools were in session, the crowd at the gym was older, serious fighters putting in the work. No adolescent grab-assing or idle laughter.

"Come by to beat up more of my paying customers?" Lucky sounded pissed off, but he always did. After you got to know him, you realized that was just the way he talked. He'd learned English from watching American cartoons on TV in the sixties. I was counting on that voice to motivate Danny.

"I came to pay my monthly dues."

His smile showed off his missing teeth. Offering him money brought out his softer side.

"Get some cardio," Lucky said to his lightweight. "Let's go into my office."

His office was small and cluttered with boxing trophies and paraphernalia from fifty years of Lucky's career both inside and outside the ring. He had signed photos of all the greats, from Cesar Chavez to Tommy Hearns, along with his own championship belt. He also had a signed picture of Tony Ayala, a local fighter who was the last great contender from San Antonio who took a turn to the dark side and never quite reached his potential. Lucky said his lifestyle killed him, but he sure had a beautiful knockout punch.

"What's up, Nick?" he said, sounding suspicious.

"I came to pay my rent." I put two hundreds on his desk, the last of my tip from Sosa.

"The rent's twenty-five a month. Ten for veterans. That's two years in advance. You're already paid up till Christmas. So, what's this about, huh?"

I explained to him what was going on and filled him in on Danny Allison. I told him my plan to lure Danny off the ranch and into town. I also let him know that it could be dangerous. *If* Danny came, he would bring backup. Lucky smiled, showing his missing teeth. The other thing that made him smile was the prospect of a fight.

He picked up the money and handed it back to me. "Keep this. Buy me lunch sometime. I think a couple of old guys can handle a little trouble." He was talking about himself and Sarge, his partner. They'd both been tough guys, but both were pushing seventy. I wondered if I could count on them in a standoff between me and Allison's well-armed security.

Lucky took a clipboard off the bulletin board and consulted the list of neatly printed names. "Check this," he said. "Danny's on the schedule tomorrow for a tune-up fight with Sarge's light heavyweight division contender. I'll tell him the fight's moved up to today."

"You think he'll go for it?"

"He'll come. He's been talkin' trash for two weeks."

He made the call. I listened in on his side of the conversation. He was very convincing. If Lucky told me I needed to drop everything and come to the gym, I wouldn't hesitate.

Now there was nothing to do but wait. Lucky went back to training the lightweight, and I decided to slip in a workout to keep my mind from overthinking the possibilities. There were too many scenarios where Sylvia's prediction was right—I ended up dead or arrested.

Lucky let out a sharp whistle as I finished a third set on the speed bag. That was our pre-agreed signal that Danny had arrived. I grabbed my towel and duffel bag and headed for the upstairs locker room. Danny stood at the front entrance along with Ricky and Lonny, the crazy-eyed rifleman.

Lucky and Sarge stood side by side on the upstairs landing.

"They'll be armed. I need Danny alone for five minutes. Can you handle it?"

Lucky nodded. A slight smile crossed Sarge's lips, like I'd just given him a present for his birthday. If nothing else, the old-timers were willing.

I checked the stalls and the showers. The locker room was empty. When Danny walked in, I moved between him and the only exit. "Hi, Danny."

His neck turned red, and he checked the blocked exit. He wore his square-toed cowboy boots and jeans, topped with an untucked Lone Star Beer T-shirt and a camo cap sporting one of those dark-colored American flags.

"Hey, Nick," he said, bouncing from boot to boot with nervous energy. His eyes were glassy like he'd popped a few cold ones on his drive in from the ranch. I wondered if he was ever sober. "I guess there's no fight today. You put Lucky up to this?"

"Don't blame Lucky. I told him what's goin' on. We didn't get to finish our conversation at the ranch. We were interrupted by your security thugs."

"I'm sorry about what happened at the ranch. That was Marcus. I mean, those guys work for Mr. Lopez." He shifted his weight again and took off his cap. "He's the one who..."

He didn't finish, and I couldn't wait. I took two quick steps toward him. Pinned him in the corner. "Marissa Luna was murdered. You know who did it. Talk to me."

He squeezed his hands into fists and tensed his shoulders, trying to work up the nerve to take a swing.

"Relax your hands or I'll put you down. Did you kill her or was it your grandpa, Patrick? Who'd you hire to warn me off the case?"

"You got it wrong. You don't know what you're dealing with." Danny's face showed the pain and fear of an animal caught in a leg-hold trap.

"Why don't you fill me in?"

"He'll get to you. It doesn't matter what you do. He won't stop," Danny said.

"So, it was grandpa. I don't care about his money or connections. He's goin' down for Marissa's murder."

Danny hesitated. The wheels were turning.

I slapped him. Not hard, but enough to pop his head back. "Talk, goddamnit." I didn't wanna give him time to make up another story.

"It's Marcus Lopez."

“Don’t start this again.” I was getting tired of his BS.

“That’s the truth,” he insisted. “I—I tried to tell you.”

“Spit it out, now. We’ll go to the police.”

“Marcus owns the police.” The goofy grin fluttered across his face.

I couldn’t tell if he spoke the truth. Every time I questioned him, he had the grin and a different story.

“Ricky and Lonny work for Marcus. There’re two more outside. All the guards at the ranch work for him, except Juan. He’s been there since I was born. Marcus hired the others to keep an eye on the family. That’s why I couldn’t say anything.”

“What about Patrick? What about your grandfather?”

“He’s dying,” Danny said. “Stage-four cancer. He doesn’t have long.” Danny looked at his boots and chewed his bottom lip.

I didn’t know how much of his story I could swallow. There had to be something more to it. Someone had shot my dog and shot at me. There had to be one big piece of the puzzle that Danny wasn’t telling me.

“How’d Marcus get control of Allison Oil?”

Before he could answer, my cell phone rang. It was Skeeter. He whispered so fast and low I could barely hear him.

“Skeeter, I can’t hear you. Slow down. Speak up,” I said.

“Marcus is on the move. Sylvia’s with him.”

I put the cell phone on speaker and tossed it on the bench. “Talk to me, Skeeter. What’s happenin’?” I pulled my street clothes from my bag and stripped out of my gym shorts.

“Marcus and Sylvia got into her Toyota,” he whispered.

“Why are you whispering? They can’t hear you.” I slipped on my jeans and boots. Danny stood watching me and listening to Skeeter.

“They’re headed for the freeway,” he said, switching to his normal voice.

“Follow them. Monitor the GPS. Don’t get too close.”

“What’s going on?” Danny asked.

I checked my watch. It was twelve ten. “Marcus is with Sylvia.” I slammed Danny back against the metal lockers. “What’s he gonna do?”

Danny’s eyes went wide. I pushed my arm into his windpipe. He clutched at his throat. I let him choke for a moment, then backed off and let him breathe.

"I don't know," he gasped.

"Stay put till I take care of the guys outside. Then go back to the ranch and wait for me."

Danny nodded while he massaged his sore neck.

"What's going on?" Skeeter said. I'd forgotten he was still on speaker.

"Stay with Sylvia and Marcus. Keep me up to date." I disconnected the call and stuffed the phone in my back pocket.

Danny collapsed on the bench, head in his hands. "There's nothin' you can do. You can't fight Marcus Lopez."

"Maybe not, but I have to try."

"Why did this have to happen?" Danny moaned, as if he was somehow the victim.

I left him on the bench and walked out of the locker room to the upstairs landing, where the two extra guards had joined Ricky and Lonny. Lucky and Sarge hadn't moved an inch. The four guards were spread out four steps below them. Ricky had a pistol in a shoulder holster. It was me and two old-timers against four armed guards.

I stopped between Lucky and Sarge.

"Danny tells me you're looking for me," I said to Ricky.

"The boss wants to talk to you." His pistol gave him confidence.

"You mean Marcus Lopez? Is that your boss?"

Ricky didn't say anything. He didn't move.

I turned to Lucky. "Are these guys about the dumbest bunch of thugs you ever saw?"

Lucky showed off his missing teeth.

"What do you think, Sarge?"

Sarge didn't speak. He rarely did. Every fiber of his five-foot-ten, sixty-nine-year-old frame was twisted into a razor-sharp weapon of destruction aimed at the four guards. I was starting to feel better about the odds.

"They work for Marcus Lopez," I continued. "The lawyer running for governor."

Lucky hated lawyers as much as he did politicians. He hated Marcus Lopez in particular because he said Marcus was going to raise taxes for small business owners. Lucky was against higher taxes.

"You *could* walk out of here and tell your boss you couldn't find me," I said to Ricky.

He shook his head. "No can do, partner." All four guards balanced on the balls of their feet. They waited for Ricky to make the first move. "Nothing personal. Just business." He pointed at Lucky and Sarge. "If you come with us, we won't hurt the old farts."

Lucky and Sarge bristled when he said *old farts*.

"I'm glad you said that," I said.

My phone rang. I used the old-fashioned ringer. Ricky and his thugs flinched.

"Don't get itchy. I'm going for my phone." I slowly reached in my back pocket. The call was from Skeeter. I hit accept.

Skeeter said: "So far so good. He's on the interstate heading west. We're past Boerne."

"Okay," I said, not wanting to tip Ricky off that Skeeter was following his boss. "I'm almost done here. I'll catch up to you." I disconnected and put the phone back in my pocket.

"It's been real, Ricky, but I gotta go." I took a step down the stairs.

He reached forward. I drove my elbow into his throat, and he fell back against the railing.

Lonny and his partner were on my right just below Sarge. Lonny made his move. He never knew what hit him. Sarge brought his right foot up and kicked him in the left ear. Lonny tumbled down the steps. His partner launched himself at Sarge and caught a knee to the face and a right-hand chop to the back of the neck. If he woke up, he'd have a mean headache. The only one left standing reached for his pistol. Lucky hit him with a stiff right that broke his jaw. It was the same punch that won him the championship belt. The whole fight lasted less than ten seconds. Lucky and Sarge grinned, like it was the most fun they'd had in a decade.

"Thanks for your help," I said. "I've gotta run. Y'all are pretty handy for a couple of old farts." They both chuckled.

"What should we do with Danny?" Lucky asked.

"Let him go. I know where to find him when I need him."

I took the stairs two at a time. A half dozen guys lined up at the bottom of the steps nodded their approval when I jogged past them and out the front door. I started my pickup and tried to think of the fastest way out of town. My phone rang.

"He's getting off at Welfare," Skeeter said.

"What the hell? That's the road to Grandpa's ranch." I waited for him to confirm. The call went dead.

I checked my watch. Twelve thirty. I tried Grandpa's phone on the unlikely chance he was having lunch inside. I hung up on the fifth ring. No such luck.

I hit redial for Skeeter. Heard: *The number you have dialed is not available.*

Either his phone was dead, or Skeeter was in a world of hurt.

CHAPTER THIRTY-NINE

The rain that had recently turned the Alamo City green evaporated just past the western city limit. The Hill Country pastures were burnt to a crisp and the sandy creek beds bone dry. As Grandpa had predicted, area ranchers were already feeding hay shipped in from greener pastures in the Coastal Plains or from irrigated fields in the panhandle to the north. I took the Welfare exit and fell in behind one of those ranchers pulling a flatbed trailer stacked with giant round bales of green coastal Bermuda hay.

That stretch of road had two lanes and as many curves as a sidewinder rattlesnake. There was just enough Wednesday afternoon traffic to keep me from passing. I turned off the radio and the noisy air conditioning and opened the windows. The blast of warm, dry air helped calm my nerves and focus my attention on the task at hand. Honking wouldn't have done any good. There was no place for the rancher to pull over. Any other day, I'd accept the shift from high stress city life to the slower country pace as a welcome change. I'd grown up on a ranch and knew firsthand that rural living came with different priorities. Animals needed attention. They relied on ranchers for food, medicine, and safety. In exchange, they provided the rancher's livelihood. Trips to the grocery store were less frequent. Spare time was spent in preparation for the next season. Today, I didn't have time to waste. Marcus Lopez was going to take out the last three people on the warning list. The three people I cared about most in the world. Since Skeeter didn't answer his phone, that number may already be down to two.

I thought about the worst-case scenario—finding Skeeter's crushed body in a ditch under his four-wheel-drive pickup. I held my hand above the steering wheel, it was solid. This was as real as any combat mission, and Allison and Marcus Lopez had made it personal. First Sam and, if my fears were correct, now Skeeter.

I moved into the left lane looking for a place to pass just as a big red semi-trailer truck peeked around the curve ahead and forced me to duck back behind the hay hauler. Then my phone rang.

The caller ID said Sylvia. I hit the switch to raise the windows and touched accept.

"Where are you?" I answered cautiously, keeping one hand on the wheel and both eyes on the narrow gap between my Ford and the load of hay. I didn't know if she was free to talk.

"Hi, sweetheart. I just got your message. You're on speaker. You'll never guess where I am." Sylvia never called me sweetheart. I could hear the tension in her voice.

"You took off early and went shopping?" I tried to sound casual. I assumed Marcus was listening.

"No, silly. I came to see your grandpa. It's such a pretty day. I was thinking about him. I wanted to bring him lunch." She liked Grandpa but would never drive out there by herself in the middle of the day.

"That's wonderful, honey-bunny."

I'd only called her that once as a joke. She'd rewarded me with a sharp punch in the arm. She wasn't anybody's "honey-bunny." If she was free to talk, she'd instantly chew me out. The line was blank for several seconds. Another sign that Sylvia was under stress.

Finally, she said: "You're so sweet. Why don't you come out and join us? I picked up barbecue at Two Brothers." She knew I loved Two Brothers' brisket.

"That sounds great!" I tried to sound enthusiastic. "How's Grandpa?"

She hesitated again. I heard a muffled sound in the background. Her hand was over the phone speaker.

"Oh, he's good. He's anxious to see you. It will do you good to take a break," she said.

"Okay, I'll finish up in town and head out there. Give me two hours." I looked at my watch. It was two o'clock. "I'll be there at four," I lied. I would be there as fast as I could drive.

"We'll be waiting."

"Bye, sweetie-pie." I let her disconnect first. If "sweetie-pie" didn't get a response from her, I didn't need any other clues to her state of mind. Marcus was going after Grandpa and Sylvia at the same time. I'd hit him where it hurt, and now he was striking back hard.

I hit my horn twice to warn the rancher I was coming around him and floored the accelerator. The rancher's hand emerged from his open window and waved me on. The coast was clear. So much for the calm, laid-back rural pace. I was kicking it up a notch.

I'd driven this road at night, in a driving rain, when it was covered with snow, and when it was invisible in the fog. Today it was clear, and I pressed my old Ford to its limit, hugging the gravel shoulders on the turns and splitting the center line on the straightaway.

What was Marcus's plan? It was obviously a trap of some kind using Sylvia as bait. Was she in on it? I thought back to her encounter with Marcus at the convention center. Maybe Danny was right. Maybe she was his girl and not mine. The pattern fit. I was always the last to know when my relationships went south. I always made the mistake of projecting my grandma's integrity on any woman who agreed to a second date with me, and I'd been burned more than once. She'd also shared details of my investigation. That part still didn't sit well with me. I tried not to let that doubt cloud what I knew I had to do. The threatening note had included her name. Loyal to me or not, she was in danger.

I unrolled the windows, gulped warm, dry air, and glanced at my reflection in the side mirror. *Keep your nerve, pard. Improvise, adapt, and overcome.* I forced a smile. I wouldn't let Marcus Lopez or the Allisons win.

After twenty minutes of reckless, all-out driving, I braked for the turn onto Grandpa's road. There was no exit. Because the terrain was impassable to the south, the road simply stopped. Anyone on his road lived there or was lost and would have to make a U-turn.

I moved the seat back as far as it would go to hide my face behind the doorjamb and slowed to just under thirty miles an hour, the normal speed for local ranchers. As a kid, I remember asking Grandpa why he drove so slowly. His irritated response was, *If I wanted to get there sooner, I'd have left yesterday.*

Hang on, Grandpa. I'm coming for you.

I studied the familiar stone fence and the clearing beyond. The cedar-post gate was open. Marcus and Sylvia were here. No one else would leave the gate open. I slowed even more to look up the gravel road leading to the house. If Marcus had his security team, I didn't have much of a chance. I'd need a plan to even the odds. My only ace in the hole was surprise. He wasn't expecting me until four o'clock.

I made a U-turn at the dead end and cruised back by the gate. Still no movement. A half mile beyond the front gate, the friendly llama stared back at me from the neighbor's petting zoo sign. There was hay scattered in the field, but no humans around. I kept going to the gas station on State Highway 290 a few miles outside of Fredericksburg. Something waited for me at Grandpa's ranch, and I had the feeling it wasn't the friendly barbecue lunch Sylvia had promised.

Skeeter was leaning against his pickup when I pulled into the parking lot. A wave of relief washed over me. Marcus hadn't gotten to him. I wasn't completely on my own. He was anxious and breathing hard, but it was good to see him alive and well. I stepped out and resisted the urge to give him a hug.

"Where the hell have you been?" I said, anger replacing relief.

He took a deep breath and raised both hands, absolving himself of any wrongdoing. "I backed off a couple of miles like you said. They turned at your grandpa's road. I didn't want to follow them into a dead end, so I kept going."

"What happened to your phone?"

He looked down at his hands. A sheepish grin came over his face. "It died."

"How does that happen?"

"I overloaded the data card on my—"

I cut him off. "You forgot to plug it in."

He nodded. "Yep."

I realized it wasn't his fault. "Shit's hitting the fan. Sylvia called. She sounded weird, like she was forced to talk. She said she took Grandpa lunch. Wanted me to meet her there."

"What's weird about that?"

"She's never done that before, and she didn't mention she was with Marcus." I told Skeeter what Danny said about Marcus being in charge.

He looked skeptical. "You believe Danny's telling the truth?"

"I believe he's scared shitless of Marcus Lopez. And if old man Allison's dying of cancer, it could explain how he was able to take over the family business."

"He could be the next governor." Skeeter's voice was hard and angry.

"That's not gonna happen."

"How you gonna stop him?"

"I'm workin' on it. First, we need to find Grandpa and Sylvia. We'll take your pickup." I grabbed my weapons, and we headed back to Grandpa's ranch. If this were a military operation, I would send in a drone to get eyes on the property or link with a satellite image. This was one of the few times I missed being in the Corps with access to high-tech gizmos and a lot of firepower and backup.

After ten minutes of silence, Skeeter said: "Now would be a good time to tell me the plan."

I stared out the window. Skeeter's eyes were on me, waiting for an answer. I turned to him and studied his size triple-X features. He had a death grip on the steering wheel, and his shirt was soaked through with nervous sweat. He didn't have the training or the skills for what we needed to do, but he was willing and the only help I had.

"The odds are stacked against us. Things will likely get messy."

"Meaning you about to go gunslinger."

"If I have to, I will. You want out, I'll understand."

His eyes stayed fixed on the road. "No. I'm with you on this. Your grandpa and Sylvia are in danger. Tell me what to do."

"Did you figure out how to load this thing?" I grabbed the shotgun off the back seat and checked the magazine. It was loaded.

"It has a seven-shot capacity. The receiver is milled from a solid billet of steel for maximum strength and reliability..." He was reciting from the manual. "...The silky-smooth twin action bars prevent binding, making it a very efficient weapon. This workhorse features—"

"Okay." I smiled. "You did your homework."

"I also watched a very informative YouTube video on combat tactics for civilians taught by a retired Navy SEAL."

I nodded, wondering how many other wannabe badasses watched that shit and got themselves killed. "Just remember to pull the trigger," I told him. "Now, let's go get Sylvia and Grandpa."

CHAPTER FORTY

Skeeter let me out in front of the petting zoo. I cleared the fence, passed the llama sign, and jogged into the pasture. The new neighbor had cleared twenty acres of cedar trees along the fence and left huge piles of brush every twenty or thirty yards. When I lived with Grandpa, the cedar thicket was home to a flock of wild turkey, a herd of white-tailed deer, and a dozen feral hogs. The new residents were llamas, donkeys, and miniature horses, all quizzically watching me run through their pasture and hoping for a handout. I kept moving.

Undisturbed cedar and live oak brush lined grandpa's side of the fence and blocked my view of his ranch house. I checked my watch. Three o'clock. Sylvia's call had come at two. I was still an hour ahead of schedule. If Marcus believed me about being in town, I still had the element of surprise.

The barbed wire fence that marked the property line was older than I was, but the wire was still guitar string tight. Too stiff to crawl through. I grabbed one of the cedar posts and gingerly climbed the wires. A stick snapped when I landed on the opposite side. The house was still fifty yards away, but I wasn't taking any chances on being seen or heard. I stopped dead still to listen. The afternoon air was stagnant. The only sound was a distant engine noise that I hoped was Skeeter. After five minutes, I inched forward. Thirty yards closer to the house, the brush thinned out, and I finished the approach on my hands and knees. Grandpa kept the family's long-standing tradition of clearing the brush around all the ranch structures. He was worried about fires, but in the old days, the biggest threat was Comanche raiding parties. The clearing helped keep both at bay. Neither one could get near the house without being seen.

I dropped to my belly and crept closer. Nothing moved in the house or in the barn. Sylvia's Toyota was the only vehicle in sight. If someone was watching from the windows, I would be an easy target. It was time to put the Skeeter diversion in motion.

I put my phone on silent and texted the word *go*. Skeeter sent a thumbs-up emoticon before my fingers were off the screen. He was anxious.

Moments later I heard the front gate rattle. Skeeter was putting all his three hundred pounds into shaking it back and forth, making sure that anyone paying attention would notice a vehicle at the gate. I'd told him to shut the gate after he drove through in case someone tried to make a quick escape. So far, he was following my instructions to the letter and maybe overdoing it just a little. I heard his pickup engine rev and tires crunching over gravel.

I studied the house and the barn. Still no movement. I caught sight of Skeeter's pickup when it came around the oak mott near the spring-fed pond. He was driving slowly. Barely above an idle. He wasn't in any hurry to reach the house. Grandpa should have appeared at the front door. I'd told him to keep it slow and easy to give whoever was in the house a chance to focus their attention on the visitor. If Grandpa was okay, he would step out onto the porch to signal his presence, a long-standing tradition practiced by remote ranchers. He didn't appear.

Skeeter parked in front of the barn. I kept my eyes on his face as he scanned the buildings. Nothing registered. He looked down at his hands. A message appeared on my cell phone. "Nobody home."

I saw movement in the hayloft and drew my pistol.

I texted back: "Don't move," but Skeeter was already out the door.

His hands were empty. He'd left the Remington 870 in the cab.

A rifle appeared in the second-story hayloft. Flame shot from the barrel, followed by a compressed air blast and a sickening thud. I returned fire, but it was too late.

Skeeter hit the ground. I was close enough to see blood on his shirt. He never saw it coming. Memorizing the specs on the shotgun hadn't done him any good. Reading about weapons and watching commando gunfights on YouTube didn't improve your odds. Experience was the best teacher. Skeeter didn't have it. I'd put him in danger and let him down when I couldn't protect him.

The vision of my Marine platoon brothers flashed through my head. I swallowed that guilty, helpless feeling and forced myself to focus on the barn and the danger inside. I had to keep moving. My mission now was to save Sylvia and Grandpa before they met Skeeter's fate.

The rifle barrel poked from the hayloft again, pointing down at Skeeter.

This time, I fired first. My bullet hit the wooden window frame, and I dove forward, running flat out for the edge of the house. An air blast from a bullet zipped past my head. I recognized the sound. It was the same shooter. The same Hollywood-quiet puff of air.

I flattened out against the worn limestone blocks, then slid around the corner of the house. I had a better angle on the barn and could see a quarter of the loft opening. The rifle barrel reappeared. I squeezed off two more shots. The barrel dropped from sight. If the shooter stayed in the loft, I might be able to get inside through the back door without notice.

Before I reached the rear of the house, Skeeter moved. He was alive. His eyes fluttered open, and his chest swelled. That explained why the shooter had risked exposing himself for another shot. It also meant I needed to move fast. From the amount of blood on his shirt, he wouldn't last long. I put two more rounds through the hayloft, then peered through the window inside the house. The kitchen was clear. The back porch was empty. I looked through the French doors to the living room. Empty. I peered through the window at the back bedroom where Grandpa slept. The bed was made. No sign of him or Sylvia anywhere.

I swapped out my half-empty magazine for a full one and sprinted for the back door of the barn. The ancient door opened without a sound. Grandpa hated rusty hinges. No shots. No movement. It smelled of dust and horse manure mixed with the metallic odor of blood. Had one of my shots connected? I hoped it had, and I hoped it was fatal.

The sun was already behind the western hills, creating deep shadows in the corners of the barn. I squatted on my heels to give my eyes a chance to adjust. Grandpa's John Deere tractor took shape. It still had the hay baler attached and a front-end loader. The workbench was scattered with tools. Something was wrong. Grandpa never left anything out of place. Whose blood did I smell?

I studied what I could see of the steps leading to the loft. This time of year, the loft was full of hay in preparation for winter. He had another barn near the airplane hangar on the hayfield, but he always filled this one first and used it for the horses. The itchy, backbreaking work to get the bales into the loft was my job until I joined the Marine Corps.

A faint popping noise came from the center support beam. I inched closer, keeping an eye on the loft, my pistol extended in front of me. The outline of a man took shape. Arms and shoulders protruding from behind the center post. There was no mistaking that khaki work shirt. It was Grandpa.

I didn't move or make a sound. The man with the rifle was waiting for me to step into the open. I'd put six rounds through the hayloft, but I doubted very much that any of the bullets had hit their mark. I opened my mouth to breathe silently, waiting a full minute.

I took another step toward the hayloft.

The metallic smell of blood got stronger. Maybe I'd hit him, and the shooter was bleeding out. Or maybe the blood was Grandpa's. I extended to my full height, trying to see into the loft opening. Nothing but hay. I took two more steps up.

"Nick Fischer," a familiar voice said.

I froze, then started to turn.

"Drop the pistol first," the voice insisted.

I placed the Springfield on the wooden step, hoping for a chance to dive for it later.

"Clever. Now, kick it off the step," the voice demanded.

He didn't go for it. I nudged my pistol off the step and heard it hit the wooden floor.

"Now, face me," he said.

I slowly turned around. Detective Peterson stood by the workbench, wearing Grandpa's khaki shirt. His tomahawk features were red from exertion, and a fresh cut marked his sharp cheekbone. He held a .308 M24 rifle pointed at my chest. Another piece of the puzzle fell into place. That sniper rifle was standard issue for the SAPD SWAT team, Peterson's former job.

"Where's my grandpa, Detective?"

"That old man's a tough nut. I'll give him that." Peterson wasn't smiling. He kept the rifle aimed at my belt buckle. I warned you, but you just wouldn't let it go."

"Where is he?"

"Pull up your pants leg. Show me the .38," he said.

I'd hoped he wouldn't remember my backup weapon. "Grandpa give you that cut?" I asked.

"Lucky punch," he said.

I showed him the hammerless .38. "So, you're on Marcus Lopez's payroll?"

He ignored the question. "Take your left hand and pull off the holster."

I did what he asked.

"Now, toss it to me."

The odds of palming the .38 and getting off a shot were a hundred to one in his favor. At this range he wouldn't miss. Peterson's finger was tight against the trigger. He wasn't taking any chances. I decided to wait for a better opportunity and tossed the .38 at his feet. He kicked it toward the back door. A fly buzzed above my head. I smelled hay mixed with blood and felt a trickle of sweat leak down my spine and into my Wranglers. My senses were on high alert.

"You're pretty good. Never saw that coming," I said, thinking of some way to buy time. "How'd you get that sound reduction?" Maybe he would drop his guard if he talked shop.

"Subsonic ammo," he said, exposing small sharp teeth. "The bullet travels slower. Don't break the sound barrier. I'm surprised an ex-Marine couldn't figure that out." He was in control and savoring every moment of it.

"That explains it." I tried my best to make calm chitchat while thinking about Skeeter wounded and clinging to life. Peterson was the same man who put a bullet in Sam's head. I couldn't let him get away with it.

"You got the drop on me fair and square. Where's your partner, Ochoa? She in on this?"

"Nah, she's too high-strung."

"You mean she wouldn't sell out."

He smirked. "Give her a few years on the job." He took a step closer.

"How'd you do it? Did you fake the investigation? How'd you get the ME to rule an accidental death for Marissa Luna?"

Peterson's nostrils flared, and his smile vanished. "Why do you give a shit, Fischer? One less knocked-up spic for the government to take care of. Probably saved the taxpayers a couple hundred thousand."

"Actually, she was the first in her family to go to college. You wasted a future taxpayer."

"Big fucking deal."

"It was to her mother."

"You *are* a bleeding heart. You'd have never made it as a real detective. You'd have ended up like your daddy, burnt up in a meth trailer."

"What the hell do you know about that?" I fought the urge to lunge for him. The comment caught me off guard.

"Everyone knows he waited for a warrant. He should've kicked in the door and opened fire."

"He was trying to save a little girl." I held myself in check.

"Like I said, you're a bleeding heart. He let the perps get away."

"You don't know that. Nobody knows what happened. Everything was incinerated."

"It was an ambush. The little girl was bait. You and your daddy are suckers for sweet little girls."

"What the fuck is that supposed to mean?" It was getting harder to hold my emotions in check.

"Think about it," he sneered.

I knew he was talking about Sylvia. I wondered if she knew she was bait. Or if I was the one being used all along. I didn't like either prospect. I had to stay focused and think.

Peterson looked at his watch. He was on a deadline. Was Marcus waiting for him? He lifted the rifle to his shoulder. I needed to think of a distraction fast or I would never know.

"There was another cartridge at the scene. I gave it to Ochoa yesterday."

"You're lying."

"Call her and ask her. She'll match it to your weapon. You know she thinks you're an asshole." He was thinking about it. That was all I'd hoped for. "Marcus Lopez will throw you under the bus. He'll be governor, and you'll be doing life in Huntsville. How long do ya think you'll last even in isolation?"

"Shut the hell up," he yelled.

"Did Danny kill Marissa, then call Marcus? Is that how it worked? Marcus called you to cover it up. Did he use that to get control of Allison Oil, he was blackmailing Patrick Allison?"

"You're not as dumb as you look," he said. "But you're too late."

"How much did he pay you? What was your soul worth?"

"Fuck you. I stopped caring about the job when they kicked me off SWAT for taking down bad guys. There's no right or wrong anymore. It's all about the money. This is just a business deal." He lifted the rifle to his shoulder. "So long, Fischer."

Peterson put his eye to the scope lens. That was the chance I'd been waiting for. It would take a second for his pupils to adjust to the light and the short distance. He'd been shooting out the hayloft into daylight from fifty yards away. Inside the barn, he would see nothing but a blur through the scope.

He hesitated. His eyes blinked. Now or never.

I dove for his knees. The suppressed .308 bullet whooshed over my head.

Peterson hit the ground. The M24 rifle clattered to the hard plank floor.

He grabbed my neck and squeezed.

I forced my hands inside his arms and broke his hold, then went for his throat. Both my hands closed around his windpipe. I brought my weight down on his chest.

"Where's Grandpa and Sylvia?"

He didn't respond. I squeezed harder. His face turned red. A minute passed. His lips turned blue.

"Talk," I ordered.

I eased my grip and let him have a lungful of air. He gasped for breath.

"At the airstrip," he whispered through his crushed throat.

I popped his head once against the wooden planks. His eyes rolled back in his head, but he was still breathing. I stripped Grandpa's shirt off him. It was the last thing I wanted him to wear on his way to jail.

That's when I noticed the blood and a hole ripped through the left breast pocket of the khaki shirt. The blood was dry and at least four hours old. Long before Marcus and Sylvia had arrived. I didn't like what that meant.

I searched the bottom floor of the barn and followed the sickening metallic smell to the last horse stall. Grandpa was leaning against the limestone wall wearing a white T-shirt covered in blood. His head was slumped forward. There was a raw hole in his chest. His hands rested in his lap. Both knuckles were scraped. Otto Fischer didn't go down without a fight.

My legs went limp, and I sank to my knees in front of him. All the air left my lungs as if sucked out by a vacuum. A lump swelled inside my chest, and a wave of emotion struck me like a tidal wave on South Padre Island.

Grandpa's skin was pale, and the creases around his eyes and mouth looked carved in stone. I crawled forward and pulled his body away from the wall. He was already stiff and surprisingly light. My vision blurred as I touched his face. This was not happening. It could not happen. I refused to believe what I was seeing.

"Grandpa?" I tried to form more words but couldn't. He had been my father and my grandfather for many years. He was my family. My only family. This man had been the rock on which I built and rebuilt my life more than once. When my father was murdered, he was there. When I returned from overseas, he gave me the courage to continue living.

"I'm sorry," was all I could mumble. I'd let him down. I lifted his lifeless body in my arms but lacked the strength to stand. I needed his advice now more than ever, and he could no longer give it.

I'd never told him how much he meant to me. How much he'd helped me. How much I needed him. I sucked in a breath of air and let out a scream that filled the empty space. It felt like hours, but I knew it was only moments later that I heard his voice from beyond death speak to me. *Get up, Nick*, the voice said. The sound was raspy, blunt, and direct, as it'd always been.

I wiped my tears with my shirt sleeve and focused on Grandpa's face. His voice was so strong and so real that I expected his lips to move. *Focus on the living*. He spoke again. His face was a stone mask. Even after his death, he was giving me the advice I needed to hear.

"How?" I managed to say. Then I heard a moan from outside the barn.

"Nick." The voice was deep and raspy. It was Skeeter. He was still alive. *Focus on the living*, he'd said. Skeeter was wounded, and Sylvia was still out there. Both, I hoped, were still alive. I stood and covered Grandpa with his favorite khaki shirt. In that moment, my pool of sorrow boiled into rage.

I heard another sound outside the stall.

This time it was Peterson.

I found him on his knees holding my Springfield pistol. A rush of adrenaline fueled my charge. When he saw me coming, he fired. The bullet hit the floor. Had it hit me, it wouldn't have slowed me down. I tackled him with a full-force body slam. The pistol flew out of his hand, and I landed on his chest.

He went for my throat. I grabbed his first.

"Why? Why'd you kill him?" I yelled.

"You killed him when you took him to the oil rig and involved him in our business."

I worked my knee up and pressed it down on his chest. I heard a rib snap. Peterson groaned and dug his bootheels into the wooden floor. This man shot my dog and my partner. He murdered my grandpa and showed no remorse. If I let him go, he would try to kill me again. If I took him in, he might get life in prison, but with Marcus Lopez and Patrick Allison's support, he might walk free. The justice system wasn't the same for men with money like Allison or influence like Marcus Lopez.

I slammed his head against the wooden planks. His face turned blue. I slammed it again. And again. I felt his bones break and his warm blood on my hands. Finally, his eyes closed. When I let go, he didn't move. Maybe I was a vigilante, and maybe I would regret it later, but right now I knew this man deserved to die for what he'd done. This was justice.

I slowly got to my feet and rested my hands on my knees, waiting to catch my breath. Peterson's cell phone chimed. I dug it out of his pocket. The caller ID showed Marcus Lopez.

"This is Nick Fischer, you son of a bitch." There was a long pause.

"Nick?" he asked, trying to cover his surprise.

"Where's Sylvia?"

"Put Detective Peterson on the phone," he demanded.

"Your man's dead, and I'm comin' for you."

"You killed a San Antonio police detective."

"He shot Skeeter and killed my grandfather. He tried to kill me."

"He was protecting me."

"From what?"

"Misguided vigilantes."

"No one will believe that. Let Sylvia go, and I won't kill you."

"SAPD will take you down when I tell them what you did." His voice was cold and calculating. "They have no reason to doubt me. I'm the future governor."

I understood Danny's fear of him. He had no limits. He didn't see himself as governor. He saw himself as king.

"Where's Sylvia?" I shouted.

"Nick, when are you going to wake up and accept how the world works? People like you can't win. You could never beat me."

"You think I'm gonna stand by and let you kill more innocent people?"

"You caused their death. You meddled in things you don't understand."

"I won't back down."

He laughed and disconnected.

CHAPTER FORTY-ONE

I staggered out of the barn, found Skeeter sprawled on the ground beside his pickup. Blood soaked the white caliche around him.

"Is he dead?" he croaked in a hoarse whisper.

"Yeah. He's dead. It was Peterson." I rolled him over onto his side.

He grimaced in pain. "Detective Peterson?"

"The one and only."

"Your grandpa?"

I shook my head, unable to say the words. My face was red hot, my scars were throbbing, and my cheeks were wet.

"I'm sorry, Nick. Damnit, I'm sorry. I should've followed them in here."

"It wasn't your fault. He was dead before Marcus and Sylvia arrived."

"Why him? He was innocent."

"He said it was just business. He was on Marcus's payroll."

"Evil son of a bitch. Where's Sylvia?"

"The hangar in the upper field with Marcus."

"Wait for the cops. He can't get away with this now."

"He owns the law. I talked to him on Peterson's cell phone. He's gonna tell SAPD I killed a cop who was protecting him."

Skeeter knew what that meant better than I did. Misguided and over-enthusiastic police work almost ended his life. They would come with their weapons up, shoot first and ask questions later.

"What're you gonna do?"

"What'd you think?"

"I wanna help."

"You did help. I'm grateful. Now, you need a doctor."

"I can't just sit here and do nothin'. Hand me the shotgun. At least I can block the gate till you take care of business." He winced in pain. He was close to blacking out. "Go. Find Sylvia. Stop Marcus."

I ripped open his shirt. The bullet had passed through his shoulder. He'd lost a lot of blood. The exit wound on his back looked clean and below the bone. It didn't mean he would live, but he had a better chance than I'd given him when he went down. He could move, and he was conscious. It took a lot to kill a man his size.

"Go," he insisted. "I'll manage."

"We have to stop the bleeding." I found a roll of paper towels in his pickup and pressed it against the wound. The sun was down, and the temperature was dropping quickly in the dry air. There was no way I was going to carry him inside. I found an old tarp in the barn and a gallon jug of water. I gave him a drink and pulled the cover over him.

"Go now. I'll manage," he said.

I dialed 911. A female dispatcher from Fredericksburg picked up, and I explained the situation. I told her Skeeter had a puncture wound from falling off a hay baler.

Skeeter didn't know what a hay baler was, and he wasn't likely to ever find out. But I wanted to hold off the sheriff's response as long as possible. I explained that I couldn't move him because he weighed three hundred pounds. She said the county rescue helicopter was two hours away taking a burn victim to San Antonio. She would have to send an ambulance.

It was less than fifteen miles, but the narrow road at night would take thirty minutes or more when they didn't know where they were going. She wanted me to stay on the line to guide them to the ranch, but I had things to do and disconnected.

"The ambulance is coming. Anybody else shows up, start shootin'." I grabbed the short-barrel shotgun off his seat and handed it to him. "We don't know how many SAPD officers are on his payroll."

"With pleasure."

"If I don't nail Marcus, he'll come after you. You were on the list. You know everything I do. He won't let it go."

"I'll be ready this time." He'd learned his lesson the hard way.

I kneeled beside him and put a hand on his shoulder. "Stay alive, my friend."

Pain marred his smile. I hated to leave him, but Sylvia was out there and so was Marcus. I secured Peterson's M24 rifle around my shoulder and took off running. It would be full dark in twenty minutes. The sky had turned from pale pink to fire orange. Deep shadows formed under the willows and scrub brush. I made it to the creek crossing and plunged into the ankle-deep water, slipping and sliding on the moss-covered rocks to the opposite bank.

When I topped the ridge, I could see the light in Grandpa's hangar. All my life that light meant that Grandpa was there working on his airplane. The light had always been a comfort. At night, I could see it from almost anywhere on the property. If I was out late hunting or working on the back fence, that light was always there. More than one night on patrol in Afghanistan, I'd see a light in the distance and imagine it was Grandpa's hangar light guiding me home. That night it was guiding me to the bastard responsible for his death.

I crept within fifty yards of the hangar, then slipped into the hayfield stubble. Muffled voices came from inside the building. I lay flat between the rows and used the night-vision scope to scan the Quonset hut.

Marcus and Sylvia were inside the office, clearly visible through the window. She was sitting at the small table that Grandpa used as a desk. Marcus was standing by the window, searching the sky. The rest of the space looked empty. No Heights Security. No backup. This was my chance. A thin glass pane and a metal window screen were all that stood between us. The fifty-yard shot would be easy. I checked the round in the chamber and put my finger on the trigger. With Peterson's subsonic ammo, Marcus would never hear it coming.

I flipped the safety off and pulled the slack out of the trigger. The crosshairs were steady on his pompous, evil face. The would-be king of

Texas was about to take a bullet to the head. It was the emotional response, but it was justice.

Suddenly, Sylvia got up and stood behind him. I eased the pressure off the trigger. One shot now could kill them both. I didn't know what part she played in the larger picture, but she didn't deserve to die. I owed her that much.

Something caught their attention in the night sky. I heard what it was before I saw it. The *thump*, *thump*, *thump* of helicopter rotors. A blast of sirens followed. I hoped it was the ambulance arriving for Skeeter. Then I realized there were too many of them. The surging wail sounded like every law enforcement vehicle within the county was on its way to Grandpa's ranch.

I kept the scope on the window. Sylvia put her hand on Marcus's shoulder. She wasn't tied to the chair. She wasn't handcuffed. She was free to move around. I zoomed the powerful scope in on her face. She didn't look scared. She looked relieved. Marcus put his arm around her. She buried her face in his chest.

I adjusted the scope to make sure I was getting a clear picture. Marcus didn't hold a gun or a knife—nothing was forcing Sylvia to act. I'd risked my life to rescue her. Skeeter was lying on the driveway with a bullet hole in his chest, and Grandpa was dead, yet there she was, clear as day in the night-vision scope, clinging to his side. One shot would end the string of lies that led to this point. The truth was written on their contented faces.

I let my breath out slowly and tightened my finger on the trigger. They were a breath away from death. Then I heard Grandpa's voice again. *That's not justice.* I blinked and eased the pressure off the trigger. The voice was so real that I felt his presence.

"That's him. He's responsible," I hissed. Either I was going crazy, or Grandpa really was reaching out to me from beyond the curtain of death. I listened for more but heard only the howling sirens and the thump of the fast-approaching helicopter. I wanted to pull the trigger in the worst way, but Grandpa was right. Killing them would make me just like Marcus Lopez. I wasn't a vigilante. True, I'd killed Peterson, but he'd fired first. Had I let go, he would have found a way to finish me off. Marcus needed to have his day in court so everyone could see who and what he was. He was responsible for Marissa Luna's death, my grandpa, Sosa, and who knew how many more. He had done it all so he could play out his dream of sitting on the governor's thrown in Austin. I couldn't take the shot. I'd have to stay alive long enough to make him face charges. He said I couldn't win, but I had to try.

The chopper burst over the hayfield. Running lights cleared the trees. Two spotlights crisscrossed the hayfield and quickly settled on me.

An electronic microphone buzzed to life over the thumping chopper blades.

A voice shouted: "SAPD. Drop your weapon!"

If I was gonna survive, I would have to run.

I carefully got to my feet, keeping my hands open and raised, not giving them an excuse to kill me. The rifle hung from the sling on my shoulder. Three silhouettes watched from the chopper: the pilot, the man with the bullhorn, and a sniper hanging halfway out the open side door. His rifle was trained on me.

"Drop the weapon," Bullhorn shouted.

I didn't move. I felt the crosshairs on the top of my head. The downward thrust of the chopper blades kicked dust and hay stubble into a cloud and filled my eyes and mouth with grit.

Another few seconds and the dust cloud would reach the chopper and obscure me from view. The sniper would shout at the pilot to pull up. A hovering helicopter was one of the most difficult places for a shooter to hit anything, especially one as small as the top of my head at night. The odds were in my favor.

When the cloud of dust and debris engulfed the chopper, I took off like Seabiscuit at the Santa Anita Handicap. A rifle shot exploded over the chopper noise and I tensed for the sudden burning punch from a bullet, but nothing came. I kept running.

The spotlight from the chopper waved across my path. I zigzagged each time the light hit me. Several more shots kicked up puffs of dirt near my feet, but I made it to the edge of the field and plunged into the thick cedar brush. I knew what it looked like from above. I'd seen it many times from Grandpa's plane. At noon on a sunny day, brush obscured the ground.

I ran to the edge of the limestone cliff that surrounded three-quarters of the hayfield. The narrow notch I'd climbed down so many times as a kid, ironically pretending I was escaping bandits or Indians, was right where it should be. Halfway down the steep incline, my boot slipped and sent gravel raining down the fifty-foot cliff. It was narrower than I remembered, or I was bigger. I caught my balance and climbed the rest of the way with my side firmly pressed against the rough limestone.

It was only a matter of time before they found my trail. They knew I was armed. Marcus would tell them I was dangerous. SAPD would remember Peterson as a fine upstanding member of the fraternity now that he was dead, instead of the corrupt asshole he really was. The SAPD chief would call Detective Ochoa and give her the bad news. She would vow to bring me in. Everyone in law enforcement would want a piece of me. Exactly what Marcus had planned. He had set a trap, used Sylvia for bait, and I'd walked right into it. If I died, that would be the end of it. I had to stay alive long enough to reveal what Marcus Lopez had really done.

The path at the base of the limestone cliff was a horse and game trail older than the ranch itself, and the only connection between the Fischer ranch and our nearest neighbor, Mr. Hoeffner. Deer and wild hogs had been the only recent users. Brush hung low over the path, forcing me to run with my hand outstretched to block the limbs from slashing my face.

The thump of the chopper was getting louder. They must have found my tracks at the edge of the brush or were methodically making a grid search of the ranch property. The law enforcement lights formed a pulsing red-and-blue dome in the night sky. I hoped the ambulance had gotten there first and taken Skeeter to the Fredericksburg hospital, and that I could get to him before Marcus's thugs did.

Suddenly, I thought of Kelly. Marcus would know I'd used her lab to match the DNA. I checked the bars on my cell phone. Zero. There was nothing I could do now but run.

CHAPTER FORTY-TWO

I reached Grandpa's boundary fence after twenty minutes of pounding the dark overgrown trail. Blood dripped from the scratches on my hands and face. The thump of the helicopter faded in and out as the SAPD crew crisscrossed the property. The fence was built with six-foot-high hog wire stapled to cedar posts. The plank gate was just wide enough to accommodate a horse and rider. I unhooked the wire latch and kept going. From there to the Hoeffner ranch house was another three miles, but it was downhill. I focused on putting one foot in front of the other and avoiding the overgrowth and loose rocks. Eventually, there would be ground pursuit, and I didn't want to be sprawled on the rocks with a broken ankle when they found my trail.

I skirted a spring-fed pond and followed the creek to within a hundred yards of the Hoeffner's barn. There were no lights. The place was deserted. So far, they hadn't started searching neighboring ranches. I stopped in the deep shadow of a massive oak tree and looked at the glow of my digital watch. Ten thirty p.m. I'd been running for an hour and forty-five minutes. When I caught my breath, I scanned the area with Peterson's night-vision scope. I didn't expect to find anyone. Senior had been dead for six years, and his son Billy lived in Houston. The ranch manager who took care of the livestock lived in Fredericksburg.

I shouldered the M24 and jogged to the barn. Hoeffner Sr. always kept a surplus WWII Jeep for running around the ranch. I hoped it was still there. The barn key was where it had always been, stuck in a crack in the limestone block over the door.

Inside, the Jeep seemed to be waiting for my arrival. Billy and I'd pushed, pulled, and dragged that vehicle over every road in the county before either of us had a license to drive. I prayed it would make one more trip to town. The key was in the ignition. Senior had a habit of getting drunk and losing the key, so he finally welded it in place. I hoisted myself into the driver's seat and cranked the engine. Nothing happened.

My stomach fluttered. My legs were already dead from the all-out run over rough terrain. The next ranch house was another four miles south. I could make it, but the new owners may not be there and there was no guarantee I'd find a vehicle. Skeeter would be easy pickings at the hospital. If Marcus's thugs got to Fredericksburg before I did, he'd never wake up.

I risked turning on the barn lights, then I pulled back the side-opening hood on the old Army Jeep. The battery was gone. I searched the workbench and found it plugged into a charger. I hoped that was the only problem. Vehicles left unattended for any length of time in the Hill Country were havens for mice and squirrels that loved to chew on electrical wires.

I attached the battery, turned the key, and held my breath. The seventy-five-year-old vehicle cranked to life, ready for battle. I cut the lights, closed the barn door, and put the key back in the crack. So far, it seemed, Saint Jude or Our Lady of Guadalupe was looking after me.

The wind from the open Jeep top hit me with a welcome blast of air that dried my sweat-soaked T-shirt and the blood on my face and arms. I pressed the gas pedal to the floor, then checked the fuel gauge. Empty. The guage'd been broken since I was in high school, chewed to shreds by a family of field mice. I hoped nobody had gotten it fixed.

As soon as I had cell phone reception, I called Kelly. Her phone went directly to voicemail. I explained as briefly as I could that Marcus Lopez was behind Marissa's killing and that she was in danger. I also told her I had killed an SAPD officer who was on Lopez's payroll. If she was at work, she would hear my name on an all-points bulletin before she got this message. I only hoped she trusted me enough to believe I wouldn't kill a police officer without a damn good reason.

In seven miles, the road from Hoeffner's place met State Highway 87, a major two-lane artery into Fredericksburg. I slowed and cut the lights. An old Jeep might not arouse much attention in this part of the country, but the missing top didn't give me much room to hide, and the inspection sticker had been out of date for twenty years. Luckily the road was clear, and I coasted through the intersection. So far, I still had fuel.

At five past midnight, I parked on the hill above the emergency room. A police cruiser making the rounds circled the building. I ducked under the dashboard and hoped he wasn't looking for an old Jeep. The headlights turned left and went out of sight. It was the usual quiet night in Fredericksburg. Weekends and Oktoberfest were the only times the town really drew a crowd.

The hospital grounds and parking lot were well lit. Two young women smoked cigarettes and leaned against a blue minivan. From the butts on the ground, they'd been there awhile. Probably waiting on a friend or relative inside. I knew how they felt. Grandpa and I'd spent several weeks in this same parking lot while Grandma slowly wasted away.

Near the entrance, I met an older man in a silver cowboy hat. We nodded at each other, and he glanced at my filthy, torn clothes without comment. I recognized him instantly as one of Grandpa's Texas-German rancher pals. It had been at least five years since I'd seen him, and he seemed too wrapped up in his own thoughts to recognize me.

"Trouble?" he asked. His raspy voice colored with a Texas-German accent reminded me of Grandpa.

"Accident," I said, not wanting to share too much. "Buddy fell off a hay baler."

His expression didn't change. "Dangerous work, bailing hay," he said. "Name's Helmut Geisler. My wife had a heart attack. The doctors try to get her stabilized." He still didn't recognize me.

"I'm Nick Fischer," I said, shaking the old man's bony hand.

"Otto's *Enkel*?" His face showed a spark of recognition.

He used the German word for grandson. I didn't tell him Otto was dead. I didn't have time to get into it, and he seemed to have trouble enough of his own. When I had Grandpa's funeral, I knew he would be there along with all the old-timers in the county. That would be my time to grieve, not now. Not tonight. I had to force myself to remain in combat mode until the mission was over. Grandpa was gone, and I needed to take down the man responsible.

I followed Helmut to the reception desk. The nurse on duty looked about nineteen, with ginger hair and a peaches-and-cream complexion under a sprinkling of orange freckles.

"Mr. Geisler, Dr. John just called," she whispered. "He's on his way. Stay as long as you want." Her cheeks flushed as she made a note on a clipboard.

I stood a foot behind Helmut, close enough for ginger to think we were together, and nodded gravely. The ruse worked. She waved us both into the back rooms.

"Y'all can go on back now," she said.

Helmut took his hat off, like any cowboy from his generation would, and we walked to the elevator. We rode in silence to the second-floor ICU. The old man studied his boots, caught up in his own thoughts and anxious to see his wife. He had a deep tan line a half inch above his ears and a close-cropped head of hair that was a shade lighter than his Stetson Rancher hat.

"I hope she's all right," I said when we stepped out of the elevator.

He looked at me with his hat in his hand and a certain resignation on his face. "This is the fourth one for her. The pastor comes tonight. He will provide what comfort he can. Give my regards to your grandpa. *Halt dich munter.*" A flicker of grief darkened his expression and was gone. Had I met him at the feed store, I'd never know his wife of over fifty years was moments from death.

"*Halt dich munter*," I repeated, feeling a sudden urge to sink to my knees. That was Grandpa's line. I'd never hear him say it again.

I let the moment pass while Helmut found his wife's room. I watched through the window as he went to her bedside and took her hand. I wondered if I would have anyone to call the pastor on my final night. I thought about Grandpa lying in the barn with no one to take care of him. He told me once that he wanted to be buried next to Grandma. When this was over, I would honor his wishes. His death left me as the last surviving Fischer. I was alone in the hallway staring at my own reflection in the window glass.

"Are you the last one?" My voice echoed in the empty space. "Will five generations of Fischers end because you can't get your shit together." I raised my clenched fist to chest level, half expecting to hear Grandpa's voice in my ear. When I didn't hear it, I spoke. "Not tonight."

I checked each of the remaining rooms for Skeeter. A woman with straight blond hair and a white lab coat in one reminded me of Kelly. I wondered if Marcus had the resources to reach inside the Lubbock police force. I guessed he would. I hoped Kelly got my message and got the hell out of town. I checked my phone. Nothing.

The next room was occupied, but not by a three-hundred-pound black man. The patient was thin, and old, and attached to the life support system. I hoped I wasn't too late. I'd already lost one member of my family and did not want to lose Skeeter. Until that day, I hadn't thought of him as my friend. He was a client at first, then my employee. Today, on Grandpa's ranch, he went as a volunteer, even though he had no training and had read how to operate a shotgun from the internet. He could have walked away, but he had my back and took a bullet because of it. If we made it through the night, I would forgive whatever debt he owed me. He'd paid in full.

Skeeter was in the last room hooked to a heart monitor, two IVs, and an oxygen mask. I breathed a sigh of relief. Marcus's thugs hadn't found him yet. Skeeter's eyes were closed and his breathing steady. Getting him out of here wasn't gonna be easy. I pulled the oxygen mask down and waited to see if the action would trigger an alarm at the nurse's station.

His eyes fluttered open. No alarm.

"Don't talk. Marcus's thugs are gonna show up any moment and try to finish you off."

He tried to smile, obviously in pain. "What took you so long?" he whispered.

"What'd I say? No talking. We gotta go."

His pants and shoes were in a plastic bag in the closet. I helped him sit up and put them on. There was no shirt, probably too bloody to keep. I tucked the hospital gown into his pants. He put a gigantic hand on my shoulder and pressed at least two of his three hundred pounds down on me.

We took the stairs one step at a time, thinking any moment Skeeter would lose his balance and plunge headfirst to the bottom. When we reached the landing, there were two doors—one to the ER and the other an emergency exit to the parking lot. I reached for the exit.

"You can't go out there," a surly middle-aged ER nurse shouted.

I ignored her and gave the door a shove. There was no sound. No alarm. The system must have been offline.

"You have to check out at the front desk," she shouted.

But we were through the door and walking toward the Jeep. I didn't look back. The door slammed in her face. Skeeter was straining with every step.

"Take it easy," I whispered. "Breathe. You're gonna start bleeding again."

He gritted his teeth and kept moving.

When I got him into the Jeep, a black Ford Super Duty with dark tinted windows slammed on the brakes near the entrance. Two men jumped out, silhouetted in the parking lamps. I recognized them as the shorthairs guarding Patrick Allison at the convention center. It was the same pickup that had been following me all over San Antonio.

When they disappeared into the emergency room, I sped south across the highway toward the high school. Suddenly, the engine sputtered. My luck had run out. The Jeep was out of gas. The engine ran for another thirty yards, then cut out. We coasted into the parking lot of the Battlin' Billies football stadium, then I jumped out and pushed it between two pickups and out of sight of the street.

Skeeter looked at me. "What now?"

I shrugged. "Wanna play some football?"

He read the sign on the high school stadium. "Battlin' Billies?"

It made sense to the locals in a county where goats used to be the leading industry. For everybody else, including our rival teams, it was a source of constant amusement.

"Back in the day we were the Hill Billies. I think Battlin' Billies was an improvement."

"'Hillbillies' makes more sense."

"Not 'Hillbillies.' 'Hill Billies.' Two words, as in billy goats from the hills."

"What's the difference?"

"That's the kinda crap I've had to put up with my whole life." I'd been out of high school a long time but being teased about the mascot touched a forgotten nerve.

"You mean, 'Billy Goats Gruff'?" He smiled.

"I don't have time to explain it to you," I said.

"Trip, trap, trip, trap." Skeeter laughed, then winced in pain.

I felt like I was back in high school. It annoyed the hell out of me, but his laughter was a good sign he was feeling better. I checked the doors of the four pickups in the lot. I had left my keys in the ignition a dozen times during high school. One of the many benefits and drawbacks to growing up in rural Texas was that everybody knew what you drove and where you were. Wherever you went and whatever you did became common knowledge shortly after you did it. If you wanted to know where Jerry was, you called his girlfriend or his aunt or his cousin Bobby. I always felt more plugged-in living in a small town than I ever did surrounded by over a million people in San Antonio.

"Who's that tripping over my bridge?" Skeeter laughed to himself while I searched for a vehicle with fuel to get us the hell out of there.

I finally found a set of keys in a Volkswagen Jetta with pink seat covers. I wondered if it belonged to one of the football players. A red-and-white graduation tassel hung from the rearview mirror along with an overpowering Christmas tree air freshener.

I ran back to the Jeep. "Hey, knock it off about the billy goats. We had a hell of a team."

I heard the distinctive roar of a Ford Super Duty. "Put your head down."

Skeeter tried to duck, but the bulk of his right shoulder wouldn't quite fit inside the Jeep. The headlights flashed in our direction. If it was Marcus's men, we were sitting ducks. I dove under the wheels and said another little prayer clutching the M24 rifle. If I made it through the night alive, I would consider renewing my church membership.

CHAPTER FORTY-THREE

The pickup flashed by without stopping. The prayer had worked, or our luck was holding. It took five minutes to extract Skeeter from the Jeep, guide him over to the tiny Jetta, and fold his giant wounded frame into the front seat. When I jumped in the driver's seat, our combined weight overloaded the springs and transformed the tiny car into a lowrider. It wouldn't get far on the rough gravel backroads without bottoming out. We'd have to stay on the pavement, increasing our chances of being spotted by Marcus's thugs or the SAPD chopper.

I turned south and pegged the little engine's cruise control on seventy miles per hour, then filled Skeeter in on what I saw in Grandpa's airplane hangar. He listened without comment. I knew his opinion of Sylvia and expected him to say, "I told you so," but he didn't. We drove south in silence for several miles.

"I wish you'd have warned me," I said, prompting a comment.

"About Sylvia? I tried. First of all, you're too hard-headed to ever take advice. And second, you were head-over-heels in love with her. She picked you out at St. Mary's because you were the alpha dog."

"What's that mean?"

"She was on her own. Away from daddy for the first time." Hearing him say it out loud reminded me that I'd known what she was doing all along. She flashed a smile and touched my arm and had me willingly eating out of her hand. And she'd done it all so that I would keep the riffraff at bay.

"You think she knows what Marcus did?" I asked.

"I don't think it went that far. Marcus used her to get information."

"I can see that. She probably thought she was doing the right thing to somehow rein me in. That I was outside the law." I found my cell phone and started to call Kelly.

"SAPD will be tracing your phone calls," Skeeter reminded me.

"I have to call Kelly."

Skeeter handed me his cell phone to use. It was one a.m. I wondered if she'd gotten my message.

The phone rang several times, then went to voicemail. I imagined she would be looking at the caller ID and see it was an unknown number. I was counting on her recognizing the San Antonio area code and making the connection.

"Kelly, this is Nick. Call this number as soon as you get this message. You're in danger." I handed the phone back to Skeeter.

"Do you trust her?"

"She helped me out with the DNA test."

"That's not what I asked. I know how you are with women. Is there any reason for her to be pissed off at you?"

"What're you talkin' about?"

"She ain't answering your call. What did you say to her?"

"Nothing. We're both Marines."

"She's still a woman. When you left her in Lubbock you probably said something stupid. You usually do."

"Thanks a lot."

"Well?" Skeeter watched me and waited for an answer.

"All right. She wanted me to spend the night."

"And you said what?"

"I couldn't. I was seeing someone else."

"And you told her that?"

"Well, yeah. Not in so many words."

"Even if Sylvia wasn't a black widow spider, which she is, you was in Lubbock, and she was in San Antonio. That's three hundred miles away.

She offered her bed, and you turned her down. Don't sound like a billy goat to me." He laughed.

"Don't start with that. I can barely handle one woman at a time. I wasn't gonna try to juggle two, even if they're four hundred miles apart."

"That's why you're the only white guy I trust. You like the ladies, but you're old school. I've known Sylvia was scamming you since I met her. Those big brown eyes and that smooth olive skin had you under a spell, or you would've known it too. You think you need a fashion model with big boobs and a thousand-watt smile, but what you really need is a woman who packs heat and dips snuff."

"A country girl. You're callin' me a redneck."

"If you shoe fits…"

"I don't want a relationship if she gets mad because I'm loyal to another woman."

"Man, you sound like one of those German settlers you're always talkin' about."

"Your mother would beat you silly if you did any different."

"That's one reason she likes you. You two think alike. You may not have the best judgment when it comes to women, but your loyalty is beyond question."

"Send Kelly a text. Say it's from me. Tell her it's life or death."

I studied the road ahead and behind us. We'd been lucky so far. No highway patrol roadblocks, no SAPD choppers, and none of Marcus's thugs. There were several feral hogs and a handful of deer on the road, but no other cars. The ranch houses along Highway 16 were tucked behind hills or groves of trees, reducing light pollution and exposing a brilliant blanket of stars.

Just as I started to relax, headlights topped over the hill behind us. It was several miles back but coming faster than the Jetta's top speed. The profile of the vehicle was unmistakable. The Super Duty had a bar of lights centered under the front bumper that lit up the highway like running lights on a commercial airliner.

Skeeter finished typing. Before he could hit send, the phone rang. "Here's your Marine," he said and handed me the phone.

"I just got your message," Kelly said, concern in her voice. "I was in the lab working the late shift. You're all over the wire. They say you killed an SAPD officer. Every agency in the state is looking for you. What happened?"

"You've gotta trust me. The guy I killed was a dirty cop. He killed Grandpa and wounded Skeeter. He was on Marcus Lopez's payroll." I waited for her to ask questions. When she didn't, I went on. "Where are you now? Right now?" I tried to sound urgent without scaring her.

"I'm in my pickup in the lab parking lot."

"Start driving. Get off campus. Don't go home," I insisted. I heard her engine roar to life. "Drive normally. They might already be watching you. Make sure you don't have a tail." I explained Skeeter's condition and that we were being followed.

While I talked, I checked the rearview every few seconds. I had the gas pedal on the floor, but the Super Duty was closing the gap quickly. They would have a clear line of fire into the windows of the tiny Jetta when they pulled beside us.

"I'm gonna hang up. I'll call you later." I rounded a sharp curve. The lights of Kerrville suddenly bloomed ahead of us.

"Wait," she said.

I put the phone on speaker and tossed it on the dash, then cut the lights on the Jetta. Skeeter sat up, alarmed. The road disappearing at seventy-five miles an hour is not something that happens every day.

"Can you see in the dark?" he asked.

I couldn't, of course, but the road was straight for the next quarter mile. I focused on the parallel fence so that I was looking at the road with my peripheral vision.

"I'm coming to you," Kelly said. Her voice was clear and devoid of any emotion, like she was giving me an order.

"That's not safe," I said. We shot past a cemetery on the right. I was looking for a turn to get us off the main road.

"Skeeter's hurt and you need backup. Give me your location," she said. She used her Marine officer voice.

I knew that tone. She wasn't going to take no for an answer. I found a road just past an automotive shop and made the turn an instant before the headlights popped back into view. I coasted to a stop behind a row of dumpsters fifty yards from the blacktop. If they saw us and made the turn, we couldn't outrun them. We'd have to shoot it out here in the turnout.

"Did you hear me?" Kelly asked.

"One moment," I said.

I reached for the M24. The Super Duty slowed for the curve. I raised the rifle and slid the barrel out the window. Before I could focus the scope, they kept going. It wouldn't take them long to realize we weren't in front of them anymore. We had managed to get away twice. The next time wouldn't be so easy.

"Nick? Hello?" Kelly was waiting for my answer.

I looked at Skeeter and remembered what he'd said about my track record with women. Kelly was a by-the-book officer. If I gave her our location, she could hang up and call the highway patrol. My gut told me I could trust her, but so much had happened over the past week that I was starting to second-guess my own instincts. She had offered to put me up for the night or as long as it took if I'd stayed in Lubbock. She'd flashed a smile and shown off her well-developed curves, something that always proved hard for me to resist. On the other hand, we did need backup and she was a Marine.

I shrugged, locked eyes with Skeeter, and said into the phone: "Meet us at Stonehenge." Right or wrong, I went with my gut. I picked the one place Marcus's thugs probably wouldn't look. They would check the motels and the gas stations, but not a replica of a British landmark.

"I'll find it. Give me four hours," she said. "Stay off the main roads and try to get some rest." The phone went dead.

"I hope you know what you're doin'."

"You and me both."

"Does she dip snuff?" he asked. I didn't bother to answer.

"We going to Stonehenge? *The* Stonehenge?"

"The closest one to Central Texas." I started the Jetta and continued west on the back road that I knew eventually turned south toward Kerrville.

"That's gonna take us a while." He leaned back in the passenger seat and closed his eyes. "Wake me when we get there. Always wanted to sample English tea."

The Stonehenge I was going to was in Ingram, a small town on the Guadalupe River which, because of growth, was continuous with Kerrville. Their version of the famous landmark was a smaller-scale reproduction called Stonehenge II that wasn't quite as impressive as the real thing on the Salisbury Plain but still evoked a sense of ancient mystery. Locals gathered at the park during the summer solstice for a festive recreation of a druid ceremony. When I went one year, the key players wore beads and flowers in their hair. When the sun rose, they all broke into a chant that I didn't understand. The air smelled like burning grass, the kind Willie Nelson wanted legalized, and by eight o'clock I left to get breakfast. I enjoyed the sunrise but smoking marijuana and chanting with a crowd of strangers wasn't my thing.

The park was dark and quiet, and the replica stones cast deep shadows in the center of an open five-acre park. There was enough parking to accommodate visitors to the replica and the open-air theater that overlooked the Guadalupe River.

I parked the Jetta facing a full-size reproduction of an Easter Island head. Why it sat next to Stonehenge, I didn't know. Skeeter was sleeping. If he snored any louder, the moai statue was going to come to life and finally give up the secret to his existence.

I leaned back in the small seat feeling hungry, thirsty, and completely spent. The adrenaline surge from escaping the helicopter and rescuing Skeeter was replaced by the chilling realization that it was only a matter of time before Marcus's thugs, SAPD, or the highway patrol found us. None of them were going to let us live. Marcus couldn't afford to, and as far as law enforcement was concerned, I had murdered one of their own.

I thought of my grandpa, the last living link to the Fischer family ancestors. In the strange shadows cast by the statue and the giant stones, I felt truly alone for the first time in my life and unable to hold back the wave of emotion any longer. In the quiet darkness, with no one to watch, my tears flowed, and my breath came in ragged sobs.

"A guilty fox hunts his own hole."

—Grandpa Fischer

CHAPTER FORTY-FOUR

DAY 7

A white flash obscured the road. The windshield exploded into my face. The ground traded places with the sky. Rushing water filled my ears. My legs burned. I willed my body to move. Nothing happened. Mangled steel pinned my thighs inside the vehicle, and a thousand tiny needlepoints stabbed my face. I opened my mouth to scream. Nothing came out.

Warm blood ran from shards of glass embedded in my skin. I saw my driver, Corporal Lorenzo, bleeding from the mouth, the steering wheel crushed against his chest. Ghost figures appeared outside the vehicle. Six of them. Weapons up. I saw flashes but heard no sound. Bullets punched holes in the Humvee. I pressed all my weight against the damaged dashboard. My legs wouldn't move. I was trapped. Faces obscured in dust surrounded me. I knew them all. All members of my platoon, except one. Skeeter joined them, holding his shotgun. They were protecting me. I screamed for them to take cover. The words stuck in my throat. The movement shifted to ultra-slow motion. I saw bullets causing wind tunnels in the dusty air, passing through the men, and exiting their bodies leaving comet tails of blood. One by one they fell to the dirt. Their lifeless faces all turned toward me.

"Live," they screamed, but their lips didn't move.

The last two men stood with their backs to me. Bullets riddled their bodies. I tried with all my strength to move. Nothing. They turned. My father and grandfather, their stern expressions chiseled in stone. Grandpa reached through the window, touched my shoulder.

"Live!" he commanded. "You're the only one left."

His calloused hand shook my shoulder as his raspy voice morphed into something softer.

"Reveille."

I opened my eyes, gripping the .45 in my lap. It was Kelly.

"Take it easy with that weapon, Marine. I'm friendly."

I took a deep breath and relaxed my muscles. "Bad dream." I blinked at her face backlit by sunlight.

The vehicle was right side up. The dust was gone, and the sky was clear, but the pain lingered. I slowly made the adjustment from Afghanistan to Central Texas. My clothes were drenched with sweat, my muscles felt raw, and the wound on my arm throbbed. The dream was so vivid and so real that I could smell the blood and the dust. I looked down at my clothes and realized I was covered with real dust and Skeeter's dried blood. Last night's events came flooding back.

"Are you wounded?" She was wearing Wrangler jeans, black tactical boots, and a tight green fatigue T-shirt. Her straight blond hair was pulled into a short ponytail and tucked into a red-and-black Texas Tech baseball cap. She looked good. But why was she here?

I sucked in another breath of the crisp, dry air and got out of the car. My hands instinctively went to my face. No blood. Only sweat. I shoved the .45 behind my waistband.

"I'm fine, just sore. The blood's his," I said, pointing to Skeeter.

"After the twenty-four hours you've been through, I'm surprised you're not tits up." She touched my shoulder again, studying my face. "So sorry about your grandfather."

"Yeah, thanks." I turned away from her to keep from breaking down again. If I did that, I might as well throw in the towel and call the DPS. Staying alive and nailing Marcus Lopez had to be my only focus. In the dream, Grandpa had told me to live. To survive. That I was the only one left. Did he mean the only one left to go after Marcus or did he mean the only one left to carry on the Fischer name? Whatever his true meaning, I wasn't going to let him down.

"Why are you here?" I asked.

"You called me, remember?"

"Yeah, to warn you about Marcus Lopez. Helping me put you in danger."

"I don't like the idea of being threatened by a scumbag. Besides, when a fellow Marine's in trouble, I don't ask questions. I'm here. What's your plan?"

I had to take her at her word. "Get the man responsible."

"I thought you already did that."

"The detective was a hired hand."

"Marcus Lopez is pulling the strings?" she asked.

"That's right."

"He's probably the most powerful man in Texas. And right now, everyone in law enforcement, and I do mean everyone, is after you. You're at the top of the most wanted list."

"I warned you to stay away from me." I used my shirtsleeve to wipe the sweat from my face. The vulnerable moment was gone. It was time to take action. I flipped the switch and pulled on my armor. I felt the emotion drain away. In its place was a cold, calculating machine that wouldn't stop until the mission was accomplished.

Kelly took an involuntary step back. The change in me was palpable. "Remind me never to get on your shit list."

Skeeter stirred and opened his eyes. "What's up?"

"The Marines have arrived," I said.

Kelly handed me a cup of coffee and a white paper bag. "Before you explode out of the starting blocks, have some coffee and breakfast. You'll need it."

I opened the bag and found a dozen fat, warm taquitos wrapped in foil.

"You are definitely on my Christmas list," I said.

"We in England?" Skeeter asked.

"England? Y'all must have had a hell of a night," Kelly said. She opened the passenger door of her dark red 4x4 Dodge Ram pickup. The grill was plastered with bugs she'd picked up on the quick drive down from Lubbock.

"I'm just glad the sun came up," Skeeter said. A pink tint lined the cotton ball clouds on the eastern horizon.

"Drink the coffee. Eat breakfast. Then we'll talk." She grabbed a Walgreens bag from the seat. "Where did you get this car?"

"From 'Billy Goats Gruff,'" Skeeter said and smiled at me.

"Whatever. We'll leave it and take my pickup," she said. "We're too exposed here. And I'm not riding in that thing."

I knew she wasn't completely sure what was going on. She'd told me on the phone about the state-wide bulletin. I'd given her my side of the story. She must have believed me, because she was here alone with a bag of taquitos and a cup of coffee. Had she any doubt, the hand that woke me from my nightmare would have been attached to a highway patrolman.

"Hi, I'm Skeeter."

She opened his door and helped him shuffle to the rear seat of her pickup.

"Nice to meet you. Let's get you out of that gown."

Skeeter chuckled. "I like her already."

"Where'd you get the name Skeeter?" she said, helping him struggle with the hospital gown. The material was stuck to the dried blood on his chest.

"I was scrawny as a kid. My cousin gave me the nickname."

"I guess you had a growth spurt." She pulled out a pair of surgical scissors from the Walgreens bag and cut the garment from his neck to his waist. She helped him sit up straight and, in one quick jerk, pulled the gown free.

"Damn! Excuse my language, ma'am."

"Forget it. I'm a Marine, remember?"

More dried blood caked the patch on his chest. Kelly pulled a roll of gauze, hospital tape, and rubbing alcohol from the sack. She opened a bottled water and soaked the blood-caked bandage until it pulled free from his skin. She kept him talking to keep his mind off his pain.

"So, why do they still call you Skeeter?" she asked. Her hands worked constantly, expertly cleansing the wound. It was red and raw like hamburger. The night's activity had broken the scab.

"They thought it was funny after that."

"What's your real name?"

I looked at Skeeter. He hated his real name and never told anybody what it was.

"Clarence," he said without hesitation. She had won him over.

"And you're the computer wiz?" She looked skeptical.

"You sound surprised," he said and chuckled to himself. He loved the reaction he got from people when they found out he wasn't an NFL player.

She took a black 4X T-shirt from the Walgreens bag and handed it to Skeeter.

"I figured you'd need a shirt. It was the biggest they had." She helped him slide it over his head.

"How do I look?"

"Like a gorilla in a bikini," I said.

"Man, you racist."

Kelly wasn't sure what to think until she saw him smile.

"I always tell the truth," I said.

The coffee and the taquitos were producing the desired effect. My head was clear, and my muscles were starting to recover. I glanced around the park. The puffy clouds had shed their pink tint and were ready to take on the day. The Jetta wasn't concealed in the daylight, and we were plainly visible from the main road. It was Thursday. All the locals who lived on the outskirts were headed into the city to work. Marcus's thugs would be on the prowl. I was sure he chewed their ass or worse for letting me slip through their fingers. They wouldn't let it happen again.

"They'll be looking for this toy car. We'll use my pickup to relocate to a secure location, then sort out our plan of action."

"Here we go. She talks like you when you go all Marine Corps," Skeeter said.

"That should make you feel safe," I said.

"What's he talking about?" she asked. She hadn't been out as long as I had, and she worked in law enforcement, so she hadn't completely made the adjustment to civilian life.

"First things first. Head call." The coffee and taquitos were making my guts churn.

Kelly reached in the console of the Ram and came out with a roll of toilet paper. "There's a tree," she said. "Go commando."

"Yes, ma'am." I grinned and took the paper.

The outdoor theater on the river was undergoing renovations, and I found a portable outhouse set up for the construction crew beside the building. I glanced around the park, checking for any sign of the Super Duty pickup. The coast was clear. Kelly and Skeeter had their heads together and seemed to be lost in conversation. He already liked her much more than he ever liked Sylvia. I admired her for coming, but Marine or not, she shouldn't be involved in what I had to do next, and Skeeter would only get in the way.

They abruptly stopped talking when I returned. Obviously, I'd been the topic of their whispered conversation. Skeeter fussed with his prosthetic hand, and Kelly bit into a breakfast taquito. I figured the best way would be to tell them directly.

"I'm goin' on alone. Kelly, thanks for the coffee and the breakfast. Take Skeeter back to San Antonio and get him to a doctor."

She swallowed a mouthful of tortilla and egg, washed it down with coffee, then wiped her mouth with a paper napkin. Skeeter looked at her, then at me like I'd just sprouted a pair of horns. Maybe I had.

"No," she said. Her voice was clear and matter of fact. She stood and faced me.

"I'm stayin' too," Skeeter said. "You can't take on Marcus Lopez on your own. I don't care how tough you think you are."

Both caught me off guard. Kelly took a step closer to me. We had a shared background, but this wasn't a military mission. I didn't want to put Kelly in harm's way or take responsibility for getting her hurt or worse. Skeeter was lucky to be alive. I wasn't going to let him take another bullet.

"This is my fight. We're not in the Marine Corps. You don't owe me anything. You came here and brought supplies. I'm grateful for that. I'll take it from here. Skeeter needs medical attention. I'm on the job. I'm getting paid to find Marissa's killer. I'm going on alone."

"Bullshit," Kelly said. "Your grandfather was murdered. They shot your dog. And you just found out your girlfriend's a lying bitch." She nodded toward Skeeter.

I shot a look at him for betraying my confidence. He shrugged. "It ain't no secret."

She stood facing me with her feet planted and her hands on her hips. She looked every inch the Marine lieutenant she once was. "You can't lie to me. You're not in this for the money. This is personal. You're in deep shit, and you need my help. I'm breaking the military's golden rule—I'm volunteering."

"That goes for me too. The hospital can wait. I'm gettin' paid for this too, and we got unfinished business."

I pointed at Skeeter. "What can you do with a hole in your chest?"

"I can shoot," he said.

I shook my head and turned toward Kelly. "You're an active member of law enforcement. You have to walk away or put me in custody right now. That's your duty. You know I'm a fugitive. I killed a police officer."

"A dirty cop working for a corrupt politician. He was trying to kill you. It was self-defense. He got what he deserved. You didn't ask me to come here. I volunteered. What happens to me from here on out is not your fault."

I held up my hands. "Listen, Kelly—" I started to protest again.

"I know what you're going through because I know Marines. You're in combat mode, shoot and move. I saw you flip the switch after you got out of the car. You won't stop till the mission's completed. I guessed, and Skeeter confirmed, that you're stubborn as a cedar post. I get that. I admire that. That's the other reason I'm here. You're one of the good guys. I've known that since we first met on deployment."

I shot Skeeter another look. He nodded and raised his eyebrows in a what-can-I-say expression.

"You don't have to protect me. I've got your back," Kelly finished.

I couldn't think of anything else to say, so I crossed my arms and stood my ground. Skeeter took that as the punch line and launched into his low baritone chuckle.

I turned to him, irritated. "You think this is funny after what happened to you?"

"You've met your match," he said. "Now, give us the plan and let's go to work."

He was right. Arguing would only waste time. I knew I was stubborn, but it was time to get over it. Both were willing, and I needed their help. "The objective is to get Danny off the ranch. Improvise, adapt, and overcome."

"Oorah!" Kelly said.

"The plan is..." They both turned to me expectantly. "...there is no plan. We'll have to wing it."

CHAPTER FORTY-FIVE

A gust of wind stirred the ragweed pollen causing my nose to run and my eyes to water, adding another distraction I didn't need. A thin layer of gray limestone dust hung in the air like ground fog above the thick cedar and mesquite brush, reducing visibility. Kelly handed me a tissue from her glovebox, along with an antihistamine.

"It gets me too," she said.

We stood beside her pickup at a remote access to the Allison ranch less than a mile from the main gate as the crow flies, but thick brush and a limestone ridge blocked our view.

We heard the pop of a rifle shot and listened for a follow-up explosion. Nothing.

"Now what?" Kelly said. She wore Oakley shades that mask the tension around her eyes.

"He's got a twenty-round magazine. Keep your fingers crossed."

I checked the rounds in my pistol and tucked it behind my waistband. Kelly clipped her Glock to her canvas belt. I lifted the M24 from the back seat and snapped in a full five-round magazine. Kelly grabbed her police-issue 12-gauge pump-action shotgun and loaded extra buckshot rounds in a black tactical backpack along with wire cutters and two bottles of water. To make the extraction work, we should have had a week to rehearse, aerial support, and at least five more men, but we had to make do with what we had.

My plan was simple—Skeeter would distract the guards by blowing up the power supply. Kelly and I would slip over the fence, grab Danny, and high run like a bat out of hell. No plan survives contact with the enemy, but desperation breeds necessity. I needed Danny alive, and I needed him to confess everything he knew. If Marcus Lopez got to him first, he would win, and I would go to prison or worse.

A second and a third shot filtered through the brush just above the wind noise. Nothing. Another ten seconds ticked by. No explosion. I shared a questioning look with Kelly. She chewed her bottom lip. The simple plan was contingent on Skeeter hitting the transformer and cutting power, if temporarily, to the ranch.

I'd left Skeeter under a small cedar tree near the front entrance and below the main transformer supplying power to the ranch. The tree provided some cover and a natural place to rest the rifle. I showed him the basics of AR-15 operation—take the safety off and pull the trigger. I left him a twenty-round magazine and a bottle of water. If he hit his mark, power to the main compound and the system linking the surveillance cameras to the guard shack would go down long enough for us to slip through unnoticed.

A fourth shot rang out. It should have been followed by an explosion or electrical pop. Again, we heard nothing. I was beginning to think this was a bad idea. Kelly was the better shot, but Skeeter's wound kept him from getting very far or moving very fast. He had to hit the mark, or this mission would be a bust.

Another shot and another miss. He was fifty feet from a three-by-two-foot target. The scoped rifle rested on a tree limb. He could spit and hit that transformer. I paced by Kelly's pickup, trying to stay loose.

The sixth shot. I stopped to listen. Nothing. We'd lost the element of surprise. The gate guard would be on the alert and calling headquarters. The window of opportunity was closing fast. I sneezed into the tissue and tossed it into the back of her pickup.

Two more shots. Both misses. We waited. I wondered if Skeeter was saying a prayer. I hoped whatever he was doing improved his aim. I held up my crossed fingers. Kelly did the same. If the saints weren't listening, we could use a little luck.

Shot number nine returned a loud ping and the sound of a ricochet. Skeeter had finally hit something, but there was no explosion. I looked through my rifle scope at the surveillance cameras over the back gate. The little green light was still on. We heard another pop. Round ten. That shot was followed by an electronic zap and a string of firecracker explosions. Bingo. After ten tries, Skeeter'd finally found the target. Kelly and I slapped a high five.

The security camera lights blinked off. Time to rock and roll. I grabbed the bolt cutters, and we sprinted to the back gate. The cutters sliced through the chain, and we were through the gate in less than a minute. Kelly pulled the gate closed, and I propped the chain back in place.

Sometime in the past ten years, a bulldozer had scraped a fifty-yard easement around the inside of the perimeter fence. Because of the drought, instead of grass, prickly pear cactus overran the space. We ran in single file to make traveling through the thorny jungle easier. A roadrunner jumped out of the scrub oak and kept pace with us for twenty yards before darting under a brush pile.

Once past the easement, we plunged into thicker mesquite and huisache brush, both equally full of thorns and both fully capable of ripping our clothes and skin. After a mile, we came to the power line that led to the house. The ground underneath had been cleared more recently, which made running much easier. We paused in the shade of a mesquite tree to catch our breath. Our forearms were covered with blood and scratches. The wind kept the temperature in the lower eighties but also filled our eyes with a fine grit.

We drank water and rested in silence. I wasn't sure how far we were from the house, but I didn't want to take any chances on them hearing us. There was no need for a discussion. We both knew stealth was our primary concern. Once we were spotted, our only advantage would evaporate. On my signal, Kelly secured the water bottle and shouldered her backpack. We took off at a slow jog.

Ten minutes later, we topped the ridge overlooking the compound. The space was teeming with activity. They'd parked a pickup sideways on the main road. Two security guards in black uniforms leaned against the bed, pointing AR-15 rifles toward the entrance. Two more men peeked from the barn loft, both armed with scoped rifles. Three men on the porch of the old house also brandished AR-15 style rifles ready for action.

Skeeter's misses had worked in our favor. All personnel were alert, but focused on the main gate, giving Kelly and me open access through the back door. We might still be able to grab Danny and be on our way to San Antonio before they realized he was gone.

Marcus was nowhere in sight. That meant we were one step ahead of him. I was betting my life and the lives of Skeeter and Kelly on my gut feeling that somewhere in Danny's twisted soul was a kernel of goodness or at least enough Allison pride to want to stick it to the man who stabbed the family patriarch in the back and stole the family land and business.

Kelly whispered in my ear, "I count nine."

I held up seven fingers. She pointed to two more in a pickup parked beside the cattle pens that I'd missed. She was good. I needed all the help I could get, but I still worried that I wouldn't be able to protect her and Skeeter if things went south. She was a former Marine lieutenant who carried herself well. But I'd never seen her in a firefight. Skeeter had taken a bullet when he jumped out of his pickup without his weapon. Being willing didn't always translate to winning. All the determination in the world couldn't make up for lack of training or poor marksmanship. I took a deep breath and let those doubts go. There was little I could do about them now.

I pointed out the old house where I'd seen Danny on my last trip.

Kelly nodded.

If we were going to take advantage of the diversion, we had to move fast. I stood and sprinted for the back corrals. Kelly followed on my heels.

CHAPTER FORTY-SIX

The original Allison immigrant built his homestead house and barn for defense against Comanches and banditos, but the younger generation had lost its connection to the past in more ways than one. The modern buildings blocked the southern view. The new barn and the garage faced inward, toward the cliff, instead of toward the sloping landscape and approaching enemies. I took advantage of the blind spots and led Kelly around the corrals and to the back of the old house.

We emerged behind a portion of the original rock wall that had once circled the building. Now, only a thirty-yard section survived that served as a landscaping backdrop for scattered rose bushes. I scanned the windows for movement. Nothing.

A Heights Security guard in a black uniform appeared on the porch, toting an AR-15 at the ready and speaking into a shoulder mic. Kelly and I ducked behind the wall and listened for his next move.

Tires crunched on gravel. The guard turned abruptly and hustled toward the front of the house. So far, so good. I motioned for Kelly to cover me. She checked her shotgun and nodded she was ready.

I vaulted the four-foot wall and sprinted to the back porch. Kelly swept right and left with her shotgun. I flattened my back against the cool limestone blocks. The door was locked, and I inched back to the window and peeked inside. The kitchen was laid out like Grandpa's—a small room with bare countertops and a long table that contained napkins and a honey jar. The only difference was the four empty beer cans on the counter. Grandpa wouldn't have allowed that. I listened for footsteps. Nothing but the muffled voices from the front yard.

One building at a time. Clear and secure. I was in military mode. Kelly was too. She was on the alert, weapon in position, and ready for anything. Only her Oakley shades and Texas Tech cap were visible above the back wall. I motioned her forward and brought my own weapon up to cover her advance. There was no hesitation. She vaulted the fence with ease and joined me by the door.

I pointed at my boot, showing Kelly I planned to kick in the door. The wooden doorjamb looked as old as the limestone blocks, and I didn't expect it would take much to splinter. Kelly held up her hand, then reached behind her belt for a Marine Corps–issue Ka-Bar knife—a deadly combat fighting tool with a fixed seven-inch blade that could do damage to anything in your way. I nodded approval. She sliced the blade in the jamb and quickly popped the door open.

Inside, we paused to listen. Wind rustled the oak limbs in the yard. The muffled voices continued, sounding anxious and agitated. Inside was quiet. The kitchen smelled like stale beer and snuff spit. Danny was definitely here. I shouldered the M24 and drew my pistol. It was a better weapon for close-quarters fighting.

Footsteps thumped on the upstairs floor. We froze. The sound moved quickly down a hall and descended the stairs behind the kitchen. I pressed against the wall. Kelly took the opposite side of the door.

The footsteps moved toward us.

I aimed my Springfield and waited.

When Danny Allison walked in, I jammed the barrel into the side of his neck.

"Long time no see, Danny," I said.

He took a sharp breath. "Why are you here?"

Kelly pulled out a pair of flex cuffs and slipped them on his wrists. I shoved him into a kitchen chair.

"I told you I would come for you."

"You were supposed to kill Marcus Lopez at your grandfather's ranch.

He was with your girlfriend. He told Peterson to kill your granddad. Why did you let him go?"

"You better start making sense."

"Grandpa said when you found out what he'd done you'd kill him and end it. Now, Marcus is coming here."

"Your grandpa set me up?" I moved the pistol to his forehead.

"No... I mean, yeah. Don't kill me." His chest heaved.

"Talk, Danny."

"He didn't set you up. He said all you needed was a little encouragement. He tracked down Marissa's mother and..." His voice trailed off.

"He sent Araceli Luna to me?"

"It was the only way to get Marcus to stop the blackmail."

"Tell me what happened to Marissa."

The color drained from his cheeks. His eyes darted toward the window. "Marcus is on his way. We have to get out of here." Tears filled his eyes.

"Then make it quick and don't lie to me again."

"Okay, okay. I met Marissa on the River Walk that night," Danny said, barely above a whisper. "I—I tried to convince her to have the baby. She wouldn't do it. We argued again. But she'd already made up her mind. I offered her money. I told her I would marry her and give her our family name. I meant every word. It wasn't what she wanted. I reached for her hand. She pulled away... and fell back into the water."

"What did you do?"

"I jumped in after her, but she must have hit her head. When I pulled her out of the water, she wasn't breathing. I panicked. I lifted her onto the bank and tried CPR. Her lips were blue. I couldn't feel a pulse. She never breathed or opened her eyes."

"Did you call 911?" Kelly asked.

"No. I called Marcus. She was dead. There was nothing I could do for her."

"You don't know that," Kelly hissed.

"What did Marcus say?" I asked.

"To leave the body and go home. He would take care of everything."

"If she hit her head, that would explain the two black eyes," Kelly said.

"Maybe you're telling the truth," I said. "What happened after that?"

"Marcus wanted money," Danny said. "The next morning, he contacted Grandpa. He would keep it under wraps, for a price."

"Even though they were partners, Marcus and your grandpa?"

"He's ruthless. He knew Grandpa was sick. Ten years ago, he wouldn't have dared challenge him. Now Grandpa's too weak to fight. He had to make a deal."

It all made sense now. Danny'd made a fatal mistake and Marcus Lopez seized the golden goose.

"As long as Grandpa kept paying, I would stay out of prison. He's bleeding our family for everything we have."

"I was supposed to kill Marcus and get him off your back?"

"Why didn't you?" He was angry now. For the second time in his life, everything wasn't going as he planned. "It'd all be over. You were our last hope. Grandpa knew that if you got involved, Marcus would push back hard."

"And your grandpa figured I wouldn't back down," I said.

"That's right. He believed in the idea of people being divided into sheep, wolves, and sheepdogs. He said you were born a sheepdog, and Marcus was born a wolf. He would introduce you and that would be it."

The front door rattled followed by a hard, insistent knock.

"It's him. It's Marcus. What're you gonna do?" He was lost. A kid without his mother.

"I'm taking you and Marcus in."

"It—it was an accident," he stuttered. "I—I didn't do anything."

"That's right. You did nothing. You should have called 911. You could have screamed for help. Instead, you called your lawyer. You let Marissa and your unborn child die without trying to save them."

Danny gave me that lost look that he'd probably used to get himself out of tough situations his whole life. It wouldn't work this time. I had zero sympathy for him.

The door rattled again. Another knock.

Marcus spoke: "Danny? Open the door." His voice was calm and conversational.

"It's too late," Danny whispered.

"I found your friend on the road, Nick," Marcus continued. "Biggest man I've ever seen in person. Unfortunately, he didn't want to tell me about you at first. Now, he's lost a lot of blood." Marcus's voice was cocky like he knew he held the high hand.

"That son of a bitch," I said under my breath.

"I have Sylvia too, Nick," Marcus taunted. "Too bad she's mixed up in this."

I caught my breath and rested my free hand on the table. Despite having seen her with Marcus and her apparent betrayal, I still had feelings for her and didn't want to see her hurt.

"It'd be a shame if anything happened to her."

I heard running footsteps in the gravel. The guards were circling the house.

"I knew you'd come here after Danny, Nick. You're smart. Danny will do whatever you tell him to do. I can't let that happen. When I'm finished, the Allison fortune will belong to me, and I'll be governor of this great state." The old porch creaked. Marcus took a step back from the door. "Let Danny come out. We have unfinished business. Drop your weapons and follow him. I'll give you one minute. Otherwise, I can't guarantee Skeeter or Sylvia will survive."

"Nick, do what he says." It was Sylvia's voice.

I peeked through the ancient red-and-white checkered curtains. She wore formfitting jeans and a white button-down shirt that was open to the middle of her chest. Her hair was curled and fell to her shoulders. She looked like she had every time I ever saw her. Flawless. Her radiant beauty turned the scene into a movie set. A movie that ended with the impossibly beautiful damsel in distress being rescued by the hero. I studied her face. There was tension in her eyes. Or was it fear? From thirty yards away, I couldn't tell. I wondered if the hero of her movie script was me or Marcus Lopez.

"Nick," Kelly whispered. "Be careful. I don't like this setup."

I glanced at the faces of the security guards. All eyes were on Sylvia.

"We're coming out," I yelled to Marcus. I took Kelly's Ka-Bar from the sheath on her belt and cut the flex cuffs from Danny's wrists.

"What are you doing?" Kelly asked. The move caught her by surprise.

I knew she wouldn't agree with what I was about to do, so I didn't try to explain. "Stay here. Wait for the commotion to start. Go out the back. Marcus doesn't know you're here. Thank Skeeter for that. Retrace our steps back to your pickup." I didn't wait for her response. "Get up," I spoke to Danny. He seemed relieved to be taking orders. "We're going outside."

"Time's up," Marcus yelled.

"Hold on. We're comin' out!" I yelled.

"Then what?" Kelly whispered. She hadn't budged. "If I make it to the truck, what then?"

"If I don't make it, haul ass. You have the DNA report. Give it to the FBI. They'll review the Luna case and find Marcus and Danny at the center of it. Tell them you tried to get me to turn myself in, but I escaped your custody."

"No," she said. Her voice was strong and clear. She pulled off her sunglasses and slipped them on the brim of her cap. "We can all go out the back."

"The house is surrounded. They'd cut us to pieces. You need me to create a diversion out front."

She held my gaze but didn't say anything. She knew I was right.

"Give me your Glock," I said.

Kelly pursed her lips. She was running through the alternative scenarios. Her eyes locked on mine. Her look was hard to read. She was defiant, but there was something else that I couldn't put my finger on. Finally, she sighed and slipped the 9mm from her holster and handed it to me. I checked the round in the chamber.

There was no time for goodbyes or explanations. "You've got fifteen rounds," I said to Danny and jammed it behind his belt. "This is your chance to man up." I tucked my pistol behind my back and hopefully out of sight. My gut instinct told me he had been waiting his whole life for someone to hand him a weapon and tell him to man up. I pointed the M24 at Danny. "You're gonna get me close to Marcus. When I grab him, pull your pistol and hold it on the guards to the left. You're gonna stand up to Marcus and make up for not standing up for Marissa and your unborn child."

He was scared, but he was gonna do it. He packed his lip with tobacco courage and nodded. "I'm ready."

I opened the door, and we stepped out on the porch together.

"Tell them to drop their weapons, Marcus," I said.

"You're not gonna shoot Danny." He was smiling and calling my bluff. He'd taken up a position behind Sylvia, using her as cover.

"Why not? I'm already wanted for killing Detective Peterson. What have I got to lose?" I stayed on the porch behind Danny. The guards kept their weapons up and ready. I counted thirteen. There were three behind the Lexus and five on each side of Marcus and Sylvia. "Danny's your golden goose. I kill him, no more money."

"You won't kill him because you want him to stand trial. Sylvia told me about you. You know she likes to gossip. You'd hate to see a rich kid get away with murder. We're a lot alike. I wanted to see him pay for killing his girlfriend too," Marcus said.

"There's a big difference. You made yourself the beneficiary."

"I merely seized an opportunity."

"It was an accident," Danny yelled, still sounding lost. "I trusted you."

"Shut up, Danny," Marcus snapped. He was full of himself, confident he held the winning hand.

The thugs who chased us out of Fredericksburg were sitting in the back seat of the Super Duty with Skeeter between them. Skeeter's eyes were open. His lip was swollen and bleeding.

"I'm takin' you both in," I said.

Marcus chuckled. "I admire your tenacity, but I don't like to lose. Turn Danny over or I'll shoot Sylvia right here in front of you, then finish off the big guy." He drew a short-barrel pistol from his coat. I hadn't counted on that. There was no chance to get close enough to grab him. This would have to be a shoot-out.

"There's money in it for you. I can negotiate a deal with the DA."

There it was. Money and influence. His two biggest weapons. I felt the cold metal of the Springfield digging into my back. That was my ace in the hole if I could reach it in time.

"Nick, please do what he says," Sylvia begged. A tear rolled down her cheek, glistening in the morning sun. I wondered how many men besides me had fallen for that.

"Okay," I said quickly. "Don't hurt her." I touched Danny's shoulder. "Stay left," I whispered under my breath. I pushed him off the porch.

The two nearest guards stepped forward. I handed them my rifle. I was counting on their lack of training. I raised my hands, palm out, level with my waist. They didn't bother to frisk me.

Marcus lowered his snub-nosed pistol. Sylvia's huge brown eyes were calm and confident as ever. Skeeter was right. She'd picked Marcus because he was the new alpha male in the pack. He was gonna be governor. I'd been the bodyguard to the lady in waiting, keeping horndog students and professors from sniffing her tail. She walked toward me. There wasn't a mark on her. No sign of a horrible kidnapping ordeal. Her clothes were fresh and clean, and I caught a whiff of her favorite Chanel perfume. I was a dusty, sweaty mess from running through the brush and getting four hours of sleep in a Volkswagen Jetta. She was ready for her closeup, from her designer jeans to her gleaming white teeth and loosely curled raven hair. Her white button-down shirt was open just enough to keep Marcus's thugs hoping it would reveal even more of her olive skin. They relaxed their weapons. For once her beauty worked in my favor.

I took another step forward and positioned myself at least four steps from Marcus. I was counting on his snub-nosed pistol not being accurate outside of ten yards. Sylvia stopped in front of me and put a slender hand on my shoulder. She arched her neck, extending her ripe lips toward mine.

"I'm sorry, Nick," she said, with no more emotion than a Walmart supervisor dismissing a seasonal employee. Had I any doubts about ending our relationship, they died with that line. I let her pull my neck down to her level and kiss me one last time.

"It was a pleasure," I said.

"Did you really think she was in your league?" Marcus raised the short-barrel pistol.

Sylvia stepped to the side, giving Marcus a clear shot.

I dropped into a crouch, pulled my Springfield, and fired in one smooth practiced motion. Marcus fired too, a fraction of a second later. My .45

slug found his Botox-enhanced brow. The back of his head exploded. Blood sprayed the Lexus. Sylvia screamed. I felt a pinch on my shoulder. Blood expanded into my sweat-soaked T-shirt. Somehow his bullet had found its mark.

Kelly burst through the front door and leveled her shotgun at the guards. Twice I'd asked her to leave. Both times, she'd ignored me. Her Oakley's were back in place and she meant business.

"Drop your weapons. Do it now." Kelly's voice was clear and commanding.

Two thumps came from the pickup. I heard Skeeter's low rumbling voice.

"You heard her," he said. He was leaning against the passenger door of the Super Duty, holding two pistols. The men that had been guarding him were on the ground. Out cold.

Sylvia was still screaming. She'd rushed to Marcus's side and touched his dead body in disbelief. His blood covered her hands and white shirt and soaked into her designer jeans.

Danny had the Glock out. He backed toward me with the pistol pointed at the five guards to the left. They seemed to recover and realize they had us outnumbered.

"Your boss's dead," I told them. "Drop your weapons and you can walk."

No one spoke. They weren't falling for it. The one nearest to me made the first move, swinging the tip of his rifle in my direction.

I fired first and hit him in the chest. I was shooting for body mass. No time to aim. A volley of shots passed over my head, close enough to feel the displacement of air.

I kept firing, each bullet knocking another guard to the ground. Kelly's shotgun exploded three times in rapid succession. I spun on my knee and focused on the next target.

Danny leveled off with the Glock on a guard to my left and pulled the trigger. Blood sprayed my face and arms. Another black uniform raised his rifle. The barrel spit fire. I pulled the trigger again and again until my magazine was empty.

I let the Springfield drop and yanked the .38 from my ankle holster. A black uniform sprinted from behind the house. His AR-15 swung toward me. Kelly's shotgun exploded. Another guard appeared behind her on the porch. I fired.

Just as suddenly as it started, it was over. Sylvia's screams turned to ragged sobs. In less than fifteen seconds Marcus and his men were dead.

I took an uneasy step. My legs turned to jelly. Stars swam in my vision. Kelly sprinted toward me.

"Nick," she yelled. "Are you all right?"

I couldn't answer. The .38 slipped from my fingers and I tumbled forward. Kelly caught my arm. My vision went black.

I saw Grandpa's hangar light and stepped toward it. We would be together again.

"It's time to put out the fire and call in the dogs."

—Grandpa Fischer

EPILOGUE

I woke to a rhythmic mechanical beeping. My chest throbbed. A hot poker jammed into my left breast. Slowly, I realized the beeping coincided with my own heartbeat. I tried to move my arms, but they wouldn't obey my commands. I tried my legs. Nothing worked. I smelled antiseptic. My first thought was of the military hospital in Germany. Then Grandpa flashed through my memory, and fragments of the last forty-eight hours played out in my head. Could he really be dead? Had I imagined running cross-country to escape an SAPD helicopter?

I tried to fast-forward to my final memory. Marcus had a snub-nosed pistol. That was a surprise. Had I shot him, or had I imagined that too? Sylvia had kissed me and stepped aside to give him a clear shot. I remembered dropping to a crouch and firing, the taste of her still on my lips. I'd pulled the .38, my weapon of last resort, emptied it, and hit the ground. Kelly was beside me. Was she a figment of my imagination as well? I remembered another name. Marissa Luna. She was the young woman found floating in the San Antonio River. I was after her killer. Had I found him? It hurt to think.

My world went black again.

• • •

When I woke again, the room smelled of lavender soap mixed with fresh flowers. I felt another presence in the room. The rhythmic mechanical sound continued behind me. My heart was still beating. I tried my arms and legs. This time they worked. The hot poker in my chest had cooled. The events of the last week flashed through my head. From the moment I met Patrick Allison in the convention center, I'd been working for him. He'd used me to take out his opponent and save his family fortune. *There is more than one way to support a candidate*, he'd said. Now, I knew what he meant. He'd used me as a sheepdog, and I'd killed the wolf. He set me up to be the October surprise in the election, to eliminate the blackmail threat, save his family fortune, and prevent his grandson from going to prison. I'd been his unwitting employee. Grandpa would be rolling over in his grave.

"Nick? Nick, can you hear me?" It was Kelly's voice.

She squeezed my hand, and her face slowly came into focus. Her eyes were red and puffy. Her shirt was different. It was short-sleeved, button-down, and clean. Red scratches covered her forearms as proof of our run through the brush. It hadn't been a dream.

"How do you feel?" she asked.

My mouth was dry, and my lips were stuck together. I glanced at the cup with a straw on the nightstand. Kelly held it to my lips. The cool liquid tasted better than water ever tasted before.

"What happened?" I croaked.

Kelly pressed the power switch on the mechanical bed and raised my head. Skeeter was there with his arm wrapped in a sling. He had a cut over his eye that was healing, and his smile was crooked from a swollen lip.

"We're twins," he said, pointing to his bandage.

Kelly explained that Danny had called in his family's helicopter to take me and Skeeter to the hospital in San Antonio. I'd come in and out over the last three days, yelling about being trapped. It wasn't pleasant.

"Sylvia told the police Marcus kidnapped her," Kelly said. "She told them he threatened to kill her, and that she was terrified you would be harmed."

"She insisted on seein' you," Skeeter said. "But Kelly told her to, ah… take a hike."

"Thank you," I whispered.

"I can't believe you fell for that bitch," Kelly said.

"I can." Skeeter laughed.

"Enough. I get it. And Danny?" I said, not wanting to think about Sylvia.

"I made sure Danny told Detective Ochoa exactly what he told us," Kelly explained. "I worked with her to piece together all the documents and evidence. The DA charged him with involuntary manslaughter. Danny lawyered up. He's already out on bail. They didn't charge Patrick Allison, even though he was obviously covering for his son."

"Not surprised. And Peterson?" I asked.

"After your visit, Ochoa started digging. He had tampered with the ME's findings. She knew he was cutting her out of the investigation. She traced that .308 shell you found in the parking garage to Peterson's personal weapon."

"How did he get to Sosa?"

"He ordered Sosa's security team out of the hospital and relieved the SAPD officers. The doctor said he probably cut off the oxygen supply. He died from asphyxiation."

"Am I under arrest?"

Kelly smiled. "The DA won't press charges. Your PI license is safe for now. Patrick Allison put in a good word for you, and Ochoa had the goods on Peterson and Marcus Lopez."

"You should get a medal for killing that bastard," Skeeter said. "He was gonna be governor."

"Danny's here. He came with his grandpa. They'd like to see you," Kelly said.

I could hear traffic outside the hospital window and see heat waves dancing over the Alamo City. I thought about Grandpa telling me to stay away from the Allison family. What would he say if he knew what had happened?

There was a knock on the door.

"That's Danny. Should I let them in?"

I nodded, and Skeeter opened the door, then excused himself and walked outside. Danny led his grandpa by the elbow. Patrick was bent over a cane, and his skin seemed barely able to cover his bones. He was a shell of what he once had been even a week ago. The ravages of cancer had taken their toll. He took off his signature hat.

"Grandpa insisted on coming in person," Danny said.

Patrick steadied himself on his grandson's arm. "Mr. Fischer," Patrick Allison said in a raspy whisper. "I apologize for what happened. Marcus Lopez backed me into a corner. Danny would have been charged with first degree murder. With Marissa being pregnant, he would have gotten the death penalty."

I cleared my throat. Kelly held the straw up to my lips, and I sucked more water.

"You don't have to say a damn thing," Patrick said, his voice gaining strength. "I've instructed my grandson to pay all the expenses you incurred during the Luna investigation, including paying for your services to my family. You earned it."

The arrogant son of a bitch was trying to pay me off, I thought. He pulled a bank envelope from his coat pocket and set it on the side of the bed. There it was, money and influence.

"Pat," I said, but he cut me off again with a weak wave of his hand.

"It's already been done. I've also instructed my secretary to pay for your grandfather's funeral. When you're ready. That was a terrible thing. You may not know this, but the Fischers and the Allisons have ties going back before the Civil War."

I nodded. "I know."

"It was a rough history. Lots of bad blood." He cleared his throat. "I'd like our families to bury the hatchet."

The old man waited for an answer. He seemed to want some kind of absolution for his sins before he died.

I stared at him for a long time. Maybe the statute of limitations was passed for wrongs committed during the Civil War and its aftermath. Maybe it was time to honor the dead and move on. It didn't excuse him from what he did—setting me up to kill Marcus Lopez. I cleared my dry throat again. Kelly gave me another sip of water.

"Get out," I whispered. "I don't want your money or your friendship."

He looked disappointed, but I didn't care. Danny started to protest. Patrick cut him off with a wave of his frail hand. An awkward silence settled over the hospital room. I handed the bank envelope back to Danny. He took it and led his grandpa out of the room.

I suddenly thought of Sam. I'd left him in the vet's care and totally forgotten about him. How many days had it been? "Sam," I croaked. "I have to check on Sam." I swung my feet off the bed.

"Stay where you are. You need rest." Kelly put a gentle hand on my shoulder. "Skeeter took care of him."

I heard an impatient whine. The door swung open, and Sam burst into the room. He bounded to the bed and propped both front feet on the mattress. His tail slapped against the metal frame. There was a neat, white bandage around his head. I leaned toward him, and he planted a wet tongue on my cheek.

"He woke up the day you came to the hospital. They called me when you didn't answer your phone," Skeeter said.

I took Sam's head in my hands and studied the bandage. "Is he… okay?"

"He'll always have a mark, but the vet said he's as good as new. A full recovery. He gave him some antibiotics to take but judging by his appetite he's ready for huntin' season."

I let Sam lick my face. "It's okay, buddy. Now, we both have battle scars." It hurt to laugh, but I couldn't help it. Then the dam broke, and my tears flowed. My grandpa was gone. I was all that was left of the Fischer family. I'd lost the one I was closest too. The light in the hangar went out for good. It was the first time I ever remembered crying in public. I'd shed tears when my father was murdered, but only when the crowd was gone. When Grandma died, I'd done the same thing, waited until after the funeral and walked out into the pasture where only the horses could see me. This time, I couldn't hold back.

Kelly put her hand on my shoulder and kissed my wet cheek. I glanced from her to Sam and then at Skeeter. His enormous frame filled the doorway. All three of them stood by me, and without realizing it, I'd let them in. Grandpa was gone, but at least I wouldn't have to deal with the grief alone.

THE END

If you enjoyed this Nick Fischer adventure, please stop by Amazon and Goodreads and write a quick review. Your support will be much appreciated.

Stay in touch with the author for future free book deals and updates on new releases.

GDObermiller.com
Facebook.com/GDObermiller
x.com/GDObermiller
Instagram.com/GDObermiller

Be sure to check out the next exciting Nick Fischer novel.

The Girl from Cali (Fall 2025)

Nick Fischer takes on the seedy underworld of sex trafficking when the estranged granddaughter of a crusty local rancher turns up missing. He tracks her from rural Central Texas to the back alleys of San Antonio. When Nick finally finds her, she doesn't want to go back. Saving her life means breaking the law but walking away is not an option.

ACKNOWLEDGMENTS

I would like to thank my daughter Ruby and sister MaryAlice, who chided and encouraged me throughout the writing process, and my friend Gus, who introduced me to the great Alamo City and taught me about suppressors. Also, I would like to thank the outstanding officers of the SAPD Citizen Police Academy for patiently answering my questions and showcasing the fine work they do to protect and serve the community. Finally, thank you to my editors and first readers Rick Beck and Lisa Gilliam, for their patience and guidance. Prost!

Because the incident on the Nueces River during the Civil War is controversial, the author would like to acknowledge two main sources of historical research. The first comes from an article in *The Southwestern Historical Quarterly* written by the historian Stanley S. McGowen, and the second comes from two eyewitness, R.H. Williams and John W. Sansom, whose self-recorded versions of the event are available on *The Portal to Texas History* website.

G.D. Obermiller is a fifth-generation Texan who has worked as a cowboy, served as a Navy Corpsman, and taught college English. He's the author of four previous novels, several screenplays, and a one-act play produced in Austin, Texas. He currently lives in San Antonio with his daughter and faithful Labrador retriever.

COMING THIS FALL:

THE GIRL FROM CALI, G.D. OBERMILLER'S ACTION-PACKED NEW NICK FISCHER NOVEL

A PREVIEW FOLLOWS

PROLOGUE

Maya Chavez and Lori Kostoch held hands to keep from falling as they raced down the narrow dirt path leading to the secluded beach on the Pedernales River outside Fredericksburg, Texas. The girls wore cutoff jeans, flip-flops, and T-shirts over new micro bikinis they'd purchased at the mall seventy miles away in San Antonio. They knew the tiny swimwear would drive every boy at the annual end-of-summer kegger crazy and make every girl jealous.

Lori was short, blond, and head cheerleader for the Battlin' Billies. She was born and raised in Fredericksburg and had been planning for her senior year since kindergarten. Maya was also born in Fredericksburg but had spent the last eight years in Southern California, a part of the world that was a foreign country to rural Texas teens. She was tall and willowy with startling green eyes and long raven hair that flowed loosely below her shoulders. Her exotic beauty was a mixture of Spanish heritage from her SoCal father and German from her Central Texas mother. Unlike Lori, she wasn't looking forward to her senior year as a Battlin' Billy. She'd never planned on returning to live with her rancher grandparents. And any hope of blending in was quickly dashed when she discovered that it didn't matter where she was born. Since she'd lived in SoCal, everyone considered her an outsider. They called her *the girl from Cali.* The nickname stuck.

The designation came with its own set of expectations. When Fredericksburg teens heard *SoCal,* they thought of popular gangster rappers on social media who romanticized drugs and gang life. Maya knew the images distorted reality. The SoCal she'd lived in did have drugs and gangs, but it also had malls, parks, movie theaters, and places for teens to hang out besides remote beaches on rivers in the middle of nowhere. But in the complicated hierarchy of high school social status, the outsider mystique put her on equal footing with Lori and the popular crowd, so she let them think what they wanted. After graduation, she would be on her own, and as far from Central Texas as she could get.

It was August, the sun was down, and the summer heat lingered in the night air like an unwanted houseguest. Cooler temperatures were still a couple of months away, and this year's *Farmer's Almanac* called for shorts and T-shirts through Halloween. The sky was clear and far enough from any big city lights to expose the hazy tail of the Milky Way.

The girls followed a well-worn caliche trail curling through prickly pear cactus, live oak motts, and spindly mesquite trees. They wound their way over a limestone hill toward the echo of a thumping bass rhythm blasting from portable speakers. The kegger was in full swing. The glow of the bonfire on the horizon drew them like moths to a porch light.

Maya carried a red-and-white canvas tote bag she'd been given at registration. It was stenciled with the stylized head of the billy goat school mascot and held a bottle of cheap vodka, two plastic quarts of lemonade, and two beach towels. She'd stolen the vodka from her mother, knowing that by this time of night, her mother'd be too drunk to remember whether she'd lost it or polished it off by herself.

Maya's foot slipped on a loose rock, and Lori caught her before she could fall.

"Don't break the bottle," Lori squealed, holding Maya upright.

"No worries. It's plastic." She reached into the bag and brought out the vodka.

Lori noticed the seal was cracked and an inch of clear liquid was missing. "You started without me."

"It was like that. My mom never brings home a full bottle," Maya said, handing it to her.

Lori twisted the cap off, took a drink, and gagged. "Gross."

"You gotta mix it with lemonade, otherwise it tastes like cleaning fluid."

She poured equal parts vodka and lemonade into a plastic cup, a recipe she'd learned by observing her mother, and handed it to Lori. "Now try it."

Lori drank the mixture. "Yeah, better. You can't taste the booze." Both girls giggled.

They paused to catch their breath on the last rocky bluff overlooking a U-shaped bend in the river. White limestone rocks covered the sandy beach below and glowed yellow in the firelight. The stagnant air was thick with pungent cedar smoke that hung in the shallow river gorge like evening mist. In the late summer, the water level was low, but the bend formed a pool nearly always over four feet deep and perfect for swimming.

Fredericksburg high school students had been partying at the river bend for as long as anybody could remember. It was isolated, and trails on both sides led through dense brush making escape easy in case local cops, the landowner, or an overprotective parent tried to raid the gathering.

"I thought this was a school party," Maya said, studying the older men around the bonfire. She didn't recognize them from senior registration.

"It is," Lori said. "Don't worry, the guys we want to impress will be here."

"You mean Owen?" Maya teased as she followed Lori down the bluff.

"What?" Lori pretended innocence.

"Don't *what* me. I saw you drooling over him at registration. You wanna cuff him."

Lori laughed. "Okay, it's time, right? We're seniors. You can't graduate without a steady boyfriend."

"Who made up that rule?"

Lori rolled her eyes. "Hello, everybody knows that. Come on." She took Maya's arm. "Owen made me promise to bring you. He said he had someone for you to meet."

Maya let Lori drag her a few steps closer to the fire. Then she realized she'd been set up and pulled Lori to a stop. "Wait, who is it?"

"I don't know. Don't worry. I'm sure he's fine. He's a friend of Owen's," she said as if that was all the explanation Maya should need.

Maya took a drink of the vodka-lemonade mix, hoping it would give her courage. She knew she needed to show off a little skin to keep up the bad girl image. "Hold on a sec," she said, dropping the bag and pulling off her T-shirt. Her bikini was bright red, with spaghetti straps and triangles of thin cloth that barely contained her small breasts. Lori covered her mouth in surprise.

Maya raised her arms and shimmied like a belly dancer. "You wanted to impress 'em? This is how you do it, girl. Take it off," Maya insisted. She felt a little lightheaded from the booze and the sudden shaking.

"No way."

"Chicken," Maya chided. "Let's blow their minds."

Lori chewed her bottom lip. "Give me some of that," she said, reaching for the vodka mix. She took a drink, then pulled off her T-shirt, revealing a strapless kelly-green version of Maya's bikini.

It worked. The young men around the fire noticed them. One broke away from the group and ambled in their direction. He was six feet tall with an angular body, muscular arms, and a cocky grin. His shock of disheveled blond hair covered his ears, and around his neck he wore a braided shell necklace. Maya recognized him and relaxed a little.

"Hey, Lori," the boy shouted over the music. "Didn't think y'all'd show."

"Told ya we'd be here," Lori shouted back. "I brought Maya." She gestured with both hands and bowed as if introducing a celebrity.

Maya arched her back, posing to give the boy a good look at her figure.

His eyes settled on her exposed skin and his grin got wider.

Lori slapped him on the shoulder. "Hey," she shouted. "What about me?"

He put his arms around Lori and kissed her. "Just teasing ya. Did you bring booze?"

Maya held up the vodka. "Of course."

He put an arm around each girl's waist and led them toward the bonfire. "Come on. I want ya to meet someone."

The music was deafening, and the throbbing bass vibrated deep in Maya's bones. She searched closely for other familiar faces. There were a few, but the group by the fire were mostly older, in their twenties or thirties she guessed. They wore long shorts that sagged below their waists. A few wore wife-beater T-shirts, but most were bare-chested, showing off a collection of tattoos. As she got closer, she noticed the men formed a circle around two older-looking women in sequined bikinis who gyrated their hips to the music as if they were on a strip-club stage.

One of the men stepped forward. His blond hair was long and tied in a thick ponytail. He was bigger than the others, with tatts covering his steroid-enhanced muscles. The most dominant artwork was a red-and-green oriental-style dragon that wrapped around his chest. The head of the beast covered his right breast, and red tongues of fire shot down his chiseled abs.

"Meet Dragon." Owen gestured toward the man with the tattoo. Owen pointed at Maya. "This is the girl I told ya about."

"You're the girl from Cali?" Dragon said in a raspy baritone.

"Yeah," she said, becoming uneasy. This wasn't what she expected. She knew she could pull off the Cali girl image if it meant intimidating a few high school girls and flashing skin at some of the local boys; they were all rednecks. But this guy was older, and she had to admit, handsome. He had prominent cheekbones and a square chin. A chill ran down her spine as his eyes seemed to bore into her. She glanced from his face to the dragon tattoo. She was attracted and repulsed at the same time.

Dragon grinned and focused on Maya's skimpy bikini top. "You ready to party?"

Maya felt her cheeks flush and hoped the man didn't notice in the dark. "Always down to party," she said, waving her arms in the air and nodding her head to the beat of the music. If she stopped the act now, she'd be humiliated.

"You're looking fine, girl," Dragon said. He took Maya by the wrists and twirled her with his powerful arms like a marionette on a string. His alpha-male cockiness and brute strength gave him total control over her and everyone there.

"Take off your shorts," he said. "Let's see the rest of it." It wasn't a request.

Maya looked around for Lori and found her hiding behind Owen.

"Don't be shy. Show us what you got," Dragon demanded.

There was no turning back now. If she hesitated, word would spread quickly that she was a fake, and she would lose her special status. Senior year would be a bust.

She smiled, hiding her nervousness, and unbuttoned the top button of her jean shorts. As she pulled the material loose, the other men pressed in around her. She let the shorts drop to the sand. Two guys tilted their heads back and howled like wolves.

Dragon shoved Owen aside, grabbed Lori, and tossed her beside Maya. "You too, girl."

Lori looked to Owen for support, but he wouldn't make eye contact. The other faces in the crowd stared like shelter dogs waiting for supper. Lori undid the top button of her shorts. Her face flushed.

Suddenly, all the men howled, then closed in around them. A hand grabbed the string that secured the tiny red top to Maya's neck. She crossed her arms as the flimsy material slipped down. The men laughed. Cedar smoke, body sweat, and cheap cologne overwhelmed her. She swooned and fought back tears. A hand grabbed her butt. Another tugged the string holding her bikini bottom. Her throat was tight. What had she gotten herself into? Maya clung to the bikini bottom with one hand and held her other arm across her breasts. She tried to scream, but the sound caught in her throat.

A rough hand grabbed her hair and forced her head down.

Then, as quickly as it began, it was over. Dragon was beside her. The man who'd grabbed her hair was on the ground, bleeding from his nose.

Dragon put his hands on her shoulders. "Sorry. These dudes're animals." He picked up her shorts and handed them to her.

"Thank you," Maya whispered. She retied her string top and pulled her shorts back on.

Dragon lit a joint and inhaled a lungful of smoke. He held his breath for what seemed like a full minute. Then he smiled and exhaled, holding the joint out to Maya.

She hesitated. She'd tried marijuana in California under similar circumstances. Someone had a joint and passed it around at a party. Dragon insisted with an expression that implied she didn't really have a choice.

"You sure you're from Cali?"

Maya nodded, put the joint to her lips, and inhaled. She tried to hold it, but immediately coughed violently. It was stronger than the stuff she'd tried before.

Dragon laughed. "Relax your throat, girl." He brushed her long dark hair over her shoulders. His smile was suddenly warm and friendly. His eyes engaging. All his focus was on her. Time stood still.

Her eyes flicked to the figures by the fire and the empty sand around her. Lori had disappeared with Owen somewhere in the dark. She was alone with a strange older man. Panic started at her stomach and rose into her throat. She knew she should run, but even if she got away from the river, she had no idea where she was.

The man saw her fear, put his warm hand on her bare shoulder, and smiled. Maya tried the joint again. This time she followed Dragon's advice and felt herself relax. A warm sensation slowly crept over her fingers and toes.

PART ONE

Missing Person

"Der Geist der Vorfahren lebt in uns."
The spirit of our ancestors lives within us.

—German Proverb

CHAPTER ONE

Dozens of Fischer ancestors scowled down at me from framed photographs lining the ancient limestone walls of my small childhood bedroom. Some were tintypes, some sepia tone, some black and white, and others were color prints yellowed with age. Five generations encased in dusty glass, and all except the ones in color were stern and unsmiling. I'd read someplace that the cold expressions in old photographs were the result of the extended period of time it took to expose the film. The subjects had to pick a pose they could hold, or risk blurring the image. This may be true, but as a kid, I thought the old folks could read my mind from beyond the grave and disapproved of my plan to escape chores and play hooky. For the longest time, I was certain Grandpa'd hung the pictures to make me feel guilty and keep me in line. It wasn't until I realized that he'd slept in this same room as a boy that I made peace with their ghosts. There'd been fewer photos seventy years ago, but I wondered if they'd made Grandpa feel guilty. It was one of the many questions I never got a chance to ask him before he was murdered.

Dawn had come and gone hours ago, but I was still in bed. The recent stint in the hospital with the hourly bed checks had ruined my circadian rhythm. A steady bar of morning sunlight reminded me of the lateness of the hour, cutting through the small window and casting shadows on the photos. The limestone block house was built by the first Fischer to immigrate from Germany over 160 years ago. With my dad and now my grandpa gone, I was the last of the family line, and the photos once again made me feel guilty. This time for not providing an heir and not protecting Grandpa. So far, I hadn't been able to hold on to a girlfriend long enough to add any more branches to the family tree. It wasn't as if I wasn't trying. My latest prospect seemed promising. Her name was Kelly Hoffman, and she was a former Marine lieutenant working for the Texas Tech police department in Lubbock. She'd helped me out on my last investigation and stood her ground with a tactical shotgun when things turned western. Had she left me alone for the final showdown, like I'd asked her to do, I'd be pushing up bluebonnets beside Grandpa instead of rehabbing on the family ranch. She'd stuck with me in the gunfight and stood by me in the hospital while they dug a .38 bullet out of my chest and refilled my blood supply. Those were qualities Grandpa would have appreciated.

I cleared my throat and spoke. "She's coming back today for Oktoberfest. So, cut me a little slack. She may be the one." I waited, but the old-timers didn't respond. They were a hard bunch to please. No matter, I had a good feeling about Kelly, but time would tell. I'd said the same thing about my last girlfriend until she double-crossed me and almost got me killed.

I took morning inventory of my battered body. Everything hurt. I crossed the morning five-mile run off my to-do list. Experience taught me that recovering from a gunshot wound was a long and arduous process. It wasn't just physical. My head was holding back my recovery. Continuing the bloodline was only one of my worries. Now that Grandpa was gone, I had to figure out whether to keep the ranch or let it go. After two months of lying on my back and deliberating, I still hadn't made up my mind. On the one hand, there were livestock to feed and daily ranch maintenance that couldn't be neglected. On the other hand, staying at the ranch meant an hour-and-a-half drive to San Antonio where my fledgling private investigation and security business was, I hoped, still waiting. I couldn't be a Gillespie County rancher and a successful San Antonio private eye at the same time. Something had to give.

The tinkling of silverware downstairs reminded me there was another problem to deal with besides the family property and my romantic relationships. The problem of an uninvited guest with her own agenda that threatened to upend any of my plans for the future.

"Breakfast!" Helen yelled from the downstairs kitchen in a shrill singsong voice. She'd shown up for Grandpa's funeral and never left. Now, every conversation included a hint at staying longer. Not just till after the Oktoberfest weekend but indefinitely. Last night, I'd found her empty suitcase on a shelf in the barn. When I confronted her about it, she said it took up too much space in her room.

The smell of pancakes and sausage mixed with coffee told me she was working overtime to worm her way into my good graces after that incident. I had to admit that I was less than a gracious host and threatened to pull the welcome rug out from under her feet. I blamed it on my weakened physical condition. But who was I kidding? For me, "gracious host" was an oxymoron. I didn't want or need a roommate.

She said she wanted to take care of me, at least until I got on my feet. The wounds were sore as hell, but I could take care of myself. I didn't want to be nursed by a woman who hadn't been around to take care of me since the seventh grade. That was the year my father was elected sheriff of Gillespie County and the year Mother Helen walked out.

"Nicky, are you gonna sleep all day?" she yelled again. Her voice sounded exactly like when I was in elementary school, same singsong intonation, and the same veiled threat that there would be consequences for remaining in bed.

What irritated me the most was that she called me *Nicky*, like I was still in the third grade. It added to the odd feeling of seeing my ancestors staring down at me from the limestone walls. They all seemed to want the answer to one burning question: *What's next?* Would I keep the family ranch and stay in my old hometown of Fredericksburg, or would I sell out and return to San Antonio where I had a fixer-upper in the King William district near the Alamo and a private eye business? Maybe I would return to law enforcement like my father, or maybe finish my last year of law school, take the bar exam, and pursue a more lucrative and less dangerous profession. I was at a crossroads and having my estranged mother around didn't help.

I stared at the old photos. "Okay, I'll figure it out. You're lucky I don't put y'all in a box and store you on a shelf in the barn." They stared back. Unsmiling. I could tell they didn't like that idea.

"Nicky?" Helen called again, using the same singsong veiled threat.

Even recovering from a bullet wound, I couldn't sleep late in my own house. I stood on the worn wooden floor and stretched my arms toward the high ceiling. Each day, I tested my range of motion, anxious to get back to one hundred percent, but knew that achieving that may take six months or longer. The thought of another week with Nurse Helen made my skin crawl.

Her sudden interest in me and the ranch was motivated by money. She couldn't fool me, and she didn't have to spell it out. The Fischer family ranch sprawled over four hundred acres along Grape Creek, less than fifteen miles from Fredericksburg, Texas, a town that had evolved from a small agricultural community into a popular German-themed tourist attraction. The transformation started in the seventies following LBJ's tenure as president. The nearby Johnson ranch was known at the time as the Texas White House and had attracted national attention. A town that otherwise would have died out like so many other small rural Texas communities now boasted more than sixty wineries, dozens of retail shops, and a handful of German-themed restaurants. It also supported a world class World War II museum named for Admiral Nimitz, another one of Gillespie County's famous sons. There was money here, and Helen could smell it. The annual weekend Oktoberfest celebration alone attracted twenty-six thousand visitors last year and the festival committee expected thirty thousand this year. Before he was murdered, Grandpa'd turned down several very generous offers to buy the ranch. The investors wanted to turn the old homestead into a bed-and-breakfast.

"Do you need some help?" Helen called. Her designer boots clacked up the ancient stone steps, and I quickly slipped on a pair of jeans and hustled into the bathroom. She was my mother, but I'd stopped thinking of her in that capacity twenty years ago, and I wasn't about to let her walk in on me in my underwear.

"I'm coming," I said, closing the door before she could reach the upstairs landing.

"Let me help you change your bandages." She let herself in the bedroom and called through the bathroom door.

"I can manage," I yelled. I stripped the bandage off my chest and winced in pain when it caught the chest hair that had started to grow back. The edges of the wound were still red and raw, remnants of an infection that only recently had begun to recede. The .38 slug was going to leave a nice scar about three inches above my left nipple. I checked the other wound on my upper arm where a .308 rifle bullet had taken out a chunk of my triceps. It was clean and healing, but still sore. The wounds were courtesy of a corrupt state politician. He'd covered up the murder of a young woman found floating in the San Antonio River because the perpetrator was the grandson of his benefactor, a wealthy businessman. I'd been hired by the girl's mother to find her killer. In the final showdown, I put a .45 round through his brain, but not before he got off one lucky shot.

I held my arm up so that the wound was visible in the mirror over the sink. The new scars added to the constellation of marks across my forehead that I'd picked up on my final overseas deployment. Being a Marine and now a private detective took its toll. If I kept this up, I'd look like Deadpool before I turned forty. "Maybe you should start wearing red tights and a mask," I said to the scarred image in the mirror. The image smiled. "At least you still got a sense of humor."

Helen knocked on the bathroom door. "You all right in there? Who're you talking to?"

"Give me some peace. I'm talkin' to Deadpool." I definitely couldn't take six more weeks of her nursing.

"Who?"

"Never mind. I'm fine. Go back downstairs. I'll be down in a minute."

"I'm just trying to help."

She sounded hurt. I didn't care. I'd been asked how I was doing more times in the weeks following Grandpa's funeral than I'd ever been asked in my entire life. I was going stir-crazy from too little activity. The ranch house didn't have a television or internet, and I'd already read the collection of history books I'd brought from San Antonio. The daily ranch work was great for increasing stamina, but it was no match for hitting the bags and taking sparring time in the ring. It'd been months since I'd stepped foot inside Lucky's boxing gym and strapped on the gloves. I missed it. The workouts always took the edge off my frustrations.

I finished applying fresh bandages, then waited till Helen's bootsteps retreated downstairs before I emerged and finished getting dressed.

When I walked into the kitchen, Helen served me a plate of sourdough pancakes topped with three sunny-side-up eggs, fresh hash browns, and a side of venison pan sausage I'd made from last year's deer meat. It was my favorite breakfast as a kid, and other than migas, it had always been my go-to morning meal.

"Thank you for breakfast," I said formally. It was easily a two-thousand-calorie meal that needed to be followed by a day of manual labor. My plan was to saddle my horse and ride the property boundary, fixing fences, then spend a few hours on my makeshift outdoor pistol range. I hated losing my edge.

Helen watched me use my fork and knife to reposition the eggs on top of the pancakes. I reached for the ketchup, not looking up, bracing for her usual litany of morning suggestions for my future.

"Would you like some juice?" She held up an orange juice bottle.

"No, thanks. I'm watchin' my weight." I said it with a straight face.

She nodded gravely. One of the many things that annoyed me about her—she didn't get my jokes. She poured herself a glass of juice and sat down to watch me eat, as if I were a toddler in a highchair. At fifty-five, she wore her hair dyed blond and pulled into a girlish ponytail. She wore jeans tucked into stylishly sequined cowboy boots and a white, long-sleeved western shirt. The silver bracelet on her wrist was embedded with turquoise and a matching pendant hung from her tanned neck. The only weight she'd added in twenty years came from silicone gel breast implants. I'd heard rumors of other boyfriends over the years, rich rancher and real estate types, but she claimed to be single now. I hated to admit that she was a good-looking woman who didn't seem old enough to be my mother.

"I thought I'd go to town this morning and pick up something for dinner before the Oktoberfest crowd gets too bad. What would you like?" She sat in Grandma's place at the end of the long wooden ranch table nearest to the gas stove. She had served me in Grandpa's place on the opposite end, but I'd moved my plate to a side chair. I wasn't ready to take over his position at the table and definitely didn't want Helen taking over for Grandma.

"I'm goin' to the festival tonight. I won't be here for dinner," I said. She was filling in dates on the calendar as far ahead as she could, another one of her calculated moves to ensure she could remain on the ranch.

"Oh, that's right. Your girlfriend is coming."

"She's not my girlfriend, but yes. Kelly is coming for the weekend."

She picked up Grandpa's stovetop percolator and poured us both fresh coffee. It was weak and undercooked because she wasn't used to boiling coffee on a burner. "I don't know why Granddad never used a coffee maker. This kitchen hasn't changed in fifty years." She topped off her cup with French vanilla creamer. "Will you two be staying at the ranch? I could cook for you tomorrow."

A family meal with Kelly and Helen wasn't on the top of my to-do list. "I found us a motel room in town. But thanks for the offer."

"I'm looking forward to getting to know her. She seemed like such a nice person when she was here for the funeral. And she stayed with you in the hospital. I think she smitten." She said the last part as if teasing me about my date to the junior prom.

I bit into the deer sausage. The flavor brought back fond memories. The recipe was as old as the homestead, and I focused on those pleasant thoughts to keep my temper from flaring.

"When are you going back to Colorado?" I decided to plunge into the deep end and sink or swim. I was raised by a no-nonsense Texas lawman and a taciturn rancher grandpa who were both blunt and to the point. What few social graces grandma tried to bestow on me went out the window when I joined the Marine Corps.

Helen stirred the creamer into her coffee. "Don't you want me to stay?"

I took another mouthful of egg and pancake, trying to decide how best to put into words what I wanted to tell her.

I swallowed the food. "No," I said, as tactfully as I could.

Helen went to the sink. Grandpa didn't have a dishwasher. There wasn't room to install one, and he scoffed at the idea of wasting money or water on modern conveniences.

"You need someone here. You're not fully recovered, Nicky." She began scrubbing the mixing bowls vigorously.

"I've been taking care of myself for a long time."

"That's not fair. You know your father had a lot to do with me leaving." Her voice took on a familiar whiny edge.

I took a bite of sausage, thinking. I didn't know that, but I didn't want to get into another argument about why she left, or why she didn't make any effort to contact me until after high school. I told myself I was over it.

"I'm sorry," she said. "I just thought..." She stopped working and leaned against the sink. "With Grandpa gone, can't things be different? We're the only two left."

I looked up from my last bite of pancake and egg. Tears were forming in her hazel eyes. She was going to pull out all the stops. I took the bite and handed her my empty plate.

"Why don't you cook that deer roast that's in the fridge? If we have time, I'll bring Kelly by for lunch tomorrow." I knew I was only putting off the inevitable. There was no "we" when it came to the last of the Fischer clan. The sooner she realized that, the better. But I didn't want to start my day bathed in alligator tears.

Before she could reply, Sam, my chocolate Lab, exploded off the porch in a rage and stationed himself in the ranch yard between us and an as yet unseen morning intruder. Sam's sunny Labrador disposition toward strangers had soured on my last case after a man broke into my house in San Antonio, offered him a tainted hamburger, then shot him in the head. He'd fully recovered, but the stranger, who turned out to be an SAPD detective, had taken his innocence. Tires crunched on the gravel and an ancient Dodge Ram slowly appeared, winding its way up the driveway from the front gate.

Helen looked over my shoulder and recognized the vehicle. "I forgot to mention, Helmut Geisler called the landline this morning before you got up."

"Why didn't you tell me?" I found my boots in the mudroom and slipped them on.

"It was so early, I wanted to let you sleep."

I waved to Helmut through the window, then called to Sam. "Calm down, boy." He ignored me and kept barking. He recognized Helmut but had an ongoing rivalry with the blue heeler perched on the toolbox in the bed of his pickup.

Helmut nodded. His expression was hard to read. He could win the lotto, witness the birth of his grandchild, or lose a family member and he'd still wear the same weathered look. Like my grandpa, he was from pioneer stock who were so accustomed to hardship that showing emotion wasn't an option.

"Did he say what he wanted?" I asked Helen.

"He wants to hire you. I told him you weren't ready to go back to work."

More of her suggestions for my future. I didn't bother to reply. The woman was exasperating. I opened the screen door and stepped outside.

CHAPTER TWO

Helmut Geisler carefully unfolded himself from the cab of his dusty Ram pickup. He reminded me of a strip of latigo wrapped in Wranglers and a faded blue work shirt. Neither he nor his sweat-stained Stetson Rancher hat had changed since I was in grade school. And no matter the circumstances, I still felt like I was eight years old when he came to visit.

His blue heeler stayed on the toolbox, matching Sam bark for bark. Helmut raised his hand. "*Platz!*" he commanded in German. Both dogs obeyed. Sam glanced at me quizzically. He didn't speak German but knew better than to cross the old man. I nodded, and Sam took off toward the stock pond. The heeler jumped down and ran after him, temporarily pausing their rivalry for a dip in the cool pond water.

"*Guten Morgen. Wie geht's?*" Helmut said, delivering his German with a nasal Texas twang. He extended a callused palm. Despite his eighty-plus years, his grip was still strong and firm.

"*Morgen*, Helmut." I knew a little more German than Sam from listening to Grandpa growing up. But if things got more complicated than "good morning," I usually smiled and nodded my head. I regretted not learning more, but by the time I went to high school, the language was long out of fashion.

He surveyed me and then the ranch yard, lingering on the patches of weeds along the corral fence, the loose tin flapping on the barn roof, and other signs of neglect that were never visible while Grandpa was alive. "Still recovering from your wounds, I see." He chastised me like a schoolboy.

What he meant was, had I been physically able, I wouldn't have neglected the ranch upkeep. It was one more thing to feel guilty about. The Geisler family'd been in the area as long as the Fischer family. He was one of the few left, now that Grandpa was gone, who still spoke Texas German, kept their ranch precise and orderly, and remembered the stories about life on the Texas frontier.

"Good that Otto got his hay in the barn," he said, chinning toward the hay loft. Otto was my grandpa. He was going to add, *before he died*, but he stopped himself. Instead, he said, "Almanac says it will be a mild winter, but we won't get much rain. Might need to buy feed before spring."

Helen'd said he wanted to hire me, but I was starting to wonder if he'd come over to make sure I wasn't running Grandpa's ranch into the ground. "Coffee's on. Come in and have a cup," I offered. Maybe he would cut me some slack and get to the point if he had a cup of coffee in his hand.

He looked past me to the front window, where Helen stood staring at us.

"Is it safe then, to go inside?" he asked with a twinkle in his eye. He knew my family history as well as I did. There weren't many secrets around the old-timer network, of which, until recently, my grandpa'd been an intricate part.

"She was just goin' to town for groceries."

"So, she's staying then?"

"For now."

He waited for me to say more. When I didn't, he let it go and nodded. "I could use a cup."

We walked inside, and he hung his crusty Stetson on the peg in the mudroom.

"Good morning, Helmut," Helen said.

"*Morgen*, Helen."

"How's your wife?" she asked.

"She's up and around. Busy with the fall garden. Says death will come when it comes." Helmut's wife'd recently survived her fourth heart attack.

"Let us know what we can do to help," she said, then put a hand on my arm. "I'm going to town. If you think of anything you need, you have my cell phone number."

Helmut and I watched her jump into her white Chevy Tahoe with green Colorado plates and kick up a cloud of caliche dust on her way to the front gate.

"You two gettin' along?" he said, pulling out a chair and sitting at the kitchen table.

"We have our differences. But you know where that comes from."

Helmut nodded but didn't say anything, his curiosity satisfied. I tested the coffeepot to see if it was still hot, then poured us both a cup. "It's weak. Helen hasn't figured out how long to let it boil."

Helmut sipped his coffee. Said, "Ya." Referring to the coffee. We sat in silence for a long minute. Helmut would get to his business in his own good time. We listened to the dogs return from the pond and shake themselves dry. Sam gave a low growl to assert his dominance on the home turf before both flopped together on the front porch. A mockingbird in the live oak tree behind the house sang his repertoire of melodies accompanied by the flap, flap, flap of the loose tin on the barn roof.

Finally, Helmut cleared his throat and said, "My granddaughter's missing." He took another sip of weak coffee. True to form, his customary stern expression didn't change.

I waited for him to fill in the details. Men like Helmut and my grandfather chose their words carefully and used them sparingly, mindful of not wasting more than necessary. I inherited the taciturn trait, which drove my last two girlfriends crazy and probably cost me a few clients, but as much as I tried, I'd never acquired the knack for idle chitchat.

"Her name's Maya Chavez," he said. "I think something's happened to her."

He plucked a picture from the wad of receipts and scraps of paper in his breast pocket that, like most old-time ranchers, he used as a filling cabinet. I took it from him and studied the young girl's green eyes and olive complexion. The picture looked clipped from a school yearbook. Her dark hair was long and flipped over her right shoulder. The smile on her face showed intelligence and a touch of youthful defiance.

"You might remember my daughter, Anna. She ran off to California when Maya was in grade school. Last spring, the knot head she married left her high and dry. She started tendin' bar and drinkin' most of her paycheck. Left Maya on her own most of the time. One thing led to another, and they ended up coming home during the summer."

I topped off our coffee cups and waited for Helmut to fill in more details. When he didn't offer any, I pressed him. "What makes you think something's happened to her?"

"She didn't take anything with her. Not even her toothbrush. All her clothes are still in her room. What girl would up and leave like that?"

"Was she angry enough to run away?"

He sipped his coffee. "Well, Maya wasn't happy to be here. I know that much." He stared out the kitchen window in a rare moment of self-reflection. Helmut and my grandfather were products of their environment, unforgiving simi-arid hill country, and descendants of pioneers who'd delt with Comanche raids, drought, disease, and bandits. They passed down a pioneer spirit that didn't include asking for help or sharing feelings. Confiding in me and asking for my help was like pulling cactus tines from his bare feet.

"What makes you say that?"

"I don't think that youngin wanted to leave California for her high school senior year," he went on. "She'd spent eight years in that cesspool of Southern California. It warped her thinking. And her mother... Well, her mother never used any discipline on her. Then she came back to Fredericksburg. Hell, you know what it's like. You grew up here. Our biggest event of the year is Oktoberfest."

I did know. Until I left to join the Marine Corps, my idea of a traffic jam was following a flatbed trailer full of hay down a one-lane road. "Did you talk to the sheriff?"

"I filed a missing person report with Detective Zeller at the city station back in August. He didn't do a damn thing. Since Maya just turned eighteen, the meathead said there was nothing else he could do. She was free to take off if she wanted."

"That part's true. Maybe she caught a bus back to California."

"That's what Zeller said, but I think that's horse shit. I told you all her stuff's still in her room. Even if she was mad enough to take off, she's a smart girl. She would've said something and packed a bag."

"Did Zeller check her cell phone records?" I asked.

He looked puzzled for a moment. Like my grandpa, Helmut had a landline in his kitchen and still wrote the occasional letter to his cousin in New Mexico.

"Ah," he said, remembering. "I gave him the number I had. He said it wouldn't help. Something about the kind of phone it was."

"A prepaid phone?" I asked.

"Ya, that's it." He dug into his shirt pocket filing cabinet. "I have the number here." He sorted through the scraps at arm's length, not bothering with reading glasses, then handed me a number written on the back of a gas receipt.

"She hasn't tried to contact you?"

"Haven't heard a whisper since she snuck out the window to go to a party on the river."

"She snuck out?"

"I told her she couldn't go. I know what goes on down there. So, naturally, she went anyway." He stroked his gray whiskers. Another moment of self-reflection. "Her mother used to pull the same stunt, and when I put my foot down, she did it anyway. She'd leave when she thought I was asleep and wouldn't come back till the next day. Crazier than a March hare."

"Did she walk to the river? That's fifteen miles from your place."

"No, the Kostoch girl picked her up outside the gate. I recognized her vehicle."

"Lori Kostoch?"

"Ya. She's a senior this year too."

"And you think Maya's in trouble?"

"I'd bet my prize goat on it. I feel it in my bones." He fixed his rheumy eyes on me. "I've tried to find her myself, but I've gotten nowhere. Hell, ten years ago, I would have turned the town inside out. But now..." His voice trailed off, displaying emotion that he wasn't accustomed to using. "It's hell gettin' old. I know you're recovering from that business with your grandpa, but if you could look around, I'd be much obliged."

I rinsed my coffee cup in the sink to give him a moment to compose himself. "I'll look into it," I said.

He stood and produced a small wad of bills from his wallet. "I can pay. I know you do this for a living."

I waved off the money. "I don't know if there's anything I can do. Let me ask around first. Fredericksburg's still a small town. You said she went to a party on the river. Somebody's bound to have seen something. If I get a lead or think I can help, we'll sign the paperwork and make it official. We can negotiate payment then.

"It's your call," he said. The brief emotional self-reflection was safely tucked back inside his rawhide exterior.

I walked him out to his pickup and waited while he folded himself back behind the wheel. "*Hier!*" he yelled to the blue heeler. The dog obediently jumped into the back of his pickup and settled down on the toolbox. Sam barked a warning, reasserting himself as master of the ranch yard.

Helmut started the engine and put the vehicle in gear. "*Danke. Halt dich munter*," he said out the window. It was a salutation I'd heard all my life. According to Grandpa, it meant something like *keep your chin up*.

"*Halt dich munter*," I said. Helmut drifted down the hill toward the front gate.

I scratched Sam behind the ears, careful to avoid the fresh scar from the bullet wound. "Rehab's over, ol' buddy. Time to get back to work."

www.ingramcontent.com/pod-product-compliance
Lightning Source LLC
Chambersburg PA
CBHW020257030826
48979CB00026B/1380/J

* 9 7 8 1 7 3 7 6 4 5 9 9 3 *